THE GARDEN OF WEAPONS

With the invention of intelligence-chief Herbie Kruger, who first appeared in *The Nostradamus Traitor*, John Gardner has established his place in the very first rank of spy-fiction writers.

Author of the Moriarty Journals, the Boysie Oakes series and such exceptional thrillers as *The Dancing Dodo* and *The Werewolf Trace*, Gardner has also been named the official successor to Ian Fleming, with the distinguished assignment to continue the James Bond series.

Fast-paced, superbly crafted, compulsively gripping—

THE GARDEN OF WEAPONS

'The spy novel in excelsis'   *Times*

'After his nightmarish look into the future
(*Golgotha*), Mr Gardner returns to today's
bad dreams and Big Herbie Kruger from *The
Nostradamus Traitor* . . . I hung in, spinning,
incredulous, tickled silly'
                                    Sunday Times

'First rate . . . deeply perceptive portraits of
the humans behind the cryptonyms'
                                    Evening News

'Sweaty tension, duplicity, violence and
racking suspense, by a writer in full
mastery of his spy-fiction craft'
                                    Tribune

'The pace increases to reach a gripping climax.
You can almost taste the grey austerity and
smell the fear in the air as Kruger hunts his
quarry while the KGB close in'
                                    Hull Daily Mail

'A cracker . . . definitely not to be missed . . .
every character comes to life and there are
more shocks in the last chapter than there are
in a dozen ordinary books'
                                    Huddersfield Daily Examiner

'Convolutions of almost psychedelic treachery
. . . le Carré in dreamland'
                                    Observer

For
Eric Major

Who has been around in many guises
From Ludgate Circus to Bedford Square

Also by the same author
and available in Coronet Books

The Werewolf Trace
The Dancing Dodo
The Nostradamus Traitor

The Garden of Weapons

John Gardner

CORONET BOOKS
Hodder and Stoughton

Copyright © 1980 by John Gardner

First published in Great Britain 1980 by Hodder & Stoughton Ltd.

Coronet Edition 1981

British Library C.I.P.

Gardner, John
    The garden of weapons.
    I. Title
    823'.914[F]   PR6057.A63

ISBN 0-340-27107-8

Printed in Canada

Acknowledgments

No BOOK IS written in a vacuum, and I have to thank a multitude of people for their time, patience and assistance. A few call for special mention. First, my editor, Richard Cohen – always tireless in pursuit, and who, in a different trade, would be my case officer: a role he assumes anyway on a love/hate basis. Dr. Vincent Pippet, of Wicklow town, who gave his time to explain certain small medical matters; Communication Control Systems, for details of commercial surveillance equipment; and, not least, my friend Charles McCarry who has allowed me to use the cryptonym, given to a walk-on character in two of his books, as the cryptonym for a major character in this one. I use this arcane name as a form of *homage* to McCarry, who is the most authoritative writer about the minds of secret men and women. To those, and countless others, my grateful thanks.

JOHN GARDNER,
IRELAND, 1980

I am not going to the green clover!
The garden of weapons
Full of halberds
Is where I am posted!

When you are in the field, God help you!
Everything depends
On God's blessing!
For anyone who believes it!

Anyone who believes it is far away.
He is a king!
He is an Emperor!
He is making the war!
Halt! Who goes there? Speak up!
Clear off!

Serenade of the Sentry from *Des Knaben Wunderhorn* by Arnim-Brentano. Set to music by Gustav Mahler between 1892 and 1895

FULLY CLASSIFIED   TO REMAIN SECURE AND
LOCKED   RED TAG

DATE AS STAMP

AUTHORITY: Head of Service
            Head of C & C
            Director Special Sources: East Germany

The following cryptonyms have been assigned to the under-
mentioned now operating under general cipher QUARTET
as directed by Special Sources: East Germany. Link with
TELEGRAPH BOYS.

Girren, Walter	ANNAMARIE
Schnabeln, Christoph	SPENDTHRIFT
Mohr, Anton	TEACHER
Blatte, Anna	MAURICE

DECIPHERED TRANSCRIPT   DATE AS HEADED
TIME CIPHERED (Cheltenham): 10.02

FOR: DIRECTOR GENERAL SIS.
FROM: SECRETARY I/C GENERAL MOVEMENTS.
        CONSULATE GENERAL. BERLIN WEST.

FLASH   SECURE

HAVE WALK-IN CLAIMING TO BE CAPTAIN KGB
EAST BERLIN WILL ONLY IDENTIFY AS PIOTR
AND SAYS WILL ONLY TALK TO YOUR OFFICER
NAMED AS BIG HERBIE STOP REQUEST
INSTRUCTIONS STOP CONSUL GENERAL FEELS
HE SHOULD BE RETURNED UNOPENED. FLASH
FLASH FLASH

CLASSIFIED HIGHLY CONFIDENTIAL   RED TAG

FROM: Director
TO: Director Special Sources: East Germany
DATE: As stamped

Dear Herbie,

   This is a letter officially informing you that the Charlton
house has been opened for your use today.

   I am required by standing orders to notify you of this in
writing and this letter will be placed on file with a copy to
the Minister and Treasury.

   It is understood that you will occupy the Charlton house
only for as long as it takes to interrogate the recent defector
TAPEWORM, and that you will have only the normal and
minimal staff required to ensure correct security and
normal care.

   I would be greatly obliged if you would vacate the
Charlton house as soon as possible, once you have ensured
your interrogation is complete.

                              Sincerely,

                              Director SIS

SIS REGISTRY: A4296/5

TO: Head of Service
FROM: Head of Registry
DATE: 10 August 1980

Following your requisition order dated as above – CS/567 –
I have today placed the following files into the custody of
Mr. E. L. Kruger, Director Special Sources: East Germany.

SZ/24   Muller, Gertrude   (dec)
SZ/25   Blenden, Willy   (dec)
SZ/26   Birkemann, Andreas   (on pension)
SZ/27   Birkemann, Beatrix   (on pension)
SZ/28   Gabell, Luzia   (unknown: pres dec)
SZ/29   Habicht, Emil   (dec)
SZ/30   Becher, Franz   (dec)
SZ/31   Zeich, Moritz   (on pension)
SZ/32   Reissven, Peter   (dec)
SZ/33   Zudrang, Julie   (believed dec)
SZ/34   Kutte, Kurt   (dec)

You will note that these files make up the major dossier of
the network run in East Berlin by Mr. Kruger under cipher
SCHNITZER GROUP c. 1955 – 1965

                                        Ambrose Hill
                                        Head of Registry

CLASSIFIED AA. FOR THE DIRECTOR AND
G STAFF ONLY   RED TAG

SIS REGISTRY: A4296/6
TO: Director SIS
FROM: Head of Registry
DATE: 10 August 1980

Following your requisitioning order as above date – AA/666
– I have today passed the following files into the custody of
Mr. E. L. Kruger, Director Special Sources: East Germany,
after making the necessary enquiries concerning the safe
keeping of this Most Highly Classified Material.

TB/1   General File. Telegraph Boys
TB/22 Gemini
TB/23 Horus
TB/24 Hecuba
TB/25 Nestor
TB/26 Priam
TB/27 Electra

PART ONE

Tapeworm

I

It was August. It had always been one of his favourite months, because they usually got out of Berlin for a few weeks. Sometimes back to Moscow. The Old Man had often turned a blind eye to the girls he took back with them.

Now he was left with only two certainties. First, there was death, the only sure thing in the lives of all human beings. Second, there was the indisputable fact that very soon his own people would be coming to arrest him. There would be no girls in Moscow this August, only a small room, or maybe a hospital ward. And endless questions.

So, at five o'clock in the morning, he viewed the situation with the exact logic learned patiently through the years from the Old Man.

He had not slept. The reality of his present condition would not allow that luxury. Instead he had gone through each step, examining every eventuality and permutation.

They would probably leave him for another forty-eight hours. That would be good psychology, and they seemed to be playing the whole business in a most classic manner.

After it had happened, a major had been flown in from Moscow to take charge. The short interrogation was friendly, even sympathetic. Some of it almost casual, as though they were really considering his feelings as a brother officer.

But then they could afford that. Time was on their side. They also had his personal luggage. "Don't bother about your things," they had said. "We'll send them on. Just take what's necessary for a few days."

That was during the previous afternoon, when the major's assistant, a very young lieutenant with acne, brought in his

17

posting. He was to report to the barracks at Karlshorst. The major came in later. "Just wait at Karlshorst for instructions," he had said. "There's plenty of work for a man of your experience and qualifications, Comrade Captain."

He knew then for certain what they were doing; and, almost without thinking, took what small action he could, arranging to arrive at the Karlshorst barracks as late as possible. The duty officer did not even seem to be expecting him; which could be a good sign. It was suggested that he report to the adjutant some time after nine in the morning. They found him a room in the officers' quarters, and offered him a meal.

He had played at being in shock, trying to convey indecisiveness. The major and his team would be busy enough; so, having packed him off to Karlshorst, they probably argued that he was safe for a day or so.

Maybe forty-eight hours. If he had been handling the affair that was what he would have done. Possibly he would leave it a little longer. The Old Man, however, would have put a watch on him, whatever his state of mind.

He was careful: dragging his heels on the way to the barracks. With his small case, and the briefcase, he had stopped many times; called in at a couple of bars; seen one of the girls; gone for a meal; used both railway and bus. All the time he checked, from the middle of the previous afternoon until almost midnight: they had nobody watching.

Today almost certainly there would be some kind of surveillance. Leave him to sweat at Karlshorst, and watch from a distance. Probably they hoped he would try to make a run for it: thereby proving complicity. They would not expect him to go quickly, though. Normally they would presume the full impact was unlikely to hit him for a day or two.

Then, if he tried to run, it would give them the ascendency, making their job that much easier. Already they must be certain that the Old Man had confided in him. You do not spend over twenty years as aide to such an officer without knowing at least some of the truth – or enough of it for the experts in Dzerzhinsky Square, at the Centre – to complete a jig-saw. Maybe, a puzzle of their own devising.

There was only one way to go, one man to approach. He hated the idea, but running was better than what would take place in Moscow. Whatever happened there, his career was finished.

Reluctant though he might be, his will to survive was strong. He had to run, and quickly. Whatever the dangers. The Old Man's legacy also included the means to get out. The means that the Old Man had, in the end, refused to use for himself.

The night had been stifling. Now, at five o'clock, it was light outside, and he could see that rain was on the way. Thunder also. The boiling, humid weather of the last few days appeared ready to break. It was as if the elements were matching his own mood and decision.

If his nerve held he could just do it; even though the reluctance was like iron in his mind. He did not suppose the British would use drugs on him, and he knew enough about interrogation to hold back, just giving them enough. In that way his conscience would be clear. He would know that, at least, he had not completely betrayed his country. There were also the Old Man's instructions – for whatever reason. The couple of falsehoods, and one piece of misdirection which he had to use.

He could take nothing. His case contained only shirts, socks and underwear. His best uniform hung in the small cupboard. Apart from these things, and his toilet gear, there was the uniform he wore, and the briefcase.

The basic needs were in the pockets of the civilian raincoat, folded neatly inside the briefcase. The other matters remained engraved in his mind. Unless they made him open the briefcase at the main gate nobody would be any the wiser if the guard had orders to turn him back.

The guard would be changed at five-thirty, according to normal routine; so he would have to leave soon. He must go when the duty man was at his lowest ebb, thinking of his time off during the coming day.

Slowly he put on the uniform jacket: straightening it, pulling it at the back so it settled neatly on his shoulders. Checking his appearance in the mirror, he experienced the same old feeling of irrevocable loss. This time it was coupled with the strange knowledge that the whole of his life was being left behind. Whatever happened now, this was the great crossroads. For the last time he hesitated, a sudden flurry of indecision; then rationalised that this was exactly what they would expect of him.

He put on his uniform cap, and it came to him that this may well be the final time he would perform such an ordinary, everyday function. Then he picked up the briefcase, went to the door and stepped outside.

Even at this time in the morning, the humidity hit him like a fine steaming mist. The clouds were low, smudged with ink blots; battening down over the city like a lid on a cauldron.

The guard at the main gate made no attempt to stop him. Nobody appeared to take any interest.

"You'll get wet, Comrade Captain," the guard shouted. "It's going to rain. A storm."

"I'll only be ten minutes," he called back, tapping the briefcase as though it had some special significance. Within ten minutes the guard would have completed his duty.

He had already decided which route to take. He would go by rail, from the Friedrichsrasse station. As long as they did not pick him up there he would be home. Not dry, though. Already thunder was rumbling in from the west. He wondered if it were an omen.

It was almost six-thirty when he arrived at the Friedrichstrasse station; but looking a different man.

Near the Unter den Linden he had used a public toilet, stuffing his uniform jacket and cap into the cistern, scuffing the well-polished brown shoes, taking the raincoat from his briefcase and emptying the pockets.

He parted his hair on the other side, adjusted the rimless spectacles, buttoned up the raincoat, leaving his real identity papers in his hip pocket, and put the passport and permit into the briefcase, together with the samples in their little boxes. The Old Man had thought of everything. *If they get me, they'll come after you. However badly you feel, save yourself. Either destroy the stuff or use it. Then do as I've told you. Guile. Remember the guile.*

Now, as he approached the station, he was transformed into a German – Hans-Martin Busch, Chief Sales Representative of a lens manufacturing firm. His business in the West was a meeting with a British manufacturer. The British firm was interested in the bulk purchase of cheap lenses for their equally cheap range of binoculars, to be sold in chain stores. It was all there – authorisation to travel; time and place of meeting; purpose – all arranged over three weeks ago. He had, in fact, filled in the relative details at four that morning, in the officers' quarters at Karlshorst – subconsciously committing himself that early. He had used his left hand to disguise the writing.

Still nobody queried anything. Only a pompous woman control officer reminded him that he had to return, through the same checkpoint, before nine that night. He assured her, in fluent German, that he would be back long before then.

By the time he reached West Berlin the rain had started; huge thunder drops hissing and exploding on to buildings, drenching the roads. He took the U-Bahn through to the Uhlandstrasse, and then ran – from the rain and from himself. He wanted to turn back. Running was the only way to get over the barricade in his conscience. By the time he reached number twelve he was soaked, his hair and face streaming with water.

Number Twelve Uhlandstrasse was the office of the Consulate General of Great Britain.

2

HERBIE KRUGER WAS relieved. There was always a sense of freedom as he left Germany – even though his bulk, and the length of his legs, made for discomfort on board a British Airways Trident. It seemed to him that the seats on that particular aircraft had been designed for transient parties of midgets.

The stewardess at the Bonn check-in gave Herbie a seat towards the front of the aircraft, allowing a fraction more leg room. Herbie Kruger, however, hardly noticed this kindness. As the Trident thrust itself from the runway, setting its course for London, he breathed a sigh, and looked around for the in-flight stewardess to see how quickly he could get his large hand around a plastic beaker of vodka.

Herbie Kruger's relief stemmed from the fact that he was leaving the country of his birth. Bonn was not his favourite city – though he would, if pressed, admit preferring it to Berlin. "Like Isherwood," he would say, "I was a very young camera in Berlin – but at a later and even more unpleasant time."

He was always glad to get out of either city: particularly since leaving proper field work to operate from London. In the past few months Herbie had discovered these most necessary trips into the Federal Republic, or West Berlin, were more and more irksome.

Once a fortnight it was either Bonn or Berlin. Everything else could be handled efficiently enough from the Annexe off Whitehall, just far enough away from the tall, steel, concrete and glass building that housed most of his colleagues.

As for the bulk of these colleagues who lived in the partitioned world of intelligence, they took the bait offered by

Department Heads: regarding Herbie with respect, and that deferential sympathy due to someone who has been a first-class field officer, but who was now blown; over the hill; facing a desk job to jog him along until pension time – which, in Herbie Kruger's case, was almost fifteen years away. The fact produced added sympathy. "He's like a great orator who's lost the power of speech," one of them said.

Big Herbie Kruger – as his natural nickname suggested – possessed none of the physical secret attributes. By virtue of his build it seemed impossible for him to move unseen, or adopt a nondescript disguise. He was the permanently visible man.

In his favour lay his deceptively slow and gentle, lumbering manner. Unless you knew the man deeply – and few did – this same quiet ungainliness appeared to have transferred itself to his mind. The eyes – set brightly into a face which appeared to have been fashioned from lumpy porridge – contained a look of almost permanent bewilderment. While other people talked, Herbie always gave the impression that he was experiencing grave difficulty in following the sentences. It was the same with his smile – slow, foolish and open. The smile, like the man himself, had been the undoing of many people. Only those who were in full confidence of his track record knew exactly how good he had been; indeed, still was.

To the innocent junior members of the Service, Big Herbie was a cuddly, hard-drinking teddy bear, inclined towards outbursts of great emotion. High-ranking personnel allowed this inaccurate and deceptive legend – including the marked tendency towards drink and sentiment – to be perpetuated. It suited them for people to imagine that Herbie was a bit of a clown; oafish or tearful when drunk. They preferred for it to be put about that Herbie Kruger was a burned-out case. These things get back.

Officially, Herbie spent much of his time on routine Eastern Bloc paperwork; a bit of vetting when necessary, and some hurried activity when trade delegations from the Soviet countries needed checking. To the very few initiates, however, Herbie Kruger was possibly one of the most important officers in the Service. Nor did he give up easily.

Having run a superb network in the DDR, mainly in East Berlin, throughout the fifties and early sixties (known within the secret files as 'the Schnitzer Group'), Herbie had finally been forced to close down all but a few of his long-term assets, and get out by his fingernails.

They had used him in Bonn for a while after that. But then there were complaints from the Federal security services that he was operating in their territory without clearance; so Herbie trekked back to London, muttering dire warnings.

"They've been penetrated. The government offices. NATO itself. Crawling with them," he grumbled to the confessors who had debriefed him at Warminster.

Later he talked at length to the Director, and some Heads of Department; and his prophecies came true. In late 1977 the first of the many Bonn secretary scandals broke. In the following two years, young men and women, compromised in the West, broke and ran for the East.

Herbie shook his head sadly. "They're still at it. The Russians are teaching us a lesson. It's bodies on the ground that count. Black box intelligence is all very well, but you need personnel." He was talking about the constant argument between electronic intelligence-gathering versus the old agent-in-place style. The black box was in favour. Yet Herbie forced the issue. "I still have six people doing one of the most important jobs in East Berlin, and they're not even being serviced properly. There are no regular handling facilities." He was told that the Service was in the midst of a job-shrinkage crisis, and money was tight. The six people in East Berlin about whom Herbie had spoken were known to a guarded few as 'The Telegraph Boys'.

In the end he won the day. The Minister – touchy about money – was finally convinced, and Herbie Kruger's office work in the Whitehall Annexe became a recruiting drive.

Now he ran servicing agents. There were four of them – infiltrated by Herbie with great success into the Deutsche Demokratische Republik, his own old stamping ground before he had been forced to get out, and return to what the Service wits called 'a grace and favour apartment' in St. John's Wood.

The fortnightly trips to West Germany or Berlin ("He's in Brighton for a few days," young Worboys usually informed any enquiring uninitiate) were debriefing sorties. Meetings with one or another of his officers who had easy access to the West.

Once every fortnight Herbie was forced to live for a matter of forty-eight hours in some small safe house, watched over by local officers in Bonn, or West Berlin, while he went through a painstaking question-and-answer debriefing. He then carried the results back home, breaking them down into a raw report before passing the details on to the evaluators and assessors. To the latter Herbie's operation was known as 'Source Six', the phrase simply referring to any information gleaned by the Telegraph Boys, then passed back to London via the Quartet. For both groups their main concern was the early warning of troop and missile movements in East Berlin and its environs within the DDR. The reports usually included highly accurate political and military policy statements.

On the Trident out of Bonn, Herbie Kruger had just left one of these debriefings. For the past two days he had been closeted with a man known as Walter Girren: a small, thin ghost of a person, with a constantly sour expression, who was especially well-placed for making regular excursions into the West. Originally Girren's parents hailed from Westphalia (he thought of himself as a Westphalian) but, in the chaos of split and displaced families at the end of World War Two, the Girrens found themselves living within the Soviet sector of Berlin. Young Walter was born there.

Girren now worked for the Berliner Ensemble as an audio technician. Naturally his education had been undertaken in the DDR, but he had been recruited and trained for the British Service while working on an exchange visit with the National Theatre in London. Almost thirty years of age, Girren had been a member of the Communist Party since his teens. Disenchantment arrived before his twenty-second birthday; so, as far as Herbie was concerned, he was in possession of impeccable bona fides.

The safe house had been a second storey apartment in a narrow street not far from the Provincial Museum: three rooms, kitchen and bathroom. Also two telephones, only one of which worked. It was a normal routine. The 'phone that worked had no number on its dial, but Herbie feared that the official tenants of all the Bonn safe houses were, in reality, whores, and therefore highly suspect. There were traces of powder on the dressing tables; some women's bits and pieces in the bedrooms; and what Herbie called, "the scent of fallen underwear and fallen women". His first action in a Bonn safe house was always to open all the windows: no matter what the weather.

They had spent a day and a half going through the minutiae of Girren's special responsibilities. It was only over lunch, almost by accident, that the other matter came up at all.

As the Trident's engines changed pitch on reaching their cruising altitude, Herbie finally got his two miniature vodkas. He then settled back to concentrate on the small and puzzling piece of information which had been nagging at him ever since Girren mentioned it.

It had its beginnings years ago; and, what seemed to be its end, only a couple of days before Herbie had left to meet Girren. In the daily digest, read by all senior officers, Herbie had spotted a Tass obituary. Brief, and without details of career, it announced that a Colonel-General Jacob Vascovsky, attached to the forces of the Deutsche Demokratische Republik, had died in East Berlin. Suddenly, of a coronary thrombosis.

The digest added what Herbie knew well enough: that Jacob Vascovsky was a senior officer of the KGB. Second-in-command of the Third Chief Directorate in East Berlin.

Herbie Kruger was oddly moved by the news of this officer's passing. He respected the man – his professionalism, dedication and the astute practice of his trade. He had dealt with Jacob Vascovsky many times.

During the years when Herbie ran his famous network, and set up the important, long-standing contacts within the DDR – with no assistance from the politicians, and only plain cover as an engineer – Vascovsky had been to him what Napoleon must have been to Wellington; Rommel to Montgomery.

In the darkness of the Cold War, Vascovsky had, time and again, set entrapments for Kruger and his people. They had fenced with one another, and in the end Vascovsky almost won. Many of Kruger's people actually went down to the Russian until, finally, the network was rolled up and Herbie got out.

When Herbie first became aware of this notable opponent Vascovsky had been a senior major. It was Vascovsky as a full colonel who had at long last caused Kruger to dismantle and jump clear – leaving some special assets in limbo.

Herbie, who in private was not intellectually modest about his own effectiveness in the field, could only acknowledge the high capabilities of Jacob Vascovsky. He had kept an eye on the man's rising fortunes ever since.

The demise of Jacob Vascovsky left an important assignment to be filled. For the Third Chief Directorate of the KGB in East Germany has responsibility for the security of Soviet forces in Germany; and counter-espionage, with special consideration for the American, British and other NATO agencies. Its second-in-command has almost total control over this latter role.

When the important business with Girren had been disposed of, Kruger placed a casual question concerning a rumour about the appointment of a new second-in-command to the Third Chief Directorate. It was meant as a feeler, a seed to plant in Girren's mind, a nudge that might bring in an answer during their next session a couple of months hence – or sent back sooner, via one of the other officers, or by the electronic fast-sender.

Girren looked as though he had been stung, loudly voicing an obscenity against himself. Then he assumed the demeanour of a schoolboy caught cheating. Cursing himself, he apologised. He should have mentioned it to Herbie before this. Only a tiny oddity, but puzzling and worth passing on. Then –

'Have you ever heard of a person dying from a coronary, and being found without a head?''

Herbie remained cool, shaking his own head slowly, as though checking it was still in place.

"Tell me." The big man was now fully alert, aware that it was from tiny remnants of information like this that something larger, more urgent, could emerge.

Apart from Girren's agent-handling duties, his brief was to

turn as many stones as possible; to look for new talent; to catch straws in the wind. In that particular line it is often relatively easy to milk simple information, over a considerable period of time, without the informant even knowing that he, or she, is being tapped. Girren was adept at this exercise, being a good mixer, a witty talker – in spite of his sour expression – and a drinker of no mean capability.

He was already a recognised regular in a number of bars and cafés in East Berlin, choosing with care those places most frequented by government employees, troops, or workers close to military establishments.

In a bar on the Karl-Marx-Allee he often drunk with offduty members of the East German Nationale Volksarmee – in particular a garrulous sergeant of the medical corps. The man was an idiot, a very heavy drinker; but Girren hoarded him against the day; reasoning that he could prove useful.

On the night before making his duty trip into the West, to attend the briefing with Herbie, Girren found the sergeant in fine form. It turned out that he had only recently been moved to the Volkspolizei Hospital, to be put in charge of the mortuary – a fact that led Girren to think they had finally rumbled the man's inefficiency.

Well in his cups, the sergeant mentioned, with some pride, that for one night he had been in sole charge of the corpse of a high ranking Russian officer. Bragging, he even gave Vascovsky's name; and later indicated that all was not as it seemed.

Girren bought him a couple of drinks, to tip him over the brink of discretion. It was then that the man disclosed that the officer was supposed to have died of a coronary thrombosis; but, to use the medical sergeant's own words: "Never have I seen a coronary case with an exploded head. Mind you, I wasn't supposed to see. Nothing left except the neck and chin. The doctors came in and put wadding and gauze where the head should have been before they flew him home to his Mother Russia and a great military funeral."

Kruger's huge hands lifted and fell, palms flat, on to his knees. He looked at Walter Girren. Neither of them spoke for a long time.

"It's water in the mouth that does it," Kruger eventually said, almost to himself.

"Eh?"

"Water in the mouth," Herbie repeated, this time for Girren's benefit. "Blows the head right off. Effective." He had read about it somewhere. If a man is determined to shoot himself but remains afraid that the bullet will not kill – leaving him only with serious brain damage – he fills his mouth with water, inserts the muzzle of the pistol through pursed lips, and pulls the trigger. The pressure of the water does the trick. The head is blown to shards.

Now, 29,000 feet above Europe, Herbie Kruger still pondered over the incident. If the mortuary sergeant was telling the truth Colonel-General Jacob Vascovsky had committed suicide. Some breach – punishable by a silent, private death – would have been dealt with in Moscow itself. You cannot *make* a man fill his mouth with water, then hold him down and push a pistol between his lips.

He could be wrong, of course; but it had all the marks of a hush-up job; and the Colonel-General was a professional. Herbie had taken the trouble to keep an eye on his file. Nothing showed. Then he recalled something else. About six months before, he had been asked his opinion about an attempted recruitment of someone around that rank bracket. The request came to him via the Director, who had been asked by the Americans. Were there any pressure points? Not one, Herbie replied, making it clear that this man was unapproachable. He recalled using the jargon – *Vascovsky's sterile*.

Suicide seemed strange. The circumstances even more strange. Without being in any way morbid, Herbie Kruger wished he had been given the chance to see the body. He then signalled to the stewardess for another couple of vodkas. He wanted to drink to the memory of Jacob Vascovsky.

At Heathrow young Worboys was waiting with a car. He looked serious, but said nothing until they were inside the airport tunnel. There was a soundproof panel between them and the driver.

"There's a flap," he began. "They've had a walk-in at the Consulate General's office in West Berlin."

"Who?" Herbie turned his head towards Worboys.

"He asked for you." The younger man sounded nervous. "They're all doing handstands."

"So? They always do handstands. Who is it?"

"Name of Mistochenkov. Captain in the KGB. Says to tell you: 'Piotr'."

Herbie's face only changed a fraction. Calmly he told Worboys to get the driver to stop at the Post House Hotel. Then Worboys was to use a public telephone. "Take care – use an open-line bit of double-talk. Get Tubby Fincher. I must see the Director as soon as we get to Whitehall. We'll need the Minister as well. There has to be a decision to bring the walk-in back here fast. You'd better stand by to fly out."

Worboys looked as though he had been hit with a rotter. fish.

"To Berlin?"

"Of course to Berlin."

In his head Kruger was weighing facts. Piotr had been his own network's cryptonym for Mistochenkov. When he first knew him – though they had never met – the Russian had been a sergeant. Like Colonel-General Vascovsky, Mistochenkov had risen in rank, though his duties had not changed over the years.

Captain Mistochenkov had been the Colonel-General's ADC.

3

OUTWARDLY, BIG HERBIE's two passions, apart from his work, were drinking and the music of Gustav Mahler. Those who knew him slightly better were often surprised at his other abiding interest – English history.

Possibly a psychiatrist would explain this by pointing out that, as Britain was Kruger's adopted country, the man's subconscious drew him naturally towards a study of his surrogate land's development. Whatever the reason, Herbie read English history with the dedication of a student committed to obtaining an outstanding honours degree. .

It was understandable, then, that every time Herbie faced the Director of his Service he thought of the *Historia Anglorum*'s description of King Henry I. William of Malmesbury, that vital monastic historian, wrote of Henry: *a man of middle stature; his hair was black, but scanty near the forehead; his eyes mildly bright; his chest brawny; his body fleshy; he was facetious in proper season, nor did multiplicity of business cause him to be less pleasant when he mixed in society.*

To Herbie, it was a living picture of the Director, whom he now faced over the desk, high in the main building which housed their particular corner of the secret world.

Occupying a third chair was Tubby Fincher – so known because of his almost skeletal stature. He looked glum. The Director, whose experience in secret affairs went back to the middle of World War Two, seemed subdued. It was not the proper season for facetiousness.

They had trekked back to the building after a visit to the Minister, from which Herbie had been barred: he sat alone in

31

an anteroom, tapping his large feet and fiddling with his hands; his whole bulk exuding frustration.

The Minister had been edgy, the Director told him. He was worried in case of political repercussions – diplomatic incidents. "He's also concerned about the cost."

"And I'm concerned about the cost to my people," Herbie replied. "Not to mention the benefits to this country." Ministers, in Herbie's experience, were all too ready to sacrifice important operatives because of funding. He asked how matters finally stood, stressing the point that young Worboys was at that moment waiting at Heathrow for instructions.

"I carry the can." For a second the Director's eyes became more than mildly bright.

"Then you can authorise?" Herbie responded.

The Director nodded, then sighed, giving Tubby Fincher a sideways glance; which meant he was asking for help. It was apparent to Herbie that they really wanted the KGB captain returned to the East. He was an embarrassment. Notes would be passed between ambassadors and consuls; words would be exchanged between foreign ministers; there would be political unpleasantness.

Tubby shifted in his chair. "What's he offering? Nothing. There's nothing concrete."

Herbie fought to remain calm, asking what the hell Tubby thought the captain from East Berlin was offering. "He asked for me, using the crypto we designated to him years ago – when he was only a sergeant; when I was in the field. *He* knew that, or remembered it; which means he has something to say about my people out there. The new people, *and* the Telegraph Boys." He went on to point out, for the third or fourth time, that he had already established something fishy concerning Vascovsky's death. The smell, he told them, had become more putrid since Captain Mistochenkov walked into the Berlin Consulate General's office.

"More to the point," said the Director, looking Herbie in the eyes, "what is *he* asking?"

"Asylum." The first syllable came out as 'Ess . . .'

"And you?" There was a note of caution in the Director's tone. The KGB man had used an old cryptonym – culled from Lord knew where – designed to bring Herbie running. "A message to you, saying that he's Piotr? Could be a lure."

Herbie shrugged, as if the Director was stating the obvious. He then said it was because of this very possibility that he was sending Worboys.

"He wants *you*. He might not come back with Worboys."

"Then we shall know. I am much more concerned with the possibility of the man having something for us. Something concerning Source Six: the Quartet and the Telegraph Boys. Something vital."

"Such as?" Tubby Fincher looked at the carpet, as though he already knew Herbie's answer, and wished to avoid seeing the big German's face as he put it into words.

"Such as a potential blow-out."

The Director picked up a metal letter opener, holding it like a dagger. "Your argument, Herbie, is that Source Six could be in jeopardy – whichever way it goes." Clearly, and with few words, he spread out the logic of the situation.

The aide to the deceased Colonel-General had come over, walked-in, and passed a message which Herbie would recognise; using a cryptonym he could only know through contact with one of Kruger's old associates. This was either a means to lure Herbie to Berlin, where they could perform a knock-down-drag-out op, taking Kruger into the East; or to pass on information indicating that the Soviets knew more than was good for any of them.

Herbie agreed. The man was there. Time was being wasted. "You know what walk-ins are like? You have to treat them as temporary mental patients."

"Quite." The Director gave him a prim look.

Subtlety stirred in the large German's mind. The walk-in had not, as yet, put any strings on his presumed defection.

"Which means we can toss him back." Tubby Fincher had a cold streak which Herbie often found exploitable.

"Exactly." Herbie gave one of his daft smiles, which did not fool either of the other two men. "Let me have him. Just for a while, eh?"

The Director coughed, a rumbling triple note, like a Morse Code S. "Berlin is worried," he began; but Herbie cut him short. Of course Berlin was worried. Hadn't he just been talking about the odd psychological state of walk-ins? Nobody was happy with a walk-in defector: particularly people in an embassy or consulate.

"All the more reason to get him back fast." Herbie's hands made what was meant to be an innocent, trusting gesture. The movement came out as one of extreme belligerence.

The silence became almost tangible. Then the Director nodded. "Can young Worboys manage it alone?"

"I'll tear his neck off if he doesn't." Herbie grinned again. "Yes, it'll be the first big chance to prove himself since you foisted him on to me. 'Foisted' is the right word, yes? A good word?"

Tubby Fincher gave a small nod, and Herbie addressed himself to the Director's right-hand man. "You get some back-up for him, Tubby? Berlin station people? Vehicles? Army? Air Force? Helicopter out of West Berlin; then a fast ride home in an RAF jet? Okay?"

Fincher caught the Director's reluctant inclination of the head, got to his feet, said okay, he would see to it, and made for the door.

Before he had reached it, Herbie Kruger turned to him again, speaking with a soft clarity that underlined his sense of urgency. "Call Worboys first, at Heathrow, Tubby, eh? Have him paged. He's Mr. Robinson, meeting a Mr. Armstrong off an Amsterdam flight."

Tubby said he would be back to report as soon as Worboys was confirmed away, and the Consulate had been flashed. It was better, now, for Herbie to spend a short time alone with the Director.

The Director did not like any of it – torn between his knowledge and the subtle pressures of the Whitehall Mafia: particularly the Minister. Yet he appeared almost relieved that the decision had been taken. He said something about not bothering to speak with the Minister until they had their man neatly tucked up at the Warminster house. "I presume you want him at Warminster?"

Herbie said he felt Warminster was too obvious. "We're on sensitive ground. Somewhere less obtrusive would be better. Say that nice little house near Oxford."

The Director sighed. "The place at Charlton?"

Herbie smiled. "Charlton, yes; like the footballer. Nice. I could take him for walks on the Downs, if the weather's fine."

"Money."—The Director looked up at the ceiling. "It all costs money, Herbie. Warminster has an allocation. Whenever I open up one of the other places it shows on the internal budget."

Herbie raised his eyebrows. "What are secret funds for?"

"They seem to be for the Treasury hounds to scrutinise and query, Herbie. When I tell them five thousand has been spent on opening up one of the houses for a special interrogation they will want to know what the profit came out at. If I give you the Charlton house, this joker had better be worth it."

"In gold to the value of his weight." Herbie did not smile this time. There was an odd glint in the usually vacant eyes. The Director looked away, then suggested that he should get Habland, of Personnel, to arrange for a pair of lion-tamers — in the constantly changing service jargon 'lion-tamers' was the current argot for minders, bodyguards, watchers and general thugs. "And the odd confessor, of course," he concluded.

"I'll do it myself," Herbie countered with a curt snap.

"All of it?"

"Unless you give me a specific order."

The Director said he insisted on the lion tamers, but would leave the question of confessors to Herbie.

"Confessors," Herbie gave another of his shrugs, the yoke-like shoulders moving in a manner which suggested a great deal of strength under the jacket of his cheap suit. "I'm an old Cold Warrior, Chief. I've had my troops stranded in the battlefield, on and off, for twenty years. They're stranded no longer. I don't want to see them cut off again.

"Your black boxes and electronics, or the American intelligence satellites, can't do it all. Twice in the past two months my Telegraph Boys have come in with Soviet movements, days, weeks, before the satellites. Now there's a man sitting, jittery in the Berlin Consulate, who knows names. I *need* him; to be certain my people are safe; and stay safe."

He leaned forward. "Does our precious Minister realise the complete operational value of Source Six?"

"He knows what he needs to know."

"That we have happy clients?"

"Yes."

"Then he should be told – maybe by the happy clients – that there will be weeping and wailing if Source Six is dried."

"He knows, Herbie."

"It should be kept that way."

The Director hesitated for a second before saying that one of the first rules of successful intelligence was to remain emotionally uninvolved with one's field staff. As he said it, he realised the error.

Herbie rose, lifting a clenched fist, bringing it softly down on the Director's desk. "Emotionally uninvolved? With respect, Chief, you weren't there. I don't want to know who else does or does not run Telegraph Boys in the Soviet Bloc. I simply know that I set up the very first six. Personally, while the Berlin crisis was boiling, and all Europe stood and watched them build that bloody Wall. I was going over every day: briefing, settling six people, six valued friends, into places where they could detect troop and missile moves long before bugs and satellites.

"Those people out there are my responsibility, and have been since 1961. I've watched them being neglected; trying to pass stuff over; having their letterboxes filched, their controls withdrawn, their lines of communication cut away, because the Treasury did not want them maintained. They're still there. All six. Still at their posts; still working. I've opened them up to full operational strength again. The Army, Navy and Air Force are more than delighted at what they're giving us – not to mention the political advisers, and the Americans. In spite of their eyes in the sky, they've been buying, haven't they?"

The Director acknowledged that the Americans had been purchasing information on troop and missile dispersal, even though their electronic surveillance provided them with proof – much later.

Herbie hardly paused in his monologue; saying that while all those with access to Source Six thought in terms of cryptonyms chosen at random from mythology – Gemini, Hecuba, Horus, Nestor, Priam, Electra – *he* knew them as people. He did not say that he had once loved Electra.

As he spoke, the faces and voices of these six people passed before his eyes. Then the faces of Walter Girren, Christoph Schnabeln, Anton Mohr and Anna Blatte overlapped those of the Telegraph Boys: the old, faithful watchers, running in a mental montage with their new handlers. For all he or the Director knew, all these people were now at risk . . .

It was at this point that Tubby Fincher reappeared, to say that Worboys was on his way, and Berlin was relieved. "Our friend's a handful, apparently."

"They're always a handful," muttered the Director.

"If he'll come out with Worboys, Comrade Mistochenkov'll be delivered tomorrow afternoon."

Herbie nodded. "Then they'd better bring him straight down to Charlton. You open it up for me first thing tomorrow, Chief?"

The Director made a motion of assent.

"Then I'll leave the lion-tamers and nuts and bolts to Tubby. I go pack. You have someone to keep house down there?"

Again the Director said yes, there would be someone.

"Good. You give our friend a crypto, Tubby?"

"We thought it better to jettison 'Piotr'." Fincher's emaciated hand made a twirling gesture. "He's now known as 'Tapeworm'."

Herbie grunted, his mind already leaping ahead to his needs for what might be a lengthy stay in Oxfordshire. "You got full sound in the Charlton house?"

They said yes.

"And a stereo? I can't live without music."

The two men smiled. Tubby Fincher said, "He shall have Mahler wherever he goes."

"You are right," smiled Herbie. "*Mensch*, how you are right." With that he went out, his bellowing laugh echoing down the corridor.

4

THE HOUSEKEEPER AT Charlton was not happy to see Herbie Kruger. Her name was Miss Adelle Sturgis, and the job was some kind of sinecure, because she was about ten years off pensionable age.

Miss Sturgis had been PA to the retiring Deputy Director, Maitland-Wood. They felt she was fully sterile, but some gabby mouth happened to tell her that he doubted if the Charlton house would ever be used. She had therefore bent the rules, and regarded the place very much as a home; even inviting friends and relatives; not just keeping to her own quarters.

Herbie was not happy but, on checking, discovered that basic security had been preserved. He took a lion-tamer called Max down with him, and they called the Service telephone people in within an hour of arrival.

Miss Sturgis was banished to her bedsitter, read a list of duties by Herbie, and instructed to tell all possible callers – both local and distant – that she could not be disturbed for the next few days. Boring relatives, and difficult old family business, was the coverall excuse. The main telephone was connected to her quarters, and a couple of new, secure lines put in downstairs. While this was being done, Herbie and Max did the rounds – checking the sound system and security locks.

The place stood well back from the road, screened by trees and a wall that had electronic eyes placed along it at intervals. There were automatic locks; the freezer was replenished: Miss Sturgis got on to the milkman and altered her daily order, also ensuring that local busybodies had wind of the imminent arrival of Sturgis relations. She even hinted there would be a solicitor present. The locals would respect a solicitor and stay clear. Likely out-of-village callers were warned off by 'phone, while Herbie sat and listened.

He then tested the stereo unit by playing the Mahler First while Max used the music to check out a pair of dodgy bugs in one of the bedrooms.

The house was modest from the outside – red brick, built around the mid-thirties, with some well-established virginia creeper crawling up its façade. The Service had made some structural changes, so that there were four bedrooms (not counting Miss Sturgis's quarters); two bathrooms; a pair of good-sized rooms downstairs; a large kitchen; and windows which gave clear views through the trees.

They were deep enough into the country for safety, yet Oxford was easily accessible should Tapeworm prove able to take in a movie, if Herbie thought he deserved a treat. Twenty minutes in the car would see them on to the Berkshire Downs. Herbie knew the value of exercise when you were into deep confessions. He wondered how Worboys was faring. Worboys should have Max's friend Charles with him when they brought Tapeworm in. *If* they brought Tapeworm in.

In spite of his confident show in front of the Director and Tubby Fincher, Herbie was well aware of the vicissitudes of walk-in defectors. They usually took the step either from desperation or from sudden decision. Sometimes they regretted the move almost as soon as they had made it. After all, a quick defection, like a quick marriage, can often end in misery. The walk-in, Herbie considered, always had to be handled with stern and fast action; before they fully realised all former ties had been severed – life, family, country. That they had committed a kind of emotional suicide.

He hoped Worboys was up to the job; praying that the local boys were on their toes.

They were.

Worboys and party arrived just before five-thirty. Herbie stayed upstairs in his bedroom with a bottle of vodka, sending Max down to help Charles get the 'patient' into the house.

On Max's instructions, Worboys came to Herbie's room as soon as they got in. He looked tired and shaken.

"Problems?" Herbie asked. "Have a drink. You got him here?"

Worboys said yes, he would have the drink; and yes, he had got Tapeworm from Berlin. But only just. "The man's a loony. Wanted you and nobody else. Threatened to stay; then to kick up a fuss; to go out and scream the British had abducted him. Bugger wouldn't believe I was taking him to you. Had to get him pissed stupid before we could budge him. There's going to be some traffic from the Berlin Consulate. The Consul General was furious. Talked of a Courts Martial. The lot."

"Take no notice. Tapeworm still pissed?"

Worboys nodded, gulping down his vodka. "Out cold. We almost fed him this stuff intravenously on the way back. Had to carry him in. Max – that the name of the other lion-tamer? – he's staying with him."

"Let him sleep it off." Herbie laughed aloud. "Get Max to feed him black coffee and a clean-out pill when he begins to come round. He'll last the night. I don't want him until tomorrow."

"And me?" Worboys seemed anxious.

"You stay here. I'll call our great hope in Whitehall and tell him everything is well. But you stay here."

Worboys looked crestfallen. It would do him good, Herbie thought. The young man had been too much of a know-all when he had come into the Service from the school. Herbie had been tough with him from the word go. He also knew that Tony Worboys was having a *liaison dangereuse* with a young woman called Noel in Registry.

"Mind if I make a call out?" Worboys asked: too casual.

"I mind, yes," Herbie guffawed. "But you'll do it just the same. Keep it to the bare essentials. None of the crudities of passion. You'll be on tape."

Worboys made a grimace and went downstairs to telephone. Herbie gave him ten minutes, then followed, to call Tubby Fincher and say things were moving.

"You started?"

"You want miracles? No. Tomorrow we start. If you want the tapes you'll have to send someone for them; and they probably won't be complete. I'll be doing a lot in the open. Repercussions?"

"Plenty, but the Director's purring at everyone." Then, in

a voice, edged with desperation, Tubby added: "For Christ's sake nail something, Herbie, or we'll all be in hock for the next twenty years."

Herbie merely laughed, replaced the telephone, sent Worboys off to get food, and then settled down with another vodka and the Mahler Fifth.

It was not a random choice. Though Herbie would never express himself with the same concentrated emotional indulgence as the composer had done concerning the Fifth.

It is the sum of all the suffering I have been compelled to endure at the hands of life, Gustav Mahler wrote of that symphony, a watershed in his life and music – twelve years before World War One. Deplored by the critics as *'angry herds of instruments stamping down fragments of melody'*, it had yet set a new path for composers of the twentieth century.

For Herbie to listen to this great piece was, in many ways, to reflect on the sum of *his* life – from the strident trumpet opening, and the funereal brass; through the grief, passion, despair and storm; to the happier Alpine dances of the Scherzo; and the sombre marches again, before the counterpoint of the grand chorale conclusion.

All this sound had special meaning for Herbie Kruger. His own true life had not really begun until the sharp blare of the funeral march for his own father.

Before that the memory was distorted, fragmentary; throwing up glimpses of nothing but love and happiness. The early recall, which coloured all that followed, was one of vague excitement: the tall, handsome father and the young mother, with her long blonde hair, appeared to have lavished gaiety, happiness and love on the boy; against what seemed to be permanent blue skies, and the comfortable little house in the Pankow district of Berlin.

From those earliest years Herbie remembered nothing but love and tenderness. There were vivid mental pictures (sometimes still coming to him in dreams) of treats and outings: picnics and boating trips at Wannsee. His mother always seemed to be laughing, ready with a joke; while the father, huge to the child, was a god in uniform, one who never stormed or ranted but showed only kindness, understanding and, above all, affection. Perhaps, Herbie wondered, this was because his duties kept him away from home for such long periods.

It was during the first ten years or so that Herbie was also taught to aim his personal affection and devotion towards the Führer and the Fatherland. Like his father and mother, these two mystical figures were, to the child, the twin staffs of life. He thrilled to the pageantry of the city of his birth – the banners, the marches, the martial music. He longed to be old enough to follow his father into the air; to wear the uniform.

In fact the only uniform he did wear was that of the Hitler Youth; but by that time he had become puzzled. Schoolfriends disappeared. Their families were taken in the night. There were whispers, and an abstract sense that all was not blue skies.

At the beginning, membership of the Hitler Youth was fun – rather like the things he had heard of the International Boy Scout movement. He began, like the rest, as a *Pimpf*, as the junior members were called during the stage of apprenticeship – having fun with athletics, week-end camps, lessons on Nazi history. He had already become a little bewildered when he passed the tests, graduating to the *Jungvolk* – Young Folk – and taking the oath:

In the presence of this blood banner, which represents our Führer, I swear to devote all my energies and my strength to the saviour of our country, Adolf Hitler. I am ready and willing to give up my life for him, so help me God.

Then the war, and with it the excitement turned to fear; and also grief. The beloved father was gone for ever, somewhere over the English Channel in 1940. Oddly, young Eberhard did not blame the British. Maybe it was the wording of the telegram, or the letter which followed, and their effect upon his mother who lost her sparkle and even some of her affection almost overnight.

His father had died For Führer and Fatherland. The twin staffs had deprived him of his father. Now other things came into relief. Scenes, only half taken in, of brutality – an old man lying bleeding in the gutter; screams of people being dragged off the streets by men in uniform. Young Kruger's mind became an insecure world of distorted images.

The bombing started. A child matured quickly in those days. He was a man – thin, tall, but strong – by the time he reached fourteen. It was during his fifteenth year that he stood in the rubble of the street in Pankow, knowing that his sad, prematurely-grey mother lay dead beneath the bricks. Kruger, at that moment, made a conscious rejection of his country, and all things totalitarian.

The Führer and Fatherland had disposed of his father and mother. Later, he understood that it was a Russian shell that laid the houses into untidy heaps in Pankow. Then, almost automatically, he ran; hid, avoided the SS squads, which searched the streets of dying Berlin for deserters – whom they hanged from trees and lamp-posts – or for young men ready to serve in the last-ditch defence of the city.

In April 1945 he was picked up by the Americans. Within three months, as the war in Europe ended, at less than sixteen years of age, young Kruger was re-educated and used by the United States' OSS to infiltrate DP Camps; to listen, watch and weed out ranking Nazis posing as innocents.

In this Big Herbie (he had already earned the nickname, filling out with good food between assignments) proved an expert. He had a natural aptitude for the work; he also learned quickly, and soon became aware that Fascism and Communism were extreme views wearing similar hats. He knew now where he stood; and worked, learning all the time, for the Americans, until the OSS was disbanded in the late autumn of 1945.

In those few months of trusted work Big Herbie had become a teenage rebel with a cause. The disbandment of the OSS was a lingering death. In fact, the boy stayed on with the Americans, was paid by them, continued in unofficial training, working undercover, until after his seventeenth birthday.

In July 1947 the American President – Truman – set up the Central Intelligence Agency, and one of the men handling the lad tried hard to get American naturalisation for him, with the idea of recruitment into the brand new service. But the area was sensitive; the applications became blocked again and again, so, unofficially, young Kruger was turned over to the British.

The officer who first interviewed Herbie was the man later to become Deputy Director of the Service – Willis Maitland-Wood. His decision was almost immediate. The British Service retrained Herbie, and completed his education.

Herbie worked on the fringes until 1951, when, with a more senior German control, he returned to Pankow – now part of the Russian Zone of Berlin – as a repatriated DP.

This infiltration proved completely successful, and, for many years, Herbie stayed undercover within the Deutsche Demokratische Republik (which, at one point, actually trained him in simple engineering jobs).

From a lone, controlled agent, gathering raw intelligence, Herbie Kruger became one of his Service's most important props in East Germany – cunning and wily; expert in his choice of targets; efficient in carrying out special assignments and, later, in the more accurate work of recruiting agents.

Towards the end of the nineteen-fifties, with political tensions growing hot and cold between East and West – particularly over the question of Berlin – there was much public talk about the nature of a possible World War Three. Pundits and military Press experts confidently predicted, with their usual macabre delight, that, should the nuclear deterrent cease to live up to its name, and become the final cause of mankind's destruction, the West would have only four minutes in which to prepare for the holocaust. The Four-Minute Warning became almost a comedian's black catch-phrase.

In fact, as far as the politicians and military strategists were concerned, the warning would be a good deal longer than four minutes. Already, electronics had progressed far enough to give considerable advance information. But an even earlier indication of forthcoming events was possible, by the covert surveillance of key military and political personalities in the Soviet Bloc; and even within Russia itself.

As East Berlin was a centre of great strategic importance, there were at least six key figures normally resident within its boundaries. Kruger's network was providing admirable information on troop movements, and, in late 1959, Herbie –

who made regular trips into the West – was given a long and detailed private briefing.

First, his masters acquainted him with the six appointments (four military and two political) whose movements were of special interest. Next he was briefed in depth concerning sudden changes in their living conditions and work loads. They gave him further tips which would indicate alterations in tactics and attitudes within these six appointments. Finally he was sent back to recruit six men and women, of his own choice, to be, in turn, briefed and handled by his network.

The surveillance agents chosen by him had to be beyond suspicion; completely loyal, and trained on the spot. Their job would be to make regular reports on the movements of the six figures they would be watching. It was also necessary for them to be able to send flash warnings should all, or any one of the targets suddenly behave in different, unrecognisable patterns. The reports from this team would constitute a true early warning of the imminence of nuclear attack – long before the fast-growing electronic devices could give closer indications.

The military and political posts would almost certainly remain constant; though their occupants would change – as individuals were promoted, demoted, died or were pensioned off. But the surveillance team had to remain regular for a good many years: their cover deep and undetectable.

These six watchers were cryptonymed the 'Telegraph Boys'.

The final moves in placing the watchers were carried out during the tensions of August 1961, and the sealing of the East-West Berlin border with the obscene Wall: the reinforced concrete blocks and bricks; wire; steel tank traps; observation towers and mines; even the strengthened façades of buildings that, in all, went to make up a compelling and chillingly active monument to repression.

Herbie managed the job; continuing to run his network for almost another four years. When it all collapsed, and they ordered him back to the West, he was shattered by the lack of consideration the Ministry of Defence, the Foreign Office and, to some extent, his own Service, gave to his faithful Telegraph Boys.

Only the constant, dripping-water technique on his superiors brought about the move allowing him to set up a new network: the Quartet – Girren, Schnabeln, Mohr and Blatte – whose main objective was to service the Telegraph Boys again; handling their weekly and daily reports, maintaining contact . . .

As the Mahler Fifth came to its moving and dramatic conclusion, Herbie thought, almost in wonderment, how the Telegraph Boys had remained constant and loyal for over fifteen years.

If anyone could have ferreted out the Telegraph Boys, Vascovsky should have done so. Herbie was plagued by the demons which so often beset intelligence operatives of great experience. The devils of intuition. He had known fear often; and it was there now, deep in his conscious thoughts, reflected by the beauties of the music – and, possibly, coloured by the alcohol he had consumed.

There was movement in the house. Worboys came in to introduce Charles, who could have been Max's twin. Herbie showed no surprise; to him most lion-tamers looked alike – big, tough, menacing young men who were also usually blessed with quick intelligence, as well as the necessary attributes of brawn.

They reported that Tapeworm had come round, been violently sick, complained of a gigantic hangover, panicked mildly, and been put to sleep, with soothing medication, by Max.

"He'll wake up as hungry as a hunter," Charles said.

Worboys, a shade cocky, assured Herbie that this would not happen until morning. Herbie pointed out, with quiet charm, that he had been dealing with matters like this since before Worboys was a gleam in his father's eye. Worboys did not argue.

Miss Sturgis provided food – an evening meal of an elaborate nature – as if trying to make up for previous lapses. Herbie gave instructions on how he expected things to be run during their stay; sending Charles off to relieve Max, so that he could be briefed separately. The question of duty rosters for the lion-tamers he left for the two men to settle among themselves.

Worboys was to keep an eye on the tapes, when Herbie worked in the house: that, and any odd job, or set-up, which might be needed during what promised to be a lengthy stay.

"I don't think he's going to give me the lot in one go." Herbie appeared amused by the thought. "They seldom do." Worboys had learned it all from the lectures, and Herbie suggested, with some force, that he should listen in as much as possible. "You might learn what it's really all about."

"You use the bedroom, I suppose?" Worboys tried to be casual in his ignorance.

Herbie's smile did not look so stupid this time. "No. We use this room, the dining room, the garden, the car – when he's ready – and the good fresh open air." He continued to give a short lecture, pointing out to Worboys that it might be best to forget all he had learned about formal interrogations at the school.

"You think this room's too comfortable?"

"Well . . ."

"You want him in a bare room? Sitting on a chair where he cannot touch you? All the old tricks? Listen, my friend, just watch your Uncle Herbie. This kind of thing is different. He has reasons for being here, but I doubt he wants to tell me those reasons. We'll get – how do you say it? – a cargo of old rabbits . . ."

"Load of old bunny."

"Yes. We'll get that first." The grin broadened. "Then Herbie will pounce, eh? Listen, mark and digest, young Tony. Oh, and don't telephone Noel too often. I cannot promise immunity from the wrath to come, should the tapes get into the wrong hands."

Later that night, in bed, with the closing beauty of the Mahler Fifth repeating itself like a looped tape in his head, Herbie thought about the work he would start with Mistochenkov in the morning. He kept thinking about what an old and valued interrogator had once advised him: it seemed most applicable in this case. The confessor had said, "Listen to the rhythms, but forget about the melody."

HERBIE HAD ORDERED breakfast in bed. Tapeworm was to be taken downstairs and given breakfast in the dining room, then placed with Worboys in the other room. Max or Charles was to tip off Herbie when all was set.

Max brought the breakfast on a tray – four sausages, bacon, egg, toast, marmalade. Herbie immediately asked about Tapeworm.

"Doing nicely," Max said, like a medical orderly. He added that, even so, Tapeworm was jumpy. "Said they promised he would see you. 'Anxious' is the word I'd use."

"Good," said Herbie, taking in a mouthful of bacon and sausage, and motioning for Max to leave. He wondered if the man were gay: he had specially asked to work with his partner, Charles. Herbie liked gay lion-tamers. They were unusually good if the going got rough.

By the time Max came in again to say that young Worboys had Tapeworm in what he called 'the library' Herbie had breakfasted, washed, shaved and dressed. He liked the bit about the library; there were at least twenty books in the room.

He had prepared a bulky file, containing old and non-confidential reports. Only the top two pages had his type-written notes on Mistochenkov and his former boss, Colonel-General Vascovsky. As he went downstairs, Herbie found himself humming.

Worboys had carried out instructions to the letter. Tapeworm faced the door so that he would see Herbie the moment the German came in. The fear in his eyes was there for only a second, as Herbie entered – which he did with speed and some drama, framing himself in the opening and giving his broad, stupid smile.

Mistochenkov had hardly changed. A few more lines perhaps; the hair starting to thin. He would be about forty now, but had kept his figure, looking slim and muscular; his long, sensitive face a shade pale. The eyes gave out fear. Apart from that, the man looked relaxed, leaning back in an armchair, an English cigarette held between long fingers.

"Well, Piotr. You searched for me a long time. Now you've come to me. I am flattered."

Herbie had spoken in German, and the Russian replied in the same language. "I thought they would not bring you. Now I'm glad. It's good to meet you at last."

Herbie extended a hand. He restrained himself from using his crushing grasp. Better to leave the handclasp weak, limpid; to let Tapeworm imagine he was dealing with an invertebrate. Retired field men often go soft. He waved Mistochenkov back into his chair, and gave Worboys the nod. Worboys took his coffee with him. There would probably be telephonic whisperings with Registry, Herbie thought.

"We often wondered why you called me Piotr." Mistochenkov seemed fascinated to be in Herbie's presence at last, and could not take his eyes off the large man.

"We knew only your initials. P: V. Mistochenkov. We thought the P probably stood for Piotr."

The Russian smiled. "Wrong, Big Herbie."

Herbie laughed aloud. "So you knew my nickname? Ah, it hasn't changed." Then, smartly, opening the folder and uncapping his pen, "Your full name then, please?"

There was a minute hesitation; a look of quick surprise before the Russian spoke, "Pavel Viktor Mistochenkov. Captain. KGB."

Herbie made the next few minutes equally efficient – "This is the official side of things, you understand" – and went on to demand age and other details, like some border control guard.

"How long do you expect to be staying in our country?" he asked at last. The Russian's fingers trembled; fear returning to his eyes.

49

"I . . . I thought they understood. I wish to stay . . ."

"On a permanent basis?"

"Of course. Isn't that why you took me out of Berlin?"

Herbie allowed his features to soften. "You were brought out of Berlin because you asked to see me. I happened to be in England, and did not wish to make the trip. You can be taken back again."

"But I thought . . . I asked for asylum."

Herbie pretended to refer to his notes. "So you did, Pavel. Yes, you did. May I ask: were you informed officially that we had granted asylum?"

"Well . . . No. I assumed . . . naturally, when they said . . ." Mistochenkov looked deeply disturbed.

Herbie said he had known Pavel for a long time ("Not personally, of course. This is our first *real* meeting"), and always imagined that he was a fully trained officer of the KGB. "You were only a sergeant when I first knew of you. Now a captain. You are a trained officer?"

Yes, the Russian said. Of course he was a trained officer.

Then he should know the usual drill with defectors. Asylum was only granted when the nature of the goods was well authenticated. "It really depends on your reasons for coming to us: if you have anything to sell."

"But I have."

"Then it'll be okay; no worries. But I have to warn you that what you think is a valuable asset may mean little to us. It would be the same if I had walked in on you. If the goods are sub-standard . . ."

"You'd send me back?"

"Perhaps. Perhaps not yet. We could hold you as stock. A KGB captain might be a good bargain." He allowed the smile to spread. "But I'm certain that will not be the case with you. Just tell me, first, why you came."

Mistochenkov gave a small shrug, and said why did any of them ever come? Disenchantment with the Party; the way things were going. In particular, dissatisfaction with the job he had to do.

"Yes." Herbie did not look up. "I was sorry to hear about Vascovsky's death. You'd been with him a long time."

"Almost the whole of my career. It was a great blow."

"And they've given you a new appointment?"

"Yes."

"Not to your liking?"

Mistochenkov repeated that the new appointment was not to his liking. He seemed about to reveal the assignment when Herbie cut in, asking about the exact circumstances of Colonel-General Vascovsky's death. Mistochenkov had drilled himself well. Not a flicker: the story straight, and repeated with exact detail.

They had been working all day and were just leaving the Colonel-General's office. He, Mistochenkov, had dismissed the driver, and was going to take his boss home. He often did. There was a bar they would sometimes visit for a drink, quietly, before going to the official apartment block where the boss lived. Vascovsky, he said, complained of indigestion. ("We'd only had time for a snack lunch that day – sandwiches and beer, eaten quickly.") Then, just as they got to the car, he doubled up and collapsed over the bonnet. "I rendered what first aid I could, but it was obvious he was a very sick man. He could hardly breathe." According to Mistochenkov, he had dashed back into the building. An ambulance arrived quickly. "I rode with him to the hospital. He was dead before we got there. They used oxygen – everything. He just died in the ambulance."

Herbie asked which hospital. The old Charité, on Invalidenstrasse, the Russian told him.

A cargo of old rabbits, thought Herbie. Aloud, he asked what Pavel thought he had to give them – "Just headings will do."

Pavel Mistochenkov said he would provide the names of six more secretaries working for the Bonn Government who were passing information, and their case officers, there was also a Federal Republic politician who had been buried deep by the KGB for a long time – *his* case officer as well.

"That should be enough to start with." Herbie nodded several times. "You'll probably think of one or two other things later."

"If I give you these? If I give them now? Can you provide me with some assurances?"

Herbie took a while to answer, then said it would be a few

days; but, yes, he thought that when Pavel's information had been checked out they could begin talking terms.

The Russian indicated that he was ready to talk now. Herbie nodded assent, then quickly asked, "You didn't tell me what your new appointment was to be, Pavel."

There was a lengthy pause. Mistochenkov swallowed. "I was to be put in charge of counter-intelligence within our own forces in Berlin. Spying on my own comrades – a job I've never done, and a job I would hate to do. A *Spitzel*." He used the German slang word for an informer, which, Herbie mentally acknowledged, was good psychology. Privately he again thought, a cargo of old rabbits.

"I understand," Herbie said with great sympathy, adding that Pavel's service had a nasty habit of siphoning people off to do dirty jobs, like watching their own.

"It's immoral, but not the only reason." Mistochenkov was covering himself.

Eventually, Herbie thought, he would get the whole political thing: the 'I choose freedom' spiel. "Now, let's have the names." He made it as jovial as possible. This was the easy bit for friend Pavel. Ten to one Herbie's Service – or the FIA – knew all about the six secretaries, and the politician; they probably also had a watching brief on the case officers.

Pavel brought out the names one at a time, coupling each with a KGB work name, to show willing. He was like a man laying out a good hand in a card game. It was supposed to convey slight reluctance.

When it was completed, Herbie pressed the bell for one of the lion-tamers, telling Pavel that he wanted to get the names flashed out immediately. He must not take his bit for granted. "Then we'll get an answer back fast. After that, Comrade Mistochenkov, I shall do some kind of a deal for you; but we must talk. A lot of talk. There are many questions; you will understand."

Pavel understood, but looked gloomy.

Max arrived at Herbie's summons, and when Pavel had been escorted away Kruger sat silently for a few moments before taking any positive action.

*   *   *

52

"Standard size for openers," Tubby Fincher chuckled when Herbie spoke to him on one of the secure lines. "But I'll pass the names on. Bet you the FIA have most of them. No MO, I notice. No handling techniques."

Herbie sighed. "Only half an hour. Thirty minutes or so talking turkey with him. I'll put the screws on this afternoon. Make him think he's giving us something important."

"Make him think that *we* think he's giving us something," corrected Tubby in a sing-song voice. "Come back to me this evening."

Tapeworm and Herbie lunched together alone, served by Charles, who discreetly disappeared between courses. Herbie made sure Pavel got the impression he was drinking a good deal, and that they appeared to be talking trivia.

Herbie began by asking the Russian when he first knew, in the old days, that they spoke of him as Piotr – this during the soup: home-made by Miss Sturgis.

"Not until we picked up your people. At the end. When we lost you. The boss cursed that. We had you quite early on – or at least suspected it was you."

Herbie nodded, saying he supposed that was when he was working for the Karl Marx Locomotive Works in Babelsberg.

"In the last four weeks we had people on to you twenty-four hours a day. How did you slip them?"

Herbie grinned inanely and said it was a trade secret.

"It's all changed now." Mistochenkov sounded sad. "All the beehives are dismantled. Gehlen's dead; the CIA're busy in the Far East, and they've had their teeth pulled in Germany. The Cold War's frozen in history now, and West Berlin's no longer an *Agentensumpf*." He used the word, current in the fifties and sixties, to describe West Berlin: a spy swamp.

The man was not a fool, Herbie thought, as Charles served the main course – lamb cutlets. Using the slang they had known during that time was strangely evocative.

"Surprised they bothered to keep the Colonel-General and yourself on the job if it's like that."

"You know it's like that."

"I know your people have caused havoc in Bonn. Plenty of human element in Bonn."

53

"It was always big in Bonn. Bonn and Munich. The Berlin thing is *kaput*."

Herbie raised his eyebrows, saying he didn't agree; then began to turn the conversation back on to the names Pavel had given him; sliding quick questions under the Russian's guard – about contacts, ciphers, drops, the kind of ops they were running, the strength of the information they were getting out.

Pavel parried, then started to answer one or two questions: gingerly at first. Suddenly he stopped. "Assurances," he said, fear clouding his eyes again. "No more about those people until you tell me I stay. That was the bargain."

"Bargain?" Herbie spread his hands wide, palms open, facing upwards. "It's all a foregone conclusion, Pavel. Names are not enough. You know that. Maybe the Americans . . . Well?" Then, as if he had only just thought of it, "Why didn't you go to the Americans? In spite of recessions and problems they would have paid more. Probably. They suck up to the NATO people more than the British."

"You came to mind. An old adversary. Your people were very good. They told us little: what they did tell was always good – about you, I mean. I thought you'd be fair."

"Me? Or my masters?"

"Both."

"Pavel, my masters are only the flavouring in the savoury now. We're squeezed between you and the Americans. We're part of NATO and the EEC. Small fry in both: small fry for big money; small fry and small influence. Me? I am an adopted son. A German with a British passport, and a British job. A World War Two boat-person whom they took in, fed and trained. You would have done better with the Yanks. How did you know I was still around?"

Pavel smiled. "Because you are indestructible. The boss, Colonel-General Vascovsky, mentioned you. Not long before . . . Well, he said you had been spotted in London."

Herbie crunched up the last piece of fat from his lamb chop, swallowing it with relish. "And you say it's all dead? To be spotted in London is to be spotted by an individual: or did they get a blow-up of me in Regent Street from one of your intelligence satellites?"

Mistochenkov made a movement with head and shoulders.

"Where there's an embassy . . ." he said, knowing it explained all things.

"It's far from dead, Pavel." Herbie wiped his mouth, his mind half on what Miss Sturgis might have conjured up for their pudding. "We may pretend; but it's all one big *Agentensumpf* now – cities, towns, villages, deserts, space. The second oldest profession. Still going strong."

Miss Sturgis had provided apple pie, cooked the way Herbie liked, with cloves liberally sprinkled into the apple. He wondered who had tipped her off about that.

During the afternoon he kept off any mention of the names Mistochenkov had given to him. They spent the time walking in the garden or sitting in the main room, with the windows wide open. They spoke of Pavel's past work, not going into anything difficult.

"Training?" Herbie asked at one point. "Where'd they train you, Pavel? Siberia?"

The Russian gave a grimace and said, yes, in fact that was exactly where they had trained him. "In Novosibirsk. On the Krasny Prospect. School No. 311. Know it, Herbie?"

Thank God he did not, Herbie laughed; then asked if they had taught him anything.

Pavel spoke at length about training – the rudiments were useful, he supposed, but it was a long time ago. They had laid special emphasis on the history of their élite organisation. He remembered they had all been a little shocked to find out that the old dreaded Tsarist *Okhrana* used similar methods of agent-handling to those they were taught. "We had an instructor who demonstrated with archive copies of case histories from the *Okhrana* files. He put them next to service copies. The similarities were striking."

Herbie commented that things changed little. "Ivan the Terrible wasn't so far removed from 'Iron' Felix Dzerzhinsky, or Beria."

Pavel hastened to add that things had changed a great deal since he was trained. Herbie gave one of his huge shrugs. "They haven't as far as we're concerned."

Dirty tricks, Pavel explained, had altered drastically. The old compromising photographs and tapes were not so effective nowadays. It was the permissive society of the West that he blamed.

Herbie said that dirty tricks were only good nowadays if you could threaten criminal action in the target's own country. Pavel was effusive in agreement. They were getting more sophisticated about doing that: using the Press, and the agencies of other countries – like they sometimes used Boss, the South African Security Agency, but without that service's knowledge. "You have probably found it also. The trick is to make it look genuine, and from an outside source. Our people are very struck on tampering with bank accounts; and false evidence in letters. But it's got to look real. The manipulation is difficult."

That evening Herbie told Tubby Fincher that their asset appeared to be settling down.

"He's sold you a pup about the case officers." Tubby's voice was deep, belying the thin, almost withered frame from which it came. "I've had long talks with the FIA boys." Tubby used the NATO abbreviation for the West German Federal Intelligence Agency, known on its home ground as the BND.

Herbie was not surprised.

"They know three of the names he's given you. The other three are double-up work names."

"Then there's nothing new under the sun."

"Well, yes. Two of the secretaries are new. They're very pleased. They're also dancing jigs about the politician. Been concerned about him for a while. Apparently showing signs of stress. They figure he's just about burned out and ready to run. You get a pat on the head for that."

Herbie said he would get as much of the operational drill as possible from Tapeworm. "I'll dangle papers of asylum in front of him tonight. Could get all that dross out of the way by tomorrow, and start on the real work. He is giving me direct misinformation about the Colonel-General and himself."

Tubby made a remark about establishing rapport, which drew a quiet, firm response from Herbie, who let him know that he had a lot of experience in establishing rapport.

Back with Pavel Mistochenkov, Herbie wagged a jovial, admonishing finger. "Naughty, Pavel. Very naughty."

Pavel gave him a blank look, which Herbie later described in his report as 'no writing on his face'.

He knew it would take a long time to get inside the KGB captain. Initially, though, he had to approach honestly. People, he told the Russian, were pleased with the names – particularly the politician. He omitted to say that the BND already had their eyes on that one, and thought the Soviets had probably finished with him anyway. It was a typical defector's trick. Some people you could lose without massive feedback. The politician, if he really was burned out, could probably be sacrificed without doing any damage.

Then he got on to the question of the case officers. "Six secretaries. Six controls, you gave me. Vodka?" He poured himself a liberal glass.

"Yes. Yes." Mistochenkov answered both questions, and Herbie went on to point out the error of the man's ways. The case officers were doubled up. Three, not six.

Pavel assumed surprise. "I only get names. It wasn't our operation."

Herbie clenched his big fists, giving them a little shake, touching his shoulders, like a movement from a Greek dance, then splaying his arms wide. "Come on, Pavel. You see everything, hear everything in the late Vascovsky's department. Names? What are names in our trade? It's the numbers that count. The BND say they add up to three, not six."

"I am passing on what I know."

Three busy men, Herbie voiced. They must be young and virile. In most cases the recruitment of young secretaries in Bonn was done by expert seduction over a period of time; until the case officers became lovers, and the targets totally reliant – emotionally and sexually – on them. "Six girls and three men, Pavel. Your people found the wonder drug? They supply the controllers with bicycles? In Bonn at night, they say, you can hear nothing but the creaking of bed springs while the secretaries are being serviced by KGB Lotharios. That's agent-handling these days."

Pavel admitted that the BND could be right. He tossed his vodka back in one draught, saying that he did not intend to mislead his inquisitor.

Herbie poured more vodka, and opened up his briefcase,

removing several forms and official-looking documents, flicking his strong fingers towards them. "Your passports to paradise" – the daft smile, on and off, like a neon advertisement of a clown. "Papers to give you asylum."

Mistochenkov's whole personality appeared to relax. For a second Herbie thought the man was going to leap from his chair and plant kisses on his cheeks. There was a great exhalation of relief, then the Russian stood up and crossed to the window.

They were in the main living room of the house, with its leather-buttoned chairs and reproduction drum tables, light coming from discreet, brass-shaded, military lamps – also reproductions. One wall was lined with books – mostly spines, bought by the yard – all leather, or imitation leather, bound and gold embossed. The French windows were partly open, and the heavy velvet drapes pulled back. Outside, dusk began to distort the trees, and the pleasant warm smell of grass and fresh vegetation filtered into the room.

Mistochenkov stood for a moment, looking out at the garden. Then Max appeared from the half light, coming from the trees like a silent killer – which was probably part of his trade.

"Might I suggest the curtains be drawn?" Max addressed Herbie in a soft, deferential voice. "One never knows. The patient could catch a nasty cold."

It was neatly timed, Herbie considered. Max knew his job. There was almost certainly no danger from showing oneself at the windows of the lighted room; but Max was a professional. He nodded, motioning the Russian back into the room; leaving Max to enter, lock the windows and draw the drapes.

A small incident, but enough to give Pavel the impression that he might still be in danger. The Russian's hand shook slightly as he took another glass from Herbie.

"The relief is great," he said quietly, relaxing in the chair again, as Max left them.

"They're not signed or authorised yet." Herbie gave him another smile, longer this time. He explained that the papers could go forward within a matter of hours if Pavel filled in some of the spaces he had omitted concerning the handling of the West German politician and the six secretaries. Quietly

Herbie asked how much he really knew about the servicing of the names he had given.

The Russian was quite good: either expert as an actor, or really distressed. Okay, yes, he knew there were only three people doing the handling of the secretaries. There were two for the politician. He did know the lot. "You understand, Herbie. You must know the effect all this has on me. It is not natural, after so many years with my Service, for me to tell everything." He patted his stomach. "It makes me feel sick, here."

Herbie told him to take a deep breath. They could stay up all night if he wanted. Just deal with it gently. "We need the fine print, Pavel."

It took until almost four in the morning, and Pavel Mistochenkov looked drained when they finished. It was probably the vodka, Herbie reflected; the people the Russian was sacrificing would not be a great loss. The handling methods were in reality nothing abnormal. If anything, some were old-fashioned.

Charles had taken over: prowling the house and grounds. Herbie left instructions for Pavel's door to be locked, and the man quietly checked every fifteen minutes – there was closed-circuit television surveillance on the room. He should be left to sleep as late as need be. Herbie would probably not want to be with him at all the following day. He would write his report. That was getting the rubbish out of the way. Once Pavel knew asylum had been granted he would relax. Over the next week or so the job would be to break him down, clean out the easy stuff; then hit him hard with the truth about Jacob Vascovsky's death.

A week? Maybe two weeks, he thought.

6

IN THE END it took almost three. Seventeen days passed before Herbie Kruger was to lay the real news on Mistochenkov. The Director – worried about costs, as ever – tried to rush Herbie. The large German, however, was not to be hurried.

Within a few days he was certain there was a good deal more to Pavel's arrival in the West than met the eye. It was also significant that the Soviets were not kicking up a fuss. There had been no Press releases on either side, and none of the usual overtures through political channels.

More to the point, the Russian was frightened. Just as with the recruitment of young girls working in sensitive government departments – 'Emilys', one intelligence expert called them – the game was to make Pavel almost completely reliant on his confessor: Big Herbie Kruger.

The strategy was simple psychology. Herbie would spend a day with Pavel, in which he would be friendly, concerned and reassuring. Then he would leave him alone, perhaps for a whole day, or a day and a half. On his return, while still showing concern, Herbie would be brusque and business-like, giving the impression that his own people were forcing the pace.

Max and Charles were instructed not to speak with their guest except when absolutely necessary. Worboys was kept in the background: though Herbie, taking pity on him, sent him off to London with the occasional odd job, allowing him to be away for the best part of a day at a time.

Herbie also tried to make it difficult for Pavel to establish any pattern in the interrogation. He would question him for an hour or so about his life – schooldays, background, recruitment for the KGB – then suddenly switch to the days when Herbie was himself involved in the field; fighting in the dark with the Russian's deceased boss.

After a week, Herbie started to take Pavel off regularly to walk on the Berkshire Downs. They visited the Vale of the White Horse at Uffington – one of the atom spy Klaus Fuchs's favourite spots – and occasionally they would watch as the trainers from Lambourn and other stables had their race-horses exercised. On one occasion they were questioned by men from a stable, who thought they might be rivals, or bookmakers' spies, trying to gauge the condition of a par-ticular horse. Herbie thought this very amusing. On each of these jaunts into the country they were accompanied, at a distance, by either Max or Charles. Both the lion-tamers carried hand guns, while there was always a folding-stock Uzi in the trail car. Herbie also went armed.

The first signs of reliance came after ten days. Between the more serious question-and-answer conversations the two men would discuss matters of mutual interest concerning the old days of the Cold War – particularly Germany, and the split Berlin. They spoke of notorious people like Frenzel, the member of the Bonn Parliament who was a Czech spy; the Otto John 'defection' case; and the KGB killer-defector, Bogdan Stashinsky, expert in the cyanide pistol technique. "His handler, Alexandrovitch, slipped up," was Pavel's only comment.

Softly, Herbie probed at Mistochenkov's political sensi-tivities. What emerged concerned Kruger even more. Pavel was unwilling to admit his defection on wholly political grounds. He tried to give political reasons, but they were woolly and ill-founded. After lengthy monologues concerning the corrupt leadership of the USSR, with its double-standards, favours, special privileges and the like, Pavel would shatter the illusion by reverting to the question of his supposed new posting after Vascovsky's death. At heart, Herbie deduced, the man was a convinced, unthinking Communist, merely dissatisfied with his lot: a KGB have-not, who, like a child, had taken to his heels out of spite.

If that was the root cause of the defection, Herbie was not at all sure that it was the mainspring. Tapeworm felt deprived, there was no doubt about that. Now he had been accepted in England his conversation would often turn to the availability of the good life – by which he seemed to mean comfort, money, beautiful women, food, drink and the latest in luxury gadgets. More than once Kruger had to caution him not to expect too much. "Our own people, like those of the rest of the world, have been through recessions. Luxuries are still far too expensive for the majority," he would claim.

In spite of such admonishments, Mistochenkov appeared to change little. An easy life is what he came for. It was his right. Behind this, Herbie detected even more fear. The man had put himself at even greater risk than could be imagined. Herbie concluded that he had a very reluctant defector on his hands; a man who had run from some unmentionable crime. Pavel Mistochenkov would, he suspected, always be looking over his shoulder.

On the sixteenth day Herbie decided the time was right. Pavel showed increasing signs of nervousness when left alone for long periods. He had also just about exhausted all his conscious – and possibly the greater part of his subconscious – knowledge. It was time to lay the truth on him.

On the morning of the sixteenth day Herbie saw him for only an hour. After that he left the Russian alone, with Max and Charles in the far background. They did not even let him go into the garden. During the afternoon Herbie had long talks with both Tubby Fincher and the Director. In the evening he ate in his own room upstairs, while Pavel was waited upon in the dining room by an unspeaking Max.

Like a monk preparing himself for some great devotion, Herbie Kruger stayed in his room for the whole of that night, planning his strategy. Then, on the seventeenth day, he briefed Max and Charles, did not see the Russian during the morning, and made his first appearance shortly before two in the afternoon.

It was a day of light winds and drizzle, so Pavel – who was distinctly unnerved by the period of neglect – appeared surprised when Herbie told him they were going out.

The two cars were in front of the house. Worboys was left in charge and – another departure from the norm – Charles drove Herbie and Pavel, while Max followed in the trail car.

They drove through the market town of Wantage, and up a neighbouring hill on to the Downs, near a stone monument which was a local landmark.

It was chilly, and the drizzle unpleasant; yet this did not seem to deter Herbie. He motioned Pavel to join him, and set a cracking pace, head down into the thin rain, arms swinging in his vaguely unco-ordinated gait. Pavel almost had to run in order to keep up with him. Charles stayed with the cars. Max followed at a discreet distance.

They padded on in silence for about two miles. Then, abruptly, Herbie turned. "That's far enough. We'll walk back to the cars now."

Max waited until they had passed him on the return leg. The wind was behind them now, making conversation easier. Half way back to the cars Herbie stopped, placing one firm hand on Mistochenkov's shoulder. It had the tight grip of a man being put under arrest, and Pavel flinched, almost pulling away.

Herbie spoke as quietly as conditions allowed. "Pavel Mistochenkov. We are now going back to the car. The boys will leave us alone. In the car you will talk to me. You will tell me the truth about two things. I know enough. Believe me. If you do not tell me the truth there is a wood down there" – he pointed to one of the many clumps of trees which dotted the slopes below. "In that little wood, there is a small well which has been bricked up for years. If you do not tell me the truth, Max and Charles will break into that well. They will then shoot you, deposit your remains in the well, and brick it up again. All documents concerning your defection will be destroyed. All those who have had contact with you – at the Berlin Consulate and over here – will suffer a severe loss of memory. Your body will never be found. It will be as though you did not exist."

Mistochenkov went white, the drizzle on his face like the sweat of fear, as Herbie continued. "You will tell me the truth about your former master – Jacob Vascovsky – and his suicide. Then you will tell me the real reasons for your defection. Is this understood?"

The Russian looked as though he was ready to make a run for it. Then he saw Charles, standing by the cars, and Max only a few steps away from them. His head fell forward, shoulders slumping. His whole body gave a shudder, and he made a small nod. Then – "If I tell you . . .?"

"We shall see. I shall personally make certain that they do not send you back." It was the only note of conciliation Herbie was to sound during the following twenty-four hours.

7

FROM THE LONG sessions – particularly concerning the Russian's childhood, and service with Soviet intelligence in East Berlin – Herbie had already gained many clues to Pavel's motivation.

Mistochenkov was an orphan of World War Two. The State had been his sole parent. It had clothed, fed, cared for and educated him. He proved to have a good, if not brilliant intelligence. In return for the State's good offices Mistochenkov had given his total loyalty: a loyalty as unthinking as it was unswerving. This unwavering allegiance to the faith made Pavel a natural candidate for many responsible jobs.

When, in due time, the KGB saw scope for a man of Pavel's talents, his parent, the State, recruited him. But then the State, in the infinite wisdom of all great bureaucracies, made a fatal mistake. The State's error lay in young Pavel's first posting: the youthful, inexperienced, energetic, zealous sergeant, assigned to be Jacob Vascovsky's assistant.

At that time Vascovsky was a rising major, proving himself to be, arguably, the best spy-taker in East Berlin. In his mind Herbie could see him now, as he had glimpsed him several times in the field: tall, slim, muscular; neat, with iron-grey hair, deceptively kind blue eyes, and a face blessed with delicate features. Vascovsky did not look like a Russian. Some said he had French blood. He was certainly elegant. A professional; a man of the world, with a distinguished war record.

When he took up his first appointment Mistochenkov must have felt as bewildered as a man coming into an unrecognisable world after a long term in prison. Life would seem so different, and almost unbelievable, working close to the gallant, secret major. "He was the first of my teachers who showed any real interest in me as a human being, as a man," Pavel had said, one evening.

Up to that time the State had been father, mother, brother and lover. Now Vascovsky assumed pre-eminence in the young sergeant's life.

If the State made an error in assigning such an innocent to Vascovsky, that error was compounded by leaving him so assigned. But such things happen. Pavel was to spend over twenty years as Vascovsky's aide.

During that long passage of years it was natural for the hard core of Pavel's duty, and belief, to polarise on the one human being closest to him. The State, which Pavel held so dear, eventually became synonymous with Vascovsky; and Vascovsky with the State.

Formerly the State could do no wrong; the State and the Party were the protectors of Pavel, the individual. As the years went by, Vascovsky could do no wrong; Vascovsky was Pavel's sole protector.

*   *   *

Pavel Mistochenkov looked a broken man, lolling, damp, in the rear of the car. Max and Charles had turned the other car: sitting front and back; covering all possible angles. Kruger had planned the final breakdown of his patient out here, on high ground, in open spaces. Within the car, surrounded by countryside, Pavel might feel safer than in the constrictive confines of the Charlton house. Herbie was sure Pavel's fear sprang from the thought of avenging KGB angels striking quickly. It was not their style any more, but Pavel's imagination teemed with diabolical visions.

The Russian shivered. He looked bleached white, and his hands trembled. Herbie took out cigarettes, put one in the man's mouth and lit it, watching him drag deeply, then remove the tube with a hand akin to a geriatric suffering from Parkinson's disease.

"Was it you who found him?" Herbie asked quietly.

Pavel gave a short nod. He had clammed up with shock. After another pull at the cigarette he asked how much Herbie

66

knew. His voice was so low that Herbie gently had to persuade him to repeat the question. You tell me your version, he smiled, then he could match it against the facts in his own possession.

The Russian clammed up again. Herbie, sharper now, said he should tell everything. "Start with finding him."

At first it came out in short bursts, as though Mistochenkov was searching for the words. The Colonel-General had an apartment near the Soviet Embassy, on the Behrenstrasse side. His wife and family were in Moscow. "It was not the best of marriages," and Vascovsky used the apartment as part office, part living quarters. He had a mistress, called Lotte Krug, but she did not live in. "The Old Man kept that side of his life in a different compartment."

Pavel was used to working at odd times. "Aren't we all?" smiled Herbie. The Colonel-General had left their office – near the Marx-Engels-Platz – early in the afternoon. Pavel's voice broke. "His last words to me were, 'Leave it until morning. Pick me up late – about ten will do. Use your key, but be discreet.' I thought he meant Lotte might be there." Pavel stumbled for words again. "So I went. About ten. Just before. I had my own key to his apartment. It was necessary with the kind of work we did. I knocked. No reply. Then I realised. It was horrible. In the bedroom."

Herbie asked why he had realised Vascovsky was dead by his own hand. "You mean you realised before you found him?"

Pavel's affirmative was hardly audible.

"Then you expected it to happen?"

"I feared it."

"What did you hope to find when you picked him up?"

Pavel seemed not to understand; so Herbie rephrased his question. Pavel had feared his chief's suicide. What was the alternative?

"I hoped that he would be taking me to the West. That we would be going together." Mistochenkov's face became a bleak mask.

"You had planned to go together?"

Discussed it, Pavel told him. "There were papers, and cover stories. In the end I came alone. I couldn't stay. The Old Man had implicated me."

"You were in trouble, then." Herbie stated it baldly. It wasn't a question, but Mistochenkov treated it as such.

"He had confided in me. I had taken no action: made no reports."

Pavel was guilty by association, Herbie stated, again not asking; using the British legal phrase.

Mistochenkov acknowledged that he was guilty because of his long association with Vascovsky; and because of the knowledge he had of his superior's actions. "Or inactions," he added.

It took an hour to deal with the details of finding the decapitated corpse: Pavel going through the moves, step by step. Saying how he called the special KGB office, which they very rarely visited, at Karlshorst. The arrivals of the officers and the doctor. His own state of shock. The waiting until the special team came from Moscow – flown in by fast jet. The sympathetic initial interrogation, and his immediate posting to Karlshorst. The knowledge that they would soon come and take him: break him. His decision to run. "The Old Man always said I should come to you if he was taken. The team from Moscow were on the scene very quickly. I think they were probably on their way before I found the body."

"To arrest Vascovsky?" Herbie asked, as if he knew exactly why they would want to do that.

Pavel repeated, yes, to arrest the Old Man. He would also have been taken before long.

"Crimes against the State, perhaps?" Herbie gave him another cigarette.

The Russian nodded. Crimes against the State; withholding vital intelligence; plotting against the State; planning to pass confidential information to the West. He went on, a list of sins which must have weighed like lead on his conscience.

"You were guilty of all this?"

"The Old Man was guilty. I knew, but did not speak up." It was the apologia of a weak man: a man in confusion between loyalty to the State and to the man who was his guide and God. Tapeworm was a good cryptonym, Herbie considered. The worm was now being drawn, inch by inch, from the gutless body. Quickly, with his usual blend of compassion and understanding, Herbie corrected his thoughts. How could you say the man was gutless? Only the facts would prove it. At the moment, Pavel was using Vascovsky as the sacrificial scapegoat: the Russian being unable to accept the responsibility of his own sins.

He asked when Pavel first discovered that the Old Man was guilty of these things.

There was a pause, during which the Russian puffed quickly at his cigarette, then stubbed it out in the small ashtray, burning his fingers and cursing. When he spoke again he appeared to have more control; his voice stronger. This time he put a question – "You know why the Old Man was so furious about losing you, Herbie?"

Herbie said he imagined it was because Vascovsky had successfully rolled up nearly all his agents, and was angry because he could not lay his hands on their link-man.

Slowly Mistochenkov shook his head. "He wanted to talk with you. He wanted to do a deal: come over and work on your side of the fence. You slipped us, in – when? – 1964?"

"Five."

"That's right. Five. Yes, April '65. The Old Man knew all about your Telegraph Boys in March of sixty-five. That was when he really wanted to talk with you."

8

THE DRIZZLE TURNED into a soaking mist outside the car windows. The wind, gusty, blew billows of the fine rain, like cloud, across the slopes, downwards towards the little market town in the far distance.

Herbie fought to recover his composure, refusing to reach for his cigarettes. Really he wanted a drink; there was also that old need – the long desire to retreat into music.

Many times, when he was in the field, that need had been so strong that the big man had curled up on his bed, in an almost foetal ball, allowing his mind to be absorbed by the music. Usually Mahler, because he knew the works so well. It was the best cover in the world, the easiest escape, to let the mind hear the score: to listen, with the ear of memory, to the sounds of Mahler's essays on life, death, the glories of nature and man's relationship with the earth, sky and elements.

Herbie thought back to an incident from early April, 1965. He had very little contact with the six Telegraph Boys: little personal contact, that was. He would respond to signals – the usual simple things, chalk marks, curtains. Electra had a special signal, a plant pot in the tiny window of her apartment. Occasionally he would clean out their dead-drops: the secret letterboxes. In the April of that year Herbie's main task was to keep hidden, and try to get the rest of his other team out. The Schnitzer Group.

Berlin Station had ordered him to clean everything; leave the Telegraph Boys in place, while they made arrangements for quick contact. He was blown, and the bulk of his agents with him.

There had been a night towards the end – perhaps the

billowing drizzle now reminded him of it – when he visited the Birkemanns. Andreas and Beatrix Birkemann both worked in the Ministry of the Interior, at the junction of Glinkastrasse and Mauerstrasse, near the apartment block where they lived. Their cover had been impeccable, and they had no idea that Electra also worked in the Ministry, holding down a responsible job. Herbie feared that, with the collapse of so many of his people, the Birkemanns were in grave danger. On top of this, there were the orders to clean up and get out. He had only about twenty-four hours left, and was seeing people in what he thought to be a correct order of priority.

He circled the apartment house twice, to make sure there was no overt surveillance, knowing that you could not be certain. If the cry was really out for him – if they had his description – there was no way to be completely sure. If they were that close, the house superintendent at the Birkemanns' apartment block would report his arrival soon enough. The house superintendents were hated, by many of the older people, with the same vehemence as they had loathed the *Blockleiters* of Nazi Germany. The house superintendents were unpaid informers. *Spitzels*.

The area appeared clean, so he finally approached the apartment block. Funny how one remembered tiny mental things. As he climbed the steps, he heard, not Mahler, but the first repetitive drama of Stravinksy's thumping, rhythmic strings from *Sacre du Printemps*. After all these years – fifteen years – to remember such a thing.

He recalled little of his conversation with the Birkemanns: except that Beatrix had remained very calm. He gave them the route they should take. The timings, the distractions that would be made. They could go tonight, though it was about five kilometres journey to the crossing point – they lived near the Brandenburg Gate, but that area was quite unsafe.

Today the Birkemanns lived on a small pension, old and crippled, in Hampshire. They had made it. Not like Gertrude Muller, or Willy Blenden. The list went on for ever – Herbie's personal roll of honour from those days: Becher, Kutte, Reissven, Emil Habicht, Julie Zudrang. All the Schnitzer Group.

71

He did remember leaving the apartment, however. Walking away, turning the corner, then feeling the clutching hand on his heart, as he saw the two men loitering on the far corner. He knew, immediately, they were security – in the street lamp it was impossible to tell if they were part of Ulbricht's State Security Ministry – the SSD – or the Russians.

One of them detached himself from the other, crossing the wet street towards Herbie who tensed himself in readiness. Any fast action would bring retribution from the other man standing only a few metres away.

The man approaching held a cigarette cupped in his hand. "A light, comrade," he called. Herbie smiled his most ingenuous grin, and used his left hand to take out the matches (always keep things like matches in your left pocket – right, if you're left-handed – to leave your killing arm free, they had taught him). But the man only wanted a light. He mumbled his thanks, saying it was a filthy night to be out. Then, just as he was moving away, spoke clearly – "Vascovsky wants to meet you, comrade. A private talk. Tomorrow, or Thursday, at eleven. Be at the Thaelmann Platz, near the press office entrance. He'll come alone by car, and wait for fifteen minutes."

Herbie had almost forgotten the incident until now. It was in his report, and they had talked about it during the debriefing. After that he had honestly thought there was no way of escape. Vascovsky obviously wanted to take him intact; thinking he might fall for some kind of covert meeting. A 'dangle', they had called it. Vascovsky was so sterile nobody could possibly have believed it to be genuine. Yet it was the kind of trick for which at least one of his people – Emil Habicht, he thought – had fallen.

Now Mistochenkov was saying it was genuine. That Vascovsky wanted to deal with him. That Vascovsky knew about his Telegraph Boys.

Herbie slid down in his seat, looking Pavel clear in the eyes. "Telegraph Boys?" he asked, face bland as a child at the font. "So what are the Telegraph Boys?"

To his credit Herbie did not move a muscle as Pavel recited the ciphers – "Horus . . . Gemini . . . Priam . . . Electra . . . Nestor . . . Hecuba . . ."

Music screamed in Herbie's head. Stravinsky's violins again; like entering the Birkemanns' apartment. He used his stupid grin and quoted Shakespeare: *Hamlet*. *"What's Hecuba to him or he to Hecuba; That he should weep for her?"*

Then Pavel Mistochenkov said something that, though he could not know it, brought him very close to death, at Herbie's hands inside the car. He smiled, unpleasantly. "Shouldn't you rather say, *What's Electra to him or he to Electra; That he should weep for her?*"

Pavel had known it. The secret within the secret. The name Herbie could not dare to breathe, let alone think about. That Mistochenkov should actually know, and voice the fact of Herbie Kruger's one true affection, seemed obscene. For a moment – a second only – Herbie felt the pain and grief; loneliness, and the unfair life that had given him one love, only to take it away, through duty and responsibility. The thing seemed worse because this seeker for easy pickings – this traitor – had said it.

Herbie gave the Russian a long, sad look, hoping the hatred did not show. He wanted to leave the car, go to Max: tell him to finish Tapeworm there and then. But his professionalism overrode emotion, like some automatic safety valve.

"Tell me what it's all about, Pavel. You're not making sense. Tell me from the start. You say Vascovsky wanted to do a deal. To me Vascovsky's always been the devoted Party man; the complete operative. Why should he want a deal?"

For a second he did not think the bluff had worked. Then Pavel began to talk. It was soon apparent the bluff had not worked completely, because the Russian made it plain that he was on secure ground.

It was as early as 1961 that Pavel noticed the change in Vascovsky. The Old Man had been on leave. To Moscow. He returned almost a different person. Pavel first put it down to troubles with Madame Vascovsky. He knew the Old Man's wife pestered him about being allowed to come and live in East Berlin. "Happily for all of us, it was out of the question. Nobody wanted even senior officers' wives to see conditions in East Germany; let alone East Berlin. His wife was a menace."

But Pavel soon discovered that the change in the Old Man was not to do with his wife. When the Wall was going up, and everything was at sixes and sevens, Vascovsky's department was working at full stretch. One night, after a particularly busy day, Pavel was asked back to the apartment. They were alone, and the Old Man started to drink. Suddenly he asked Pavel if his aide ever questioned whether they were right.

"I didn't know what he meant. I asked him, 'Right about what?'" Vascovsky laughed, hurting Pavel by coming out with what Herbie knew all too well; saying that Pavel was a political innocent. He kept repeating the word 'oppression'. "Look at this damned Wall we're building," he ranted. "To keep people in. To stop people thinking for themselves. When did you last think for yourself, Pavel?"

At first Mistochenkov had been frightened. Then he listened. Vascovsky still did his work with ability, the same devoted expertise. Yet there were subtle changes. He did not seem to enjoy the chase; the sifting of facts; the manoeuvres of the secret fight. They talked more – alone, late at night. "We all speak with great pride about the Revolution," the senior man would say. "So we should be proud. The society which bred the Revolution was degenerate, corrupt, unfair. The men and women of 1917 were right. Change, revolution, had to come. But what has happened since then, comrade Pavel? The creed of Communism is all very well: it is similar to the creed of Christianity. Yet neither of these creeds works. For religious and political creeds to function, there must be freedom of choice. Where is your freedom, comrade? Where is your choice?"

He told Pavel what politicians in the West called the frontiers around the Warsaw Pact countries – "The Iron Curtain. That make you happy, living in the freedom of the Iron Curtain?"

Pavel boasted that, on several occasions, he had argued with his superior, and once – he thought it was around the end of 1963 – had asked him why he did not go and seek his beloved freedom, in the West.

Herbie asked what Vascovsky had replied.

"It was night. We had been drinking, but talking most seriously. I could follow his arguments. I saw his viewpoint. In a way I agreed."

"But you didn't report these conversations?"

Pavel looked away, saying no. That was wrong; he should have reported them. Then he excused himself by claiming that, as a junior officer, he would not have been believed. In any case, the conversations were private. Vascovsky was more than just his chief. He was more like a father.

Herbie pressed him about Vascovsky's answer to Pavel's taunt about fleeing to the West.

"I can give you his exact words. He repeated them many times. Almost right up to the end. He said, 'I dare not go to the West, little Pavel. I would be too important to them here. You've seen how we try to do it – without much success. They would keep me for a few hours, then smuggle me back with promises. Promises for my old age. A safe retreat, if I go on doing my job and provide them with information. They are as ruthless as ourselves. Twenty-four hours and I would be back, with a good cover story, and it would be I who made dead-drops, and passed information in the streets and cafés.' He was afraid, Herbie. Afraid of being sent back to penetrate his own service for you. Would you have done such a thing?"

Almost certainly, Herbie told him. The picture was starting to become brilliantly clear now. "You knew he wanted out. He told you as much, Pavel. He capitulated at last, and planned to go: right? What about your conscience?"

The Russian said he had become confused. Vascovsky almost convinced him. There were days when he saw, with his own eyes, that the Old Man was right. Other days he wondered.

"But you came in the end. After his death. You even used papers, and a disguise, provided by him. You must have been party to a conspiracy, Pavel. Consider it carefully. You blame Jacob Vascovsky. You say you ran because he was guilty, and therefore you were guilty by association. You were as guilty as hell, Pavel. You were party to some conspiracy. There must have been some agreement between you about coming to the West."

It was as though Herbie's words were the first to make any real impact on Mistochenkov's conscience. The Russian sat stock still, his face a mask of shock, his mind revolving around the realities which he had refused to face, possibly until this very moment.

There were tears clouding the Russian's eyes. Under other circumstances Herbie would have felt compassion. Deep within him was the explosive hatred of what Mistochenkov had said about Electra: what he knew about Herbie's own private life, those many years ago; and, most of all – because Kruger's dedication lay in his work – the fear which blossomed from that list of cipher names, enumerating the Telegraph Boys with such accuracy.

9

THE TEMPTATION WAS very great. Herbie dearly wanted to call Charles over, and drive back to the house. He would have preferred to complete the interrogation in comparative comfort. But there was no safety in it. Having brought Tapeworm this far along the road, the thing had to be completed. Mistochenkov was in an unstable state. The drive back to Charlton might clam him up again – this time for good.

"You were party to some conspiracy," Herbie repeated. "There must have been some agreement – between yourself and Vascovsky – about beating it to the West." He continued, calmly; reminding Mistochenkov of his own earlier words, when talking about finding Vascovsky's body.

"When you went to the apartment you told me your hope was that the Colonel-General would take you into the West with him."

Pavel nodded again. Behind the eyes the fear turned to anguish. He repeated that they had discussed it.

"You did more than discuss it, Pavel. You prepared it. You had papers, sample lenses to prove your story – that you represented a manufacturer meeting a British businessman. Did Vascovsky have papers also?"

"Yes. After finding his body I burned them. Flushed away the ashes. I knew where they were kept." His voice rose, suddenly, angrily. "It was his fault. He became dissatisfied. His whole life seemed to be built on lies."

"In our world we live on lies." Herbie tasted the bile in his own mouth.

Pavel said it was not just a question of his work. "He lost all respect for the Party; for the State; for Russia itself. He would tell me that we had taken the wrong turning long ago. The dreams of Marx, Lenin and the rest had been twisted: that the fight for peace was a charade."

"And what's all this about – what did you call them? – the Telegraph Boys?"

Mistochenkov laughed, telling Herbie not to play the innocent. Then he shrugged. Okay, he would play games: pretend Herbie knew nothing about the Telegraph Boys.

They had worked as a close, élite team – Vascovsky and Mistochenkov – almost from the start. The structure of their department demanded that all information should be limited to a few people only. The same need-to-know principle used by the Americans and by Herbie's own Service.

Towards the end of 1962 Vascovsky told Mistochenkov that he had made a breakthrough on the British front. "We knew your people were running a long-term network: recruiting; subversion; political, economic, scientific and military intelligence in the DDR. We knew the centre was in East Berlin. The Old Man came up with a sheaf of work names. It was your lot, Herbie. Vascovsky told me we should keep it to ourselves: just the two of us."

Over the next few months Pavel knew that his chief had made some kind of contact within Herbie's network. "He was very private about it. A year, a good year, went by before he told me what he knew. Even then there were no names to begin with. Only the work names."

"And the Telegraph Boys?"

"Much later. Not until March 1965. No names, though. I knew the work names long before the real identities of your people. The Old Man only gave out the real names when we took action. Early in '65. Karl; Vixen; Peter and Paul – they were that couple, yes? The Birkemanns? Vascovsky let them go. But he knew them all, very early on. All members of what you called the Schnitzer Group."

"Yet you did nothing?"

"Vascovsky did nothing. He had the knowledge. They were neutralised."

Like hell, thought Herbie. He knew the full strength of that. His Schnitzer Group had been far from neutralised. At least, not until a few weeks before the blow-out. If Vascovsky had penetrated his group as early as '62, or '63, he had let them get away with murder.

Pavel suddenly laughed aloud. "Schnitzer" – the laugh rising – "Schnitzer. Blunder. That was you, Herbie, wasn't it? Blunder?"

Herbie gave a slow nod. He asked how many people knew details of the network. Only Vascovsky and himself, Pavel told him. "We kept it sealed up. Hermetic. The Old Man knew real names: identities. I knew only the work names. Until he fingered you. March '65. When he found out about the Telegraph Boys."

"So the pair of you knew about the Schnitzer Group – my group – for about two or three years: a long time. But it was not passed on for action."

Pavel shook his head. In the mid-sixties he had finally fallen in with the Old Man. Rightly or wrongly, he came to believe Vascovsky. Mistochenkov agreed that he was also disenchanted with the way things were going. "We decided to try and make contact. We used subordinates. But nothing was kept on file; nobody knew names except ourselves. That was when we began to search for you. The Old Man wanted to talk to you – to make certain that, if we came over together, there would be no plans to play us back. He needed to be clear on that."

Vascovsky married up the work name, Schnitzer, with Kruger at about the same time as he found out about the Telegraph Boys. "The Old Man's contact within your group kept some of the cards close to the chest. Then – that was March '65 – he got another lead. New information. But even that one held out on him. He told me about it one evening. I got a 'phone call to go to his apartment."

Lotte was there, but they had quarrelled about something. Vascovsky sent her packing. He drank a lot, sat Pavel down, and gave him the full strength on Schnitzer's Group: names and everything. He knew where most of them could be found, and where they were placed. Then, after more drinking, he told his partner that he had a new contact. Schnitzer had recruited six special operators, back in 1961. He gave Pavel the ciphers – Priam, Horus, Electra, Gemini and the others – and disclosed their purpose. "It was a clever move."

"Did he say where the information came from?"

"One of the six. He sometimes became boastful, particularly when he'd had a few drinks. He laughed a lot, and said he had Schnitzer by the balls: he had spun one of his group; and now he'd spun one of these Telegraph Boys. They would do a deal. *You* would do a deal to save your people."

That night, in the apartment, the two KGB men made their plans. They would draw Herbie out of cover. The last thing they wanted was to arrest him. That would have made it too official.

"You went along with him, then?"

"By then I was sure he was right. Herbie, that was my last moment of peace. It was the Old Man's last moment also, I suppose. There was no turning back."

They had to let Herbie know his people were blown. Sitting in the car, looking at the sombre drizzle, Herbie remembered very clearly how he had first got the message. Julie Zudrang was arrested. Then, a day later, a whole crop went – Reissven, Kutte, Becher.

· He flashed Berlin Station and waited, for nearly twenty-four hours, before a courier came over. He was a man they often used, a tub-like fellow with thick glasses. He had been killed in a border shooting a few months later. Herbie never knew his real name, calling him Blucher. The man looked like a bullfrog, but was really a bit of a chameleon. Blucher gave him orders. Not instructions; direct orders from London. He was to close up shop. Keep the Telegraph Boys in place, but reassure them. London did not think they were in danger: there was a list of emergency communication measures. The Telegraph Boys were Herbie's priority. It would take a day, at least, for him to go through the various cut-outs and drops; get new instructions to them. Blucher said Berlin was arranging new handlers. After dealing with the Telegraph Boys Herbie was free to issue warnings to whoever was left; then get out himself.

Herbie recalled how Blucher had neatly gone over London's choice of his own people – the ones *they* would prefer out – as they sat talking, in one of the only two safe houses the network kept in East Berlin. This one was above an *Apotheke* near the

Alexanderplatz, and smelled musty, damp. Chemical odours rose from the little dispensary below.

London suggested the Birkemanns, Emil Habicht, Moritz Zeich and a girl called Luzia Gabell. Herbie agreed, did his rounds of the Telegraph Boys in quick time, then went for Habicht – because he happened to be the nearest.

Habicht had already gone. An important meeting, his landlady said. A man had come. Emil left soon after. Herbie went straight on to the Birkemanns, and had the experience with Vascovsky's messengers.

Of his whole network, only the Birkemanns and Moritz Zeich got away. Luzia Gabell went missing. When he got to Zeich, there was news of Emil Habicht. He had been shot down in the street. Herbie remembered being shaken, because it had happened near the safe house, close to the Alexanderplatz. The story said Emil was stopped by a policeman: asked for his papers. He appeared to be loitering, but the policeman let it pass – one of the ubiquitous Vopos. A car had come up. Emil approached, then suddenly changed his mind. They had shot him from the car.

"Habicht?" Herbie asked Mistochenkov, wanting to get the truth about Emil's death.

Pavel grimaced. "The Old Man thought Habicht was the reason you didn't come to the Thaelmann Platz. Our people had orders to pick him up. You knew he was sensitive?"

This was news to Herbie.

"Having an affair with one of our girls. A German. Only a secretary, but she worked in Vascovsky's department. No access to confidential material. It was a threat, though. We had a couple of men watching for him. They moved too soon. The Old Man was furious: thought the business would scare you off."

"He really believed I would meet him?"

Pavel said he did not know. There were contingency plans. "We had surveillance on you. You lost them."

There was a faint trace of Herbie's old grin. "I know."

He went back over the ground again, scraping the barrel of Pavel's memory; asking about Vascovsky's informer within the original Schnitzer Group. Pavel maintained he did not know who it was, any more than he knew either the true name, or the informant, from within the Telegraph Boys.

"The one from my people?" Herbie finally asked. "What happened? Did Vascovsky get him out? Or deal with him in Berlin?"

"Or her," Pavel looked tired. "Or her," he repeated. No, he did not think whoever it was got out. He thought Vascovsky took care of the informant.

Treading on glass, Herbie asked if Pavel could remember the work names, and real names, of the Schnitzer Group. The Russian started to tick them off on his fingers. Herbie repeated the process. Then again, until he was satisfied. "You're certain there wasn't another?"

They were all Pavel could remember, so Herbie gave him the missing name – "Theodor?"

No, there was no Theodor on the list.

"Vascovsky was playing it close to his chest as well, Pavel." Herbie now knew who his traitor had been in the sixties. He also had a fair idea of the inducement. Classic. Easily checked. "And you failed to make contact, Pavel. You were both locked behind the Wall, with no safe key out; and with treason on your dossiers."

Mistochenkov said that was about the way of things. Fifteen years was a long time. Neither Vascovsky nor Pavel had made a report about the half-dozen Telegraph Boys. They were just left to function for fifteen years. Herbie once more probed Pavel's knowledge concerning the six names.

"Only the ciphers. That was all I knew; except what the Old Man told me, one evening, about you – you and Electra."

Herbie let it pass. The shock had gone. "You're telling me the truth, Pavel? You don't even know which of the six was keeping your boss informed?"

"You have it all." His voice dropped to a whisper. "All except how it came to an end."

"I can guess. Vascovsky's agent from within the Telegraph Boys found a new handler? Right?"

Mistochenkov said it was near enough. The Old Man was getting very tired. About five weeks earlier he had given Pavel the documents and cover to get out; intimating that he would probably go as well. "He was still frightened of leaving cold.

Past his prime, but a proud man. He still thought you might send him back. It worried him."

Did Pavel know why Vascovsky suddenly reopened the idea of leaving for the West? He did. Some top brass had been down from Dzerzhinsky Square. There was talk about the Colonel-General being given a desk job in Moscow. The informant from the Telegraph Boys got to hear about it. "Maybe the Old Man said something. Whoever it is – Priam, Gemini, whoever – threatened to find a new handler in our Service. The Old Man, as I said, was tired. He had a relationship with the Telegraph Boy. There was no question of death. Of murder. Whoever it is has been a convinced Party Member from a long time back. Had trusted Vascovsky. Thought he, or she, was doing a service to Party and country."

Herbie filled in the rest. The mud would fly. Moscow would want blood.

"So would the Telegraph Boy." Pavel's misery appeared more acute than ever. Soon, he supposed, the one informant among the Telegraph Boys would talk to somebody in Moscow: from the Centre.

"Didn't Vascovsky make any contingency plans at all? He thought of going to the West. You agreed –"

"We were trapped. He told me to go if they got to him first."

"Then he chickened out, and got to himself."

"He did say he had instructed the Telegraph Boy?"

"In what way?"

They had been making provisional preparations for the flight West. Vascovsky went through each step twice – once for if they were to go together; then once if Pavel was forced to run by himself. Pavel asked him about the source among the Telegraph Boys.

"I've told the asset there is danger," Vascovsky replied – the asset was the Telegraph Boy the Colonel-General had in his pocket. "The asset thinks there's been some kind of penetration. The instructions are that new contact will be made if anything happens to me. I've even given a word cipher."

Herbie sat up, shifting his bulk quickly from the slumped position he had adopted. Vascovsky had told Pavel the words.

Any new handler appointed by Vascovsky's friends would slip a quotation into the conversation. Gorky. From *The Lower Depths*. "A man can teach another man to do good – believe me."

"Pavel," Herbie creased his brow. "The Old Man told you to come to me, yes?"

Mistochenkov acknowledged it.

"He was sending me a message, Pavel; and you have wasted a lot of time. Why do you think Vascovsky's asset would spill it all out to someone in Moscow?"

The Russian said that it was his experience with stranded assets. "They do not hold out for long. There will be a lot of fuss. Why, the Old Man's death must be spread all over the newspapers; and my defection, also."

Herbie gave a small, frustrated, sigh. "The Telegraph Boys held out for fifteen years. You seek glory, Pavel? You have lived in our world for a long time, yet you do not seem to have grasped the rudiments. Vascovsky's death did not make much of a ripple, a small column in *Pravda*. A tiny mention in *Neues Deutschland*. Twenty-eight words in a *Tass* report. As for you, Pavel Mistochenkov, would it surprise you to hear your Service thinks so highly of you that it hasn't even asked to have you back? Nobody has mentioned you."

He lowered the window, beckoning to Charles, who came at a run over the soggy turf.

On the way back to the house in Charlton, Herbie threw various names and phrases at Mistochenkov: asking if he had heard them used, or was conversant with any. The Russian replied with negatives to each one. He seemed genuine enough, three times asking for a word to be repeated. Most of the words, names and phrases were meaningless. Into the middle of the group, Herbie Kruger threw 'Quartet'.

Pavel Mistochenkov did not even ask for it to be repeated. Odds on that they at least had gone undetected.

The afternoon's interrogation was over; Herbie's next business was in London.

*   *   *

Ambrose Hill, the Head of Registry, must have been well past retirement age, but nobody asked him to go: even under the strict rules of the Civil Service.

It was known that he had, for three years now, been training two of his admirable, younger assistants. But Ambrose Hill had been with the Service for a long time, the possessor of an encyclopaedic memory. At the top, they knew it would be a bad day when the Head of Registry walked through the door, set the time lock, then went into retirement.

Herbie Kruger was one of Ambrose Hill's special favourites: a man after his own heart, who had given the whole of his active life to the Service. When Herbie caught him that evening, just as he was leaving, Ambrose was only too willing to pull out all the Schnitzer network files.

Herbie leafed through them, his eyes creasing with pain at some of the remembered faces. He finally selected one dossier, signed it out and took it down to Pix, where he stood over Bob Perry – 'Mr. Pix', as they called him – while a copy of the photograph from the dossier was made.

Then Herbie, carrying his briefcase, and stepping with a sprightliness unusual for a man of his size and bulk, walked over to the main building and demanded to see the Director.

One did not usually demand to see the Director, but Herbie was in no mood for hanging around. He was worried, concerned, not only for his people in the field but also for the first line of defence. Source Six had become a major contribution. Even a NATO General had remarked on it at a meeting of the JIC, to which that particular General had been an honoured guest.

There was no time for haggling. He came straight to the point, told the Director the facts as he saw them, then submitted what he felt was the only possible solution.

The Director was concerned, both with what Herbie had cleaned out from Tapeworm and the proposals the German now made.

"It's too bloody dangerous, Herbie. I can't authorise it alone, you know that. It'll take at least a full session of the Foreign Office Intelligence Committee, and you also know what that means – the Treasury'll be in on it. They'd never let you go in."

"Over the hill?" Herbie mused.

"You're blown."

"Then I'll spin myself."

"For real?" The Director looked pained.

"Of course not for real. But they might just fall for it."

"No time to set you up."

"I can walk in. We can arrange some sort of story."

"It's too dangerous."

"Then what do you suggest? Close down my people? Get them out? Pull the shutters on the Telegraph Boys?"

"Well, there are others . . ."

"Not with the same yield. You know it, I know it, the Joint Intelligence Committee knows it, and, if they use their brains, an FOIC will realise it."

The Director tapped his desk. "Herbie, someone else can go in."

"Nobody else has real access. They're my people. Besides . . ." He paused, his shoulders drooping. "Besides, it's my fault. I have a right to correct my own errors."

"It's old history, Herbie. No one's going to —"

"Hold me responsible? You joke. Of course, if it comes out, I'll be responsible. I personally chose the Telegraph Boys in East Berlin. I . . ." He thumped his chest. "I made the decisions; I took the responsibility. It's still my responsibility."

"And you can still deal with it. Long range."

Herbie looked bigger than ever, like some animal with the ability to swell in a courting or fighting ritual. "When I kill, I like to do it at close range."

"Now that kind of talk . . ." The Director paled, clutching the corners of his desk.

"I am only joking. Please, Chief: fix the Foreign Office Intelligence Committee for me. I'm pleading. I need to deal with it myself; and if you think I like the idea you must be a fool."

People did not usually speak to the Director like this; but the senior man knew well enough what it meant to Herbie, who steered clear of Berlin at the best of times. The confessing of Tapeworm had certainly produced a change in Herbie Kruger.

"I'll do what I can," the Director promised.

Herbie did not believe him. On the way back to Charlton,

with Worboys driving as smoothly as he ever did (which to
Herbie meant, "Like a demented tractor driver"), it crossed
Herbie's mind that a refusal to let him clean up his own,
long-standing error would absolve him from responsibility.
The thought was tempting, but did not salve his already
blistered conscience.

Mistochenkov was getting ready for bed, Max said, when
they got back to Charlton. "Then get him out, and down here;
fast," snapped Herbie, clicking open his briefcase.

Pavel was brought down in dressing gown and slippers. The
dressing gown was of heavy wool, and a size too large for him.
He had turned up the cuffs.

Herbie made him sit, then placed the photograph in front of
the defector. It was the one from the Schnitzer Group dossier.

"Okay, Pavel. Who's that?" he asked.

"She looks a lot younger there . . ." the Russian started.

"Who is it, though? You know her, don't you?"

"Yes. Yes, of course I know her. It's Lotte Krug, the Old
Man's bit of skirt."

"Wrong." You could almost see the bitterness flowing with
the words from Herbie Kruger's mouth. "That is a photograph
of one of the Schnitzer Group. Work name Theodor. Her real
name was, I thought, Luzia Gabell."

Under his breath, in Russian, Pavel breathed, "The clever
old bastard."

Herbie turned away, moving with that quaking agility
which always amazed people like Worboys. As he reached the
door, ripping it open, he turned his huge head. "And *I* am a
stupid old bastard," he said, the venom spraying from his lips,
his spittle caught in the ring of light from one of the military
lamps.

10

MAX AND CHARLES left with Mistochenkov early the following morning. He was to be worked on, in due course, by the Warminster people. The order came straight from the Director.

Herbie, with Worboys again at the wheel, drove away from the Charlton house a little after eight. They could not start any work at Warminster until he delivered his full report. To Herbie the report itself was second in priority. He wanted action on the facts.

He was angry, mainly with himself; the legend he had created, as a cold warrior of great ingenuity, lay shattered. He recalled, in exact detail, how he went about the recruitment of the attractive young blonde student who called herself Luzia Gabell.

Until the early sixties, when the Berlin crisis finally bit hard into the lives of Berliners – in both the Eastern and Western Zones – it had been comparatively easy for a man like himself to retain deep cover. For a time at least, during the formation and early years of the Schnitzer Group, Herbie was looked upon as a staunch supporter of the Communist régime. There were those in Pankow who even avoided him because of it. Walter Ulbricht – the *Spitzbart* (Goatee), as he was derisively called – led a ruling party detested by many.

In those days even card-carrying supporters were not stopped or dissuaded from working in the Western Zones. Except for the anti-Party riots in 1953, it was not until the end of the decade and the final two summers – '60 and '61 – that the going got rough. For at least three years Herbie Kruger took on the role of a *Grenzgänger* – a Border Crosser, living in the East, working in the West.

The fact that his 'job' in the West was manufactured by the Service never came to light. These were crucial years, when Herbie spent days and nights co-ordinating, arranging lines of communication, recruiting and training members of the Schnitzer Group.

They were almost happy years. The American agencies were in the ascendant, and some of his own British Service people seemed to imagine they were playing a polite game of tennis. In the decade and a half following World War Two the Service appeared to contain more enthusiastic amateurs than good, solid professionals. A fact they lived to regret. Herbie was later to watch cells and networks being blown – from East Berlin to Dresden, from Weimar to Rostock – because of careless recruiting and poor handling.

Agents, working under deep cover – often of German descent – sometimes appeared to recruit at random. In those days clandestine recruitment was based on information from tipsters, who pointed you in the direction of possible, quick-witted intelligent men and women who were potential material. You made some kind of contact, sniffed out the land, then passed the whole thing on to the scrutineers who worked in what was jokingly called 'the Rummage Department'.

The scrutineers were supposed to do a deep survey – an all-embracing examination of the prospective recruit's background, true political stability, ability and weaknesses. The job meant turning over every stone; following each twisted lead.

Quite early in the recruitment stage of the Schnitzer Group Herbie discovered that scrutiny was lax in the West Berlin department. Compared to the United States, they were under strength. Corner-cutting, the desire to please London by producing impressive payrolls, became the order of the day.

The Americans were more thorough, so Herbie, taking his lead from them, performed most of the scrutinies himself: making certain that he was not being sold a dud, long before he passed names on to official hands.

Until now Herbie believed this attention to detail had been one of the solid reasons for the Schnitzer Group's consistent success in the DDR. Pride, he now thought, using the old cliché, comes before the fall. The Schnitzer Group remained intact and working until 1965. It was his doing. Now, Pavel Mistochenkov had shattered the myth. The pretty blonde Luzia Gabell had been spun, to become Vascovsky's mistress, Lotte Krug. So the Schnitzer Group, held up to Service trainees as the ideal network, was shown to have been monitored by at least two KGB bigwigs for the bulk of its active life.

Herbie took more than normal care in the recruitment of women. Special care with Luzia. Yet she had fooled him. The bone stuck hard in his throat, even after so many years. Herbie Kruger's operational marvels within the DDR had been achieved only by kind permission of the KGB.

As they arrived at the Whitehall Annexe, Herbie looked back on his East German career. If the past was poisoned the way ahead appeared to be blocked by a similar contagion. Now – and he had no doubt about Pavel's information – there could be no true reliance on the Telegraph Boys. He even began to reflect on the personal choices made for the Quartet, operating at this moment within the DDR.

It was in this commixture of icy frustration and personal rage that Herbie arrived at his office, to find the IN tray piled high.

He knew the priorities were wrong, but the Tapeworm report had to be done first. Worboys was dispatched to Registry with a requisition order for the Schnitzer and Telegraph Boys' files. Herbie lifted the IN tray from the desk, dropped it on the floor, placed his notes in neat order, slid a new cassette into the Grundig, then began to talk through his report. *The truth about the worm in my soul, on magnetic tape*, he thought with a wry smile. It would make grim reading, and he did not spare himself any of the minute details.

It took almost three hours, during which he did not stop for lunch. His only pause was when Worboys returned with the files, demanding Herbie's countersignature.

With the unpleasant chore completed, Herbie took a brief look at the files brought down from Registry – all the Schnitzer Group material, and the red-tagged folders, denoting restriction and classification, and containing details of recruitment, handling and field reports on the Telegraph Boys since their conception.

The files went into Herbie's briefcase, which he stowed in the office safe. It was time to put pressure on the Director. Like a good employee, Herbie had done the rough work. Now the action must start. As though by some form of ESP the interdepartmental telephone bleeped.

"Herr Doktor," Tubby Fincher said into his ear. Fincher tried to sound happy, but Herbie caught the misery in his tone.

"I need to see him," Herbie took the initiative.

"He needs to see you. Now." The 'phone went dead. If the Director had been going through the voodoo rituals of their trade, the chicken entrails must have come out stinking, thought Herbie. Tubby's voice signalled a bad omen.

*　　*　　*

"You're too much of a liability," the Director said, fiddling with his letter opener: further imaginary dagger thrusts. Herbie decided this was body talk. The usually placid Director's stabs at thin air were acts of violence. Possibly against the Minister; more probably against his wife.

Herbie looked uncomfortable. Is this the way it ends? He thought to himself. A lifetime cut away by a paper opener? "You want my resignation?" Somebody else's words. He could hardly recognise his own voice.

The Director puffed. "Good God, Herbie. Nothing like that."

"You said I was a liability."

The Director's sigh seemed to come up from the soles of his feet. "I mean you're too much of a liability for the kind of operation you've put forward. It can't be risked. I saw the Minister this morning."

Herbie asked if he was permitted to put his case before a Foreign Office Intelligence Committee. The Director said the Minister had declined to call a special meeting.

Herbie laughed. "He does not want the cat let from the sack, eh?"

"Nor does he want you to place your head on a block, so that the Whitehall mandarins can tear you to shreds."

"My life's work is already in shreds. I have inherited the

wind." Herbie gave a long sweep of his arm, to show that the melodrama was intentional. He laughed again. "So the Minister prefers to keep up the myth? That I ran the best beehive in East Berlin for all those years? That Source Six is untainted?"

When the Director replied he chose his words with the care of a connoisseur selecting wine. In spite of the latest developments, Herbie could not deny the large contribution made by the Schnitzer Group over the years – whatever the circumstances as they now knew them. Nor could he deny the proving of Source Six. "Your pride's been hurt, Herbie; and revenge isn't part of your nature."

Herbie thought differently; but did not say so aloud. How could the Director gauge his depth of personal hatred for both the Gabell woman and whoever was doubling within the six Telegraph Boys? Yes, Big Herbie Kruger wanted revenge. It went beyond that; he needed to be the man who wreaked havoc on the Gabell woman. Herbie Kruger had to be the one who would gouge out the cancer within the Telegraph Boys. It was the only way he could be certain, and retain his own confidence.

The Director still mumbled on about the Telegraph Boys. The main thing now, he droned, was to remove the problem: put the six agents out of danger.

"If they're not already blown." Herbie sounded diffident, as though the Ministerial decision had removed all responsibility.

"Herbie," a slightly admonishing note. "We'll all know soon enough if they're blown."

That was true. A clean-up committee from Moscow would not hang around to discuss matters, once they discovered the extent of Vascovsky's and Mistochenkov's duplicity. There would be arrests in the DDR's Berlin Ministry of the Interior; in the Soviet HQ at Karlshorst; the Soviet Embassy, on the Unter den Linden; in the DDR's Political HQ at Niederschonhausen Castle; the HQ of the NVA – the National People's Army; and, further afield, at Zossen-Wunsdorf – the HQ of the Group of Soviet Forces in Germany. These were the six firmly-established bases where the Telegraph Boys held down jobs. Some menial; others highly responsible.

"We just sit and wait?"

"I didn't say that." The Director settled over his desk, leaning on elbows, cupping the fleshy cheeks in his square palms. "You recruited each one of the Telegraph Boys, Herbie, with your usual most efficient care. I take it that each works in isolation. You would agree, therefore, that it is unlikely that any one member of the Telegraph Boys has knowledge of the other five?"

Herbie said it was not likely. On the other hand it was not impossible.

"Under normal working conditions, knowledge of other members of a network like this would not matter." The Director sounded like a lecturer at the school.

"It matters now," Herbie snapped. "If one Telegraph Boy – the double – knows the other identities, it would be through his Russian handler: Vascovsky."

The Director wanted to hear the equation out.

Okay, Herbie told him. It was the old story. Once the Schnitzer Group left the picture, those all-important Telegraph Boys had been badly – spasmodically – handled. "You know what happened." The people who did the handling, who brought information out, and cleaned the letterboxes, were not constant. Under pressure the Service modified the system. The same dead-drops – letterboxes – were used by more than one Telegraph Boy at a time,

Herbie said that the maggot within his Telegraph Boys only had to pass on the location of his own letterboxes, or the places where he made exchanges of information. If Vascovsky was patient enough it would only be a question of time. The faces would all eventually repeat, again and again. "It's like looking at a person's bank balance to see where the pressure points lie. Like we've all been taught, Chief. A quick glance at six months of a balance sheet tells you everything – if he drinks too much; what he does away from home; his mistress; his wife. All the figures become faces. Under Vascovsky's surveillance the trails would eventually lead back."

True, Mistochenkov had said Vascovsky played it close to the chest. "He also said the Colonel-General 'had a relationship' with his Telegraph Boy. You know what that means in the language Moscow Centre uses? There aren't any sexual innuendoes. It means that Vascovsky was gaining the rotten apple's confidence: power-sharing. If it was me I would give him all the names, and probably a few more innocents for luck."

The Director straightened up in his chair. Far away a police klaxon sawed through the traffic sounds. "The Minister has instructed me to seal off this breach as quickly as possible . . ."

"There is only one way." Herbie thumped his chair with a balled fist. "Let me go in."

That had already been ruled out: unthinkable. "However," the Director cleared his throat, "I'm putting you in charge of limiting the effects. You've got a meeting with one of your Quartet runners in ten days' time?"

Herbie nodded. He had looked it up in the Secret Diary on arrival that morning. Meeting with Schnabeln, exactly ten days from now, in West Berlin.

"Can that be brought forward?"

Herbie said he could try. What was in the Director's mind?

"That I make you what used to be called a Director in Residence. For a limited period; and for a special operation."

Herbie chuckled, saying he was already virtually a Director in Residence: Director for the Quartet and the Telegraph Boys. Residence: London, Bonn, West Berlin.

"I'm talking about a clearing operation. A unit job. Strictly on the QT as far as the military and Berlin Station are concerned. You take Worboys; technicians; equipment: anything you need. Act as a puppet master. Hose the whole thing out from the West, using the Quartet. Or, at least, one member of the Quartet."

Herbie pounced on the obvious flaw. "It would spread the area of knowledge." He had been devious in training and briefing the Quartet.

"The Quartet imagine the handling of the Telegraph Boys to be something of relatively minor importance: a chore that must be done with security; but one of routine. They do it with more than adequate zest; very efficiently. Probably because I played it down." Herbie said that to let the Quartet know the full strength now would be inviting trouble.

"And if you went over, Herbie? On your own? You wouldn't attract danger? Jesus, man, you were blown in the sixties. They have long memories. You'd be tagged within twenty-four hours. I doubt we'd ever see you again."

There was truth in that, and Herbie knew it. Yet . . . Yet . . . Yet he still knew, deep in the core of himself, that he was at his best when exposed, in the field. He could at least give them a run for their money. He put that into words. "I'd give them a good race for their money."

The Director raised his voice for the first time. He would not tell Herbie again. The answer was no. Nobody could be responsible for sending Herbie over the Wall. "However . . ." He launched into the only possible solution. What if Herbie had been given the green light? How would he have used the Quartet?

"As a back-up team, of course."

"Just to watch your arse, Herbie? Get you out of trouble? You wouldn't have briefed them? They would have remained innocent?"

"Naturally."

"Who's your most trusted man in the Quartet? The best?"

Without hesitation, Herbie told him Christoph Schnabeln.

"Who you meet in ten days' time – or sooner if it can be pulled forward?"

Herbie agreed. He knew exactly what the Director had in mind.

"Then you take a team into Berlin. You bypass our locals. We'll provide cover, all the gear, and a house. Then you brief Schnabeln. Lead him through it. Put your mind into his mind; your thoughts into his thoughts; lead him by the hand; be the magician, Herbie; play the warlock and guide him through the operation. Give him your knowledge, and direct him. Let him become your zombie. Let him clean up the mess through you. Hose them down, sterilise them, but do it through him."

Technically Herbie would later admit that this was the most sensible suggestion. The one flaw the Director could never grasp – even if Herbie talked to him all night – was that Herbie could not put his own heart into Schnabeln's heart. Everything else, yes – the knowledge, methods, chess moves and counter-moves. All apart from the one essential piece of the equation.

In the days to come, Big Herbie Kruger realised that he really made up his mind at that moment. "Okay," he said quietly.

If the Director had not been so relieved he might have reflected on this relatively easy victory. A fast pushover where there had been steely resistance. One shrug and the barriers were down.

"Okay," Herbie repeated. "We'll try it your way. What happens if that doesn't work?"

The mildly bright eyes went dull. "Your Quartet lifts them." No emotion in the Director's voice. "They lift the lot. We do a bring-'em-back-alive caper and sweat the buggers until they break."

"Dismantle?" Herbie did not conceal his dismay.

"Win a few, lose a few. Yes, close down and start again, from scratch."

If Herbie had any doubts about the plan lurking in his mind at that moment they disappeared with that rejoinder.

The Director called in Tubby Fincher. They talked about Herbie's requirements. He would take Worboys, naturally. A couple of heavies would be a good idea, just in case the opposition got wind and tried a snatch.

"Can I have Max and Charles? They were very good with Tapeworm."

He could have Max and Charles.

They would need a house. High, and as near to the Wall as possible. A large apartment would do. There had to be some clear frequencies for the radio traffic. "Not the ones the Quartet use."

Indeed not, the Director agreed. They had to bypass West Berlin Station. For this, a most important part of the operation, Herbie had to have the two best technicians available.

Nothing but the best, Tubby promised. He would take care of it. The briefing in London as well. They would handle that under field conditions. Herbie finally made his excuses. If he was to advance the meeting with Schnabeln it was necessary to move quickly. He would try now.

"We can be ready in a couple of days," the Director suggested tentatively.

Four, Herbie thought. "Four days at least. It's complicated. Has to look natural." He explained that Schnabeln's own East German employers were always under the impression *they* arranged his visits to the West.

The Director looked concerned. "He's not playing the double, is he?"

Herbie said of course not. "It's a question of his work, his cover," and so departed – happy, but with a mind reeling full of personal details: as secret as the grave. As he rolled down the corridor, arms flaying, Herbie hummed the snatch of a tune. Listen to the rhythms but forget about the melody.

Locking his office door, in the Annexe, Herbie used the sterile telephone that was his direct link with West Berlin. It was as untraceable as you could make them. He only used it to call the Quartet's West Berlin field contact – Uncle Klaus. Herbie was the nephew, Timmy. They had spent weeks working up a progressive double-talk act. The double-talk would be difficult to penetrate if the link suddenly became unsterile: always on the cards in these advanced days of the micro-chip and printed circuit.

Uncle Klaus would call him back that evening. No, the nephew said, he would be out. Could Timmy telephone his uncle tomorrow? Uncle Klaus decided that might be better. He would have seen Aunt Girda at the hospital by then: maybe the doctor also. They were both very worried about Aunt Girda, who had been subjected to a number of surgical operations over the past few months. Tomorrow then, Uncle Klaus agreed. Tomorrow, the dutiful nephew, Timmy, promised.

Then Herbie called Worboys in and gave him some instructions: acting on the correct assumption that he scared the living daylights out of his young assistant. "You just watch my arse, eh? And you don't breathe a word: no notes, no reports, no nothing, or I blind you, make sure you have no fun again with your little girl in Registry. Noel. Right?"

"Right," said Worboys, meaning every letter.

Herbie was going home. He left instructions with the duty officer, checked for messages at the Information Room, took the bulging briefcase from his safe, and lumbered towards the street.

Herbie Kruger did not go home.

A taxi carried him as far as Oxford Circus. From there he took the Underground to Tottenham Court Road, changing to the Northern Line, and booking through to High Barnet: the end of the line. In fact, he got off at Camden Town, only five stops on.

Herbie thought he was clean, but took the precaution of running a few back-doubles before emerging into Camden Town High Street where he finally entered a small shop. The shop sold, and repaired, watches and clocks. It had an old and tired look, as if the mechanism had run down, or the mainspring broken.

Behind the counter a small man – a fragment from the rock of ages – peered hard through thick pebble glasses.

"My God," the little old man said in German. "Is it . . .?"

"Yes," Herbie said, quickly. "It is Siegfried, making a rare visit to the Nibelungen. Put your sign up. You were going to close soon anyway, huh?"

Yes, of course he was going to close up. The little old man hobbled out from behind the counter in a state of high excitement. "In the back," he nodded to the door behind the counter. Herbie had to stoop to get into the small room – a cluttered, dusty mixture of workshop and living quarters.

"Drink?" asked the little old man. In spite of the hobble he moved fast, like a scuttling crab.

"Do seeds need rain?"

"Schnapps? Vodka?"

Herbie said Schnapps. Good. The old man moved some books from the only chair large enough to accommodate Herbie, flicking his fingers a few inches from the faded velvet seat, as if to discourage the dust.

"Anyone been asking for me?" Herbie sat down, still clutching his briefcase.

"Nobody. Not for years."

"You tell me the truth?" He accepted the glass of Schnapps, deciding not to worry about the film of dust which rose to the surface of the liquor.

"Always. Not since the old days does anyone ask. I hear nothing."

"You get your pension on time?"

"Regular as the clockwork. More regular. The clockwork is going out, Herbie. All electronics, digital watches these days. Stupid little batteries. No hands, no dial. Figures that pop around. Will it last, I ask myself?"

"You still do work on the side?"

"You asking me official?"

"No. I do not ask. Understand?"

The old man threw up his hands in a dramatic gesture of surprise. "You go private, like me?"

"You went private because of a Vopo bullet."

"A Grepo bullet," the old man corrected.

"You get a Kruger bullet if you talk. Okay?"

"*Prosit*," the old man raised his glass.

"*Prosit*." Herbie drained his Schnapps and looked reflectively into the bottom of his glass. "A Kruger bullet if you talk to anyone. One thousand pounds, sterling, if you do the job."

"You got me for life, Herbie. What should I do with one thousand pounds sterling? Women?"

"Once it would have been."

The old man gave a tired smile. "Who said, 'I can't do it any more, but I still have the desire'?"

Herbie smiled, feeling a twinge of his own sadness. Women? What had he known of women? Only one who mattered. He looked at the little old man and thought what a change the years had made to him. Less than thirty years ago he had been small but so attractive to women that the young girls, it was said, lay down in his path. He must have been in his forties then.

The old man did his scuttle towards Herbie, grabbed at the empty glass, which he refilled and handed back, moving all the time, as if to keep beyond the range of Herbie's grasp. "Okay, what I do for you?"

Herbie told him. In detail.

"But your own people . . .?" the old man began.

"Should not be troubled or consulted." Herbie's finger came up to his nose in a conspiratorial gesture. "This has to be untraceable." He gave his stupid grin. "Don't worry. It's only unofficial for my own reasons. The money will come from the usual place."

"So I'm in business again. The old firm."

"Exactly, only you mustn't say it aloud. Not even to the old firm. You can do it? Up to date? The very latest?"

"No problem. I have two sons still there. I keep up with the times, my friend. For just such an emergency."

"Four days. Three if possible."

"Three will be easy. No worries."

"I'll telephone."

Herbie Kruger then left the shop and, finally, went home to his flat in St. John's Wood: doing the back-doubles; using a bus and two taxis.

Worboys arrived ten minutes later. "Clean as a whistle," he said.

There was a time when Herbie would not have taken the chance of being covered by Tony Worboys. But he had personally trained the man since then. If Worboys played his cards correctly, he might even become moderately good at the job.

The 'grace and favour' apartment smelled musty after Herbie's time at Charlton. He opened the windows, cooked himself an omelette, shovelling herbs into it on a one-to-one ratio with the eggs. Herbie then uncorked a bottle of Burgundy, and sat down with the tray.

Burgundy was wrong with eggs, but what the hell: he felt like Burgundy.

After the meal, he planned to work – revive painful memories by going through the Telegraph Boys' files. For that he needed background music. He thought, perhaps, the Mahler Tenth – the incomplete symphony, available in the performing version which was the genius of Deryck Cooke, musicologist extraordinary.

11

IT WAS STRANGE for Herbie to reflect that, during his formative years, he had lived within a society in which Mahler's music was banned. The fact that the composer was a Jew wiped his work from the Nazi calendar at the stroke of a pen: even though, in Hitler's early years the future Führer showed great excitement at Mahler's direction of Wagner in Vienna. Hitler had also enjoyed the composer's own work at that time – but then he had loved Mendelssohn also. Madness.

As with sexual experience, it was another fact of life that Herbie remained a musical illiterate until well into his teens – the interest being first sparked by his American case officer. Later, as his education was completed with the British Service, music became an abiding passion.

As Mahler's Tenth Symphony – in its performing version – was not heard by the public until 1964 (over half a century after the composer's death), Herbie Kruger did not experience it until the Schnitzer Group crumbled, and he was back safely in the West. He loved what he heard: the piece becoming more poignant to Kruger because its composer had completed the general symphonic sketch while in deep psychological crisis: already overtaken by the disease which would bear him to an early grave in 1911.

Herbie remained unaware that he always listened to the Tenth Symphony when he was also going through deep periods of stress. It was a fact noted by the Service psychiatrists, who, with the other medics, thoroughly monitored all senior personnel every eighteen months.

Now, with the meal eaten and dishes washed, Herbie seated himself in his favourite chair, the bottle of Burgundy, still half full, at his elbow. Lately he had made a conscious effort to cut down on spirits: turning to wine in the evenings.

The files were out of the briefcase; placed on the floor, in two piles – one for the old disbanded Schnitzer Group, the other for the still active Telegraph Boys.

The first passionate viola notes of the symphony flooded from the speakers. For a few seconds Herbie closed his eyes. The strings joined the violas, grasping at the first haunting melody of the adagio.

Taking a gulp of wine, he reached down, sweeping up the whole pile of Schnitzer files in one great paw, dropping the folders on his lap, and flicking through them with an indolence which belied his personal concentration.

As each faded, black and white ID photograph came into view, so Herbie heard voices from the past – incidents – words – fears. The Schnitzer Group had been his whole life for so long. His whole life, before Electra – Ursula Zunder – came into his private world.

Fifteen years? Friends, comrades, colleagues in the secret war. Now, all but three of the faces were gone for ever – bones and skulls: only God knew where they lay, and He was unlikely to turn informer. Only the Birkemanns and Moritz Zeich were available, living on their pensions, in English retirement. Zeich and the Birkemanns – and one other: the girl Herbie had known as Luzia Gabell: the girl with no name, or two names: Luzia Gabell – Lotte Krug. She would be in her forties now: alive and out there, as far as Herbie knew, behind the Wall.

The adagio rose to its rending crescendo, the orchestra becoming one great organ-like thunder. Herbie heard the other voice in his mind. Pavel Mistochenkov's laugh – *Schnitzer. Blunder. That was you, Herbie, wasn't it? Blunder?*

Herbie smiled to himself. Yes, Schnitzer. Yes, Herbie was Schnitzer, he supposed. Schnitzer never existed. A name only. A figment. Schnitzer, the German word for blunder. Ironic now.

For all Herbie's adherence to conformity, to care in the field, the Schnitzer Group had been run against the established rules. It caused headaches, and gave the big man extra problems. But the circumstances demanded it.

The rules maintained that the director, or controller, of a field network, that was unlinked to an embassy or consulate, should not expose his identity to his agents. The classic structure was a network, divided into cells, of two or three persons. The director kept contact through couriers. These were usually postmen, or brush-men – people who picked up the cells' messages, or documents, by brush passes; or cleared out the dead-drops – letterboxes: hiding places where documents or messages could be concealed.

Perhaps the techniques were better, but the general pattern went back for centuries. Controls and agents were like lovers, with go-betweens carrying their passions to and fro; arranging meetings – clandestine trysts.

For Herbie's Schnitzer Group, the old system was not possible. First, he had returned to the Soviet Zone of East Berlin in 1951, under his own name. The documentation was too good to waste, London argued. They had only to cobble up a story and a couple of documents. Herbie had the rest for real – his old ID, the deNazification certificate, a whole series of papers which showed he had been moved around from camp to camp. London merely had to fill in the last few years.

Young Eberhard Lukas Kruger was the genuine article, returning to his old home, now a mass of rubble, still lying waste: flowers, weeds and grass growing from the bricks and slates, once the stable domicile of that long-ago happy Kruger family. Returning, Herbie took a small, two-room apartment, not far from those nostalgic roots. There were still people around who remembered him as a child. Herbie Kruger had built-in deep cover.

From then until early 1955 Herbie Kruger worked as a singleton: establishing his bona fides, paying lipservice to the régime, training in simple engineering, making new friends, discovering the strange new life of East Berlin. In fact, London was grooming him for stardom.

Herbie met his case officer – either in the Alexanderplatz safe house or in the West – about once a month. He supplied standard information: mainly gossip and observation. His real duties, they said, would begin later. In the meantime he was to keep alive to the possibility of recruits.

For the intelligence and security services of both sides, it was the time of cowboys and Indians. The secret war did not stop at arrests for treason or espionage, but exploded into back-alley jobs, where operatives' lives were lost to the silenced pistol, the knife or 'swatting' – crushing against a wall with a speeding car. It was the open season, and to be suspected as a trained agent meant sudden death rather than arrest.

After three years London instructed Herbie to begin gathering in a stock of potential recruits. In 1954 he became a *Grenzgänger*, making his daily trips to his 'job' in the Western Zone, and doing detailed research on prospective clients for the network. At the time Herbie did not realise he would be controlling these people on the ground, but he knew what was required, and cast his net wide, so that it covered almost the entire Eastern Zone.

Willy Blenden and Gertrude Muller were his first prospects. So Herbie did his own detailed research on the pair before putting their names forward, establishing his own particular pattern: making certain of people before the scrutineers in the Rummage Department could make any errors.

Luzia Gabell was also an early choice. Part of Herbie's present bitterness was, he considered, caused by the facts of her recruitment, and their own personal friendship. She was the only agent Herbie ever tried to trap into the web through the love-reliance ploy. That this approach ended in ludicrous disaster only drew Luzia closer to him as a person.

When they first met Luzia had only recently started work: as a typist in the press office on Thaelmann Platz. Now Herbie reflected on the tiny fact that Vàscovsky's abortive secret meeting with him had been called at the Thaelmann Platz.

He supposed, thinking back over the time, that it really was the girl's sexual appeal which first aroused him. Petite; short blonde curly hair; mischievous face of a guttersnipe; body in good proportion to her height, and what a drinker at the Rialto in Pankow once described as "The best little ass this side of dreamland".

Herbie, who had been talking to the drinker at the time, looked and decided that it was, indeed, a bottom of considerable nubility. As little Luzia wriggled her way through the tables Herbie had been immediately attracted to her. It was purely physical, and he was far from being the only man whose eyes followed the complicated series of movements. Luzia Gabell attracted men as a magnet draws iron filings: the original honeypot.

She was also uncaring about what she said. Her visits to the Rialto were regular – two or three times a week. Within a fortnight Herbie had spoken to her – even warned her about talking the way she did. At that time the Rialto was a favourite haunt of those who worked for the Ulbricht administration: card-carrying Party members, people who belonged to the GSDF – Society for Soviet-German Friendship – and even the occasional Russian officer. Yet Luzia made no bones about her feelings. She hated the Communist régime and was not partial to Russians. "I may not have been long out of the cradle," she would say loudly, "but the bastards raped my mother and shot my father. They're worse than the Nazis. *Arschlöcher*," and Herbie would shush her. He even argued with her – being a Party member himself: a fragment of his overt cover.

"If you don't like it, why stay?"

"My old aunt is the only one left. I have to help."

"Then why work for them? You could find work in the American or British Zones. In the West."

Her aunt would worry. They had lived in the same area – her family – since Noah's ark. The aunt would go crazy if she worked anywhere west of the Brandenburg Gate.

She lived, with her aunt, in the nearby Weibensee district, and her aunt was a character. Luzia would have Herbie doubled up with laughter about her aunt, whose hearing had been affected by the bombing.

Luzia would ask the aunt if she was going out, and the aunt would always reply by telling her the time. When the public telephones were still working properly, the aunt had a great friend who went down with scarlet fever and was taken to the Charité Hospital's isolation ward. Each day the aunt would trot to a public telephone, carrying a small bottle of antiseptic in her bag. She would scream down the telephone to the isolation ward for news, then carefully clean the instrument with the antiseptic, before hurrying home to gargle, lest this form of communication should transmit the disease to her.

"She never goes up past the Brandenburg Gate," Luzia said. "She really believes that the people who live on that side of the city are strange. She's never been to the Ku-damm in her life."

Herbie continued to caution her about loud anti-Soviet or Party comments – particularly at work, or in places like the Rialto. "You're okay with someone like me. But if the *Spitzbart*'s SSD hear you there'll be trouble. Not just for you, but for your aunt." The East German SSD was a natural extension of the old Gestapo. Only the political viewpoint changed. The methods of secret police seldom alter.

It was ten days after they met before Luzia went home with Herbie one night. They slept together regularly after that – though she never stayed away from the aunt for the whole night. Herbie was barely twenty-five, far from being a virgin; but Luzia Gabell, young as she was, had a way in bed which showed great experience – probably from a very early age.

Herbie concentrated on all that his teachers had told him. The job entailed making the potential agent reliant on the seducer alone. It was, of course, impossible.

One evening, returning from a session in the West, he saw her going into an apartment block, not far from the broken and bombed Cathedral, near the Marx-Engels-Platz. Herbie waited and watched half the night. She came out five hours later, standing on the steps of the building almost wrapped around a man, kissing him more than just a fond farewell.

It was two days before he saw her again: time enough for Herbie to discover the man's identity. He was harmless enough. A factory worker, as vociferous as Luzia in his condemnation of the Party.

On their next meeting Herbie said nothing. They had a few drinks at the Rialto, then went to his apartment and made love. Looking back on it now, from the age of fifty-one, Herbie almost blushed at the things they did – he, and this lusty nymphet. She was as critical of her lover as of the régime: telling him what she liked, what to do next, then taking over the whole proceedings, mounting him and sitting astride, as though she was galloping a horse towards the winning post.

After it was over Herbie asked her about the other man. She laughed at him. "Darling Herbie. Please, do you think you are the only one? I'm sorry." Then, in a small panic, "You're not in love with me?"

He told her, no. But he was getting fond of her. She grinned, sadly, resting her hand affectionately on his loins. "Don't, Herbie. I'm my own girl. I don't intend marriage. I'm really not capable of fidelity – sexual fidelity, that is. If a man attracts me, I'll have him. Is that so terrible?"

Herbie said he understood, and she told him the only men she stayed away from were Russians. "Though you probably think I'm a little whore, now."

No, Herbie did not think she was a whore. The promiscuity was a drawback, but she was still excellent agent material. If she could be controlled, her sexual desires and agility could be harnessed. "Sex is a sport," she would say. "Like football for two." Then, "You want to score another goal, Herbie?"

Later, after she was recruited, she changed the tune and would giggle, "Sex *used* to be a sport. Now it is a pleasant duty." She also confided, in later years, that she liked Herbie more than most. She was paid to tempt men into indiscretions now, but never felt like a prostitute, because the payment came through Herbie.

Odd, he thought now, from the vantage point of the present, how sexual activity pervaded the secret world. Not so much as ploys in field operations, for the days of the Japanese Hall of Pleasurable Delights, of the Delilah and Mata Hari honeytraps, were long played out. The sexual reliance ploy still worked, but Herbie was more interested in the way in which the whole enclosed life remained orientated towards sex. Operational men and women were, by nature, lonely, and sought comfort in either passing, quick relationships or full-blown affairs.

Going through the file, now, in London, Herbie knew there had been a risk in her recruitment. Her indiscriminate choice of partners was a danger in those days. But her character was strong; her hatred of the Russians, and the Communist Party, genuine. Herbie took the trouble to put a trace on her parents. All she told him was true. Documented. The father had been killed on the Russian front, the mother had been raped. The aunt she cared for had also been a rape victim, and was as scatty as Luzia claimed. He discovered that the child, Luzia, at twelve years of age, had been present when a group of drunken Ivans invaded the house. Luzia had also been raped.

Eventually he put her name forward. It came back, cleared, like eleven others from among those he submitted. This was in 1955, when Herbie received final instructions to take over the network of twelve agents. Normally the twelve would be split into operational cells of three or four; but, apart from the married Birkemanns, Herbie wanted no interrelation between individuals. No cells. So he argued it out with his masters in the West. It would be best if each individual in the Group remained unaware of the others.

The hierarchy agreed, but only up to a point. "You're asking for trouble not using couriers," Maitland-Wood – who was present at one conference – told him. In the end Herbie agreed to use two couriers. The pair he knew and trusted best – Muller and Blenden – but only on the condition that they were kept unaware of Herbie's situation. Like the others, they were to think Herbie was also only a courier.

So it was that Schnitzer came into being. The imaginary Schnitzer – with no documents, no address, no being – became the Group's director; while Herbie Kruger, together with Gertrude Muller and Willy Blenden, was a mere courier.

One by one the newly-recruited agents were smuggled into the West – during week-ends and vacation periods: sometimes only for a day at a time. They were taught the principles of their trade, given special instructions – the total harvest to be as much information as possible on morale, troop movements, barrack-room gossip, the political and economic system. They were also engaged in acts of political and economic sabotage. The Schnitzer Group was a front-line force against Ulbricht's DDR. So said London and the West Berlin Station.

In the St. John's Wood apartment Herbie checked and rechecked Luzia Gabell's record, trying to see what should have been clear during the Schnitzer years. He cross-checked dates and times, trying to recall any glaring worries experienced over her. Herbie's memory was good; and long. She had done her job with zest. Her capability was without question. In black and white, here on the pages of reports and dossiers, was a record of her contribution. It was excellent, showing that a great deal of solid, raw intelligence had come directly from her.

Herbie played the Mahler Tenth right through, three times, as he worked on the puzzle. Not once had he suspected her; never had she jibbed at an assignment. The spot-checks always showed her clean. Never had there been a hint that she was in touch with people like Piotr and his boss, 'Vasily' – the Group's ciphers for Mistochenkov and his spy-catching chief, Vascovsky.

Had he been blinded by his fondness for her? The wry, almost laughable way in which he had sought to seduce her to the trade? As he thought about it Herbie caught a glimpse of the elfin girl, naked on his bed, body as supple as a fish. He remembered the others, also: the one-to-one meetings in the safe houses; the alleys; the fluctuating fear. It was not possible to blot out the one real act of violence they had carried out – the killing of an SSD man who was getting suspicious of Blenden and the Birkemanns.

Herbie had done it himself, with Willy Blenden driving the car. It was dark and messy: the stuff of which nightmares are made. He did not like to dwell on it. But then he did not like dwelling on Luzia Gabell's treachery.

No, the real weakness came later, after he had found happiness with Ursula Zunder, knowing for the only time in his whole life the true feelings of a woman: and his love for her also. In the end they had proved it. He wondered how Ursula had fared over the fifteen years . . .

Herbie put down the Schnitzer files and took a deep breath, which turned into a sigh. Luzia Gabell had fooled him, making a mockery of a decade; yet he still could not see how she had managed it. Again, for a second, he saw himself in a small bare room, crouched over the radio, earphones in place. Luzia with him as he signalled West Berlin Station. Blenden, moving a magazine from hand to hand in the street. Gertrude Muller, approaching down countless alleys. Habicht, laughing over coffee in the Alexanderplatz house . . .

Ursula was there, in his mind, now. Ursula laughing;

talking. The thought raised no desire. After fifteen years his impotence was total. Not that he had ever found the courage to approach a woman in that time. Neither the courage, nor the desire.

Once more the Mahler Tenth reached the drum strokes of the second scherzo. *Only you know what it means*, the composer had written to his wife in the score's margin. Then, later, *Farewell my lyre*.

But, after one walk with the great Freud, Gustav Mahler had recovered his potency, a remission only to be overtaken by death. There could be no such walk for Herbie Kruger.

He dropped the Schnitzer Group files, taking up the hefty batch which dealt with his recruitment and operation of the Telegraph Boys. Herbie knew, before opening it, that the first file would be the one on Ursula. There it was. Ursula Zunder. Cipher: Electra. His last recruit among the Telegraph Boys. Operational, September 1961. Place of Occupation: Ministry of the Interior. East Berlin. DDR. Recruitment forced on him by circumstances. Recruitment against his judgment or will. They were lovers for over a year before it was ordered. No escape from that.

Herbie opened the folder, looking down at Ursula Zunder's picture – Electra's image – solemn, the oval face with strong cheek bones, large eyes, copper hair and sensual mouth. There was no colour; the photograph could not convey the woman. He remembered Ursula as she really was: the flooding enthusiasm, constant enquiring mind; the laugh, and arching of the eyebrows; the pursed lips and troubled eyes, when she was concerned or angry; the wide, overpowering look which embraced him, even at fifty paces, when things were right. The talk and stimulus; the drive. The loving? Oh yes, and the loving.

He leafed quickly through the other five dossiers. The ones chosen before the panic. The four men and one woman trained after a toothcomb selection. Little Moritz Winter, whom they called Gemini, with his jokes, constant imitations and risque stories – storeman at the Karlshorst Soviet HQ: gabbling away so that you could hardly get a word in. The tall, thin, bespectacled Otto Luntmann, who people called the

Professor, and the Service knew as Horus. Otto was a civilian messenger for the Soviet Embassy.

Peter Sensel, a chubby, scruffy man, whose appearance did not match up to his intelligence. A labourer (a one-time builder); now foreman of the German maintenance staff out at Zossen-Wunsdorf, the Group of Soviet Forces HQ. Priam, to the Service.

That left Nestor and Hecuba – Nikolas Monch, a filing clerk at the National People's Army HQ. A grey silent man who appeared to have been born that way. The only other woman Telegraph Boy, Hecuba: Martha Adler, who held a prime job at the DDR's Political HQ. Ash blonde, long legs, sensual in a very obvious way. Herbie always suspected she was a teaser with men.

There they were, the full half-dozen: and one of them rotten, though they had all held their jobs – some even getting promotion – for twenty years or so. Until the present flap there had been talk about new recruitment. At least two of the six would be coming up to retirement soon. Now, who knew? One would be retired early.

Five Herbie had recruited personally: arranging their handling with the Schnitzer Group. He was mulling over possibilities for the sixth at the very moment the DDR began to pressure the Border Crossers. Three Party Committee members informed Herbie, in no uncertain terms, that he was a disgrace to his country. Members of the Workers-and-Peasants State should labour in the East. Kruger was forced to leave the 'job' in the West, taking on work at the Locomotive factory. A foreman's job, true, but communications were not easy. Then the axe fell. The Border was closed; the barbed wire went up: then the Wall. One Telegraph Boy short. Ursula was the only answer, and Herbie thought, maybe, it could be temporary. He did not count on having to get out to save his life. But that was another story, one on which he would not dwell now. Soon, Herbie knew, it would be borne in upon him at close range in Berlin. The dreams would return; the sweats and nightmares.

For a brief second Herbie questioned what he was planning to do. Was it really to put right his errors made long ago? Or was it to give himself a last chance with Ursula? Perhaps even to bring her back – find the way that could not be found fifteen years ago? Was it really all duty and vindication? Or the need to see if his Electra still had the power to clear his mind, and his body also? To sharpen the appetite of a middle-aged, big, ungainly German?

The spasm of doubt passed quickly. He tried to bring reason to the events. The sin lay in his first error – the recruitment of the Gabell girl. Long before the Telegraph Boys were even thought about. With a start, Herbie realised that Luzia Gabell had known of his relationship with Ursula. They made no secret of it: why should they? The best secrets are kept by leaving them open to the world.

Over coffee at a regular meeting place, Luzia had touched Herbie's hand, saying how happy he looked. She had seen them together – Ursula and Herbie. "You looked like an old married couple," she had laughed.

"Not old, but we feel married," Herbie said.

Christ. He remembered all the conversation now. Luzia had asked her name. Off his guard, Herbie told her – "Ursula Zunder. A fine girl."

Luzia Gabell's information would be an added bonus for Vascovsky. Once he had been approached by the weak link in the chain of Telegraph Boys; then had traced and identified each of them, Luzia Gabell could tell him – "That was Schnitzer's piece. That was Big Herbie's woman, the Zunder."

He rose to switch off the tape. Yes, he would carry out his plan for duty, because his marriage to the Service was like that of a monk to his vows. Yet, in the far dark corner of his mind, Herbie Kruger knew that, if the Telegraph Boys were utterly blown, he would move mountains to get Electra out of East Berlin. Into the safety of the West. Into his safety.

He returned to the files, revising the dossiers and faces of all the Telegraph Boys, like a man bent upon winning some competition – to spot the odd man out. Winter; Luntmann; Monch; Sensel; Zunder; and Martha Adler. Who, out of these six, could he have so mistaken all those years ago?

At around one o'clock in the morning, with the street noises almost quiet, Herbie knew that no amount of digging or probing into the files would track him to the rogue Telegraph

Boy. It was a field job. In the silence of the night he opened a window and looked out on London.

The Six Telegraph boys would have to be put to the question. Maybe he should have one more go at Pavel Mistochenkov, to make certain the question was correct. Gorky provided the key. The correct lock could only be found in East Berlin, and there was one man, alone, who would be able to act as locksmith.

PART TWO

Trepan

TIMMY, THE DUTIFUL nephew, telephoned his Uncle Klaus in West Berlin shortly before ten o'clock the following morning.

The news was much .better, Uncle Klaus assured his relative in London. Aunt Girda would be coming out of hospital on Friday – only four days away; much earlier than they had hoped. She would have to take it very easy, but the doctors' prognosis was good. She would eventually have to go back, into a convalescent home, but Uncle Klaus expected her to stay with him for at least two days.

Timmy said he was very pleased. If he could get off work he might even nip over and see Aunt Girda. Would she like that? Uncle Klaus sounded miserable. Timmy knew what she was like. Already, still in hospital, she was making plans: wanting to spend his hard-earned money. Still the same old spend-thrift. Wanted new curtains for the apartment, even though she hadn't seen it in weeks.

Spendthrift: Schnabeln's crypto. The bit about curtains meant there was a lot of activity. It was a low-grade alert sign. Something was stirring in East Berlin.

So, Herbie thought, Schnabeln would now be in West Berlin on Friday and Saturday. Today was Tuesday. He would be unable to leave before paying another visit to his old friend in Camden Town, and that could not be until to-morrow night at the earliest.

He called Tubby Fincher on the internal closed line, and gave him the days. "I see Spendthrift Friday and Saturday. You can arrange it?"

"Everything's fixed. I've only got to fill in the dates." Tubby *had* moved. "The Director wants you at half past eleven. Can do?"

Up in the Director's office, at eleven-thirty, Herbie saw just how quickly Fincher had activated the whole thing. Perhaps the Director wanted things under way before Herbie changed his mind. Herbie was to brief the entire team that afternoon. Already they were moving, in ones and twos, into a house maintained by the Service in the West End.

"Everything organised?" Herbie asked, surprised.

"Almost everything," Tubby told him. "We've requisitioned the equipment we think they'll ask for. Most of it's already on the way. Anything extra, your technicians can ask me. We'll have it over by jet within twenty-four hours."

The Director was behind his desk. Tubby Fincher sat in the corner, a clipboard on his bony knee. Worboys stood near the door, looking puzzled.

The Director had lapsed into his senior officer mood. "Calling the show *Trepan*," he chuckled. "Good, eh? Gouging out the cancer. *Trepan*."

Herbie looked puzzled, and Tubby Fincher had to explain. Though the word was obsolete now, a trepan used to be a surgeon's drill, boring into a patient's skull before brain surgery. Yes, Herbie agreed, *Trepan* fitted very well.

"You've got Max and Charles," the Director said – still the general briefing his troops for battle. "And I've laid on the best two technicians in the business. Scoffer and Tiptoes."

Herbie asked if Scoffer and Tiptoes were cryptos.

"Scoffer Grubb and Tiptoes Corn," Tubby again explained. "They're particularly good at long-range stuff; know all the tricks; do an electronic homer track standing on their heads. Excellent at dodging monitors and intercepts. Best in the business."

The Director shot a sly look towards Worboys. "You were worried about the spread of knowledge," he began, sliding his eyes back to Herbie.

"Our young friend here does not know it all. Not by half," Herbie replied. "But they'll all have to be given the general picture. The whole damned lot. I still don't like it."

"Then I leave it to you. You decide who should know what, and how much."

Herbie looked at Worboys; then back at the Director again. Of Fincher, he asked, "We have a house?"

"For *Trepan*? Yes. Top storey apartment. In the Kreuzberg district. Near the Mehring Platz."

"Very easy for the American airfield – Tempelhof – teeming with Yanks." Herbie did not sound happy.

"Borrowed it from them," Tubby smiled.

"Had it swept?"

"Yes, and knowing Scoffer and Tiptoes they'll go over it again. It's okay. The Yanks think we need it for a skip-trace outfit. They think we've lost somebody."

"It should be a dark alley job," Herbie mumbled. It was *going* to be a dark alley job, only this lot were not to know that. "You arrange the tickets?"

"Everyone goes tomorrow. Different flights, of course. Max goes with you, Herbie: minds you all the way."

"Not tomorrow he doesn't."

"Herbie . . .?" The Director sounded a warning.

"Okay." Herbie made placating gestures. "Max can mind me, of course. I mean I don't go to Berlin tomorrow. I go at the last moment – Thursday."

"Thursday," Tubby repeated, as though all his careful schedules had just been blown apart.

"Late Thursday. I got things need doing. Max minds me – okay. Tomorrow I want to see Tapeworm again. Not for long: a few minutes. At Warminster. I also got paperwork to do. Max can mind me to Berlin, Thursday night. I start with Spendthrift on Friday." He went on to explain that he needed all Friday and Saturday with Spendthrift: the whole of his agent's time in the West. There was a great deal to be done with Spendthrift.

The Director understood. If Herbie was to do a real Svengali on Schnabeln he would certainly need all the available time.

"At this moment he's only handling Priam and Hecuba." Herbie was firm. "That leaves four to cover. I also wish to play close to the chest. Schnabeln handles only two. There has to be an enlargement of *his* knowledge. He will have to change the handling arrangements on the other four. It will take time. Then I have to put the fluence on him. Is that what you would call it? Putting the fluence on? I read it somewhere."

"The Black Arts," the Director mumbled, to nobody in particular.

"Yes, Director. The Black Arts. Pity old Ramilies isn't still around. He was the one for the Black Arts, eh?"

Ramilies was a World War Two legend in the psychological use of agents: a manipulator, held in great esteem within Service mythology.

"Okay." Tubby ceased doing calculations on his clipboard. "I'll book you out as late as possible on Thursday, Herbie." He then gave Kruger the address and location of the top storey apartment in the Kreuzberg district. "I've got a chart," he fished into a briefcase. "That's for the technicians. Give them the height of buildings and all the local interference guff."

Herbie took it, sticking the large folded sheet into an inside pocket. They would fix him for a trip to Warminster? Yes, the Director would see to all that; and the technicians could deal direct through Tubby.

"One more thing," Herbie rose from the chair. In the confines of the Director's office he seemed to dwarf everyone. "I use the same house as normal for Spendthrift?"

They told him, yes.

"You'd better have a good excuse for the Berlin Station people. Max can mind it. Nobody else, on Friday and Saturday; and I want assurance that the tapes won't be running."

"Herbie," the Director's face went through a slight spasm. "That's a bit of routine tradecraft. For your benefit as well as ours."

"No tapes, or no Herbie," Kruger grinned. "I mean it; and don't think I will not check it out."

There was general capitulation. At three o'clock Big Herbie was to meet the *Trepan* team.

*　　　*　　　*

The house maintained by the Service in London's West End was really only a flat. In the old days they were always houses. During the cut-back of the last few years the houses had gone. Flats were in. This one was above a smart outfitter's in Jermyn Street.

Herbie made his usual careful approach. He seldom disregarded the rule, even on home ground. Not these days. It was partly the habit of a lifetime; partly security.

The interior lay-out suggested the era of Noël Coward and Ivor Novello, though this was not borne out by the furnishings – drab and functional. Herbie identified most of the stuff as old WD surplus: ranging from barrack-room tables to the kind of armchairs and sofas from officers' married quarters that were in vogue during the fifties.

Max and Charles were already there – bounding to the door in stylish soft jeans, expensive sweatshirts and handmade moccasins. They reminded Herbie of two playful young tigers.

With them was a small man, dressed neatly, even fastidiously – a person, Herbie considered, who had dragged himself up the so-called class ladder to a point at which he could mentally equate with those who were considered professionals. He had that hard, nut-brown leathery look of one who spends much time on beaches, or under sunlamps, and he wore tinted spectacles in heavy black frames.

It was hot, but this did not stop the newcomer from staying in what was obviously his uniform. The suit was very Saville Row – dark and chalk-striped; set off with a white shirt and rough-silk, claret tie. A handkerchief, of the same colour and material, hung foppishly from his breast pocket.

Max and Charles vied with one another to do the honours: introducing him as the famous 'Tiptoes' Corn.

Tiptoes gave Herbie a dazzling smile. One might have known that his teeth would be perfect. He then spoke, destroying the outward illusion. "Brought me back from bleedin' Benidorm," he said. "This one had better be worf it, Guv'nor. I done me whack this year. They 'ad to convince me this was a special."

"Convince, or order you?" Herbie grinned, disguising his mistrust of Mr. Corn. Inclined towards lippiness, he thought, grasping the man's hand, reflecting surprise at its strong grip.

"Well, if you put it like that, Guv'nor. We never worked together before, 'ave we? You know the Service; yes, 'ordered' would be the better word."

Herbie decided that he would check on Tiptoes Corn's

record when he got back from Warminster. Aloud, he announced the obvious: that they were two people short – "My own lad, Worboys; and your partner, Tiptoes – er, Scoffer Grubb. I understand that is his name."

"*His* name? *His* name?" Tiptoes shook his head. "You bin with this firm long, Guv'nor?"

Herbie gave an intimidating glower. "All my life, Tiptoes. Since twenty years old. Less. I started in the business when I was fifteen. You beat that?"

Mr. Corn shook his head.

"All right, then. It's just I don't get much chance to work with technicians."

Tiptoes, slightly subdued, said that would account for it; returning to his seat, chuckling and mumbling something unintelligible about Scoffer Grubb. "*Him?* Be pleased about that, bleedin' Scoffer will."

Herbie announced there was no point in starting until they were all in. They waited some ten minutes before the doorbell rang, Max springing out to answer it. He returned, ushering a tall, decidedly elegant young woman into the room.

"Whatcher Scoff, me old love," effused Tiptoes.

The girl gave the small man a haughty look before turning to Herbie with a mixture of deference and sexual interest, in equal parts, as she extended a soft hand. "You must be our boss. The legendary Big Herbie Kruger." The voice was pitched low, devoid of regional accent or affectation.

She was a looker: dazzling. Around thirty, Herbie thought. Medium height, but with a figure kept in trim, and all there for the eye and mind to see or imagine under the linen pants suit. The dark hair was cut short, and had that bouncy look which is the envy of girls with unmanageable locks in TV commercials. Behind the large gypsy-black eyes lay the watchful intelligence which Herbie usually noted only in the eyes of old trade hands. Born into it, he thought to himself, wondering what her real name might be. She certainly had the look of an instant professional.

"Miss Grubb, sir." Max introduced her, doing his butler-in-waiting act.

Tiptoes laughed. "'Scoffer' to her mates, eh, Scoff?"

"Miriam," she looked steadily at Herbie. "Miriam Grubb.

My last name has produced an unfortunate appellation. Hired help, like Tiptoes here, find it amusing."

"Thought you was a fella, did Mr. Kruger." Corn gave out a burst of laughter.

"Well, now he knows I'm a woman. Normal. Full of the joys and ready to work." She gave Herbie another beautiful smile which twisted into a small, lopsided smirk as she turned to Corn. "Whatcher, Tiptoes, me old mate. Good to be workin' wiv you." Then, again to Herbie, her voice modulated once more. "Just to show that I can lower my standards once in a while."

"Long as that's all you lower, girl," Tiptoes leered.

"Sod off," she flung back. "In spite of appearances, Mr. Kruger, the little man and I work well together. I merely have to keep him in line."

Herbie remarked that he had been told they were a good team; at which moment Worboys arrived, making a great point of letting Herbie know he had particularly waited until everybody was in safely. "Tubby's got minders outside," he whispered, as though – following the trip to Camden Town – the pair of them were held together by the chain of some dark secret.

There was only one telephone in the whole place. Herbie went to it, dialled a number and asked for Tubby by his work name. There followed a lot of double-talk, in the course of which Herbie was reassured that the apartment was clean, and the minders there merely to be on the safe side. When put into plain language Tubby was reinforcing the fact that *Trepan* was highly sensitive. He also reassured the big German that the whole team was cleared to a stratospheric level.

Herbie returned, to find that Miriam Grubb had organised everybody. A table stood in the centre of the room, with six stand chairs around it, and a place for Herbie at its head. His five subordinates were already seated. They all had small notebooks at the ready.

"No writing," Herbie commanded. "Nothing on paper. You have been told this is sensitive?"

They murmured affirmation.

"The crypto for the op, and for ourselves, is *Trepan*."

They knew that also. "Okay, I brief you. Simple. Questions and planning later."

They sat, like students at a seminar: attentive and deferential. Herbie had already decided how much they should be told. Certainly no names, and only the cryptonyms that were absolutely necessary. He would not use the term Telegraph Boys, for instance.

"Here beginneth the lesson," he started. "It came to pass that, in those days, there was a clumsy Kraut who worked for the Service. They called him Big Herbie Kruger and he lived, like a gopher, looking after a nest of agents in East Germany: mainly in East Berlin. These were the days of the Cold War.

"Then the Lord, in London, sayeth, 'Herbie, we have a special job to give unto you. You are to go forth and multiply your agents, without the rest of your spies knowing. The number of your agents shall be six. Each will be trustworthy and well-placed. None shall be aware of the others. Each must be placed so they can view the comings and goings of those in high positions, with the Deutsche Demokratische Republik. For, lo, there are six people in East Berlin who will do certain things, if the Philistines of the Soviet Bloc prepare to move against us with their mighty weapons.'"

Herbie had judged the *Trepan* team correctly. The sombre looks disappeared, their interest was roused.

"So, God gave the order. 'The six people shall guard, and watch over the comings and goings of these important men – who are both counsellors and warriors. They will report on the movements in the usual manner. Your people, already in the land, shall be their handlers. They shall have no knowledge, but they will take messages from letterboxes; they will pick up words by brushing against each other in the throng. The messages will be sent at all speed to our wise men, who shall ponder over them, and so have knowledge of war-like movements well in advance.'

"So, the clumsy big Kraut went abroad: into the highways and byways; into the castles and council chambers of East Berlin; and he selected six persons to do these tasks.

"His own agents went about their daily business; but, in addition, they handled the secret words of the six watchers. And it came to pass that Big Herbie Kruger's nest of spies was smitten to the left and to the right. Many were killed, and only a few escaped in their socks.

"The six watchers continued to do their work: yea, even under the difficult conditions which prevailed; for there were few to handle them. For many years the watchers laboured in the vineyard of East Berlin; and in their loneliness they often sat down and wept. Herbie also sat down and wept for them: by the waters of the Thames, and in the Lord's council chambers. Until one day the Lord sayeth unto Herbie, 'The watchers that you left in East Berlin are still able to give us warnings – Yea, even in advance of the giant celestial machines which whirl above the firmament. Go, choose four men and women. They shall be sent forth into East Berlin; but with cunning they shall be made to think they go as ordinary spies. To their duties you shall add the handling of those who have watched so long, as there will be a proper conduit for their intelligence.'

"And so it was, brethren, that Herbie sent forth four spies, who brought back messages from the watchers; and who handled them like babies; even though they knew not what they did.

"And the Lord in London was pleased, as were those from over the mighty ocean; and the warriors who call themselves NATO. For the warnings they received from the watchers still came many days in advance of those from the celestial bodies.

"But lo, an enemy changed sides, being a turncoat, bringing news which made both the Lord and Herbie fearful. One of the watchers – set by the bungling Kraut, Herbie – had been treacherous and full of falsehood, from the moment of his, or her inception: and they knew not who this traitor was.

"Neither did the turncoat know, but he passed words to Big Herbie. Words which, if used with guile, can reveal the maggot among those who watch." He paused, looking around the faces.

"There you are," he grinned. "One of the handlers is coming into the West on Friday. I will see him and send him back, armed and primed. We need to track him. In turn he will track our mystery man; let us know the identity. We will then tell him what to do." He made an expansive gesture – "All this in secret, with nobody – either military, or our Service in West Berlin – knowing."

"Search and destroy," Miriam said.

Herbie nodded, then asked for preliminary questions.

The technicians immediately proved themselves high grade. Tiptoes asked if the handling was all done on the ground – by which he meant through dead-drops or clandestine passes. Herbie said yes, though recently those he called the watchers had been issued with micro-squawks – instruments no bigger than a matchbox which, if activated, would alert Berlin Station to a most immediate need for contact.

"And the handlers?" Miriam Grubb leaned forward. "How do they get the stuff over?"

The watchers, Herbie told her, had access to microdot facilities, and could also make screech tapes – small cassettes on which they recorded ciphered messages. The tapes could be played on fast-senders, small high-powered radios, tuned to particular frequencies, transmitting the screech tapes so quickly that they came out as a short squeak, or distortion, which could be recorded, then played back at a normal speed to produce the correct message.

"The handlers have fast-senders?" From Tiptoes.

"Two. Two of the handlers only."

"Frequencies?"

"Automatic change of frequencies, on a random machine linked with West Berlin Station."

"Whom we wish to bypass?"

"Exactly." Herbie gave his most stupid look, as though all these technical matters were far beyond him. "Berlin Station has to be bypassed."

Miriam said they would need another fast-sender in the East. Herbie thought that was already being arranged. "Just tell my friend Worboys here. He will arrange for everything."

She immediately went into a huddle with Tiptoes, and they started to throw the names of technical equipment at Worboys who appealed to Herbie, asking permission to put it in writing. "Just to get the requisitions. I can't carry all this in my head."

Herbie relented.

"We'll need a detailed chart of our own operating area." Tiptoes was demanding, not telling. Herbie produced the chart already provided, and the technicians pored over it. They continued to throw technicalities at Worboys, who fielded them adroitly, repeating the part numbers and names as though he knew their exact purpose and use. Herbie raised his eyebrows.

It was Miriam Grubb who brought up the question of the homing device. "We're situated fairly high up in this place" – tapping the map – "but there's still going to be the hell of a lot of interference. We can deal with the fast-sender – beam it directly in to us. No problem. There's a new scrambler that'll do the trick. Berlin Station won't even hear it."

"I do want all this contained." Herbie spoke softly.

Miriam hardly paused. "It'll be contained. But the homer's going to be a bitch. To track your man properly we really need a bouncer." She was talking about a homing unit which bounced signals back from one of the communication satellites. It was a small, battery-powered device: operational over a long range, but with a life of barely twenty-four hours.

"Done." Worboys looked pleased with himself. "Already organised. They're clearing a frequency for it as from Saturday night."

"Then we can track him to Moscow and back."

Herbie coughed. As he would be making delivery of the homer he insisted on a pair. "We'll test them on site. My man's time is very limited. I don't want to send him with a dud."

They agreed that a standby duplicate was in order. Herbie was certain Tubby Fincher would query it, but kept his fingers crossed. For what Herbie was about to do he needed at least two homers.

Tiptoes then asked about the types of antennae they needed to monitor the whole operation. Had anyone thought about that? To Herbie's surprise Worboys came out with a string of jargon, rattling it off parrot-fashion, which signalled to Herbie that his assistant had spent a number of hours under Tubby Fincher's tutelage.

The question and answer session, and cross-checking of the technicians' needs, went on for nearly two hours. Max and Charles looked bored. Finally, when everybody was happy, Worboys read out their departure and arrival times, handing out the tickets. Both the lion-tamers and the technicians had worked in Berlin before. There were no language difficulties. They knew the city, so times and methods of arrival at the Mehring Platz apartment presented no problems. Herbie went through his own movements.

Max already knew he was minding Herbie. "Have to behave yourself, old darling. Got eyes in the back of my head, I have. No footling around with the Fräuleins."

Herbie pretended to enjoy the joke at his own expense. He would arrive in Berlin, late on Thursday night. Max would be given the address of the house they would be using. "It's a fair distance from our *Trepan* place; from the Mehring Platz." He let them know about the crypto of their subject – Spendthrift. Herbie would be working with him all day on Friday, then would come over to see them at the Mehring Platz. On Saturday he would again work with Spendthrift, and see him off that evening. They should not expect to find Herbie taking up residence with them until Sunday morning at the earliest. "On Sundays I do not rise at dawn. I do not expect much action until late in the day."

Worboys was to tie up any loose ends. In the meantime Herbie had work to do. He would see them all in Berlin. "Except me," Max reminded him archly. "I pick you up Thursday. Your place or mine?"

He was told to follow Herbie out to the airport from the St. John's Wood address. "Be ready for me at least two hours before departure time. I shall try not to keep you waiting." The last order was curt and pointed.

"Got a bark worse than his bite, that one," Max said after Herbie left. Worboys suggested that Max take care.

"He's big, but slippery as an eel. Done it all. You've seen enough of him in action to know that, Max." As he said it, Worboys realised the insecurity of his aside. Both the technicians – fascinated by Herbie – immediately plied Max for details.

The lion-tamer was not to be drawn. "Did a job with him, that's all. Young Tony's right. Ruthless as they come. Beware the Krugerwock, my son! The jaws that bite, the claws that snatch."

Out in the streets of London, Herbie walked slowly up to

Piccadilly, where he used a pay 'phone to call his old friend in Camden Town. Yes, the clock was in good working order now. He could pick it up any time after five tomorrow. Herbie said he would be there.

He took two different taxis back to St. John's Wood, leaving the last one to walk the final half-mile back to his apartment building.

Check. Double-check. He appeared to be clean.

Herbie arrived home feeling the vague onset of depression. No doubts were left in his mind. He was doing the right thing. The only thing. There might be some disciplinary action when it was all over, but that did not matter.

His thoughts, at that precise moment, turned to Schnabeln, and the arranged meeting for Friday.

2

CHRISTOPH SCHNABELN'S CHEEKS glowed a bright rosy red. Someone had once likened them to English Red Delicious apples. But then no matter what ailed him Schnabeln always looked healthy. People would say how well he looked even when he was dropping with influenza.

He had the same hale and hearty look now, early in the morning, sitting on his bed. Nobody would have dreamed that Schnabeln was unusually anxious.

Though a decade younger than Herbie, Christoph Schnabeln had been in the business for a long time; he too had home-grown cover, and was German by birth.

Of the four members of Kruger's Quartet in East Berlin Schnabeln was undoubtedly the most comfortably placed. Walter Girren lived in two poky rooms above the Tauben Strasse; Anna Blatte had what the British called a bed-sitting room in one of the older blocks overlooking the Treptow Park; while Anton Mohr occupied two rooms in a crumbling villa on the outskirts of the Köpenick district – sharing a bathroom with an elderly, sick woman, her husband and a young pair of newly-weds: sombre convinced Party members.

Christoph Schnabeln, however, lived in comparative luxury – a permanent resident of East Berlin's newest and best hotel, the Metropol. The rooms were spacious, the furnishings and fitments excellent. The décor was pleasing to the eye: particularly the polished light-coloured wood which betrayed the hotel's Swedish design. In fact, the Metropol was a jar of jam for the tourists who still came – out of morbid curiosity, Schnabeln felt – in good numbers from abroad, and the West.

It was one of the many places in East Berlin where you could spend only foreign currency: desperately needed to keep the DDR's foundering economy above water.

The room, bathroom and restaurant facilities at the Metropol went with Schnabeln's job. He worked in tourism, and had done so for the past ten years. In fact his recruitment to the British Service had almost coincided with the first appointment of any major importance by the Ministry concerned with tourism.

Schnabeln's advent to the tourist trade began when he received an invitation from the Ministry asking for his assistance in their "expanding industry of interchange with other nations". As always, Schnabeln knew the invitation was really a command. He spoke several languages, and was good with people. Eventually, he feared, either the SSD or the Russian KGB would make an approach. Strangely they left him alone (though he had faithfully carried packages under orders: facts which he immediately shared with his British masters, to their mutual advantage).

In all, his overt career had been good. Three years in Prague; fleeting visits to Moscow and New York; another three years in East Berlin, followed by a two-year posting to Bucharest. Then another year in Berlin preceded eighteen months in London, where, despite the occasional random and snap surveillance, he had completed his Service training, and worked closely with Herbie Kruger, preparing to be a member of the Berlin Quartet.

Schnabeln even had the notion that it was part of Herbie's strange magic which had caused his present appointment: East Berlin liaison officer for a respected West Berlin coach tour firm that provided twice-daily tours of the Eastern Zone.

The morning tour was a straight sightseeing trip. In the evening the coachloads of tourists came to visit plays at the Berliner Ensemble, or sample what passed for East Berlin's nightlife.

The Party representatives never ceased to remind Schnabeln that his was an important and responsible post. He knew why it was important. Everybody knew why. Foreign tourists, even on a few hours' coach trip, brought in and spent their currency. Tourists were always welcome, as long as they paid in dollars, deutschmarks from the West, even sterling or, particularly, Swiss francs.

The job accounted for his living conditions, and a free-of-charge run of the Metropol Hotel, plus a brand new Wartburg car, and the special permits to visit the Western Zone.

The permits were, of course, only granted when it was essential for him to attend meetings with the West Berlin company; but Schnabeln's duties included travelling, at least three times a week, with the coach tours. He was also responsible for arranging schedules concerning the nightlife. This latter duty made him a popular figure at the few available nightspots and restaurants, who looked to him for inclusion on the list of places visited by the tourists.

In this respect he was given a good deal of freedom by the Party Committee member who was his immediate boss – a plump and genial fellow within whom a thin, mean autocrat was desperately trying to get out. As long as Schnabeln did his job, was in the hotel when needed by visitors (who used his services to get advice and bookings), and at his post during the visits of the coach parties, Hoffer, his boss, did not complain.

This left Schnabeln plenty of time to carry out his more clandestine work. It also meant that the pattern of his life could not easily be charted. Always alert to potential surveillance, Schnabeln was well aware of his priorities. The Quartet was interrelated, each knowing – within a rough spectrum – the duties of the others. Schnabeln was too old a hand to be completely taken in by Herbie's blandness regarding the handling duties assigned to the Quartet.

Though Herbie always spent a large portion of the regular debriefing sessions, in West Berlin, dealing with the intelligence-gathering and recruiting nature of their jobs, they always ended up with a hard, concentrated session on the handling of their special contacts.

Spendthrift had known this was the real priority within his first couple of months back in East Berlin. His two contacts – Priam and Hecuba – were about the most professional operators Schnabeln had ever encountered. Priam lived out of the city, therefore most of his information came through by letterbox, dead-drops; though they had seen one another on several occasions. Hecuba delivered most of her stuff by direct passes.

The letterboxes, and the passes, were always varied and were imaginative to the point of being blinding in their ingenuity. Not for these people the old chestnuts behind radiators in public buildings or in wall cracks. They made Schnabeln really work – the purchase of some cheap ornament; or the tape left in an empty cigarette packet in a litter bin. This last caused Schnabeln nightmares, lest the bin be emptied before he reached it.

On one occasion Hecuba had sat next to him, chatting about art, in a bar for a full hour before leaving, then dropping a particularly difficult package straight into his lap, without bartender or customers being aware of it. That was the trouble with such professionals, Schnabeln considered; they were so good that it was sometimes difficult to keep up with them.

Girren, with whom he spoke from time to time in one of the safe houses, drew the analogy of a young and inexperienced actor playing a difficult scene with a really accomplished performer. The expert would give a great deal, but the tyro had to learn fast in order to remain in character. Girren knew about such things, working backstage at the theatre as he did.

Schnabeln was also aware that Girren, and himself, were the two most important members of the Quartet. They had to retrieve material dropped, or passed, to Anna Blatte and Anton Mohr. Girren and Schnabeln were the only two with access to the West. They were also the only two equipped with the most important, and dangerous, tool of their trade – the fast-sending screech boxes. To be caught with one was something upon which Schnabeln did not dwell.

The screech-boxes looked like small, innocent radio sets. They were in fact transistorised transmitters. Even the most casual examination would yield the truth very quickly.

Their operation was simple enough. You did not have to worry about tuning to some prearranged frequency. The boxes tuned automatically to frequencies which changed daily. One merely had to insert the mini-tapes, switch the box to the 'on' position, and depress a play key. The tape would whip through in sometimes less than a couple of seconds.

Berlin Station would record the minor squeal, or seeming interference, and send it directly through to London, where the wizards would slow it down and decipher the message. The problem was sticking to a schedule of sending times, which rarely allowed more than five minutes' delay; and the necessity of actually sending from a different place for each transmission.

Schnabeln usually did his sending from the Wartburg, always in a different area of the city. He had even done it while accompanying coach parties on their night tours. It never ceased to scare him, though, for he was well-primed about the lengths to which KGB and SSD Direction Finders would go.

Now, sitting on his bed in the Metropol Hotel, Christoph Schnabeln was not worried about using the fast-sending machine. His anxiety sprang from the telephone call he had just received from his boss, Hoffer. It seemed that the coach firm in West Berlin required to discuss new schedules with him on Friday of this week. There was to have been a regular meeting next week. That had all been arranged. Herbie would be there, with the usual cover story for him to take back to Hoffer. This call to a special meeting was something different. It worried him. Hoffer said the coach firm had spoken of it as an emergency. Permits were being granted for him to leave on Friday and stay overnight. "You can return with the evening tour coach on Saturday," Hoffer told him. It was to do with the revision of timetables.

"You will do everything in your power to ensure there is no drop in the number of tours," Hoffer said with a nasty edge. "In fact I shall be extremely disappointed if you do not bring back news of an increase."

Schnabeln tried to point out that this was unlikely in view of the continuing rise in fuel costs, and the Western inflationary spiral.

"If there is a drop in the number of tours I shall make a special report to the Ministry of Tourism," Hoffer threatened. "Then we shall see what happens. I hold you personally responsible."

That did not worry Schnabeln one bit. His well-spring of anxiety was the sudden change of plans. The word *emergency*, dropped so innocently into Hoffer's ear by the coach firm, indicated something more sinister.

He would have to leave the usual messages, to let Priam and Hecuba know he would not be available on Friday or Saturday. That was simple enough. They still used Indian signs – the chalk marks on walls, the particular angle of a scratch on a park bench. Personal contact, on the other hand, had to be made with Girren. He smiled, thinking of Girren as Annamarie, his crypto. He always smiled when he thought of Girren as Annamarie. Teacher – Anton Mohr – was easy. They already had a meeting planned for later in the day. But what of Maurice? Maurice was convinced she had a ripe potential on her line: she also had a pile of photographs. Schnabeln did not like carrying photographs into the West.

A call on Maurice was always a pleasure, though. Anna Blatte – Maurice – was in her late thirties, and on constant heat. Herbie had been advised of this possible pressure point, but had assured Schnabeln that the busty Anna was quite capable of controlling herself. She rarely did so when Christoph Schnabeln was around; he was glad to say. A trip over to Anna Blatte's place would be truly pleasant. She would be in this morning; Tuesday was her free day. He could kill two birds with one stone. It might cheer him up, quell the anxiety.

Schnabeln shaved and dressed, then made his way into the hotel lobby. He was half way to the main doors before he spotted the long legs and ash hair of Hecuba. She had not seen him, as she sat, deep in conversation, drinking coffee with a man whose face appeared to be vaguely familiar to Schnabeln.

Their heads were bent together. Probably one of her contacts. Pumping him quietly over coffee in the lobby of the Metropol. Hecuba was a cool one, sure enough.

It was only when he was in his little Wartburg, driving out towards Treptow Park and Anna Blatte, that Christoph Schnabeln remembered where he had previously seen the face of the man, now in close conversation with Hecuba.

The face had been on a photograph, and the photograph was one they had all studied with Herbie Kruger in London.

He could even put a name to the face. The anxiety deepened. What would Hecuba be doing, sipping coffee, cosy and chummy at the Metropol, with a KGB major usually only to be found at the Moscow Centre?

3

"Tubby Fincher told me I should watch you." Worboys was driving them to Warminster.

"You tell him anything?" Herbie did not even look at Tony Worboys. He watched the road.

Worboys said of course he said nothing, but what did it mean?

"It means that I have a reputation of sometimes cutting red tape into little ribbons and scattering it all over Whitehall."

"You're doing that now?"

"You must wait and see. Just watch, and learn from me." Herbie placed a large hand on Worboys' knee, pressing hard. "But never stop me, young Worboys. Loyalty to the Service is one thing. I am your immediate superior in the Service. We are together on a most sensitive matter, so sensitive that you don't even tell yourself about it. Just be a good boy and do as you're told – which means you do what I tell you."

Worboys had already pledged himself to Big Herbie. He did not like the way Tubby Fincher had taken him to one side after the whole requisitioning order for *Trepan* was completed.

"There's some highly emotive connection for Herbie in this one." Fincher's voice contained a warning note. "You'll have to watch him; make sure he doesn't do anything silly – go off at half-cock. Got me? I'm warning Max as well."

"He's warning Max as well," Worboys said, taking a corner a shade wide.

Herbie flinched. "Max doesn't worry me. Don't you get concerned, either. I'm a professional, remember? Berlin's my patch." At least, he thought to himself, they would not be able to warn Schnabeln.

For no apparent reason, Herbie's mind slid back to his thoughts concerning the enclosed life of the Service and sex. His brow creased: then he realised the trigger had been Worboys. Worboys and the girl Miriam Grubb. A look, a spark between them? Was it Miriam eyeing Worboys, or the other way around?

"Your girl, the one in Registry . . ." he began.

Tony Worboys grunted.

"Noel, is it?"

"Yes." Defensive.

"Everything okay?" Gently, thought Herbie.

"Fine. Why?"

"Like to see my people happy. You going to miss her?"

Worboys supposed he would miss Noel Richards, but it was only for a few days. He had not thought about it.

"Give you a tip," Herbie grinned. "A few days under field conditions can seem like years. There's another woman in the team. Happens, you know, particularly when you are young."

"What happens?" Worboys kept his eyes on the road, but had a sudden desire to turn and show anger. In a way he was bewildered, for Herbie had touched some raw nerve he did not realise existed.

"Casual screwing. Can lead to problems."

Worboys exploded, raising his voice, twin patches of red on his cheeks. "You know all about that, do you, Herbie? You a big one for sex? I heard you kept away from women. Nobody's ever suggested that you're the other way, but it's Service gossip. Big Herbie's not a man for the ladies. You're giving me sex instruction, are you?"

Herbie mumbled an apology. The little outburst hurt. He could not know that Worboys could have bitten his tongue off.

*   *   *

The Warminster house was large; guarded by military police, dogs and electronic body-sniffers. This was also a property which held a particular mystique for everybody in the Service. The Warminster house upset some people; others shuddered at its mention. Some smiled, knowing the legend to be more colourful than the facts.

Pavel Mistochenkov looked in startlingly good health. "It's the vitamin shots they're giving me," he told Herbie; and Herbie's suspicious mind gave a silent chuckle.

He wanted to ask one or two more questions of Pavel. First, Lotte Krug. How often had Vascovsky seen her? Once a week? Twice? More?

"How should I know?" Mistochenkov gave a slight shrug. "I didn't sleep with him."

Herbie asked how long the affair lasted. Years, Pavel replied. "From '56 or so; and still going strong when he . . ." The pause again. Herbie had noted, when Pavel was at the Charlton house, the Russian could not bear to say that Vascovsky was dead; or that he had committed suicide.

"Describe her," Herbie snapped.

Pavel laughed. What did he mean, describe her? He had seen the photograph. That was her; only younger than when he last saw her.

"Then describe Lotte Krug as she was when you last saw her."

"Looking tired," Mistochenkov replied.

Herbie forced the pace. Finally the Russian said she was a small woman. "Nice figure, though. Face like a sprite; but lost her looks quickly."

"You saw a lot of her?"

"Only when I had to call at the apartment and she happened to be there."

"Anything else?"

"She was good at making people laugh. At least I think so. She made the Colonel-General laugh a great deal."

"You told me she did not live in Vascovsky's private apartment."

Pavel made a grimace. No, she did not – except possibly over week-ends when the work-load was light. "She stayed there for nights. I took no notice. Many of our senior officers had girl-friends. There was no problem."

"Where did she live?"

Pavel did not know. He thought Vascovsky arranged things. Fixed an apartment for her.

"Think, Pavel. Think hard. This was a long affair. When it first started, where did the girl live?"

Light dawned on Mistochenkov's face. That was easy, he smiled. "I drove her a lot in the early days. Used to pick her up and take her home. She lived out in the Weibensee district. Had a funny old aunt. Used to give me a drink. The Old Man was jumpy about her in those days. I always did the pick-ups and returns in different cars – we had a big car pool then – and always in plain clothes. It was like handling an agent."

A cloud crossed Herbie Kruger's mind, blotting out any lingering hopes. Why, he worried, did I not know? Why did we not pick up some scent? There were occasions, during that time, when Vascovsky was watched – for days on the trot. No hints; no reports. That Luzia Gabell and Lotte Krug were one and the same was not in doubt. Far away, as though coming faintly from the past, Herbie could hear Luzia, in bitter anger, talking of her hatred for the Ivans: her father killed by them; her mother raped (though she never mentioned her own childhood experience at their hands).

Herbie changed the subject, turning to the question of the one Telegraph Boy who was Vascovsky's agent. He wanted to make absolutely certain of the way in which Vascovsky had arranged for new handling.

It was not proper handling in the first place, Pavel answered. "You knew that: we went through it. The Old Man knew it all; he received reports from your Telegraph Boy. But we sent nothing on. It remained *our* secret."

"Your secret? You saw some of the material, Pavel?"

"I saw nothing, and I've told you everything. It all came through the Old Man. I didn't even know who your Telegraph Boy was. Nor do I know if anything was written down on paper."

"At the end . . .?"

"At the end the Colonel-General told me he had taken measures. We've been through this already."

Herbie raised his voice a fraction. That they had been through it once or twice did not mean they would not keep up the questions. As far as he was concerned, it did not matter if they went over the same ground a thousand times. "Vascovsky told you he had instructed this person: this Telegraph Boy?"

Okay, Pavel said, he would lead Herbie over it once more. He was concerned, because he felt, once he and Vascovsky jumped over the Wall, the Telegraph Boy would go running to the first new contact he could find. "I still think he will. I think he's spilling his guts out now. Maybe in Moscow."

"He? He? You're certain about that? You did not say it was definitely a man before."

"He or she, then." Pavel's good humour disintegrated quickly. "Yes, I got the impression it was a man. The way the Old Man talked. It could have been a woman, though. I just don't know."

Vascovsky had said Pavel was not to worry. The Telegraph Boy had been given detailed instructions. If anything happened to Vascovsky the asset was to close all contact. To wait. New contact would be made. "That Telegraph Boy, you must understand, imagined every report was going straight through to Moscow. You know what you do with doubles, Herbie. You make them feel they are indispensable. They become reliant."

"They also become difficult, Pavel. Did the Old Man hint that his tame Telegraph Boy was difficult?"

There were occasional difficulties. Doubles like to try it on; but it paid Vascovsky to keep the asset happy. "He was storing up goods to help in our journey to the West."

"It is better to store up treasure in heaven." Herbie spoke in a whisper. Then: "In your statement to me you said that Vascovsky had neutralised his asset – the Telegraph Boy. Told him to wait for a new contact, if he disappeared."

"Or if anything happened to him, yes."

"Those were his words? The Old Man's words?"

"His words to me."

"And he actually gave you the new contact sentence, Pavel?"

Mistochenkov was puzzled. Yes, the Colonel-General had told him the words passed on to the asset. "The lines from Gorky. They were to be the signal that the asset had a new handler."

Herbie quoted again from *The Lower Depths*: "A man can teach another man to do good – believe me." Mistochenkov said, yes, those were the words. Put into a conversation, the asset would know they came from someone trusted, or sent by Vascovsky.

"And there was no answer-back?" Herbie gave a snort. "Why do you think he told you, Pavel? Why *you*? You were going into the West, whatever. With the Old Man, or, if something went wrong, without him. In the end you came alone. But why did he tell you?"

Insurance, Pavel presumed. "If I was caught. If you tried to double me back I would have a bargaining point."

Herbie laughed at the nonsense, then shook his large head. "No, little Pavel — that's what the Old Man called you, didn't he? — little Pavel? Vascovsky gave you the words, the cipher, so that you would tell me. Don't you think so?"

Mistochenkov did not know. He did not see the point.

"Then there are other points you should try to see, little Pavel." The laugh had left Herbie's face; not even the trace of a smile. Worboys thought he had never seen the big man's eyes go so cold. "The Telegraph Boys, as you call them; you were never given proper names, only cryptos?"

Pavel said yes, of course: again repeating they had already gone over all that.

Herbie ploughed on, oblivious to the Russian's remonstrations. "And these cryptos? Vascovsky gave them to you: told you? When did he do that?"

"Christ in heaven," Mistochenkov raised his hands. "March 1965. I told you."

"Repeat the cryptos, Pavel."

"Repeat the . . .?"

"Yes. Repeat." Herbie moved in closer, towering over the Russian, who took a step back, then, opening his mouth twice, rattled off the six names. "Priam-Hecuba-Electra-Horus-Nestor-Gemini."

"And where did your good Colonel-General Vascovsky get those names, I wonder?"

Pavel Mistochenkov shrugged. From the faithless Telegraph Boy, he presumed.

"Really?" Herbie gave the Russian a friendly push with his huge paw, smiled, then cocked his head at Worboys who followed him, like a sheepdog, from the room.

Herbie's smile camouflaged mental confusion. The puzzle split, divided itself, the parts chasing around his brain. The Telegraph Boys had, from their inception, been carefully segregated: no one member of the six had knowledge of the other five – either by true name or cipher. Certainly during that long period of sporadic, and poor servicing after the Schnitzer Group left town, their faces might have been identified by dedicated surveillance. Yet no single Telegraph Boy could have given Vascovsky the cryptonyms; and it would be harder still to marry the ciphers with the true names.

Luzia Gabell could have given neither true names nor cryptonyms to Vascovsky: even if she had been able to let him see any of the material. In the days of the Schnitzer Group the Telegraph Boys' handling was so tight you could not move.

Until Herbie's Berlin Quartet moved in, some eighteen months before, only half a dozen people were even aware of the cryptonyms, and only two could have married them with real names – the Director and Herbie Kruger himself. The Director was like Caesar's wife; while Herbie's store of secrets was endless, and locked away deep in the cradle of his memory.

So, Vascovsky's asset within the Telegraph Boys could not have passed the names in the March of 1965. Nor could Luzia Gabell. Yet Pavel Mistochenkov claimed to have had them – via Vascovsky, via a Telegraph Boy – at that time.

Herbie's brow creased as the anxiety blossomed. Could Vascovsky have pieced the six cryptos together through radio intercepts? Unlikely, for only a small portion of the Telegraph Boys' traffic had gone through radio in those days.

With freezing logic, Herbie considered the alternatives: that all six of his Telegraph Boys had been turned from the outset – odds heavily against; that by some wizardry, Vascovsky had obtained a spectrum of intercepts, revealing the ciphered names as early as 1965; that Pavel Mistochenkov was deliberately misleading him about the dates. If this last was true, it could mean that the Russians had only recently learned of the six ciphers: from one of the new Berlin Quartet.

It was this last possibility which struck a chord of anguish within Herbie Kruger. Already he was discredited through the Schnitzer Group and the Telegraph Boys. If one of the Quartet had also gone, then his whole status collapsed: his reputation was triple-shattered. More, it threw a new hazard of horrifying dimensions into the ploy he was about to play.

Worboys got no hint, as they left Warminster, that the slump of Herbie Kruger's shoulders signalled the fear of complete defeat. Herbie said little on the drive back to London. His head buzzed with the permutations, and his mind constantly slid on to the technicalities which the *Trepan* operation posed. He hoped that Tiptoes and Scoffer were as good as Tubby Fincher claimed. Certainly they seemed to be efficient; but the testing time would be from Saturday night onwards.

He visualised a room he had yet to see – high on the top storey of the apartment block near the Mehring Platz. The transmitters and screens: the small, high-powered dish antennae hidden on the roof, seeking for the homer blips from Schnabeln. The pair of technicians picking up the blips, doing their sums and pinpointing, tracking, the man on a large scale map: following him invisibly down streets, into buildings. Charting his progress; waiting for the screech. He had taken Worboys through the screech cipher. "Just to be on the safe side. In case I'm called away, or anything happens," he told his assistant, without the hint of a betraying smile. "It's always better to double up on this kind of thing. That screech has got to be slowed and deciphered on the spot."

Worboys felt elated. Herbie was, perhaps, starting to trust him at last. The screech, when it came, would give them the name of the person they were after. The blip, charted by the progress of the homing device, would provide the exact location. Big Herbie must have something up his sleeve – some method of communication with his man in the East; so that action could be taken straight away. But Worboys had enough sense not to ask about that.

They went straight back to the Annexe where Herbie spent half an hour with the Director and Tubby Fincher. He put in requisitions for two more small pieces of equipment, then went to look at the paperwork in his office.

At just after four Herbie instructed Worboys – who was due out to Berlin on the last flight – to do a final minding job: once more cautioning him to silence.

"I've got to pack . . ." Worboys began.

"An hour at the most. Quick in and out. Just let me know Tubby's boys aren't watching; okay?"

Tony Worboys saw no surveillance on his boss. Herbie was quite clean all the way, he told him, back in the St. John's Wood apartment. They had gone out to Camden Town High Street again. Taxi-cab and bus, this time: Herbie clutching his fat briefcase. Underground and taxi back.

"Okay, young Worboys. Have a good trip to Berlin. I see you Friday night. Look after the others; and I'm not to be disturbed unless there is genuine danger."

Worboys understood, and left Herbie alone with his thoughts, and the package he had collected from the shop in Camden Town.

Herbie spread out the newly collected material on his table, examining it with care. The American and East German passports were really high grade merchandise; as were the various pieces of ID, the permits and passes. He would get by with this stuff; unless he was expected, which was always a possibility.

Later that evening Herbie sat back in his favourite chair and went through his plan again. He had to be word-perfect with Schnabeln, and the timing was critical. The whole thing would have to be completed by Sunday night. Twenty-four hours was the maximum. Otherwise there really would be problems. Herbie knew he would return either a hero or in disgrace. There was a third possibility – that he would not return at all. For a second he wondered if either Tubby or the Director had seen through his innocent requests. Well, he'd know that soon enough.

Mahler's songs from *Des Knaben Wunderhorn* – *The Boy's Magic Horn* – played softly in the background. The composer had dipped again and again into this massive anthology of German folk art – which so enchanted poets, musicians and philosophers – using, or altering, poems and songs to include in his symphonies and cycles. The twelve-song cycle Herbie was playing contained a whole range of subject matter from the military to the blatant sensual overtones of *Verlor'ne Muh* – *Wasted Effort*, a dialogue suggesting adolescent seduction, the girl making the moves and the boy rejecting her –

All right, shall I give you my heart?
Will you always remember me?
Take it, dear little boy, take it, please!

Crazy little wench, I certainly don't want it.

Herbie nodded to himself. He knew the poem, the song, by heart. Ursula had spoken the dialogue with him: part of their love-play. She, trying to titillate, where no arousal was needed. He feigning disinterest: a verbal chase-me-round-the-bedroom.

As though suddenly recalling something from the past, Herbie wound the tape back to the first song – *Serenade of the Sentry*, or, more accurately, *The Song of the Night Sentry*.

Trumpets, joined the strings for the first verse, in which the sentry bemoans his lot. He must stay awake; he must be sorrowful. His lover answers. There's no need to be sad; she'll wait for him – in the rose garden: in the green clover. Then –

Zumgrunen Klee geh ich nicht!
Zum Waffengarten
voll Helleparten
bin ich gestellt.

Yes, Herbie thought. That's exactly it –

I am not going to the green clover!
The garden of weapons
Full of halberds
Is where I am posted.

4

Tony Worboys left Heathrow on a Lufthansa flight. Charles, with Tiptoes Corn, went earlier, by British Airways. Miriam Grubb was on Worboy's aircraft. He spotted her in the terminal building. On the aircraft he saw the back of her head, and the curve of one shoulder, some six rows in front of him in an aisle seat.

The familiar devil of lust rose in Worboys. At his first sight of the elegant, attractive girl – in the Jermyn Street house – he had fancied her: and this in spite of the deep sexual involvement in which he was entangled with Noel Richards of Registry. Herbie Kruger had hit a confused but raw nerve during the drive to Warminster.

Worboys was an only child: a loner since he could remember, and prey to all the parental blackmail prevalent in one-child families. "You're all we have, you know, Tony," his mother would often remark wistfully, seated in the drawing room of her well-appointed Surrey mansion, among the antiques and silver passed down by young Worboys' grandfather, together with a large and healthy portfolio of stocks and shares.

Both parents set a high store on what they called "the purity of the body", by which young Worboys understood to mean, at first, washing. Later he realised they were referring to the more pleasant duets of the body – disapprovingly. Naturally he rebelled, but still occasionally found himself twitchy with inlaid guilt.

That guilt was present now, in double portions, because of Noel Richards, who had opened some novel doors to Worboys. She was small, blonde, wore long skirts, sandals, and an expression that suggested butter would not melt in her mouth.

Two days after an initial meeting – while Worboys was running messages between Big Herbie and Registry – he had lured her to the cinema, and, in turn, Noel lured him to her little flat in Maida Vale. There his eyes were opened. Unlike Miriam Grubb, Noel had short legs which she would wind tightly around him, like a wrestler. He also discovered that, though Noel looked prim, she wore nothing under her outer clothes, used graffiti language as they made love, and was a sexual glutton. It was all new to Tony Worboys, whose former conquests had been as inexperienced as himself.

Now, as the aircraft trembled in a small pocket of turbulence, he allowed himself to wonder at the potential of Miss Grubb, and struggled with fantasies in which the slender nubility of Miriam vied with the muscular tensions of Noel Richards.

At Tegel – West Berlin's civil airport since Tempelhof had become a United States military base – Worboys loitered by a bank of telephones until he was certain Miriam Grubb had safely left the terminal. He emerged after fifteen minutes, heading straight for the taxi rank.

He took a cab to the intersection at Mehringstrasse and Yorckstrasse, walking the rest of the way; lugging his suitcase, and going through interminable stops, checks and window reflections to ensure he was not under surveillance. Trying to memorise car numbers and passing faces is not easy when humping luggage through city streets. Hence the School's dictum that a street man should always travel light.

The building was just south of the Mehring Platz – a modern, concrete slab, built obviously for the use of multinational companies with their head offices in New York: no soul, and precious little to please the eye. There was a security man in the lobby, who nodded, showing no sign of interest when Worboys asked for "Mr. Calder's offices".

Herr Calder had made arrangements on the top floor. Number Twelve-twenty-two, the guard said. Twelfth floor; the right hand elevator.

It was a large suite on the top floor corner, so that the balcony gave them spectacular views, back across West Berlin, and angled to look out towards the East. Miriam Grubb let him in, cocking her head towards the main room, furnished like an office, but cluttered with crates and heavy cardboard boxes, half unpacked. They had pushed two large tables against the longest wall, between windows which opened out onto the balcony. Some of the equipment was already set up on the tables.

Charles and Tiptoes struggled with a ladder, making final adjustments to wire grilles around portable electronic bafflers which they had just installed.

"Not clean?" Worboys asked.

"Clean as a whistle, squire," Tiptoes leered down from the ladder. "Swept it myself; but it's best to be on the safe side. Never can tell what the buggers'll try on. We ordered bafflers, so we use bafflers. Cuts the odds."

Worboys nodded. Electronic eavesdropping was a complicated art, and one sweep did not a summer make, nor rule out devices operated from a distance. The electronic bafflers, like humming fans, would do the trick.

"Where we sleep?" He put down his suitcase. Miriam Grubb laughed.

Tiptoes leered down again, assuming an American accent, "We go to the mattresses; like the Mafia wars."

"Bedrolls," explained Miriam. "Tiptoes insists on staying with the equipment in here; Charles has already allocated the best of the other two rooms for himself and Max – when Max arrives. That leaves one room; one kitchen, and a bathroom."

Worboys nodded. He would doss down in the kitchen. Miriam Grubb smiled. Almost casually she said they could share the other room. "I won't eat you. Unless that's what you want. I'm certainly not staying in here with Tiptoes; and Charles wouldn't appreciate me."

"Why don't you get us some food, Scoff?" Mr. Corn shouted down from the ladder, trailing a cable through the final grille.

"Just 'cause I'm the only woman doesn't make me a galley slave. You want food? You get food – yourself."

"I'll get the food." Worboys felt it was the best, and least, he could do. At the door, in search of the kitchen, he asked where Big Herbie would sleep when he arrived.

Charles nodded towards a large leather armchair. There was a table beside it with a Sony Stowaway machine, a set of headphones and a box of tapes. "You don't think the old love'll sleep, do you? Maybe he'll listen to music, but I expect he'll spend his time pacing like a lion, and leaning on Tiptoes and Scoff."

Worboys felt suddenly depressed. He could be tucked up, cosy, with Noel now; instead of here in this bland set of offices, high above Berlin. He found the kitchen and looked at the stocks. Plenty of tinned stuff; and a refrigerator crammed to the door.

He was opening four tins of soup when Miriam Grubb came up behind him.

"Take no notice of the lively banter," she grinned. "It's always like this with Tip. You wouldn't think it, but he's a repressed old closet queen. Bloody good with the magic boxes though. Here. I'll give you a hand." She took a saucepan and began to pour the contents of the tins into it, switching on the electric stove with her free hand.

A smile moved in Miriam's eyes, though her mouth remained solemn. Worboys decided she was an enigma: he would never be able to tell when she was joking.

He said she was pretty good on the magic machines herself – "So I've heard."

Miriam claimed it was a challenge. "This kind of thing's quite easy, really. In a few years it's all going to change. We'll be filching stuff straight out of the Centre's computer banks; and they'll be trying to do the same to us. Big Herbie's wrong, you know."

"How come?"

"Networks – field agents – they're a dying breed. Maybe another few years: I don't know. But there'll be cuts and retirements. One field man for each country; that's all we'll need. One man, or woman, trained in the technology."

"Like you?"

She nodded, silently, stirring the soup. Then – "They get you at university?"

Worboys told her, yes, but no more. She gave him a quick, appreciative look. "Me to. Enough said."

Worboys asked if her whole life was given over to the magic

boxes. She shrugged. "I like books, poetry, progressive jazz, the songs of Jacques Brel, and old movie scores. That's what it says on my file."

"Men?" Worboys still did not know if she had been serious with him before.

This time, the corners of her mouth turned up, showing the smile on her lips as well as in her eyes. "I always choose, Mr. Worboys; and I never make commitments. Life's too short. I'm known for being a bitch of a lady. What else're we eating?"

They had the soup, and plates of tinned salmon, with tomatoes from the refrigerator. Charles opened a *Bocksbeutel* of Riesling, and the four of them sat on the floor to eat, avoiding the cables that now trailed like exposed roots over the plastic tiles. The bafflers emitted a distant hum, not enough to drown the city noises coming from outside and below.

Tiptoes had already set up the scanner on the table. The scanner was a large, powerful, complex and more sophisticated military version of the commercial A-7 Panoramic Surveillance Receiver which had been adapted from its large brother by Communications Control Systems – suppliers of electronic hardware. It looked like a medium-screen TV set, mounted above a metal panel of controls, switches and VUs. Worboys also identified the fast-sender receiver, complete with its own tape machine. Another machine was yet to be uncrated – the one they would use for slowing the screech-tape, and deciphering its message – known in the profession as a portable unraveller.

Worboys hoped, almost with prayer, that he would not be called upon to operate that machine, as Herbie Kruger had suggested – *Just to be on the safe side. In case I'm called away, or if anything happens.* Worboys rehearsed the daily ciphers in his head, as Herbie had given them to him; so he would be able to set the decipher key if necessary.

In case I'm called away, or if anything happens. Big Herbie had said it so casually. *In case I'm called away.* The words began to take on a new, sinister meaning. He remembered Tubby Fincher warning him to watch Herbie, because of the emotional involvement – whatever that meant. Now, Tony Worboys wondered if he should have tipped Fincher; whether he should still tip him? In the event he tried to dismiss it from his mind and join in the general conversation.

They talked about their flights into Berlin; about the latest scandal in the life of a much-married pop star; about such mundane matters as the price of food in England; but not about the operation. Tiptoes and Miriam Grubb exchanged a few technicalities concerning the equipment.

By the time they finished eating, the darkness appeared to have closed in around their tower block. Miriam took Charles off to do the washing up, while Tiptoes conscripted Worboys to help with "putting up the soup plates and rods", by which he meant the small bowl antennae – four of them – and the main reception antenna, disguised as a TV aerial.

The dish antennae had to be sighted properly on the roof, so that they would pick up the signals, relayed by the communications' satellite, from Spendthrift's homing device, once he was in the East. These signals would pass into the scanning machine, pinpointing Spendthrift's exact position in the Eastern Zone. The main antenna was there wholly to receive the fast-sender transmissions.

It puzzled Worboys: all this wizardry was one-way traffic. They would discover Spendthrift's exact location, and get the identity of the maggot within the Telegraph Boys. After that the elaborate electronics were of little use to anybody. The intelligence would be received, with an exact pinpoint on the man who was relaying it; but intelligence is of little use unless you can act upon it. The equipment in this penthouse suite did not include a transmitter. He could only presume that a large segment of Herbie's plan, to gouge out the pustule within the Telegraph Boys, had been hidden from all except the Director and, possibly, Tubby Fincher. Once more Tubby Fincher's warning dug into Worboys' mental ribs. He shrugged it off out of loyalty to Kruger. Big Herbie was too wise a bird, too old a hand, to neglect the end-product of the *Trepan* operation.

Tiptoes led him out on to the balcony, strewn with the antennae components, plugs, cables, and a rope ladder fitted with steel grapples. Tiptoes carefully folded the ladder, took hold of the grappled end, leant back and, heaved it with one arm, so that it uncoiled, tracing a dark upward curve on to the roof ledge some thirty feet above them. Tiptoes made it look as easy as throwing a paper streamer. The grapples took hold, and the little man tugged, swinging on the ladder to test its safety.

Worboys glanced out over Berlin. The lights in the Western Zone reflected a dull red glow against the low cloud crawling in from the East. There was a sticky smell of rain in the air, and from the balcony corner Worboys could see the zig-zagged snake of security lights stretching like a jagged and spiked chain, marking the boundary of the Wall.

There was no time to take in the sights. Tiptoes called, snappy, anxious to get on with the work. "I want me bed, mate, and I'm the one doin' the circus act up the ladder and on the roof. All you have to do is make sure I get the stuff up in the right order."

The little technician had forsaken his smart suit. He wore black cord jeans and a sweater; thin black leather gloves, and a belt with a leather hold-all. Around his waist there was a thin nylon rope, with clips and hooks at each end. He went through the routine once, talking slowly, ending each sentence with "Got it?", making Worboys repeat the instructions.

Only when Tiptoes was satisfied Worboys would do the job without having to ask, or hesitate, did he go towards the ladder. Worboys glanced down from the balcony, thinking "rather Tiptoes than me." A slip on the rope ladder would almost certainly send the little man over the side of the balcony rails, down the building's cliff face into the street below. Twelve storeys. The danger unaccountably seemed to arouse Worboys. He held on to the bottom of the ladder, putting his weight on the lowest rung to create tension, as Tiptoes swung onto the rope.

The little man went up at speed. Worboys felt the weight on his own arms and legs as he held the ladder, fascinated at the quick, spider-like ascent. Tiptoes was on the roof in less than fifteen seconds. Ten seconds later the strong nylon rope curled down from the parapet.

It took under twenty minutes for the rope to go back and forth, with the various attachments: the tubular sections of the main antenna, the small dishes, with their detachable bases; and the cables, rolled neatly and held together with plastic clips.

Half way through, Miriam came out to watch for a few seconds. Worboys was sweating slightly, as the rope seemed to come down again almost as soon as he watched one item disappear over the wall.

"Rapunzel, Rapunzel, let down your hair." She gave a throaty laugh, then disappeared into the suite again.

After an hour, with hardly a noise coming from the roof – Tiptoes moving silently, setting up the antennae – the technician began to let down the cables, each one marked with a colour-coded tab; then all of them gathered together at a point just above the main balcony door, tied and secured on the roof's edge.

"Right," Tiptoes came down the ladder, faster than he had ascended it. "'Nuff for one night, squire. We'll plug 'em in tomorrow and hope to Christ they work." His right hand gave a flick on the rope ladder which dislodged, waterfalling on to the balcony, Tiptoes catching the grappled end before it could hit the stone and make any noise. The little technician gave Worboys a friendly nod of thanks, and went into the main room.

Worboys followed him, silently wondering at these strange skills, which were the simple legerdemain of people like Tiptoes Corn and Scoffer Grubb.

Miriam Grubb was playing cards with Charles, both squatting on the floor and laughing a great deal. She had changed from the elegant suit, and the make-up was now scrubbed from her face. In trim jeans and shirt she looked younger, her hair slightly tousled, falling over her face so that she continually pushed it back with her right hand. An automatic gesture – "Like a woman putting a record on the gramophone," Worboys thought, remembering distant strains of T. S. Eliot.

"Out," said Tiptoes, not unpleasantly. "I need me beauty sleep."

Miriam made the obvious riposte, drawing her legs under her: rising in one athletic movement. Charles yawned. "Early beddy-byes. Won't do any harm, I suppose. Oh, I do hate being alone. Always hated sleeping on my own since I was a child." He paused at the door. "How I loathe the dark," he said. Then – "In the last words of the Master, 'Goodnight, my darlings.'"

Tiptoes was in the bathroom. Miriam said Worboys could use it next; she wanted a word with Tiptoes, leaning over the cables which came in from the roof; sorting through them, separating them, like a weaver unravelling strands of different coloured wool. "The bedrolls're in the hall; and the pillows. Take a set in for me, would you?" She did not even look at him.

Worboys stripped, washed, put on his old towelling robe, then humped two sets of bedding into the one spare room. He could hear Miriam Grubb and Corn talking in low voices.

He laid out the two sets of bedding on the floor: well apart from one another; lit a cigarette, and opened the paperback he had tried to read on the flight over: even though he could neither read nor sleep in airplanes.

Miriam Grubb came in half an hour later; just as he was getting drowsy.

She looked at him, and closed the door without watching what she was doing. The lock made no sound, and Worboys realised what she and Tiptoes had in common – they were both silent movers: everything they did, from walking between rooms to putting down a cup, made little noise. It was as though they had been trained to work without being detected.

"Don't you look sweet, all tucked up and cosy." She smiled and began to undress without any sign of embarrassment. The texture of her skin seemed to have a depth to it, as though the pink smoothness went on for several layers. Naked she was very different from Noel: the body proportioned to the long slender legs, the skin stretched taut, without blemish or wrinkle; breasts high and firm. She paid no attention to Worboys' blatant gaze as she walked to her bedroll, slipping between the blankets.

"You said you liked jazz and poetry." He felt he had to contribute something.

"You've put us a long way apart." She was propped on one elbow, looking at him. "Is that a warning? Hands off?"

Worboys shrugged. This was something for which he had not bargained. "Poetry," he repeated. "Modern poetry?"

"Not necessarily. It's not a passion, just an interest. I have catholic tastes."

"Such as?"

She paused, giving a grunt of frustration. "Oh – okay. Frost. Do you go for Robert Frost?

> 'Some say the world will end in fire,
> Some say in ice.
> From what I've tasted of desire
> I hold with those who favour fire.'

"Do you favour fire, Tony Worboys?"

"I'm not quite . . ."

"Well, get up, go and switch the light off, then show me."

"I . . ."

"Yes, you're being seduced; and I'm very wicked. Either do it or go to sleep."

About an hour later, Tony Worboys felt he had undergone his final initiation ceremony. His noviciate was over. She asked him, as they lay together in the afterglow, why he was laughing.

He had remembered a line from an old Bob Hope movie, he told her. *Paleface*. When Hope, imagining that he was a hero – those around him thinking the same thing – was carried shoulder-high into the saloon, Hope curled his lip and said, "I wonder what the cowards are doing?"

5

AT THE MOMENT Tony Worboys was discovering the unexpected delights of Miriam Grubb's body, Herbie Kruger was dialling Tubby Fincher's private number, on his own CC600 – the most sophisticated telephone security system, which remained locked in a metal shelf below his normal telephone. The CC600 was standard issue in the homes of all senior officers.

He had listened to the tape of *Des Knaben Wunderhorn* several times, and gone over his notes again.

"Tapeworm," he said when Tubby greeted him.

"Yes?"

"They boxed him yet?" He meant, had they put Mistochenkov through a lie detector test? 'Boxing' was arcane CIA jargon, now outdated in favour of 'fluttering', but in vogue with Herbie's Service which tended to be conservative in its argot.

The Americans gave all their employees a lie detector test once a year. It would be standard procedure, almost straight away, with any defector. The British Service had resisted the practice, as not really being their style. Only recently had they done limited tests, and then not with the old polygraph system.

In any case, all services were changing from the polygraph nowadays. It was accurate, but being superseded by new developments, including the PSE – the Psychological Stress Evaluator: an instrument which did not require electrodes, or any wires linking with the body of the person being tested.

Tubby said he thought they had done the standard questions that afternoon.

"I would like them to run another batch first thing tomorrow," Herbie lowered his voice. "Just the ordinary things, but I want a couple of mine slipped in. I need the results before I leave."

Anything, Tubby told him. Anything that would help.

Herbie put the questions simply. They were to do with times and information. When exactly Pavel Mistochenkov had been told of the Telegraph Boys' cryptonyms? Herbie still found it hard to believe that Vascovsky and Pavel had known those details as early as 1965. There were also a couple of test questions about his relationship with Vascovsky, and the germination of a plan to defect to the West. "Should have been done before this," Herbie added.

"The graphs aren't one hundred per cent accurate," Tubby reminded him. "Particularly inaccurate, as we know to our cost, with highly-strung people who've only just spun themselves."

Herbie replied that he knew all about that. The Americans had been caught on the hop with it as well, but enough time had passed. Tapeworm should be receptive; and he had to know.

"Have it for you before lunch."

Herbie replaced the receiver, nodding to himself. He went straight to bed. He dreamed, and remembered the dreams on waking, sweating, in the middle of the night. He dreamed of a set of ruby drinking glasses, perfect with facet-cut stems, standing in a cabinet, together with a Meissen figurine of some eighteenth-century dancers: though, in his dream, they were not the real thing. He also dreamed of a Dürer woodcut, small but alive with detail – an avenging angel, the horse rearing up over strewn bodies, heavy cloud in the background, the angel's face set purposefully, carrying out the orders of a ruthless and unforgiving god.

These things, Herbie remembered in his drenched wakening; and, in remembering, knew what they were, and why he dreamed them. He thought of Berlin, trying to quell the reasons for the dream; the anxieties that had begun to explode inside him.

He thought of the *Trepan* team and wondered how they were, high in the penthouse above the Mehring Platz.

Particularly he thought of young Worboys. Was he missing his little blonde from Registry? Possibly not, Herbie thought. He had taken the trouble to read through Miriam Grubb's personal file. He had been right, she was born to the trade and Grubb was not her real name: the daughter of an officer only recently retired, with an unblemished record. Miriam Grubb, however, was – so her personal file claimed – 'an unashamed sexual scalp-hunter: but always within the Service, therefore considered safe'. Well, good luck to them both.

But these thoughts failed to reduce the anxiety racing through him. It was as though there was a special brand of tangible nervous expectancy mixed with his blood. He could feel it pumping along his veins and arteries. At four in the morning Herbie got up. This time tomorrow he would be back in Berlin, in his home town, preparing for Schnabeln's arrival. Schnabeln would be at the safe house, in the West, by eight-thirty.

He prowled the living room, all sleep banished, the anxiety remaining, throbbing and as consistent as his steady heart-beat. To calm himself he switched on the tape deck, turned off the speakers, sitting down with a cup of black coffee, head-phones over his massive skull, to listen to the Mahler Fourth – the most easily digestible of the composer's works, harking back to Haydn and Mozart. Mahler's longing for simplicity was Herbie Kruger's longing also. In the back of his mind, as he listened, Herbie vaguely recalled some Viennese critic writing, after the first performance – *'Unless you become children you will not enter God's realm.' Mahler's G Major Symphony is a work for children and those who will become children.*

As the music ended, so Herbie found a fragment of peace again, and sank into a half doze.

*　　　*　　　*

In Berlin, Worboys woke at about five o'clock, his arm numb, alarmed for a moment, not realising where he was, or whose shoulders the numb arm encircled. His body throbbed as Miriam Grubb moved a thigh against him, her hand, like a small animal, scuttling in half-sleep towards him. Worboys swallowed, partly with amazement, but mainly the same bewildered surprise of the previous night.

Now, first her; then Worboys. They were both fully awake when it was over, and she snuggled up to him. "You're a nice man, Tony," she whispered. "A darling man. Would we could know each other better."

"Can't we?" He felt in thrall to this dark-eyed witch; as though Miriam Grubb had practised the magic arts of the electronics, in which she was so well versed, upon him: that she had, somehow, hooked him to one of her black boxes, and taken his senses into her as she had taken his body.

Her eyes were clouded; little crusts hung in the corners, from sleep, as though tears had dried and hardened there during the night. "I told you. I'm a bitch of a lady. I take when I need. Then I let go. That's how it is with me; and there's no changing it now."

"But why?"

She put a finger to his lips, shaking her head. "I'm sexually very potent . . ."

"I'd noticed. Miriam, I . . ."

"And I'm careful. I'm not the tart you might think. There's been nobody for two months. Treat me as an experience, Tony. You were here; I needed you. Be a love. Enjoy me, and I'll enjoy you. No strings."

He tried to probe once more, but saw a hint of anger flicker in her eyes, so kissed her, gently disentangling himself. "We touched on poetry last night. What about the other interests? The progressive jazz?" He reached for the cigarettes.

"I'm into a guy called Keith Jarrett at the moment." She was curt, and didn't want to talk, turning away from him. Worboys smoothed her shoulder, innocently: a soothing gesture. He felt the shoulder shake under his arm, and knew she was weeping. His scant experience with women made him feel emotionally impotent.

Eventually she turned to him, holding on tightly, saying she was sorry; how could he understand? He reminded her of someone, that was all. Someone who *had* understood, and knew her; loved her, and was the only thing that mattered.

"And he's gone now?"

"Of course he's fucking gone," she spat. "What do you think I'd be doing here if he hadn't gone? Oh, sod it, Tony Worboys, isn't it enough that we've . . .?"

"Possibly for you. Maybe not for me." He saw Noel's face in his mind, and thought how little he knew: about himself or others. He had imagined himself in love with Noel. What the hell was that all about now?

Miriam wiped her eyes, and slipped from beside him, gathering up her clothes. "Come on, I'll make you something special for breakfast," she beckoned. Even that movement took on sexual connotations. Worboys, in his robe, padded after her into the kitchen. She said the others wouldn't be awake yet. They'd have a feast of their own. "Honeymoon Potatoes," she said, selecting four or five potatoes from among the vegetables, going to the sink and starting to peel them; giving Worboys orders, telling him to find an onion, and some bacon and oil.

"Honeymoon Potatoes?" he asked.

She had a friend. A girl of her age who had married, young – "In love, like no two people ever before; or ever will be. There's sentiment for you." The girl had expected they would be honeymooning in some smart hotel – on the Riviera, or the Costa Brava, or the Riviera dei Fiori. It was her husband's style, and he kept the secret of where they were to honeymoon. It turned out to be a cottage in the English Lake District. "Miles from anywhere. It was a lovely idea. He thought she would find the change and solitude – just alone with him – beneficial."

The one problem was that, on their first day, the girl had to admit she could not cook. In her father's house there had always been servants; they had moved about a lot, mostly in the Mid- and Far-East. Nobody had ever questioned if she should be taught to cook.

"So" – Miriam's eyes were slightly clouded, Worboys noticed – "So, on that first morning, he gave her a cooking lesson – there were a lot more later, and she became a good cook. This is the breakfast they had, and they called it Honeymoon Potatoes."

She cut the peeled potatoes into small square chunks; heated oil in a pan; chopped onion and bacon; then tipped the whole lot in, seasoning them well, then stirring all the time as they cooked.

Worboys knew she had been talking about herself, but said

nothing. They sat across the table from each other and ate the platefuls of food. Worboys told her, truthfully, that it was delicious. Miriam Grubb just nodded, her hair falling over her face again. Then they heard Tiptoes Corn stumbling around in the main room.

*   *   *

In London, Herbie Kruger set out for the main building at ten o'clock. He would look into the Annexe later. His case was left on the bed at the St. John's Wood flat, only half packed. The documents collected from Camden Town were in a secret place where nobody but a determined expert could find them. Already he had done a little preparatory paperwork – things which had to be set up before he saw Schnabeln.

In the Director's office Tubby Fincher told him he had just received the results from Mistochenkov's 'boxing' at Warminster. "It's all positive," he said. "The machine tells us that Pavel Mistochenkov and Jacob Vascovsky had a longterm understanding to attempt a crossing of the Wall. It also says that he's been telling you the truth – that Vascovsky knew the cryptos of the Telegraph Boys in March 1965."

Aloud, Herbie said it did not make sense. "I began to think they were pulling an enticement on me. Recent intelligence, with Pavel nudging me in by saying they had known for a long time."

The Director coughed, looking concerned. "There is marginal evidence, from a couple of extra questions we put to him under the PSE."

"So? Marginal evidence? What the hell does that mean?"

"It is possible, from what Tapeworm says, that Vascovsky knew the cryptos of the Telegraph Boys at an earlier date. Almost when you set them up."

Herbie swore. It was a ghostly impression he had also received while confessing Mistochenkov.

The Director went through the *Trepan* operation in detail; just to be certain they understood one another. "As soon as you get Spendthrift's analysis of the situation, you uncover and flash me from Berlin Station."

Herbie's great head moved in a slow nod. The Director

spoke firmly – the admiral on the bridge, as old men-of-war moved to action stations. "*I* make the decisions. You will give me an hour. You'll have time to get back to the *Trepan* group, and check Spendthrift's exact location – make sure he's reached the place we agreed."

Again Herbie nodded. He said nothing aloud.

"The *Trepan* group close up shop, and you will get my instructions via Berlin Station. Head of Station will know once he's confirmed with me. If there's cloak and dagger needed, Berlin'll do it, Herbie. If there's a rescue operation, Berlin'll do it. You, I want out: quickly. Berlin'll give you priority."

Herbie merely looked gloomy.

"Hell, Herbie," Tubby Fincher came over to him. "At least you'll know the worst, or the best, by then. Leave the bother to others. You agreed it was the safest way."

"Yes. Yes, I agreed. Okay." Herbie got to his feet. He said there were one or two things he needed to do at the Annexe. He would be back to pick up the homing devices sometime early in the afternoon.

Outside, in Whitehall, the mandarins and their minions were heading to lunch appointments in clubs and bars throughout the city. Herbie went on foot, walking down to Trafalgar Square, doing a few turnoffs. He was clean. Anyway, who would worry about a shopping expedition. He hailed a cab, and headed for Oxford Street.

In a chain store which catered for the passing American trade he bought some checked slacks, and a sports coat of many colours which appeared to be masquerading as the tartan of the Black Watch. In another store he purchased shoes; in a third, some expensive spectacles with heavy horn rims, and lenses which looked normal but, according to the makers, adjusted in various lights to avoid glare.

These things Herbie carried out to St. John's Wood, before making the return trip in to the Annexe. He checked the IN tray, dealt with a couple of minor administrative matters, then went over to the main building where he was to pick up the homing devices. The requisition chit was signed by Tubby Fincher, and the technical expert on duty at Stores passed the equipment over without a query. "You know how they work?" was all he asked. Herbie assured him that he knew all about these matters.

The homers were transistorised: embedded in digital watches. They operated by pulling up, and then depressing, one of the two buttons usually used for adjustment. To switch off, you performed the same function with the other screw.

"They're only armed when the battery's in place," the technician reminded him. "I've kept the batteries separate." The equipment was packaged in three small boxes, and the watches looked slightly different. One emitted a series of long bleeps, the other a dot-dash tone. They had both been pre-set to the correct frequency.

Herbie had many contacts within the world he had inhabited for so long. Some were known to his superiors, others, while known, had long been buried in the files. One of these had a job with security at Heathrow Airport. On his way back to St. John's Wood, Herbie Kruger stopped at a public call box and dialled Heathrow, giving a particular extension number. His contact was on duty that day, and expecting the call. Herbie had briefed him almost as soon as he made up his mind on what course of action to take.

The conversation was brief, but it calmed Herbie. What he had asked to be done had been seen to; all was arranged.

With things in order, Herbie returned to St. John's Wood to complete packing. The batteries for the homing devices were in his shaving kit, loose inside an electric razor. He wore one of the watches. The other went into his briefcase, in a small compartment that even the alert security people were unlikely to unearth.

Last of all he folded the newly-purchased clothes, after carefully removing all the labels. The car arrived at six. His flight was due out at seven forty-five. As they drove away Herbie did not need to look back; he knew Max would be in a chase car, well behind. He also knew that Max had a special permit and would not go through the usual security screening. He would also be armed. Herbie, on the other hand, was under strict discipline: the Director was edgy because of his personal involvement.

Herbie checked in at Heathrow, and, unusually, his flight

was called on time. At the security tables they took special care with him. Max was nowhere in evidence. At the check-in desk Herbie asked for a particular seat number, and found it was already reserved for him.

In the cramped space of the aircraft Herbie's bulk appeared to have been taken into consideration. The seat next to his was vacant. He saw Max nowhere.

Putting his briefcase on the cabin floor, Herbie deftly undid the catches, slipping a large hand up under the seat. Below the lifebelt pack a flat polythene-wrapped parcel had been lodged between the retaining straps. Herbie slipped it into the briefcase which he snapped shut in one movement. Stewardesses and passengers were too busy settling people into their seats to notice.

Herbie smiled to himself. The parcel had been arranged by his old secret contact at Heathrow, who regarded it as a correct security matter: for Herbie Kruger's bona fides were impeccable. Now a flat, deadly, .9 mil Browning automatic, with three spare magazines, lay snug in the briefcase.

6

IN THE PENTHOUSE suite, high above the Mehring Platz, the *Trepan* team spent the day wiring up the equipment, talking, playing cards. The scanner, and receiver for the fast-sender, could only be hooked up to their respective antennae, plugged in, then the circuits checked. No proper tests could be done until late on the Saturday afternoon, when Herbie was to run a screech tape, and bleep the homers, before seeing Spendthrift back into the East.

They uncrated the portable unraveller, setting it on the table to the right of the scanner, in front of the receiver, and its large open-reel tape deck. This piece of magic would deal with the screech tape, slow it and – if one correctly keyed the right daily cipher – translate the whole thing into a legible message. It looked like a miniature typewriter with a cassette tape machine attached. Above the tape deck was a small, oblong screen; behind that, a print-out roller. The screech tapes were never convertible to normal commercial speeds – each set of fast-senders, their receivers, and the unravellers, being pre-set to different speeds on each day: just to confuse any long-eared sound-stealer.

Worboys looked at the unraveller with concern. He had operated one before – under ideal conditions, during the communications course, as a novice at the school. Once more he hoped, most fervently, that things would go to plan. He did not relish the prospect of Herbie not being there to direct operations and, at least, offer guidance with the unraveller. He pictured himself with the unraveller, in a confusion of unlockable ciphers.

During the afternoon, Tiptoes and Charles put their feet up and dozed. Miriam Grubb gave Worboys a long look. There was no mistaking her meaning. He nodded, and they went silently to their room. Miriam locked the door. "I won't cry again," she promised. "Do you lack respect for me, Tony? In the old days, men were supposed to feel that a girl was no more than a useful piece of furniture when something happened – like last night."

Worboys told her not to be silly. It wasn't like that any more. "I understand," he added, not meaning it; wondering if he would ever comprehend women. All day he had found difficulty in keeping his eyes off her. He scarcely allowed Noel to enter his mind: there was no room there for both women, and his consciousness buzzed with the need to know what had happened, in the past, to this poised, intelligent, self-contained girl. He wanted to delve into her background, talk with her; discover her mind, and the environment in which she moved, just as he had discovered her body. The frustration burst again, now, as they stood alone. He asked her straight out, looking steadily into the dark eyes.

She pursed her lips, closing them tightly, as though wrestling with the words within, shaking her head like a child. Anger burned, almost red, in her eyes. 'You have Big Herbie's ear, Tony. Get him to let you squint at my PF. It's all there for anyone who has the eyes to see." She made a movement towards the door.

Worboys caught her, clasping her in his arms, half-expecting the fury to turn physical – perhaps a knee to his groin. She stood, stiff and tense, in his embrace; but it passed, and they moved towards the bedrolls, which she had now placed close together on the floor.

*   *   *

At ten-thirty that night – when they had eaten the evening meal – the one telephone in the main room rang three times: stopped for a minute, then rang again.

Charles answered. "Yes." He spoke with his usual, disinterested, languid diffidence. "Good, yes. Yes, the plumbing *is* in. Tomorrow night as arranged. Okay." Cradling the receiver, he turned to the others. "We're on. The Surgeon's here. Calling on us tomorrow evening; as per schedule."

Herbie Kruger – or 'Surgeon', as they had jokingly cryptonymed him for *Trepan* – was back in Berlin. He had arrived about half an hour before the telephone call, at the house they normally used for meetings in West Berlin – a comfortable four-roomed apartment on the second floor of a building on the Dahlmannstrasse, off the Ku-damm – at the end furthest away from the Uhlandstrasse: for the Consulate General's office preferred Service premises to be kept as far as possible from their own place of work.

The building which housed the apartment was squeezed between a bar and a branch of Kutzler's Foto Kino. Four bar-hostesses, who worked shifts at the Eden Saloon, occupied the first-storey flat. The ground floor was owned by the Service: usually manned by the listeners during meetings. Berlin Station used the house all the time.

Herbie had his own key, letting himself in with the stealth of ages. Leaving his cases in the middle of the room, he went straight to the places where the microphones were usually secreted. The wires had been cut and sealed, but he made a careful run around the place, examining the heavy gold and red wallpaper, looking for any tell-tale marks, in case the Director and Tubby had instructed a new set of voice-activated bugs to be installed.

Unscrewing the telephone mouth and earpieces, Herbie checked for anything like an infinity bug, knowing he would find nothing. If the Service were determined to listen, it would find some other way. Max would have a sniffer with him; but they would know that in London. If they were really determined there was nothing he could do about it. Well, almost nothing.

It was unlikely that anyone would be manning tapes on the ground floor, but it would be out of character for Herbie not to check. They did not know he possessed a key to the ground floor apartment.

He went to his usual bedroom, opened the briefcase and unwrapped the Browning and clips of ammunition: stowing the gun away in a metal waste bin, crumpling copies of the newspapers, bought at Heathrow, around it.

Herbie let himself out of the apartment, going down to the ground floor, fiddling with his key-chain. The apartment at the bottom of the house was empty, but the tape machines were there – unplugged, with the leads to the apartment above severed and sealed off. Everything bore the hallmark of the Director taking Herbie seriously.

Max arrived ten minutes after Herbie returned to the second-storey apartment. In that ten minutes the big man had hung his clothes in the bedroom closet and locked it, with the briefcase inside.

Max greeted him jovially: all set to be chatty. Herbie knew the psychology of dealing with men like Max. "Okay, Max." Herbie appeared to have withdrawn from the kindly iron hand in a velvet glove. Now only the iron hand showed through. He stood erect, the face grave, eyes stone hard. "You pick up the 'phone, Max, and call the number I'm going to give you. Let it ring three times, close the line and call again. Right? Your friend, Charles, should answer. You tell him the Surgeon has arrived, and will see them tomorrow. You ask if the plumbing is in. Okay?"

Max nodded, looking wary, noting the change in Big Herbie. This was not even the Herbie he had known during the heavy part of the interrogation of Tapeworm. He did as he was told: passed the message back and asked what was needed next. Herbie told him that he had personally gone over the place for taps – "They told you we weren't to have any sound? Yes?"

Max said that was what he had been told.

"Reassure me, then, Max. You got a sweeper?"

The minder nodded, unzipping his bag. He went over the place inch by inch. Herbie would not let him go into the closet in his bedroom – "I got personal things in there. Important for the man we're meeting" – so Max swept it with great care, from the outside. After an hour Max pronounced the whole apartment disinfected: "Hygienic as a bottle of Harpic, love. Nothing here to worry us."

Herbie had looked at the sight lines from the window. There were binoculars and night glasses in the apartment. He went over the possible windows and rooftops, across the street, where people could set up a hide, or use parabolic listeners. Herbie checked that these points were visible from one of the other rooms, which would also afford Max a good view of the street.

Max asked if they were going to eat. "I only had one of British Airways' plastic sandwiches."

"Go and get some take-away." Herbie told him there was a place on the corner he often used when in residence. "It's open till all hours."

"I'm supposed to be minding you."

"I won't run away. Tubby Fincher had you carry something in for me, yes? I'll have it before you go."

Max passed over the package he had brought through the clear channel, avoiding a security check. It contained the fast-sender Spendthrift was to take into the East. Then Max dumped his bag in one of the three bedrooms and went out to get food.

Herbie unwrapped the parcel and took the machine out of its polystyrene coffin. It was no larger than a normal hard-back book, and about four inches thick. In fact, Herbie carried a book in his luggage that was slightly larger and deeper, hollowed out for the purpose of carrying the gadgetry over the border. Cloak and dagger: old hat stuff; movie business, Herbie thought. Some of the old ways, though, were just as effective as ever – bars of soap, shoe heels, tubes of toothpaste, orifice hides. All still viable, and used.

The fast-sender was set to the *Trepan* frequency. It also had a built-in microphone and a speed dial – more sophisticated than the machines Schnabeln and Girren already used in East Berlin. Herbie packed it away with the homers and his false documents. He then retrieved the Browning, undid its wrapping, weighed the weapon in his hand, slid back the mechanism, felt the firing pin, stripped the whole thing down and put it back together again. He slid a magazine into the butt, thumping it home with the heel of his hand. He then put the gun, together with the remaining spare magazines, into the pockets of the lurid American jacket in the closet.

By the time Max returned with the food Herbie was settled in an armchair, a huge glass of vodka snug in his paw. He dreaded bed, wanting to remain as active as possible, taking his mind off the fact that he was now back in the city of his father and mother; back, within a short distance, of the one person who mattered – who had mattered for so long, unseen;

Ursula Zunder, to whom he had not spoken, whose face and body he had not seen, for fifteen years.

It was extraordinary, Herbie considered. Absence, time, usually dulled the memory – or distorted it – as with death. Yet Electra lived and breathed in his being, to the point where he could almost see and hear her: the laugh, the voice with its particular inflection – the hint of a lisp when she was excited. There were occasional nights when he could even feel her skin and flesh, soft but strong; the muscles firm under the smooth, almost translucid epidermis.

These visions pumped blood in his head, but did not rouse him sexually. Herbie knew that condition could only be treated by reality. Fantasy had never played a large part in his real life. Until he had her store of personal memories and her physical being close to him once more he would not be cured.

The main room in which Herbie now sat was out of joint with the times – great dusty red velvet-covered armchairs and a settee; a heavy ornate table and sideboard, solid uncomfortable stand chairs, and a sprinkling of rugs: cheap and threading imitations of Ispahan designs, badly knotted, strewn on stained wood. Surrounding a gas stove was a heavy marble mantelpiece, filched, probably, from the ruins. This was crammed with old photographs in silver frames – men in Kaiser Bill uniforms and moustaches; women staring, bewitched or bothered, frightened by the lens; a child – fourteen or fifteen years old – pretty in a pinafore, long ringlets of hair draping the shoulders, on a long-gone garden swing, her legs stretched out straight, parted slightly; buttoned boots pointing at the camera as though trying to shatter it. Herbie knew somehow the photograph had a subtle sensuality, but could not quite place the reason. In one corner there was a second table: a small, ugly piece, cluttered with more photographs, and some cheap ornaments. The whole effect was of some Victorian spinster's sitting room – only the photographs did not match the period. The paintings, however, reflected Victorian popular art at its most abominable: several large canvases depicting mountains and woodlands. Herbie considered that they would be Wagnerian if a little better done. They looked dark, dirty and gloomy as the grave.

Max brought rolls filled with *Weisswurste*, and the raw spiced pork spread called *Hackepeter*. He drank only lager. Herbie refilled his own glass of vodka.

As they ate so Herbie Kruger went over matters with his minder. Conscious that Max had already been privately briefed by the Director and/or Tubby Fincher, Kruger now thought it time to perform his own briefing. Psychologically Max might react more strongly to a hard and firm set of orders from Herbie, on the spot, and so lose sight of London's instructions to keep a careful eye on the German.

He went through the best look-out point – the window in Max's own chosen room: far from this room, where he would talk with Spendthrift; the time and method of Spendthrift's arrival tomorrow; telephone signals; body talk; house talk, including signs which meant that Max was free to enter the room when Herbie was with Spendthrift; or forbidden, apart from cases of genuine emergency and danger.

Max sat, chewing on his rolls, taking it all in, repeating the signals, but with some hint of deceit behind the eyes. Herbie now knew, for sure, London's eyes and ears were on him through Max: or as near sure as he could be.

"You're under my control now, Max?" he asked at last.

"Of course, old love. You know that. I'm to mind you and the bloke coming in."

"Level with me, Max. They told you to watch me special, yes? Said I was slippery."

"Well, you are a slippery big thing, aren't you, Mr. Kruger?"

"They gave you direct orders, though? About me?"

"Only for your own good."

"Forget it. You're here to do my bidding now. Just remember that and we'll have no unpleasantness. Don't let London confuse you. We do a job, okay? Let's make it a good one."

"I'm here to see that you're kept safe, that's all."

Herbie shook his head. He would be safe. They would have a few days of concentrated work. After that, back to London. "Tomorrow night we go to see your friends," he smiled, cunning creasing the corners of his mouth.

Max said that would make a change, then suggested it was

time to turn in. "Your asset'll be here by eight-thirty, won't he?"

Herbie nodded, giving Max a dismissive goodnight. He did not want the loneliness of the big feather bed with its smotheringly soft duvet. He went over to the window, throwing it open, smelling the air. It is funny how all cities have their own smell. Below, a couple of men were escorting their ladies into a car; from some cellar up the road a band played – guitars, the bases turned up, the throb of drums and discordant tinkling of an electric piano. In a pause of silence, Herbie thought he could hear another sound, further off: a violin sobbing and wailing a threnody of remote grief.

Funny, he thought again, how each city had a different odour. In the old days even West and East Berlin smelled differently. He liked neither side – deploring all the East stood for, and considering the garish, fleshy, consumer-beckoning of West Berlin to be a propaganda affront to any thinking human being.

Undressed, lying on the bed with no sleep, Herbie's mind rotated slowly in the past. Back to Berlin as it had been just before the panic: in the months prior to that gigantic exodus from the East; when the reception centres of West Berlin, like Marienfelde, could hardly cope with the influx. In late 1959 none of that sudden anxiety for escape had permeated East Berlin. But, in his daily work in the West, Eberhard Lukas Kruger was just receiving instructions to mount his team of Telegraph Boys. The Director flew in for a week, and Herbie was closeted with him, the Head of Berlin Station, and a thin spare quiet man from Military Intelligence.

In one of Berlin Station's offices, from the windows of which one could just see the shattered memorial that had once been the Kaiser Wilhelmskirche spire, they had enumerated the targets – the official jobs, or appointments, which had to be covered by surveillance. Later they got down to specifics: the trends and behaviour patterns that had to be noted by the watching Telegraph Boys.

At first sight, Herbie recalled, the list struck him as impossible. The Director of Liaison – usually at least a General – at the Karlshorst Soviet HQ; the Soviet Attaché at the DDR's Political HQ; the DDR's Minister of the Interior; the Military and Air Attaché at the Soviet Embassy; the General in charge of liaison between the NVA – the National People's Army – and the Soviet Forces in East Germany; the Commander-in-Chief, General Soviet Forces in Germany. The list of targets seemed, at first hearing, to be reaching for the moon.

He was not to use any of his Schnitzer people. These new watchers were to be recruited fresh – turned over and clean, absolutely free from any taint of flying false flags.

The briefing on the targets went on for about a week, as Eberhard Lukas Kruger made his daily journey – a *Grenz-gänger* – backwards and forwards between East and West. It was autumn. Almost exactly twenty-three months of freedom was left to East Berlin, before the August of 1961 and the closing of the border: the building of the Wall.

Two weeks after the initial briefing Herbie had his first stroke of luck. A chance meeting, as they so often are, with the chubby and scruffy Peter Sensel. Sensel was celebrating in a bar in the Stalinallee – as it still was then – buying drinks for everyone. He had been down and out for months, after losing his own little three-man building firm, now absorbed into the reorganised labour force on Party orders – which meant Walter Ulbricht's orders.

"I don't care if it's working for the Ivans," Sensel had declared. "It's a good job; steady hours; the money's fair, and I get my own accommodation out there."

Herbie soon found that "out there" meant the General Soviet Forces Headquarters at Zossen-Wunsdorf, about forty kilometres to the West, in the heart of the Deutsche Demo-kratische Republik. "I might even put a spanner in some of their works," Sensel had grinned, arching eyebrows, and shrugging his shoulders with a curious, lopsided smile. It was an effeminate movement from someone who looked as clod-hopping as Peter Sensel.

Herbie began turning stones straight away: burrowing into Sensel's past. "Doing some ferret work," he called it. Sensel always came to the same bar at week-ends. He said he would probably not break the routine, now he was to work out of town. "Even if I make good friends there. Old habits, you know." In fact, he returned on most week-ends. Herbie played him slowly; let Sensel make the running, before starting to draw him in. Sensel was recruited as a Telegraph Boy six months later. Peter Sensel had, all these years, been Priam.

It was in the same week that Herbie stumbled over a second possible convert. This time on his own stamping ground – at the Rialto in Pankow. He had known the girl by sight for a long time – Who did not know her at the Rialto? Men surrounded her, for she had an aura which spoke of high living in the bleak austerity of the DDR.

The night Herbie met her for the first time she was escorted by a young Russian: a pleasant, harmless junior officer wearing the collar patches of the armoured troops attached to the 20th Tank Army, who had their Headquarters at Bernau a few kilometres up the road. The girl was a stunning looker: tall, ash blonde, with incredibly long legs and a walk of acute sensuality. She made Herbie – in those days well-active – reel with pleasure when she passed near him. At close range you were always aware of the silken rustle of her thighs.

Herbie remembered the details with some clarity, if only because she was the last woman prior to Ursula Zunder. It was a Saturday night, and the Rialto was crowded: noisy with music and talk, the air clouded with smoke.

The young Russian officer was already a little drunk when he arrived with the girl. Herbie, standing near them, could not miss the fact that she was angry, and the Russian was making matters worse. Eventually the officer said something which really upset her. She became abusive – loud; not caring who heard. People were looking at the couple. The Russian spat something obscene at her, and she hit him: a crack over the cheek which seemed, in its ferocity, to silence the room. The young officer hissed an intake of breath, turned on his heel – Herbie could plainly see him now, half staggering on the turn – and left the bar, crimson-faced, trying to retain some dignity.

Herbie moved in before any other man could get near to the girl. Was there anything he could do? Did she need help? Martha Adler said another Schnapps would be pleasant. She appeared unconcerned. Good riddance to the lieutenant: he was nothing but a schoolboy anyway. She must have been all of twenty herself.

Several men came up – she seemed to know most of them by name – including a Russian captain, from the same outfit as the lieutenant. He apologised for his brother officer's boorish behaviour. Martha Adler treated all these solicitous men politely, but dismissed them quickly by carrying on her conversation with Herbie Kruger.

The Schnapps had a mellowing effect. She started to appraise Herbie with her eyes. As they talked she began touching him from time to time: her slim hand resting, for a moment, on his wrist; or closing around his arm, in a gesture of affection, as she made some point.

Martha was always a beautifully groomed girl, her clothes fashionable and obviously bought in the West, the ash blonde hair rarely out of place – a toss of her head would send it flying, only for it to drop heavily back into place again. Herbie recalled how, even then, he felt like a lumbering, clumsy oaf when next to her in public.

They talked about the eternal subject of the times – politics: the zoned and split city of Berlin; the future of their country, which had now become two countries; and the discontent on both sides; the possibility of another war. "Just because I work at the Political Headquarters doesn't mean I agree with all they're trying to do," she told him. Bells rang in Herbie's head. Martha Adler was a secretary at the Niederschonhausen. "For two pins I'd settle in the West," she said. "It's a job, that's all: not a political commitment. I do as I'm told and keep my thoughts to myself" – something she was not doing at that precise moment.

Martha had a small apartment nearby, in a block reserved for secretaries at the party Headquarters. "It's the only really good thing. Goes with the job. If they kick me out or I throw it in then I lose my home. They have a girl by the armpits," she giggled.

Herbie found her a voracious lover, but – after the disaster with Luzia Gabell – had no thought of doing a dependence act with her. In fact, looking back on it, she was more honest than Luzia. She left Herbie in no doubt about her philosophy and attitude towards men. She always had a lover: she was always faithful to him. Between lovers it was open season. At the moment of her meeting with Herbie, Martha Adler was between lovers. Another would appear soon. After one night in her company Herbie knew that it would not be him. He would not have wanted that in any case.

She hinted that, until the right man came along, Herbie was always welcome – to talk; drink, eat, or have her. She was a woman who craved for affection and love. In bed she became possessed with the necessity of being needed, "Lie to me," she cried out when Herbie first had her. "Lie to me, please. Tell me you love me, and that there's never been anyone else. Please, Herbie, please tell me . . ." This sentence rose to a choke as she climaxed, thrusting her body at him, pleading for him to go on through the experience.

In all, Herbie only slept with her three or four times. She was perfect material for the Telegraph Boys – if she could be trained, and trusted to control her tongue. He saw her at least once a week – even after the sexual jinks stopped, and she took a new, permanent lover. The lover was a convinced Communist: a German called Martin Schtemm, one of the male secretaries working for 'Red' Hilde Benjamin, the ruthless Minister of Justice in Ulbricht's régime. Martha Adler now received invitations to visit the exclusive residential compound for government heads at Wandlitz, where the leaders of the Ulbricht administration indulged their less proletarian passions.

It was from these visits that Herbie learned of the Minister of Justice's ebony-panelled music room; the Deputy Prime Minister, Willi Steph's, huge collection of ancient and valuable weapons; the aging socialist, Otto Grotewohl's extensive, and priceless collection of carpets, paintings and antiques. It seemed that the old standards of the Nazi hierarchy had been passed on to the new élite of the Communist leadership. Ulbricht, Martha told him, was the only one to show any sign of restraint.

Martha Adler remained Herbie's friend. Though she enjoyed the higher standard of living, obtainable through her Communist lover, the hypocrisy of it sickened her, closing her mind to any political claptrap Martin Schtemm might pour into her. Within a few months her secret thoughts were essentially anti-Party. Herbie taught her, by slow degrees, to keep silent. In all it took seven months to get her fully recruited and cleared; but Martha was worth it in the end.

Now, Herbie knew, she had long been the PPS to the Minister of Defence, within the Political Headquarters, and so had constant access to the Soviet Attaché. She had reported on him with clear and consistent accuracy for years. Out of all the Telegraph Boys, Martha Adler had, during the time when there was only sporadic servicing, been one of the most hard-working. She had even found alternative ways to get her reports into the West. Martha Adler was Hecuba: her material high grade.

It was about a month after that first meeting with Martha Adler in the Rialto that Herbie met Ursula Zunder for the first time – so altering his emotional life out of all proportion, and sealing the sadness of his future.

It happened on a chill November evening, when the city air was damp with mist, and the odd scent of woodsmoke crept into the streets. Herbie was returning from a day crammed with work in the West. He travelled back on the S-Bahn, his mind still active, alive with possible names for the team of Telegraph Boys.

Now, somewhere a long way off, outside the apartment on the Dahlmannstrasse, came the echo of a girl, probably tipsy, laughing a high melodic sound: as though she had lost control, prostrate with mirth.

In his sleepless state, Herbie heard Ursula Zunder's laugh, mixed with this unknown girl's peal of merriment.

Herbie Kruger could have wept at the images that particular sound drew from the memory banks of his past. The well-stored feelings, pictures and senses from that happiest of times, could never be controlled. He tried to quell them, push them away, deep, like drowning kittens. But they returned of their own volition, almost every day; triggered by innocent things – a musical note; the sound of a train; a door closing; footsteps on stairs; the sight of a head in a crowd; or, as at this moment, a laugh from a darkened Berlin street.

Ursula Zunder and Eberhard Lukas Kruger had first met with laughter.

7

WHILE WORKING UNDER the cover of a *Grenzgänger*, in those late days of 1959, Herbie Kruger made certain that he always left the East by either the S- or U-Bahn stations on the Friedrichstrasse. He did not return religiously by the same route, but made sure the journeys home terminated, each evening, at the same Friedrichstrasse station.

On that particular evening he took the S-Bahn from the West Berlin station at Bellevue. It was a slightly longer route than usual, as the line loops over the Spree, then back again across the river in the East. On that day it was, however, more convenient. Herbie had spent the afternoon not far from Bellevue, in a liaison meeting with the Head of Berlin Station, the sombre officer from Military Intelligence, and a pair of researchers from London.

When he thought back to that evening – as he did many times over the years – Herbie knew he had only partially noticed the young woman seated opposite him on the train. Initially he recalled the trim, neat figure; an oval face, capped by short blonde hair – not really blonde, but more of a peppery gold. 'Copper' was her own description. She was dressed simply in a grey skirt and jacket, visible because her thin raincoat lay unbuttoned, spread back, open.

In reality this was a kind of background picture. He spent most of the journey peering through the window's darkness, glimpsing the lights; thinking how quickly the buildings were rising in West Berlin, compared to the programme in the East. He remembered the days just after the war ended, when the *Trümmerfrauen* – the women of the ruins – worked long hours, cleaning and clearing the bricks and rubble. On his few brief visits to the city, after joining the Americans, Herbie had seen them at work.

When he now saw young women in London – fighting for rights, proclaiming lost causes: or the svelte, elegant ones who nagged and worried over the trivia of some minor inconvenience, Herbie would think of the *Trümmerfrauen*. The young, neurotic, pill-ridden society had it all to come; as surely as dawn would break.

It was only after they got to the Friedrichstrasse S-Bahn station that Herbie took any interest in his fellow passenger. They both left the train at the same time, the woman walking ahead of him. It was the walk that first caught his true attention: an unnatural movement; stiff from the waist down. He wondered if she had been injured, yet it seemed odd, for her body was proportioned like an athlete; even that of a young boy. Her arms and shoulders moved with grace, and in a slightly different rhythm from the waist and legs.

They were separated from the main crowd, with people bunched behind and in front, approaching the exit gates where a pair of Vopos stood, watchful: waiting. The Vopos and Grepos often picked people, indiscriminately, from disembarking passengers. Documents were examined; also packages, baskets – there were even body searches. People brought goods over from the West every day. Sometimes if they were caught the goods might be confiscated, and that would be the end of it. Occasionally there was a clamp-down on 'subversive literature' – which covered a multitude of books and magazines, newspapers and periodicals. People were more careful about these.

The woman ahead was slowing down. Herbie hung back: there was something odd here, and he did not really want to get involved. Herbie remained about four paces behind her. Others passed him, and even overtook the woman. Then she faltered. Herbie thought he heard a small noise of desperation start from her throat. Then her walk became even stranger, a shuffle of short steps, before – with unexpected swiftness – a copy of *Paris-Match* descended from under her skirts, hitting the ground in front of Herbie with a flutter and thud.

Instinctively, Herbie lunged forward, scooping up the magazine, thrusting it under his coat, jamming it between arm and body. Hardly had Herbie straightened into his stride, when *Harpers* slid from between the girl's legs, sprawling on the damp concrete, open appropriately – Herbie thought as he flicked it up beside *Paris-Match* – at a double spread of underwear ads.

He was still in a crouched position, not more than an arm's length behind the girl, when a whole sheaf of paper cascaded from under her skirts, trailing behind her as she walked on, as though trying to pretend the worst had not happened. There was *Time*, *Newsweek*, two copies of the *New York Times*, and a periodical which seemed to be concerned with photography.

The material was all of a nature frowned upon in East Berlin, and the girl had no option but to continue walking, spreading the batch of magazines behind her, like a 'hare' in a paperchase. Herbie was reminded of a light aircraft on a leaflet drop. He did not even pause to think, but continued to move forward in his crouch, sweeping up each of the journals or magazines, throwing them, one after another, into his coat, where they lay, precariously grasped, but out of sight.

People crowded in the exit, and the Vopos were so busy scrutinising faces that they appeared not to have noticed the cascade of printed matter. Herbie rendered up his ticket, still keeping his left arm tightly to his side, clutching at the literature. Once clear of the Vopos he thrust his right arm under the coat to steady the load; then set off quickly after the girl. She had now increased her pace: walking with a normal and definitely agile swing.

"I think you dropped something, Fräulein." He fell into step beside her.

"Me? No, I don't think so." The eyes, oval, like her face, glinted with fear. She imagined they had spotted her: probably visions of the SSD prison, not far from the Alexanderplatz, were already grim in her mind. You did not know who to trust these days. Never, Herbie, thought back; never had there been any time, since the beginning of the world, when you could trust another human – unless they proved their love for cause or person.

He smiled, telling her that, truly, it was okay. He had her magazines; opening his coat to show her, explaining what he had done. "I was behind. I was behind you when they fell from under . . . from . . . Well, I picked them up and brought them through.'' His arms made a gesture: a man lost for words.

She slowed her walk, turning towards him. Her face, he saw, caught in the dim glow of a street light, appeared white with fear. Then the dark, grey-flecked eyes suddenly lit up as she accepted his honesty – the eyebrows arching. She had a straight, Italianate nose, which now wrinkled as the corners of her mouth tilted – showing deep tiny crescents of laughter on each side, bracketing the lips.

"Oh my God. I thought I'd be in such trouble." She began to laugh. "It's the first time I've ever tried to bring magazines over. I only wanted to gloat at the photographs: the lovely things women can get in America; and in France, now." The laugh burst into a bubble which seemed to catch her breath. They stood there, in the damp street, Herbie chuckling, and Ursula – though he did not yet know her name – giggling at the thought of how ridiculous she must have looked, with the magazines falling from under her clothes. She put a hand out, holding on to Herbie's arm as though to steady herself. Herbie felt its warmth, even through his greatcoat: another warmth, intangible, spreading between them.

At last he said that she must have been shaken up; would she like to come and have some coffee with him? There was a place he knew, not far; on the Friedrichstrasse. That was unless her husband or . . .?

She had no husband. They introduced themselves to one another, with a formal gravity; then broke up with laughter again, for that also seemed ludicrous. She thanked him, and they walked together to the restaurant. Herbie tried to match his own, heavy strides with the languid, easy lope which, later, he was to know and love so well: her body always under control, but relaxed and easy.

The waiter did not seem happy at them just ordering coffee, so Herbie persuaded her to eat with him. They had immediate rapport. She laughed easily, even teasing him as the meal brought them closer. It remained unsaid, but they were happy in each other's company: at home as they talked.

That night, Herbie simply took her back to the door of the block in which she had a small apartment. They shook hands:

again very correct. With Martha Adler, even a few weeks before, he had not hesitated: no second thoughts about walking up to her apartment; even circling her waist with his arm, pulling her close.

Now, with Ursula, Herbie would have given anything to go with her: he would have also given nothing for himself. He desired the agony of waiting for the moment. They had talked, and laughed, for over three hours. When he left her – with a date to visit the cinema on the following Saturday – Herbie stood, for a minute, watching her almost skipping towards the door of the apartment block: like a child, clutching the magazines in front of her. A child with new toys.

As he lay, now, under the duvet, in the bed above the Dahlmannstrasse, Herbie recalled the sensual thoughts that had coiled around him at the first parting. She turned at the door, blowing him the kiss he had not claimed. He thought of holding those magazines: his hands on the shiny paper, touching it, where it had touched her: under her skirt. It was the most sensual thought he could ever remember.

That day had been Ursula Zunder's monthly free day. She had week-ends, and one free day a month, working as assistant supervisor to the secretarial pool at the Ministry of the Interior building – flanked by the Maurstrasse and the Glinkastrasse – not far from where the Birkemanns lived. Indeed the Birkemanns also worked there. Ursula Zunder was a definite possible for the Telegraph Boys: but Herbie dismissed the idea as soon as it came into his head. This girl, with her trim body, laughing eyes, sparkling intelligence and humour, had to be kept separate from his work. It was an immediate decision; made with no hesitation. A luxury never before allowed in his life.

Until then every person he met had been weighed-up for potential or danger: a safe bet or a risk. It would not be like that with Ursula Zunder.

Herbie knew, that first time, when he walked away from the apartment block. He detected something in her eyes; and divined the same sense in himself. As she left him Ursula had the look of a person who has searched for something over a long time, and was now within an ace of finding it. Herbie had lived so many secrets already, that he had not known, within his own being, that he also had followed a quest. Ursula Zunder was the gold at the end of his invisible rainbow: the Holy Grail of his own seeking.

Nothing stirred now, outside in the Dahlmannstrasse. Herbie Kruger, the big, tough yet sentimental man – with an icy intellect, and reputation, in his own world – felt the pricking at his eyes. In the darkness, he allowed the tears to come, at last falling asleep, guilty at the indulgence of his own weeping.

Max woke him gently, bringing coffee. It was seven in the morning. In ninety minutes Christoph Schnabeln would arrive.

Herbie lay there, adjusting to his dreams – of Ursula's lips finally on his, a few days after the first accidental meeting. Her small firm hand, later, in his huge paw; or resting on an arm. His own arms around her; their bodies close. He knew, also, that he had dreamed once more of the set of ruby drinking glasses; and the Dürer woodcut of an avenging angel.

Lying back in the warmth, sipping coffee; listening to Max clattering around in the kitchen, Herbie recalled, unwillingly, the weeks of courtship – for it had been a courtship in the real sense. Respect had flowed from one to the other. There was no easy giving or taking between them; no matter gone into lightly. Their times together, in those months, had helped Herbie through one of his most trying periods of work – when most of his days, and a number of nights, were spent searching and vetting likely recruits for his team of Telegraph Boys.

They did not sleep together until three months after meeting; and, while Herbie was aware that Ursula would have preferred marriage straight away, their joint conclusion was to allow the relationship time to build and flower before taking the final step. She had no idea of Herbie's true work until the disaster days of 1961; and even then no full picture of it until the catastrophe of 1965. Until then the bond between them was stronger than any natural marriage: even though the living was somewhat peripatetic. She would be at his little flat in Pankow for some of the time; but the bulk was spent at her apartment, which became home for both of them.

It was during their first seven months that Herbie made

real progress in the preliminary stages of filling the Telegraph Boys' appointments. He found the rake-thin, tall, short-sighted Otto Luntmann – known as 'The Professor' (grey-haired at twenty-eight: once a schoolmaster) – a natural because of his well-established job as a civilian messenger at the Soviet Embassy in East Berlin. Luntmann eventually became Horus – watcher of the Soviet Military and Air Attaché at the Embassy.

Herbie was also able to commence a trace on the joky prankster, Moritz Winter: a man full of bounce, like the stock uncle known to all large families; forever playing practical jokes, doing imitations, a source of embarrassment to his friends when they met in public places. Moritz reminded Herbie of a man he had once seen jump from a French railway carriage at Dijon station at three in the morning – Herbie was doing a quick run across Europe by rail from Paris, for a courier link in Cannes. The railway station at Dijon was deserted, but for a solitary old man selling bottles of wine, minerals, and rolls, from a wire trolley. Yet the japester had leaped on to the platform, cupped his mouth and shouted at the top of his voice, "*Avez vous la moutarde?*" That was just such a man as Moritz Winter.

Winter was still in his place now: moved up the ladder a little, to chief storeman at the Soviet HQ at Karlshorst; working, with several other civilians; under a Russian quartermaster, seeing to the regulation issue of door frames and lavatory seats; paper and pens; booze for the officers' mess, and mirrors for the private soldiers' ablutions. For so long now Moritz Winter had been Gemini – watching and reporting on the Soviet General in charge of liaison with the senior staff officers of East Germany's National People's Army.

Through all that time Ursula became Herbie's one constant: the source of his content, the stimulant for his weary mind, and the solace of his body.

Herbie tried to throw off the memories, as he now pushed back the duvet and lumbered into the bathroom. He shaved with great care, for his face, for any kind of razor, was like a tank trap, with its bumps and lumps, and troughs of skin. Rarely did he get through the morning ritual without nicking himself at least once. Back at St. John's Wood the bathroom litter-bin was spotted with bloodstained tufts of cotton wool. This morning his hand was steady. Behind the depression of the past night's haunting a sun of hope began to rise.

He went into breakfast, wearing his usual loose grey suit, that fitted where it touched: the jacket hanging sloppy, and the trousers riding at least an inch high. Today he sported a floral tie, at odds with both suit and shirt.

"Christ, Mr. Kruger," Max set ham and eggs before him. "Hang about while I get me Polaroid sunglasses. Did you choose that, or was it some malicious present from the opposition?"

The joshing was lost on Herbie, who thought the tie rather smart. He took a mouthful of food, and heard Ursula's voice from the past — "Darling, you should give blood for the Party" (this after his shaving). "Herbie, sweetheart, you really can't wear that tie. Red, and a blue-striped shirt, don't go together." Since leaving the East he had lost all sense of colour combinations.

The small, apple-cheeked Schnabeln – Spendthrift – arrived on the dot of eight-thirty. He looked concerned, but kept to the ritual: exact timing, and the three double rings on the bell. He had left the Metropol Hotel at seven; crossed into the West at eight; gone straight to the approved meeting place with the Coach Tour firm – in at the front door, straight out of the back. By the book. It had always worked in the past. To their knowledge he had never been spotted. Berlin Station street men would see him in and then leave, knowing of the meet, but not the hunt.

"Something is wrong?" he asked immediately, and Max chimed in quickly – "Not in front of the hired help, dear. I speak the lingo, you know, and this is all highly confidential, I'm sure. Eat first."

While Max was getting food Herbie quickly tried to allay Spendthrift's fears. "A job. Came up sooner than we thought. Took us by surprise: with the trousers down."

Schnabeln said he had been very worried, because the meeting had been called forward. Nothing to concern him, Herbie soothed. All over by Sunday night. They had the best part of two days. There was some equipment to be taken over;

certain routines to be run. He stressed the routineness of the business. A report to be flashed back. All over. Painless, like having a filling with an anaesthetic.

The trick was playing everything like a normal debrief. While Max cleared the plates away they waited, talking inconsequentialities, or lapsing into silence for periods. Herbie went to the window and watched the street. He wanted Max in position before they began in earnest. Schnabeln fiddled with his briefcase, while Herbie refreshed his mind on the last Telegraph Boys' reports he had glanced through before leaving London.

There was movement in the East. Gemini reported a number of meetings with the DDR people that had suddenly come up. His target was bobbing to and fro like a yoyo. Out at the General Soviet Forces, Germany, in Zossen-Wunsdorf, Priam had disturbing news. All the baloney concerned with arms limitations in 1979 had come too late. The salt had lost its savour. The Soviets had already stock-piled enough lethality. The talk at Zossen-Wunsdorf was of new warheads coming in for the advanced SS-19s, and smaller SS-14, ICBMs in the East. The delivery rockets could remain unchanged for decades; what really mattered were the warheads. Priam talked of superior warheads, some – about a quarter – with chemical fillings, some multi-purpose. There were also to be changes in the armoured regiments in the DDR. New equipment was rumoured to be on the way.

Electra, Hecuba, Nestor and Horus reported a rise in meetings of strategic planning between their targets. Otto Luntmann – Horus – had flashed a last minute brief to say that the Military and Air Attaché at the Soviet Embassy was scheduled to attend a General Staff conference in Moscow.

Electra reported the Minister of the Interior spending more and more of his time at Political Headquarters; and Hecuba echoed this, adding the attendance of Soviet military at the meetings.

The picture was one of a large-scale refurbishing of Soviet units in the East: possibly ready for a hardening of the political line.

Nestor, the grey, silent filing clerk – Herbie's last recruitment to the Telegraph Boys, before he was forced to include

187

Ursula – added a flash only three days before. He was at the National People's Army Headquarters, though his flash – on a screech tape – concerned the military-air situation. DDR Air Force fighter units were being retrained. He had sight of the instructions. Some pilots were already on their way to Russia, converting to the Foxbat – Mig 25s – until now used almost predominantly by the Soviet Air Force.

There was a great deal of bustle. An air of new brooms and girding of loins.

Max reported everything clean – the street showed no signs of watchers; all possible hides were covered; no tapes running.

Herbie gave him a short smile of dismissal and settled back. "What news on the Rialto, friend Spendthrift?"

Schnabeln opened his briefcase, passing over a small sheaf of flimsies. They were all in the form of typewritten letters to the Coach Tour Company, with one or two addressed to theatrical audio firms. Each would have a microdot embedded somewhere.

"Telegraph?" Herbie raised his eyebrows, already knowing.

Schnabeln nodded. The latest; all picked up last night. Herbie would see they got to Berlin Station quickly. "And your own work?" he asked, as though this was more important.

Schnabeln began a recitation. He handed over Anna Blatte's photographs, which detailed meetings between a high-ranking KGB man and two faces that Herbie easily identified as visiting firemen from the West German Federal Intelligence Agency. "Who's setting up who?" he asked of nobody.

Walter Girren had a request to tap into the National People's Army's field intelligence offices. He claimed to have had some overtures.

"You tell him not yet. I got to get clearance for that kind of thing."

Schnabeln nodded again. He was like a man waiting for sentence. Not much hard stuff to report. Troop movements – some exercises to the East of Berlin. Nothing spectacular. "Why the change, Herbie?" he asked twice; and twice Herbie fobbed him off. "Plenty of time. It's easy." The large hands unmoving, still on his knees.

They did a long question-and-answer session during the morning. Requirements mainly – film, money; the usual things. Then Schnabeln mentioned having seen one of his assets with a KGB major.

Herbie went silent, then asked for details. Schnabeln, who did not know Martha Adler by name – only as Hecuba – recounted the sighting in the foyer of the Metropol. "Probably a contact, but he's usually at the Centre. Rarely comes out. He's on your list, Herbie. You briefed us on Major Kashov. In London, you had his photograph."

Herbie asked if it was definitely Kashov with Hecuba. No doubt in his mind at all, Schnabeln replied; so Herbie played his first ace. Did Schnabeln recall the situation over Colonel-General Vascovsky's heart attack? Well, things were in flux. Something was going on; Herbie knew it, because Major Kashov had come to Berlin with particular instructions following Vascovsky's death. London knew he was there. Did Hecuba still get about?

"You mean men?" Schnabeln allowed himself a smile.

"Yes. She still put herself about?"

Schnabeln said he was not her keeper, but . . . well, yes. He got the impression she did it for friends, and had few enemies. Russian officers a speciality; officers of the political branches, and NVA, as hors d'oeuvres and dessert. Schnabeln presumed that was her job.

After lunch Herbie asked Schnabeln what he thought *his* job really was. The text book reply came back – recruitment, military, political, economic intelligence; and the servicing of deep penetration assets.

Herbie, armed now with a post-prandial vodka, asked which of these jobs Schnabeln considered the most important. "Come on, you're not a fool. Tell me straight. What do you think?"

"I think we're really in for one thing." Schnabeln gained confidence: relaxed. "We're handlers. The Quartet is there to service your special assets – two for me; two for Girren; one each for Mohr and Blatte. I spend most of my time picking up, dropping, and farting around risking my liberty with screech tapes – all from the special assets."

Herbie gave a big, wise nod. Did the others think the same?

Girren almost certainly – because he had the transmission jobs with Schnabeln. He doubted if either Anton Mohr or Anna Blatte had wind of it. Schnabeln used only the work names.

"You're right, of course." Herbie slowly started to reveal the nature of the work done by the special assets. He went into no true details, but said they had been there for a long time – for a lengthy period without proper handling facilities. "The Quartet was designed to fill that breach. It seemed that all six of our long-term assets were sound. There's no need to give you the small print, but one of them is unhealthy."

"Jesus. We're blown?"

"Not necessarily."

"We know which one?"

"Not yet."

"But it's certain?"

"There is no doubt." Herbie leaned forward, hands clasped together around his glass. "This is why I called you over early. I would trust you with my life, Christoph. You will go and rout out the cancer."

"But . . .?"

Herbie was well ahead of him. He knew it may mean a complete dismantling of the apparatus – the long-term assets, and the Quartet. "We shall see. There is a way – a sure way – to smoke the double. The smoking is to be your job. London directs it. I am to give you all six names – real as well as the cryptos." He went on to explain London's plan. Herbie said he would give Christoph Schnabeln everything he knew about each of the assets. He would direct him. They even had equipment that would track him into East Berlin: follow every move. He told Schnabeln about the sophisticated fast-sender, and how it was to be used. In due course he would also tell him how the entrapment would work: the words he would use and the response. "You'll have to be alert. I shall give you a place, a map reference, from which to send the screech tape. We shall act upon what you tell us."

Schnabeln asked if he would have to finish off the double. He did not like the idea of violence.

"It will be done for us, Christoph. London will analyse the information. They will make the decision. London does not like violence any more. They may just decide to decamp everybody except our man . . ."

"Or our woman." Schnabeln spoke again of seeing Hecuba with Major Kashov. Kashov was always thought of as the director of operations concerning assassination.

Herbie nodded. He was not thinking of Kashov. Herbie Kruger had more violence in his soul at this moment than ever before. He had seen men killed; and killed them himself; he had directed 'wet operations', as they used to be called, and sent men into situations knowing the circumstances would bring about their ultimate deaths. There had been times when he had locked himself up for days on end after such things: when he had got drunk to forget. But now his conscience would not be troubled. He wanted the person who had betrayed the Telegraph Boys; also Luzia Gabell who had made rubbish of his own life.

"You must do exactly as I tell you, Christoph. You must not deviate a fraction. I shall know, because we have machines that will be watching you . . ."

Max tapped at the door. Earlier they had telephoned for a courier from Berlin Station. Now he had arrived to pick up the latest Telegraph Boys' reports and the other material brought over by Spendthrift. Herbie told Max to go ahead, give him the stuff, and get rid of him. The bunch of papers, Anna Blatte's photographs – together with a short memo written by Herbie – were all sealed in a heavy brown envelope. Max took them without a word, giving Schnabeln a curious look as he left.

Max was both minding and listening – a living bug in the safe house. All right. Herbie was playing the whole thing as they would expect: going by the book. Word perfect. Normal and obedient to his London masters. In the few seconds while Max was seeing the courier to the door Herbie's hand dived to his pocket; a small piece of paper passed between him and Schnabeln. The look in his eye told his colleague it should be read later. It contained instructions: things Schnabeln would have to do in secret, while Herbie was away with Max, seeing the *Trepan* team, and later – tomorrow – when the going would get tough. Herbie prayed he had not misjudged Schnabeln: that his man, Spendthrift, really was *his* man.

Now he sat back, and began to play the Svengali with Christoph Schnabeln; taking each of the Telegraph Boys in turn; moving back and forth over their personal histories, as he knew them. He annotated their likes and dislikes; their strengths and weaknesses. Whoever was to act as beater for the guns on this shoot had to be on the most intimate of terms with every scrap of information: to be inside Herbie's boots; while Herbie Kruger had to walk inside him.

For the moment he did not give Schnabeln any hint of the Gorky phrase; or the reactions he might expect. Herbie concentrated on filling the man with knowledge: of the people involved, and their pressure points.

Towards six o'clock, when they had covered a great deal of ground, Herbie said it was time to break. As he spoke his eyes lingered on the pocket in which Schnabeln had placed the clandestine paper. Schnabeln nodded. "I have to go out for a while," Herbie told him; then called for Max. "You will be left alone. An hour or so. Open up to nobody, Christoph. Just do as I say."

Schnabeln gave the ghost of a nod, and Herbie asked Max to arm Schnabeln. That had been part of the arrangement. Max produced a weapon – a little Italian gun. Herbie reckoned it would not have Service handwriting all over it. People like Max had private sources: just like Herbie.

Now, Max would not leave Big Herbie's side for an instant. They would visit the *Trepan* team in the eyrie above the Mehring Platz. Max told Spendthrift he should stay away from the windows. "Nasty draughty places, windows. Catch your death."

They went out into the evening, Herbie praying that the Service had cut at least one corner on this job, and not left another minder to lurk outside of the building.

Max had a car ready; spirited from nowhere. "Max the Magnificent," Herbie chuckled.

"No, old love, Max the client of Avis rent-a-barouche. Think I'd better drive. You watch, eh?"

Herbie settled into the front of the rented Merc and, ostentatiously, fastened his safety belt.

"Like that, is it?" Max pouted.

"I remember the time, sonny," Herbie's voice cut like steel.

"I remember the time when you couldn't go a hundred metres in this city without the Russian hoods trying to bang you up against a wall."

"Chance would be a fine thing." Max pulled away from the kerb. Herbie was doing a fast recce on possible watchers. It looked okay: then he reminded himself never to be deceived by looks, and silently prayed that Schnabeln would use his common sense.

8

FOR THE *Trepan* team, that Friday was one of dull waiting. "Doodling time," Charles called it.

For Worboys the day started badly. As the hours passed, so his anger mounted: he was annoyed, both with himself and Miriam Grubb. The fury directed against himself had a lot to do with the discovery of personal vulnerability – the knowledge that he was hopelessly obsessed with Miriam.

He watched her all the time, hanging around as a pupil will manoeuvre himself to be near a worshipped teacher. She was there, in the penthouse, all the time. Mentally, she did not leave Worboys' mind for a minute; and the very fact throbbed in him, like a boil drawn by a hot medical fomentation. Worboys knew he should be able to treat the business with Miriam like some shipboard romance. But his growing bewitchment would not allow that.

With Miriam the problem lay not in the undeniable sexual pleasure but in her attitude – the stubborn refusal to open either heart or mind to him. She was like a wall. If only he could smash down this barrier, Worboys considered, Miriam might reveal her true self. Once that happened there was the possibility of choice. He could make up his mind; analyse true feelings; separate the obsession from reality, make a frontal attack on the future – either forcing a continuation or an end to the whole thing, once and for all.

In some ways it had already ended. Only the gnawing obsession lingered on, nibbling his mind and peace. There had been a row early that morning – inevitable, for they had gone to bed on the previous evening, with Worboys smarting and surly. Outside the bedroom Miriam Grubb treated him as if he was not there: hardly speaking to him; rarely acknowledging his presence. Miriam, he thought, was using him, just as so many men use women – something Worboys had, in truth, never done.

She woke him, in the early hours, kissing him to consciousness, pressing her body close to his. After an initial response, Worboys had suddenly felt his mind flood with the stored resentments.

She asked what was wrong – wet and close to him, her naked breasts against his chest as he drew away. The operation would be starting tomorrow; Big Herbie was visiting tonight. Once they began there would be no time for "fun and high jinks".

Worboys said he was not really certain if that was what he wanted – "fun and high jinks".

"I hadn't noticed. You've not complained before." Her voice was throaty, her skin hot, even feverish – the temperature of arousal. Though the voice and mouth smiled at him, Worboys saw the invisible steel shutters coming down behind her eyes. He had noticed it before: the eyes dissolving into cold points with nothing showing behind them. He had seen the same look in a silent killer who now lectured at the probationers' school. She spoke again. "We've enjoyed ourselves, haven't we? That's the name of the game, I thought."

Worboys, glancing towards the window, with grey light showing that it was well past dawn, said he did not think it was the name of *his* game.

"When you've got it, you don't want it," her laugh was forced: unpleasant.

"Oh, I think I want it, Miriam. But not on your terms."

"They're the only terms you'll get." Her hands came up to fondle his neck, and he caught hold of her wrists. He wanted her to hear him out. She nodded, as if to say that she would listen, but much good would it do him.

For about ten minutes Worboys talked quietly; telling her about his upbringing, the very few women in his past, his feelings, likes, dislikes; and the strange metamorphosis that appeared to have taken place – his obsession with her.

She sighed, breaking the grip of his wrists. He was like all the others, she said. "You take them, and they either despise you for it or think they're in love with you."

Worboys told her he had not said he was in love with her. Obsessed was the word he used. He simply could not relate to this kind of situation; it was outside his experience. If she would only talk, open up to him, then he might cope.

"It's not on, Tony. I've told you. You're a darling man . . ."

"You wouldn't think so from the way you treat me out there," a thumb jabbed towards the door.

"You're a darling man, but I've got personal rules. I don't intend to break them, not for you, not for anybody."

He asked her to tell him about the rules – "Two can't play unless they both know the rules" – but she said that would mean going over everything. She did not intend to air her personal problems, even with him. He had been so kind to her: gentle; considerate. "For me you're a natural lover. Know that?"

Worboys had not experienced enough of women to know it. He was aware it had never been as good for him. "That's not the point, though, is it? Yes, it began as a sexual lark." For him that was not enough. Or maybe it was too much. He wanted to know her in ways other than Biblical. Miriam was running with a devil at her heels, he felt. If she went on behaving like this, keeping herself bottled from talk, only giving her body, the devil would catch up, and engulf her. He realised this was the kind of language Big Herbie might have used. They say dogs grow like their masters.

"You could be right, at that," her eyes briefly flashing, like sun striking ice. "If I'm engulfed, so be it. Let it happen. Who cares?"

"I might. But, if that's how you feel, there's an end to it," Worboys shrugged. "You and me, Miriam: we've paddled in the surf. Maybe I want to go out and play with the big boys and girls, in the deep end. It's obvious you've already done that. What happened? You get cramp and nearly drown? Or did someone push you under?"

"You . . ." she began, stopping, running a hand through her tousled hair. Worboys thought he saw a slight movement in her eyes: as though he had conjured some horror: raised a ghost she had put to rest a long time ago. She gave a short nod. "No, I don't like playing in the deep end. I do my job. That's living enough – life enough – for me."

"So I'm your chosen summer playmate. The little boy you splash with in the surf, and ignore on the promenade. Well, that's an end to it, Miriam. You either show some trust, take my hand, swim out into the deep, or I go alone. The chances are that we'd both want to swim straight back to the shore, and go different ways in any case. Tell me. Talk to me."

Slowly she shook her head. He was a terrible romantic. It almost sounded like a sneer, as though romantics were lepers.

"That's an end to it, then. Tonight I'll sleep in the kitchen." He picked up his clothes and stumped out, leaving Miriam looking pensive, and a little puzzled.

All day, even though he stayed near her, his mind reeling, Worboys did not exchange a word with Miriam, except on a professional level. Once or twice he caught her looking at him, with an expression of indecision. When she saw him Miriam looked quickly away.

If Charles and Tiptoes noticed the atmosphere they did not show it. All four of the *Trepan* group were drinking coffee when Herbie arrived with Max. It was just after six-thirty.

When they left the Dahlmannstrasse, Herbie had not been in the car above two minutes before he knew Max had lied. The vehicle was not rented; it had 'Service' written all over it – from the bonded bullet-proof glass to the hairline cracks below the dashboard, indicating a stowaway panel for communications gear. There were also locked pockets on the door interiors, for hand weapons.

All this signalled that the Director and Tubby Fincher were breathing down Herbie's neck. Max would be in constant touch with London, and could call up Berlin Station at speed, if London so ordered. It meant Herbie's fears were well-founded. Max, the minder and listener, would not be alone. The Dahlmannstrasse house would be on a round-the-clock survey. Once more, Herbie prayed quietly that Schnabeln could accomplish everything without leaving the building.

There was no tail on them during the drive to the Mehring Platz. Herbie stayed alert, though nobody would have known it, to see him, slumped in the passenger seat. He looked more like a tired, stranded whale. In his mind he went through all the possible permutations of the Director's thinking.

The last time there was defector trouble – from within the Service itself – Herbie had been deeply involved. He had also made one small error, and the target was missing for a few days. Herbie had failed to be his brother's keeper, and double-check on a telephone tap that was not there for twenty-four hours.

Now, with the new information about the Schnitzer Group, and the cancer within the Telegraph Boys, his credibility was shot. His superiors would, naturally, be cautious. Maybe, they would think, Herbie really was over the hill. The legend had been crippled by Mistochenkov's revelations.

He pondered on Pavel Mistochenkov. There were still many things that failed to add up, from the information given – particularly the dates when the Russians claimed to have known the Telegraph Boys' cryptonyms. It did not make sense. The Director would – if Herbie knew the man at all – be doing his own cross-referring even now. It stank, the whole thing; and it stank at a time when the Telegraph Boys were starting to prove their real worth: the prior early-warning system, possibly the most important intelligence assets possessed by the West. Blown. Penetrated. Herbie Kruger's big bloomer; Herbie's blunder; Herbie's *Schnitzer*.

Max parked the car a block from the Mehring Platz building. Almost as soon as they arrived Herbie shrugged off the queries that dotted his mind. It was a happy, boisterous reunion. Max got into a huddle with Charles, whispering close together in a corner, while Tiptoes went through the electronics with Herbie. It all seemed most satisfactory; though Herbie became quickly aware of the coolness between Miriam Grubb and young Worboys. Lovers' tiff? He grinned inwardly. Perhaps they had not hit it off at all. Alas, poor Worboys.

Herbie tried his chair for size, nodded contentedly at the Sony Stowaway with the headset, and looked through the tapes. "Ach, that is not so good a recording of the Mahler Third." He discarded a cassette with the look of a man sniffing sour milk.

Finally he gathered the team around him: sitting in his

chair while they squatted at his feet. A Service guru giving spiritual advice to the converted. He told them there had been most fruitful conversations during the day with their friend from the East. He was uncertain as yet what time the man would leave on his return journey, but suggested the team should stand by from about four o'clock onwards, tomorrow.

"Early as that?" Max looked surprised.

Herbie turned off the charm, looking at Max with the uncertain, swift gaze of a Gila Monster. "Yes, Max, as early as that. Do you mind? You wish to run this, or will you leave it to those who know?"

Max said he thought the departure would be later. "Sorry I spoke." Piqued.

And you, thought Herbie.

Herbie would give them a wrong number telephone call, about ten minutes before he was ready to test the equipment. "We shall do the homers first." The second digits on the watches indicated if the devices were working correctly, giving a pulse to show the strength of the signal. Herbie gave them the signals – a series of long bleeps for one of the devices; a dot-dash tone for the other. They would test both. If they were operating normally they would then give a fifteen-second burst with the one Spendthrift would use back in the East. "So you will see both come up, one after the other. Then one. This last will be Spendthrift's signal."

After the homers Herbie would run a screech tape. "I shall prepare some nonsense tonight, using tomorrow's key word. A good test for you, Worboys. Convert and decipher the message, and I shall mark you for accuracy when I arrive." He had in reality already prepared the tape. But who's counting? he thought.

He asked for any questions. There were none. They all knew what was to be done. "You're clear, are you, Worboys, in case Max drives me into a lorry on the way here? You could handle it?"

Quite buoyantly, Worboys said it would not be beyond his capabilities. He'd show bloody Miriam.

"At this point, before going into battle, the commander usually gives a pep-talk. It is a good English tradition – 'This day is called the Feast of Crispin', 'Once more unto the breach, dear friends, once more'; all that kind of thing, do not you know?"

Miriam laughed aloud.

Herbie wagged a finger, beaming around the group: a disarming look. "You aren't going to escape the pep-talk. I think, in this case, it's very important. I was flippant when we last spoke in London. Made a joke out of it all. It is not a joke. Understand that. This operation is vital. I cannot stress this more highly. Absolutely vital; because it concerns the defence of the West." In the old days, he told them, the business in which they were engaged was known as The Great Game.

"That is, to me, a most unfortunate term; for this is no game. Games are physical trials or tests of intellect. True, our job concerns both such elements. But games are for fun. We play for keeps. If any one of you regards this as a nice cosy game – baddies versus goodies – forget it. Go home now. I have already suffered enough at the hands of totalitarian administrations.

"We are engaged in something that goes beyond personalities," he told them. The people they had in the East were part of an important link. Now, through duplicity, they were at risk. In the field people accepted being at risk. It was part of their job – being expendable. "We are all expendable, because freedom must not be thrown away lightly." Herbie said he was not using the word 'freedom' in any sentimental sense, nor in the jingoistic terms pumped at them from bad movies and TV programmes. "I speak of truth, even though the word has lost currency. To me, freedom is a question of choice – even if it is sometimes a limited choice, these days in the West. Even limited, you *still* have a choice – to decide, to write what you wish, to speak without too much fear. The basic ideology held by the Soviet Bloc is excellent in theory: crippling in practice. Have no doubt that they wish it on us also. In dealing with the Soviet Bloc I believe we are dealing with a plague. Anything that restricts basic freedom is a plague.

"This operation – as with all our work – is surgery and disinfection." Worboys had heard the speech before. It was from one of Herbie's lectures at the school. "Remember," Herbie said. "Our masters sometimes talk of soft-pedalling;

of detente; of peaceful co-existence. That is all very well; but at those times one must be on guard. Remember, there is always peril."

*   *   *

Before leaving Herbie managed a quick word with Worboys, who had spent a lot of the time hovering, as though wishing to talk.

"Okay?" Herbie asked.

Worboys said that things appeared to be going smoothly. "Sorry about the blow-up," he added.

Herbie looked blank, asking ingenuously, what blow-up?

"On the way to Warminster." Worboys, plainly embarrassed.

"Ach. Women. Yes." Herbie allowed one of his fast, daft smiles before asking if Worboys had encountered some unexpected difficulties.

"It's complicated." The young man shifted his feet. "Bit of an emotional problem."

"I can help?"

Worboys shook his head. "Time I grew up in that department." He gave a nervous laugh. "Thought I had. Just wanted to say you were right about women in the field. Need – emotions – that kind of thing."

"You'll cope – that the word? Cope?"

Worboys said yes, that was the word; and yes he would cope. Herbie was pleased. He would make something of Tony Worboys yet. Time and experience were the only real teachers.

*   *   *

Back in the Dahlmannstrasse house Christoph Schnabeln read through the paper Herbie had clandestinely passed to him. At first he was shaken; he had to read the entire sheet twice before taking in the full extent of Herbie's propositions.

The writing was small, but neat and legible. First, a warning that Max was probably listening; there might be watchers on the house: all Service people. Then the propositions, listed under separate headings, as a series of instructions.

After the instructions came the reasons for this unethical action, together with possible suggestions of how the venture could be managed. If Schnabeln thought he could organise on the hoof, ad lib, he would obviously need extra time. When Herbie returned there were phrases, and bits of body talk, Schnabeln could use to denote it could be done, and what extra time would be needed. If this meant leaving the Dahlmannstrasse house early then Herbie would have to know. But they must cut it as fine as possible.

If it was really necessary for Schnabeln to use a telephone to make arrangements now – while Herbie was out with Max – he should not use the instrument in the house. There was a booth on the corner – but only if it was really essential. *Remember we are probably being watched. For all that we believe in, my friend, I beg you to take no chances*, Herbie wrote. The message ended with advice to burn the paper. If Schnabeln would co-operate, he was to place the large glass ashtray at a particular point on the table.

Christoph Schnabeln thought for a while. He considered the true desperation that would make a man like Herbie Kruger resort to actions such as these. He understood, so began to work out times. If they left the Dahlmannstrasse at four forty-five tomorrow, Saturday afternoon, it could just be managed. He would not have to use a telephone. Not yet.

Christoph Schnabeln picked up the heavy ashtray, placing it firmly on the appointed spot. He then read through the document again – just for insurance – took it into the bathroom, and destroyed it, tearing the paper and burning each piece, before flushing the charred bits, singly, down the lavatory.

9

As soon as they got back into the Dahlmannstrasse house Herbie noticed, with a lifting heart, that Schnabeln had given the ashtray signal. The relief was quickly followed by a sense of great tension. Herbie had tipped his hand: committed himself. The rest would be a matter of luck and professional expertise.

Max went off to prepare a meal, and Herbie said he and Spendthrift should talk again. In the first few minutes of the conversation Spendthrift gave him the signals. In order to get to the Coach Tour Company offices in time to arrange things he would need to leave at four forty-five.

When the messages had passed, Herbie returned to the briefing, keeping strictly to the limits and instructions London had given him. First he ran a question-and-answer routine: a rehash of the day's work with Spendthrift – the real names and personalities of the Telegraph Boys; their individual characters; the way he would expect each to act, or react, in certain given circumstances.

Even in the kitchen, preparing a meal, Max would have some device working: Herbie was certain of that. When the food was ready he banished Max from the table – "Time's going fast, and we've still got a lot to cover."

No skin off Max's nose, he said.

They ate simple fare, as one usually did under these circumstances – tinned soup, some cold cuts with salad, and a rich cake Max had stopped to get on their way back. Herbie, becoming infected by field paranoia, was convinced Max had really made a drop for London while getting the cake.

Herbie went through the communications equipment. Spendthrift would take the fast-sender over in a book – they would go into that tomorrow, as it was a different make of machine: more sophisticated. Fifteen minutes' instruction should be ample. There were two homers; one for insurance. Herbie explained the test signalling, saying – as he had done at the Mehring Platz – that he would make up a test tape tonight. He then gave Spendthrift the key words, for the days over which the operation would run – Saturday and Sunday. They had provided keys for Monday and Tuesday; also for insurance. He then sat back and asked how Spendthrift would contact each of the assets, meaning the Telegraph Boys.

There were two safe houses still used in East Berlin – one in the Behrenstrasse; the other, not so good, up in Weibensee. Schnabeln could make immediate contact with the other three members of the Quartet.

"You can do that on Saturday night, once you're back in the East?"

"Within the hour. We've got a good alarm system. And the whole Quartet can get in touch with their individual assets – you know there's a crash signal: a method."

"So you'll do it straight away?"

Spendthrift said, naturally. He would set up individual meetings, at one or the other – or even both – safe houses for the Sunday.

"For God's sake leave plenty of time between each meeting," Herbie was talking almost for real now. Schnabeln knew how it was going to work out. "You don't want them bumping into one another on the stairs." Herbie smiled, remembering how the story had spread through headquarters like wildfire. London ran a whore – several if the truth was known – with a good clientèle from the embassies. One afternoon, her case officer was leaving after a debriefing, in the trade sense, when he bumped into a senior Treasury official on the way up. The Director passed a hush-hush list of the Service whores around the main Whitehall ministry buildings after that – initials required, the list shown to people by hand, then taken back to Service headquarters for filing.

Schnabeln asked about the unmasking routine, but Herbie was not giving him any of that until the last minute. He did not want to tell him the Gorky phrase at all; but with Max listening it was essential.

It was after eleven when Herbie sent Spendthrift off to bed. They would start at eight in the morning. He wanted Spendthrift oiled and running like an automaton before he left. Spendthrift grinned. Herbie grinned back, then went into his bedroom, extracted the fast-sender and a tape and concocted a nonsense screech for Max's benefit. He had no doubt that Max would have some way of letting London hear the test before it was even supposed to be played out to the Mehring Platz.

He used the Saturday code, and did Hey-Diddle-Diddle, with the Twelve Days of Christmas as an encore. Then Herbie stashed the tape in his briefcase, inserting the one already made up in London into the machine.

Once *that* tape went out, and Worboys got his head around it, all hell would break loose. Herbie felt more relaxed: himself again. He was working, and it did him good. He slept soundly, waking without any memory of dreams.

*   *   *

In the meantime, in the *Trepan* suite, Worboys was having an uncomfortable night. The kitchen was draughty, the floor less yielding than that of the room he had shared with Miriam.

Sleepless and chilly, at about one in the morning he put on the light and got out the cigarettes in a small flurry of anger. Damn Miriam, he thought. Or damn himself. Was he normal? A normal man would take what was offered – enjoy himself. No tears, no fuss, hooray for us, and thanks for the memories.

Like all the *Trepan* team, Worboys had been armed by Charles after their arrival. The pistol was under his pillow – into his hand as soon as he detected someone in the passage. Perhaps Tiptoes, or Charles, was going to the bathroom; but Herbie had taught him to take no chances.

The pistol pointed steadily at the door as it opened, silently. Miriam stood there. She wore a tiny pair of briefs and no bra. Worboys saw her nipples were erect; but that could be the chill air. Then he looked at her face. Miriam Grubb had been crying.

"Yes?" he queried, as dispassionately as possible.

"Come back," she said. A husky note. "Please come back. I'll tell you. Tell you everything."

She wanted him to make love to her first, but Worboys, through the passage of his anger, had found strength to resist. "I'll respect your privacy, Miriam. It's cost you a lot to come to me. I know that. You've been playing at personal freedom: making your own rules. For Christ's sake share them with me now. We make love – you'll put it off again. Back to square one."

She took a deep breath. The tears had gone from her eyes now, and they lay side by side in their old room. "It's just that I don't like talking about it. Simple as that. I've been thinking all day, and you're right. I have to tell someone, though there's nothing spectacular to tell. Not when you boil it down against all the anguish in the world."

She began, hardly looking at him, her eyes fixed on the ceiling. Her father was Service. "Only recently retired. Good street man in his day. Got past it, though, so they brought him back to London; agent running: Scandinavia. You know how it is? His name would mean something to you." She told him. Worboys knew immediately. Her father had lectured at the school – "I sat at his feet" – Grubb was her married name.

Her father and mother split up when she was still only a child. "The Ma couldn't stand the lonely nights, when Pa was away doing some piece of nonsense like this." She paused and apologised, remembering Herbie's speech. "Anyway, Pa came home unexpectedly one night and caught her at it. Sensitive time. The bloke she was fucking turned out to be Service – a brother officer and, when you come to breaking rules, as you well know, that's the ultimate sacrilege. Scandal."

Miriam spent her adolescence shuttling between the separated parents, who saw to it that she had good schooling. She had an eye to the future, and her father had his own eye on her. She was good Service potential. "The lovable old bugger played me like one of his own assets. I went up to Oxford to read physics, and ended up specialising in electronics. Pa did that. He could read the stars, knew what the future held. They recruited me at Oxford – openings for people with my kind of skills. That was about seven years ago, just when the Service had its big love affair with electronics. My own first job was putting all these bloody great Registry files on microfilm." The laugh was genuine now. "Isn't it bloody silly? They've got all that microfilm, yet they still use the paper files – talk about a builder running out of money. Treasury's never allowed cash for the whole system, and they're not sanctioned to use the secret vote for it. Waste of time and energy."

Worboys knew all about that. He said the old guard felt unhappy about destroying the files. They did not trust the microfilm computers. "Each generation resists change. It'll come. They all laughed when Christopher Columbus . . ."

She agreed, then continued. She met a bloke. It happened towards the end of her noviciate with the Service. As she put it, "I was just about to take my vows of chastity and obedience – oh, and poverty; *that* government was in." Anyway, she met a man, and the impact devastated her.

"I'd had blokes, of course; but this was the shape of things to come. Immediate explosion. An overnight success: made for life, or at least a very long run. Rave reviews. Within two days I was the star, walking around singing the lyrics: word perfect."

Her bloke worked in the Street – by which she meant Fleet Street. "Foreign correspondent. Name of Grubb, so he couldn't use it as a by-line because of its connotations: Grub Street and all that. You'd know his nom de plume." She took another of Worboys' cigarettes. He had given her one at the start; now she chain-smoked her way through the private ordeal.

The Service gave permission for a wedding. "Quiet. Only a hundred or so guests." A pretty grimace. "Even the Ma came, with some horrible little man from the city. She and Pa didn't even exchange a spit. It was one month to the day after we first met – wedding bells, Mendelssohn, a three-tiered cake, the lot. Bliss . . ." For the first time Miriam faltered – a slight choke, the eyes damp again.

They had two and a half years of the bliss. But tragedy was on hand, as it nearly always is.

"Happens all the time; only when it happens to you, you cry, 'Why me?' You just get happy when the old man with the grey beard comes along and cuts it all down."

Her lover-husband – she called him Richard to Worboys, though there was no way of telling if that was correct – being a Foreign correspondent, was away for long periods. "But I was busy, and happy. In some ways it made us better. The partings

were hell, but the homecomings . . . well. I wasn't like the Ma."
She used this strange expression, 'The Ma', whenever speaking of her mother. "There was nobody else. There *is* nobody else who can take his place. He was the one I needed. He fed my mind and body. Lord, Richard *was* my mind and body. Never a dull moment. It sounds like a bundle of women's mag clichés – the diary of a happy child bride. Richard was all *I* ever needed." She thumped her chest with a balled fist at the '*I*'.

Two and a half years. Then all over. He had a sudden assignment. "Just called me at the office. Going to Tel Aviv. Three days. Back Thursday afternoon. See you then. Keep everything warm for me. I love you."

The next morning, the Director sent for her. "A car from Pangbourne where I was doing some trials in the Lab: Soviet mikes some fink had swapped for the usual thirty pieces of silver. They wouldn't let me have the radio on in the car, I remember. The thing I've never really understood is that nobody let on he was Service. Between husband and wife there's supposed to be intercognisance. Richard never let on. The Director said it was because he only used him from time to time – a temp: not full-fledged. That wasn't true, I found out later."

Richard had arrived safely in Tel Aviv. They knew that. It was all they knew – all they ever knew. Except for the fact of his body, found next morning, smashed up by three nine-mil bullets, in a stolen car parked in some back street. "Richard had been doing one of his occasional black bag ops. I was in a wasteland."

Naturally they offered her leave. She refused. In the evenings she went home from the electronics shop at Pangbourne and methodically packed up everything that had belonged to her beloved husband. "I had him in my head. There was no need for the physical reminders." She disposed of the lot. "People said it would pass. Give it time. But I knew myself – and Richard. It wasn't just an emotional phase: not simply grief clogging the valves. Nothing could ever be the same again with another man. It cannot."

For a year she had lived chaste, like a nun. "But the sex drive is strong in a woman like me. It returns. Not the same, mind you. Just for comfort, and the warmth of somebody beside you, and inside you." When the year was over, Miriam composed her set of rules.

First, she would be her own woman, within the confines of Service discipline. Second, she would never again allow herself to become emotionally involved with a man. Third, she would be dominant. If there was a man she fancied then she would take him; make the running; avoid all emotion and sentiment. There was, of course, a codicil to this last. She would have no man outside the Service, and would stick to the dogma which said you could not commit adultery with the husband – or wife – of any other Service officer: the law her mother had broken, long ago.

Miriam Grubb had kept to her rules.

Worboys let the silence lie between them. His mind circled the facts of how little he knew of life – the sheltered upbringing, lack of real pain. Did he even lack conviction in the job he was now doing? Behind him there were only thirty-odd years of dross. Nothing you could call a real crisis.

Slowly he reached forward, taking her in his arms; wishing he could bear some of the twisted pain. He rocked her, as one lulls a baby into sleep. "You poor old love," he said; then repeated it, "You poor old love. I understand. Thank you for telling me. I do understand now."

After a while she stirred and answered; eyes quite dry as she looked into his. "Yes, Tony. I believe you do. I really believe you do."

"I certainly know the devil now – the one you're running from. It's the way to destruction, Miriam."

"As long as I do my work as well as I'm able; up to the end; I've still got the right of choice. Freedom. Big Herbie says so. Does it matter so much if, eventually, my way turns me into stone, or a pillar of salt? Richard was destroyed."

"It might matter to me. I don't know." He kissed her lightly on the mouth.

Miriam folded herself against him, returning his kisses. He could feel damp patches on his cheeks, and knew she wept again. They made love for a long time, on the bedrolls, and with Worboys concentrating all his efforts on exorcising the devil of grief, and bitterness, chattering in the black shadows of her mind.

10

It was four o'clock on the dot when Herbie Kruger telephoned his wrong number routine to the *Trepan* team. Max had been told they would need the car ready to drop off Spendthrift, they were then to go on to the Mehring Platz at four forty-five.

"But he doesn't leave on his coach before six-thirty," Max objected.

"Then he'll have plenty of time to run the back-doubles. Be there well in advance; avoid suspicion, Max." Herbie smiled genially, then heavily underlined the four forty-five by putting it another way – "A quarter-to-five, Max. Exact."

Saturday had turned sunny. Berlin and his wife would be out in force, strolling the Ku-damm, looking at the goodies in the little glass kiosks; shopping; going for picnics, and a spot of boating at Wansee; hand-holding in the Tiergarten; drinking in the bars and cafés. No such luck for Big Herbie and Spendthrift. They worked all day. Herbie did everything the Director suggested: the whole Svengali routine, the psychological black arts, a brain transplant – knowledge, intuition, method, technique. If Spendthrift really was going to unearth the broken link in the Telegraph Boys' chain he could not have been better prepared.

Herbie thought to himself that if Max was sending reports every hour, on the hour, to London, both the Director and Tubby Fincher should be well pleased. Maybe, by mid-afternoon, they would feel happy enough to take the rest of the day off – the Director to his butterflies; Tubby Fincher to the kites, which everybody knew he flew from Kensington Gardens on his off-duty week-ends.

Charles answered the telephone when Herbie did the wrong number bit.

"Stand by, babies," he called; and the rest of the *Trepan* team began to get themselves organised.

Tiptoes and Miriam Grubb seated themselves in front of the wizardry equipment, Miriam giving Worboys a small, affectionate smile as he took his own seat to her right. He was an innocent when it came to the scanner, but they had explained the rudiments; and the receiver – which was his job – presented no mystery. Worboys switched on and ran an eye over the green and red lights which popped into life. "Like a bloody fun fair." Miriam leaned across, double checking the frequency setting; watching Worboys as he locked-on, set the four-hour open-reel tape running, and turned up the volume. He put the headset on, then let it drop from his ears, draping around his neck.

Tiptoes knocked the switches on the scanner, and a fuzz of snow made a blizzard of the large screen. "Come on, girl," he looked at Miriam, "let's get the film in."

The film was a thin sheet of microfilm the size of a paperback novel, set into a plastic frame. Miriam took it gently from its case, sliding it into a slot in the control consol. The microfilm was an entire map of Berlin – West, East and environs.

Within the complex body of the scanning equipment a small high-powered lens tracked over the microfilm, projecting it on to the screen, where it came out full size – its scale over four times that of the old British inch-to-the-mile Ordnance Survey maps.

The frame around the film snapped home, and Tiptoes played with the focus. The screen went bright and settled. Above them the map section around the Brandenburg Gate came into sharp relief: everything showed on this map, up to the number of strands of barbed wire, and individual tank traps, in the *Todesstreifen* – the death strips – on the Eastern side of the Wall.

Miriam switched to manual, slowly tracking the picture by hand, running it backwards and forwards over the screen. Even the trees were marked in, for the map had been made from high-fly recce photographs and satellite pictures.

When the technicians were happy with the picture Tiptoes selected automatic, setting the frequencies to correspond with those of the homing device. The homers would bounce their signals, on a cleared channel, to one of the communication satellites. In a fraction of a second they would relay the pulses to the dish antennae on the roof. The four antennae passed the signal into the box of tricks, which would do a rapid triangulation, then swing the lens straight on to the area of the map from which the signals were being sent. Tiny bright lights, and accompanying sound, would give an exact location. To Worboys it was a miracle he accepted; but could never begin to understand.

"Big Herb said it should be about ten minutes after the call," Miriam sounded calm, eyes not moving from the screen.

Tiptoes nodded. After a while he said it should be any minute now.

Almost as he spoke the screen moved, and a series of long bleeps started, so loud that Miriam reached out quickly to adjust the sound. The screen showed the Ku-damm, and a bright pinpoint of light coming from half way up the Dahlmannstrasse.

In the background Charles said he knew the house well.

The long bleeps stopped. Five seconds later the pin of light began to pulse again: dot-dash. "Dip-Dah, Dip-Dah," the tone said through the speaker.

"And for my next trick," Miriam leaned forward, "we get the answer. Which one is it to be?"

The light bleeped again. Fifteen seconds, as Herbie had said. The series of long bleeps.

"Okay, Spendthrift's using the long bleeps. Just so we know if anyone tries to be funny and latches on." Tiptoes turned sharply to Worboys; telling him he had better get the earphones on: the screech would be through any minute.

There was background interference, mainly static, in the headphones. Worboys tried a little squelch to reduce it, pushing in a filter as added help. He hoped that was the right thing to do. In reality his communications training was barely adequate. He need not have worried, the screech took him by complete surprise, and he knew by the afterburn in his ears that the volume setting was too high. Two seconds. Less. A swish of sound. Very strong. There and gone. "Got it," he said, a shade too calmly, pressing the stop key on the recorder.

"Have fun," Miriam said, filching one of his cigarettes. Worboys now had to relocate the screech on the tape, transfer it to a cassette, then run it through the unraveller at his elbow. Transfer. Slow. Key-in the day's word; then watch the numbers come up. Tear off the print-out, and tap away at the numbers on the small keyboard. The *en clair* should then show on the small oblong screen above this little miracle of science, together with a print-out.

With a sigh, Worboys began to concentrate.

In the Dahlmannstrasse Herbie pocketed the watch containing the dot-dash tone homer. "I get packed up now," he said. Schnabeln strapped on his watch. It looked suitably cheap and used. The book, containing the fast-sender and tape, lay on the table. "You got everything now? In the head, I mean," Herbie said for Max's benefit, tapping his forehead like someone insinuating that another is crazy.

Schnabeln touched his own head and winked. Herbie had given him the Gorky phrase only just before they did the test runs with the homers. He repeated it now because Herbie's eyes asked for it. "A man can teach another man to do good — believe me."

As Schnabeln said it, Herbie heard the whole quotation in his mind — *Jail doesn't teach anyone to do good, nor Siberia, but a man — yes! A man can teach another man to do good — believe me.*

As he lumbered away to complete his packing Herbie wondered what dark ironies had made Vascovsky choose that particular phrase. When he heard it in his head — in its entirety — it was the voice of an actor. The line took on a stagey feel. He could not place the actor for a moment, then realised it was his old favourite, Anthony Quinn. The words would sound good in Quinn's Zorba voice. *Am I married? Are not all men foolish?* Homespun philosophies such as the Gorky phrase hung in that actor's voice like comfortable, adequate watercolours in a room one recalled with love.

Herbie unlocked the closet, taking out his suitcase and the briefcase. He arranged things, delving into secret places for the papers – from the cobbler of documents, in Camden Town – putting them in his inside pocket. The horn-rimmed spectacles went into his jacket. Making sure of everything else, Herbie took out the Browning, pushing it into his belt, banging the butt down so that it almost touched his genitals, the barrel pointing out and clear of the body. In the movies they shoved the things into their waistbands, muzzle down. "The quickest way to lose a foot – or your future," they used to say at the school.

Clutching the two cases in his great hands, Herbie clumped out of the bedroom, shouting for Max in the loudest, most commanding voice he could muster.

"He's getting the car," Schnabeln said. "You sure this . . .?"

Herbie silenced him with a look. Always be suspicious: survival depended on it. Herbie was all for survival. Why else would he put himself at such risk now? Between them Vascovsky and Mistochenkov had ruined his pride, his life, and, maybe, holed the Service he held in such respect. Yes, he knew the black box intelligence lobby would finally win, but – for a time at least – his Telegraph Boys, on the ground, had kept the Service in information, giving them an edge on the black box boys. Even the Americans were impressed. Not an easy accomplishment.

Max came up. The car was ready. Herbie nodded to the bags. With a small hesitation Max took them. In the street he shoved the bags into the Merc's boot, while Herbie settled himself in the front passenger seat. Spendthrift got into the rear. Max acted with the grace of an unruly ape at a wedding.

"I do the directing, Max," Herbie said quietly. "A few passes from my youth. Just for the hell of it."

"Where we going to drop him off, then?" Max started the engine.

"I'll lead you. Straight ahead, Max. Then turn right at the Niebuhrstrasse. There are some side streets there. I'll run you through them. It'll be an education." The Niebuhrstrasse lay almost parallel to the Ku-damm; a couple of blocks removed. Unless they had done a lot of rebuilding since his day Herbie knew of one or two alleys off that street which would serve his purpose.

They drew away into the traffic, and Herbie turned, nodding to Schnabeln who pressed his homer switch – a ten-second burst.

The bleep sounded, showing clearly on the screen in the Mehring Platz. "They're off," Miriam said, like a racing commentator.

Worboys had the screech on a cassette now. He sat back and lit a cigarette. There was plenty of time. He could unzip the thing in less than half an hour. Herbie would not be with them for at least an hour.

"Where next?" Max asked, sounding edgy.

Herbie told him, quietly, there was a narrow turn coming up. Not this one. The next. Here.

The Merc swung to the left, and Herbie prayed he had got it right: a cul de sac, running between two buildings, and walled in at the end. Max swore – "Wrong, love; wrong. Bloody dead end" – and with delight Herbie saw the old red brick wall ahead, laced with cement, and some half-baked political slogan daubed in white paint. Max put on the anchors shifting his body to get a good view of the rear for the reverse.

"Sorry about this, Max." Herbie had the pistol nudged into Max's ribs. "Switch off the engine."

Max looked at him, puzzled. Then, "Bastard. They said to watch you."

"Like an eel, they said," Herbie sounded cheerful. "Terribly sorry, Max, but it's for the good of Service and country." He coughed, which was the prearranged signal, and Schnabeln, from the rear, chopped hard to the back of Max's neck. Herbie winced, putting out a hand to stop the minder falling across the wheel.

They tied him with his own belt, took his gun, emptied it and pocketed the spare magazines. He was not miked-up, which had been Herbie's main worry.

Nobody lurked in the alley. People passed in the sunshine on the main street, but today was a day for minding your own business. Gagging Max was easy; Herbie saw to it while Schnabeln disconnected the ignition and horn. They locked the doors, went round to the back and hefted Herbie's cases from the boot.

"*Hals und Beinbruch*," Herbie told Christoph Schnabeln — break your neck and leg: good luck.

"If there's no booking for you by six I'll write one in," Schnabeln told him. "Otherwise, plain sailing. Don't worry. I'll do everything."

Timing, thought Herbie. Timing was everything now. They went their different ways, Herbie walking at speed — a sight to see, the rolling unco-ordinated gait, dodging and ducking through the crowds. He did not see Schnabeln leave. The man just disappeared, like a spectre.

Herbie stopped three times on his way to the Bristol Kempinsky Hotel. Once to buy cigars, and once to purchase a camera and film. He knew exactly what he wanted, and the shop assistant did not argue. The last stop was to pick up a hat — a little trilby with a feather in it. Herbie did not usually wear hats. It made a great difference; so it was not the old Herbie Kruger who walked past the wall tanks, full of tropical fish, in the lobby of the Kempinsky — hat on head, heavy glasses, cigar stuck between his teeth, camera slung around his neck. The two bags were removed, very smoothly, by one of the porters. The staff saw him as the lone American traveller and hoped for largesse.

He had a reservation. Made by 'phone from London. The accent was German-American — he alternated words and sentences. Herbie was good at American-born Germans. Name of Krust. Elmer L. Krust, "Like in bread. Ha-ha."

The very correct assistant at the check-in desk smiled thinly. American humour was a closed book to him.

Herbie registered as from Denver, Colorado, signing his name with a flourish, cigar smoke curling. "A bath. I gotta have a bath or a shower." Then, suddenly, as if it had just come to mind, Herbie said that, as he was staying for a few days only, he wanted to make a trip into the East. "They do coach trips, don't they? See the nightlife?"

They did. The coaches left at six-thirty from depots near the Friedrichstrasse. There were several firms. Elmer L. Krust said he had one that was recommended, giving the name of the firm for which Schnabeln worked.

They would try and get him on tomorrow's tour. "They are heavily booked, Mr. Krust. Always difficulties."

Hell, tomorrow was no good. Tonight. Get him on tonight. They doubted the possibility, but would try. If he would go to his room, they would call him.

From the window of his room, Herbie could see the rising radio tower of the Funkfurm, its red light winking at the top. It was no time to look at views; or remember. Big Herbie, the quick-change artist. Out of his loose grey suit, into the checked trousers, an ill-matching shirt and the tartan jacket. Go through the pockets: tick off the list.

The telephone rang.

Mr. Krust was lucky. The firm had one place left on tonight's coach, but he would have to hurry. The coach left at six-thirty. Get him a cab. Mr. Krust would be down in three minutes.

Herbie looked at himself in the mirror. *Tannenbaum*, he thought. A bloody Christmas tree. He was going clean: no cases, not even the briefcase. Clean as the proverbial whistle. Only the Browning, because he might well need that. In tonight, out by Sunday night, with the job done. Schnabeln would see to the legwork: put a call out for Luzia Gabell, or Lotte Krug, or whatever she called herself these days; arrange the safe house meetings with the Telegraph Boys, even Electra, whom he would try and clear tonight . . .

The Browning lay snug in one of his rear pockets, the spare magazines in the other. They didn't check individually on the coaches. The firm took the passports in, and the Vopos came out to return them on the coach. You filled in all the forms before boarding in the West. Virtually a head count.

Downstairs, in the early evening bustle of the Kurfursten-damm, a cab waited for the big, overdressed American. It sagged visibly as he climbed into the rear, and took off into the traffic.

They got there with only five minutes to spare. Schnabeln talked and smoked with the driver; coming over to assist Elmer L. Krust to fill in the form, which the American did with ill grace – "What the hell they want to know how much money I got?" Regulations, said Schnabeln. You had to put down the exact amount. "And your passport, please, Mr. Krust."

On the coach there were other tourists – some English, and

217

a lot of Americans. "My family originated from here," Elmer Krust confided in a little old lady from Des Moines. "I come on a visit. Promised my grandpa when I was a kid. Good, eh? Europe's like coming home. Three days in London, two in Berlin, then back to Paris, and last of all Rome."

The Eternal City, the old lady from Des Moines commented.

"No, Rome," said Elmer L. Krust. "Where the Pope comes from."

Somebody said not this Pope. He came from the East; and the coach started off, heading towards the Friedrichstrasse checkpoint: Checkpoint Charlie, of other days and other lives.

11

In London, on a corner near Westminster Bridge, a young art student – doing a special project on modern architecture – was setting up his camera and tripod. He glanced at his light meter, certain he could get a good dramatic shot of the tall, oblong concrete and glass building.

He squinted into the lens, making the necessary adjustments to the mounting. He was the genuine article: innocent as a babe. It was a shock, therefore, when the unmarked police car drew up with a squeal, disgorging a pair of uniformed police who asked him, without courtesy, what in hell he thought he was doing?

He told them, truthfully, what he was doing and why. They examined his Student Union card, and one of the policemen returned to the car, to see if his name showed up in CRO. This usually only took a couple of minutes, because Criminal Records Office is now fully computerised. It took a mite longer in this case, because the police officer asked for a political check as well.

The boy was clean. "On your bike then, son," one of the policemen told him.

"Why?"

They said, no real reason. But he couldn't take any pictures of that particular building. "There are people who work there that don't like their pictures taken, lad. Right? So leave it alone, eh, there's a good boy."

The security officer on the eighth floor had spotted the student and called up the patrol. It was standard practice. At the Service Headquarters they did *not* like having photographs taken.

The Director and Tubby Fincher had not gone off for a Saturday afternoon, to their butterflies and kite flying, as Herbie had hoped. It was better, they argued, for them to be on tap in the top floor offices.

At Headquarters the top floor was where the Director lived, moved and had his being; but it was not really the top floor. The top floor was the penultimate floor. The next storey had windows made of black glass which no lens on earth could penetrate: that was the real top floor – where the communications people worked: 'C & C', they called it – Communications & Cryptanalysis.

At the moment the police were warning off the young student one of the cipher machines clattered out a signal in the C & C rooms. This particular message was long-haul, via Finland, to one of the Service's receiving stations in the far north of Scotland, thence to the main Cipher Station near Cheltenham. There, on starting to unzip the cipher, a senior cryptanalyst spotted the designation: *Head of Service or G Staff Only*. He had handled this traffic before, so dispatched it, direct, on a scrambled cipher machine to the C & C floor in London.

At the London end the operator picked up his telephone to ask where the Director was – surprised to learn that, on a Saturday afternoon, his chief was actually in the building. The Duty Head of C & C glanced at the signal and took it from the operator, heading for the lift, carrying it personally to the Director's office. Only the Director, or some designated officer, would be able to turn the groups of letters, typed on the blue signal sheet, into an *en clair* message. The Duty Head of C & C, a small sharp Welshman – known to all in the headquarters building as Jones the Spy – had also seen signals with this designation before. He had no idea of its origin: nor did he wish to know.

The Director knew, immediately. "Flash, urgent, from Stentor," he threw the information at Tubby Fincher, while half way between his desk and the safe, in which, among other things, he kept the Stentor ciphers.

In the *Iliad* Stentor was the herald, before Troy, with a fifty voice-power: hence Stentor being the cryptonym of the Service's deep penetration agent inside the First Directorate of the Russian Intelligence Service. It had taken years, and a series of devious ploys, to establish such a man deeply within Moscow Centre. Stentor was used with immense care: as infrequently as possible. *He* came to them, as a general rule. Only rarely did the Service go to him. Because of Stentor's age, and the method employed to place him, the man had only a couple more years of active life in him. Urgent flashes from Stentor invariably meant trouble.

The Director sat at his desk – the safe door still open – with the cipher books next to the signal: untangling the groups, his pen flicking between the blue flimsy and the lists of figures and letters, running in precise columns, in the book. Tubby Fincher watched the square face become more grave as he translated. Finally, in silence, the Director read through the signal twice, before passing it over to Fincher.

The urgent flash for Head of Service only, read:

AIRWAVE ERASED. LONG TERM BOIL ABOUT TO BURST DRENCHING TELEGRAPH BOYS THROUGH CIPHER TRAPEZE. NO KNOWLEDGE TRAPEZE. REGRET PROBABLY TOO LATE SAVE. ADVISE ATTEMPT. STENTOR

Airwave was a group of three agents, doing exactly the same early-warning job as Kruger's Telegraph Boys: though Airwave worked within Mother Russia itself.

The Director already had his hand on the telephone. He would have to go naked, as he called it: a direct open-line telephone conversation, through normal channels, to the top floor of the Mehring Platz building. There might still be time for Herbie to warn Schnabeln. If not, Berlin Station would have to be called in for a bring-'em-back-alive caper: lifting the Telegraph Boys into the West. He doubted the feasibility of this last option; but, whatever, Kruger's *Trepan* operation, to disinfect the Telegraph Boys, would have to be aborted.

*　　*　　*

The coach stood at the East Berlin end of Checkpoint Charlie, its passengers waiting patiently for their two friendly guides to return from the control and security offices. These days, in spite of the tightening of regulations, the East Berlin authorities made it as easy as reasonably possible when it came to coach parties of tourists.

Grepos, armed with Kalashnikov machine pistols, stood in pairs, occasionally glancing at the coach. One of them had, half-heartedly, pushed a mirror, mounted on wheels, attached to a long pole – like some child's toy – under the coach. Two others made the driver open up the vast luggage boot, which was empty.

A German officer came out with the two guides, carrying the passengers' passports and documents. He climbed on to the bus, the guide calling out names, the officer returning the passports to their owners, wishing them a pleasant evening in East Berlin. "You will enjoy yourself," he said to each passenger. It sounded like an order, but the whole business was most courteous.

The huge American, Elmer L. Krust, sat by patiently. He knew this place only too well, and memories jostled each other in his mind, quickening the tempo of his thoughts, so that he could almost hear them, a chaos, in his head.

Herbie did his best to neutralise this building cacophony of memories: of the times he had travelled East-West, and West-East. Of that hot August night in 1961 when the Wall went up, and the border closed, almost trapping him in the West. Of the years of clandestine shuttles; and the final debacle.

Faces floated through his mind – Julie Zudrang, Emil Habicht, shot down in the street; Willy Blenden; the Birkemanns making their escape; Gertrude Muller; Becher; Reissven; Kutte, and the treacherous Luzia Gabell. For a second he imagined he was going back to them. Then normality returned, and his mind locked on to the Telegraph Boys – the true reason for this dangerous, unauthorised, journey.

For a second he railed within himself, on the complacency of the man in the street within his adopted country. They slept with their glossy dreams – the house on the HP, the television, the car, the right to work; cheap package tours; the demos, escorted by police to show that demo meant democracy as well as demonstration.

On his way to the coach offices in the Friedrichstrasse the taxi had been forced to pull over as four police cars and vans dashed past, sirens wailing. In his assumed American-German Herbie asked what that was all about.

"Terrorists again," the driver shrugged. "Young idealists with their eyes closed to reality."

Four young men had hit one of the smaller government buildings, holding some civil servants and a minister to ransom. "They want two of their colleagues released and sent to Egypt, or somewhere." The driver made a hopeless gesture. "Tomorrow they'll be dead or arrested. But they'll be saints to their cause."

Herbie tried to marshal his thoughts: concentrating on his Telegraph Boys, wondering what each of them was doing at this very moment. In fact, all six were getting on with their individual lives, in different places, all of them not so very far from where Herbie Kruger sat, as Elmer L. Krust, in the coach at Checkpoint Charlie.

Martha Adler, Hecuba, was dressing in her bedroom. She knew well enough who the Russian major was, but he would serve her purpose. Major Kashov could be of great value, and she had no doubt about what he was after. Russian officers – even seasoned KGB people like Kashov – were not over-subtle when it came to dealing with women. The present he had handed to her, as she left the Political HQ just after five, was wrapped in gold paper. Silk stockings and underwear. French labels; real silk. Probably brought back into Russia by one of Kashov's team of travelling acrobats. What was it to her? She put it all on, admiring herself in the mirror. For her age her body was still very good. She would meet Kashov at eight. He would give her dinner and, later, the clothes would all come off. His presents were not really the kind of things women put on to wear, but to take off. Hecuba shook out her long ash blonde hair, twirling in front of the mirror. Not bad at all.

At the Soviet Embassy, on the Unter den Linden, 'The Professor' – Otto Luntmann, Horus – was just going on duty. Being on nights pleased him. As a civilian messenger he found there was never much work to do at nights, and he helped out the security guards, giving him the chance to ferret a little.

Better than that, it allowed him long periods of solitude during which he could sit back and read. The schoolmaster's stamp had never left Otto Luntmann, and the stooped shoulders signalled many hours of poring over books. At the moment he had dedicated himself to a complete study of the Roman Empire, and was ploughing through a translation of Gibbon's *Decline and Fall*. That evening he checked in at the Embassy with the happy thought that he would probably be able to finish the section on The Pagan Counter-Reformation. This pleased the scholar in him. Within his other life he also looked forward to a brief peep into the Soviet Military and Air Attaché's office. The secretaries were not good on security: occasionally gems were to be found in the litter bins.

Nikolas Monch, who had been cursed with grey hair since the age of twenty, was in his bath. Today, during the laborious work of wheeling filing trolleys from point to point along the avenues and corridors of the Nationale Volksarmee HQ, he had chanced on a dossier of some interest. The file contained more information concerning his most recent reports about pilots of the DDR's Air Force being in the process of converting to the Russian Foxbat fighters. The file in question listed most detailed data on the number of pilots to undergo the conversion courses; dates; and training areas. There was also a note concerning delivery of the Russian fighters to the Deutsche Demokratische Republik, their dispersal and reorganisation of the DDR's Fighter Wings.

Monch had a good memory. As he lay in his bath he went over the figures, places and dates. Later, after a meal – there was a small piece of stewing steak cooking – he would settle down to compose a report and transfer it to cipher. Tomorrow he had a drop set up, on his way to collect the milk. Every other Sunday was a free day for Monch. Tomorrow he did not have to go to work.

In her neat little apartment Ursula Zunder sat crouched over the table, composing her next cipher. It was important; her target – the Minister of the Interior – had now been summoned, after all those countless meetings at the Political HQ, to a special delegation in Moscow, on the third of next month. She gathered that the Moscow trip had something to do with reorganisation of Soviet and East German forces.

Ursula paused, in the middle of completing the first half of the cipher, her mind suddenly alert, as though she expected something to happen. Her nerves were on edge. It had been like this for the last few weeks. She had dreamed a lot of the large man whose heart she still held within her own. A wave of misery clouded her for a few moments, before she pulled herself together. Life was not fair: fairy tales did not always have happy endings. Not asking for love, she had found and lost it – irretrievably now. Yet, there was a stirring in the air. The scent of the past, redolent in her nostrils, as though she could smell her old lover close at hand.

Moritz Winter, the joker, was already well on the way to being drunk. As chief civilian storeman at the Soviet Army HQ, Karlshorst, his duties finished at noon on Saturdays. He had nothing particularly new to translate into cipher, or put on a tape; so today Moritz had gone home, bathed, put on his best bib and tucker, then set out for a crawl along the bars.

At this moment he was drinking in the Wolff bar on the Karl-Marx-Allee, with its ugly Soviet architecture, the workers' flats and shops and the wide pavements. Winter had known the Karl-Marx Allee from before it was even the 'Stalinallee'. It would be a good week-end, he thought. Plenty to drink, then, perhaps . . . well, who knew? He leaned over the bar to tell the barman a story he had heard at Karlshorst; about a Russian General, a farmer and the farmer's daughter.

Out of Berlin, within the perimeter of the headquarters of General Soviet forces East Germany, Priam – Peter Sensel – was in bed with his Russian lover. The Russian was assistant adjutant to the Commander-in-Chief: a lad really, ten years younger than Sensel.

Both were aware that discovery almost certainly meant the end for them. What they were doing was still considered to be a weakness and perversion within the Soviet army. But the young officer was, in his way, deeply in love with the chubby, scruffy German maintenance man. They kissed affectionately and clasped each other.

Sensel wished beyond measure that he had been born a woman. There were nights when he could weep at the manner in which his body and mind could never be reconciled. Since his teens Sensel had dreamed of the wonders of sexual fulfilment by having a man implanting his seed to grow within *his* body. He longed for the organs which should, by right, at birth have been his – breasts, and the female parts with which he had not been blessed.

He took his young Russian in his arms, and began to make love to him for the third time. In the back of his mind he knew the officer would soon have to return to duty, while he would make his usual week-end journey into Berlin.

Almost since taking up the job at Zossen-Wunsdorf Peter Sensel had managed to find Russian lovers. That part of him which was Priam made certain the lovers were all close to the Commander-in-Chief – or at least within his office. The Russian officers seemed to like German civilians as lovers, and there were only a few months, out of all the time he had gone about his clandestine duties, when access to the C-in-C could not be had through a man who shared his bed.

Priam, Horus, Nestor, Electra, Hecuba, Gemini; Herbie thought, waiting in the coach. Moritz Winter; Otto Luntmann; Ursula Zunder; Nikolas Monch; Peter Sensel and Martha Adler. They were all out there, somewhere in front of him: going about their overt, and covert, lives – and one of them was a tiny plague-bacillus he had to destroy.

The guides, and the officer, had almost completed the formalities, the officer chatting genially with Schnabeln's colleague.

Herbie thought, not for the first time, that the small, apple-cheeked Christoph Schnabeln reminded him of someone he could not quite place. Now, as the coach moved forward, and the barriers were raised, he made the connection. The study of English history again. Henry II, and Sir Richard Baker's *Chronicle of the Kings of England: He was somewhat red of face, and broad-breasted; short of body, and therewithal fat, which made him use much exercise and little meat.* Herbie smiled. Christoph Schnabeln as King Henry II of England. He chuckled again. *Henry Shortmantle.*

East Berlin rose around them on either side, as the coach proceeded down the eastern end of the Friedrichstrasse. Herbie glanced to his right; eyes searching ahead. Yes, it was still there, the little café – looking more dilapidated now, peeling paint and wood, but open all the same. The place where he had taken Ursula Zunder on that evening of their first meeting – the coffee that turned into a full meal.

Herbie's great body gave a shudder: the muscles relaxing and tightening. For a moment, darkness covered his thoughts; only to be replaced by excitement. He looked up and saw Schnabeln raise his wrist to note the time, scowling at the adjusting screw; then depressing it.

The bleep would, now, be plotting the coach's position on the screen, in the Mehring Platz control room. He wondered if young Worboys had deciphered his screech; and if so what kind of panic was going on.

With the mischievous sense of a schoolboy Herbie lowered his eyes, touched the button on his wrist-watch, and gave the Mehring Platz a fifteen-second burst of his own Dip-Dah signal.

*　　*　　*

Worboys had been flirting with Miriam Grubb instead of getting on with the work. Enjoying the attention, and looking almost radiantly happy, Miriam kept one eye on the scanning screen, while Worboys whispered – sometimes lasciviously – into her ear. At last, with a giggle, she winked and reluctantly told him he should really unzip the screech, or there would be hell to pay when Big Herbie arrived.

He had the screech on a cassette, fully slowed to the speed of the day. He had even listened to it – Big Herbie's voice, vibrating in the cans, reading off the groups in over-precise English. Transfer. Slow. Now he keyed-in the day's word, which happened to be 'Plate' and pressed the run-through. Magic. The groups coming up in red on the screen: the print-out clicking away like a mini telex.

The unraveller gave a little squawk to show that part of the job was complete.

Worboys tore off the print-out, placing it beside the machine, switching to manual decipher. He took his time, making certain that he tapped out each group correctly on the keyboard, occasionally glancing at the little oblong screen, where the groups showed red, then flashed into words – electric blue, the print-out clicking away again.

After eight words his mouth started to dry. As the message progressed, he managed to get out a soft, "Sweet Jesus."

Tiptoes looked across sharply, worried, asking what was wrong; and, at that moment, Miriam called out, "There he is. Spendthrift's through. He's through Charlie."

The bleeping of Spendthrift's homer came out clear, and the pin of light pulsed on the screen, the map shifting with a whirr on to the Friedrichstrasse section. The pulsing moved forward, just as the coach travelled up the East Berlin section of the Friedrichstrasse.

Then – "Christ," shouted Tiptoes. "What the hell's this?"

Everyone's eyes went to the screen. For fifteen seconds, Spendthrift's homing signal was joined by the other signal, the dot-dash: both sounds clashing in the speakers.

Worboys had the completed screech now, ripping the print-out from the machine. "That's what it is. Oh my God. Herbie's gone over. He's over the Wall with Spendthrift."

Miriam Grubb snatched the print-out from Worboys, reading aloud. As she read, in a fast jumble, running the words together, so the homer signals cut out. They were expecting Spendthrift signals at about half-hour intervals from now.

"*Sorry*," Miriam read from the print-out. "*I have to do the job myself with Spendthrift's help. Max in car. Undamaged. Will use spare homer. Back Sunday night. Apologise for inconvenience. Surgeon.*"

"Jesus," Worboys kept saying.

At that moment the telephone began to ring, and Charles, looking as if someone had hit him, dived at it. A second later he had his hand over the mouthpiece. "I've told him Herbie's not here. He wants to speak to you." He looked at Worboys, who asked who wanted to speak with him. "The Director. 'Phoning on an open-line." Charles held out the instrument as though it was some kind of explosive.

Worboys heard the Director out – if Kruger had not yet arrived he had to take charge. *Trepan* was to be aborted. Soviet agent Trapeze – no knowledge – was about to pull the watchers. Tell Kruger to signal, immediate from Berlin Station.

As calmly as possible Worboys broke the news. There was silence for a few moments, then the Director said Worboys was to keep track of the situation. Berlin Station would be informed from London. Somebody would come out. Then the Director asked him to read Herbie's screech. Unheard of – clear on an open-line.

"My God," was all the Director managed, before closing the connection.

*   *   *

The coach's first stop was at 'a typical tourist shop', where the visitors could buy souvenirs. The shop was kept open especially for the coach party, and they would have twenty minutes to do their shopping. Only foreign currency would be accepted. After this they would be going to the Budapest Bar.

"Guess I'll meet you all at the Budapest Bar," Elmer L. Krust told the old lady from Des Moines. "Can't stand tourist shops."

"You think that's allowed?" she asked. "They have regulations."

"It'll be okay. I'll have a word with the guide. I got me a street plan before we left. Budapest's not far from here." Herbie did not want any alerts from other passengers – particularly if they might affect Schnabeln, who was smilingly seeing the passengers off the coach. The other guide was already with them, in the shop. The driver had climbed down to stretch his legs.

"You go on ahead," Herbie told the old lady, who said he was kind and considerate.

Herbie was the last to leave the coach. He paused, nodding to Schnabeln. Okay? Schnabeln gave him a nod, and Herbie, as he lowered his head to leave the coach, groped under the front seat, grabbing the handles on a small canvas Adidas holdall. Schnabeln's brief had been to get the bag, shaving gear and a large raincoat. The holdall would be enough to prove Herbie had luggage when he arrived at the Metropol, where Schnabeln had arranged a room – 'phoning from the coach firm's offices which had a line through to the hotel. In place of the Adidas bag Herbie left the Krust passport. They would at least see it at the checkpoint. Schnabeln, swiftly picking it up, knew that the headcounts were never very efficient on the return night coach trips.

Without another word Herbie swung down the steps. Schnabeln went after him, going around the coach and into the shop, where the tourists bought cheap souvenirs, including a number of traditional Russian gifts – the hollow dolls that fitted inside one another; medallions; tins of caviar. He would place the Krust passport with the others.

Herbie, shielded from their view by the coach, now walked upright and with speed, knowing exactly where he was going, sniffing the air, completely orientated, back in his old environment. It held no fears for him now, this part of the city: memories by the score, but no fears. Even his rolling, shambling gait disappeared. He had used that disorganised walk for the whole time he worked in East Berlin, and still affected it daily in London. But now, as an American tourist, the bearing was almost military. At speed it would take him about ten minutes to reach the Metropol. People did not even stare at the big figure in the loud clothes; he was so obviously an American visitor. The second US passport, cobbled together in Camden Town, had a visa stamp for that morning – hours before – and was in the name of Herbert Kagen.

Half way to his destination two youths stopped him to ask if he had any dollars they could buy – offering fifty per cent above the official rate. Herbie pretended not to understand. He wanted the comparative safety of the hotel, and a place to stash the Browning.

Every vista seemed dominated by the Russian-built television mast, ugly and functional, with a bulbous restaurant in the tower. A lot of building had taken place since Herbie's last visit, but he could still find his way – like a blind man working through extra sense and feel. Banners proclaimed the old clichés, using the same words he remembered, but sometimes in a different key – "Forward With Good Deeds and Higher Productivity". The ugly white barrack blocks of apartments sickened him; yet they were very familiar, even in their newness.

They were expecting Herr Kagen at the Metropol. Herbie had organised that well in advance. One might be in the West here: the lavishness and order. The staff jumped when you spoke; they showed courtesy, even if they despised you with their eyes. The room was large, well-furnished and pleasant. He could not have wished for better. Schnabeln would come to see him around midnight. In the meantime, Big Herbie Kruger would take a trip down memory lane.

PART THREE

Trapeze

1

In LONDON THE Director put down the telephone, staring at Tubby Fincher for almost a full minute before speaking. He looked, thought Fincher, like a man who had just witnessed an appalling accident. Bewildered and angry.

Eventually he said that Big Herbie was on the loose. He spoke flatly, as though it was a personal affront. "Gave Max the slip."

Tubby Fincher pursed his thin lips, emitting a little hissing noise. It was always on the cards, he mumbled. "Really thought we had him tied up, though."

"Gone over," the Director repeated several times in a sort of chant. "In East Berlin now. At this very moment. Christ."

Tubby Fincher, lifting his skeletal body from the chair, opened his mouth to ask what kind of action the Director had taken. The answers were supplied before the question was even out. Worboys was holding the fort; the Director had promised somebody would be over, *et cetera, et cetera.*

Deep within his silent logic the Director knew exactly what he should do. This was a serious situation; one to be played by the book. In terms of the book there was only one way: a complete shutdown. Pull the *Trepan* team out; leave Herbie to stew. By the book, they would have to deny Herbie Kruger; for he had denied them.

So far the whole operation had been limited to a circle which encompassed only the Director, Tubby Fincher, Herbie and the *Trepan* team. All the thinking had been one of containment. Herbie's chances of getting Schnabeln to sniff out the person the Director called "the rotting plant in the East Wing's cellarage," would have been reduced if Berlin

Station had access – spoiled by allowing their street men the opportunity to offer a helping hand. A friend in need, someone once said, is a pest.

The major error was now very clear. There should have been some strictly controlled two-way radio traffic. Gloomily the Director realised that Herbie had outmanoeuvred him by not suggesting it. Sins of omission were often the most deadly.

They had cut out two-way traffic because of the decision regarding containment: relying on Herbie and the *Trepan* team to track Schnabeln with the electronic wizardry. Berlin Station assumed the Kruger-Schnabeln meeting was routine. They would only be brought into play for the end game, when the entrapment was complete.

The whole thing was planned and double-checked in this very office. Herbie had agreed: all professional and smooth. Schnabeln's homer would guide them. His screech would give the name and details of the traitor among the Telegraph Boys. Once Herbie was satisfied with the screech – which included him being certain it came from Schnabeln, fast-sending from a designated point – he would personally go to lay the news on the Head of Berlin Station. In turn, Head of Station would verify with the Director.

They had allowed a four-hour lapse between reception of Schnabeln's screech and the end game. Four hours, with half-hour fallbacks. Schnabeln's job was to identify, and then snare the guilty Telegraph Boy, leading him to a pre-determined spot – near Treptow Park. The rest would be up to Berlin's trained street men operating in the East.

As for the details, the Director had been confident they could be left safely in the hands of Herbie and Head of Berlin Station. Once Herbie had the full facts the decision would not be too difficult – though the options were limited. With Schnabeln as a lure the target would either be eliminated there and then or lifted: snatched, hidden up and smuggled out. After that, the ultimate decision – whether to pull out the remaining Telegraph Boys and, possibly, the Quartet – would be the Director's alone. The heavy work would be done by Berlin street men. Simple. No mess. Containment until the last possible moment. As for the final instructions, it had been the Director's intention from the beginning to whisk Herbie out of Berlin the moment the target had been neutralised, one way or another. After that, the order regarding both the Telegraph Boys and the Quartet would go from London: with Herbie safe, and not able to baulk at the possibility of seeing the last remnants of his East Berlin teams being hauled out.

That was academic now. The advent of the unknown, cryptonymed Trapeze, together with Herbie going rogue on them, altered the situation. Any former plans might just as well go into the shredder.

The Director's hand hovered over the telephone. By rights he should flash Berlin Station now. Put them in the picture, remove the *Trepan* team, and close the shutters – send Herbie to the isolation ward; which meant almost certainly sending the faithful Telegraph Boys and the Quartet with him. "I told Worboys that someone would be out," the Director looked at Fincher as though appealing for help.

From where? Tubby Fincher asked. From here or Berlin Station?

The Director shrugged, not answering, but taking his hand away from the telephone. "We can't even warn the idiot," he spoke to the window. "Could haul him back with the help of Berlin, I suppose. But I think, if we have to deny – when they get Herbie – it would be best if Berlin knew nothing at this stage. You know about muddied water, Tub. Young Worboys is there – capable – just needs a parental hand on his shoulder. Someone who can organise a quick dismantle if it does fall apart."

"You looking at me?" Fincher raised a hand, the fingers like a claw, all bone and no flesh. Then he continued, pointing out that his chief had just contradicted himself. *When* they get Herbie, the Director had said. *If* it does fall apart, the Director had said.

Both men were aware of the reasons for the apparent double-think. They knew Herbie's limitations. They were also well versed in his tremendous experience and will to survive. The Director pointed out that Kruger knew the ground and the personalities better than anyone in the Service. It was as though the senior man was trying to lift the ghastly situation a couple of notches into optimism.

"It's the emotional thing," the Director grunted, muttering

like an old man trying to make a decision, eking out his pension in a supermarket. "Emotional business. Worrying. Worried me from the start."

Tubby Fincher's shoulders rose and fell. "You want me to go and hold Worboys' hand. See it through." He was not asking, but stating a fact.

"It would still contain things, if . . ."

"If Big Herbie happened to pull it off?" Fincher actually laughed aloud. "Okay, I'll contain it for as long as possible. Rorke's Drift, what? I'll go, if that's what you want. Contain, then wrap it up the moment it explodes." He added that he was certain it would explode. Herbie Kruger could not last long in East Berlin. "Give him twenty-four hours. Probably less. Our Herbie's a known commodity. Passage of time means little to Moscow Centre. They mark your card, it stays marked. Give you the Black Spot, that's it. For life."

The Director agreed about the twenty-four hours, but said Herbie might just manage it in the time: clinging on to straws. Then, without warning, his fury burst. "I'll have his balls for this: stupid, sentimental, big, idiotic Kraut."

Tubby was always one for rationalising other people's thought processes. Now he found himself doing it for Herbie. If you put yourself into Herbie Kruger's brain, the thinking was rational enough, he argued. With the confessing of Tapeworm, Herbie would consider his career fully blown anyway. The myth and legend had shattered. Within those given circumstances the revenge motive would be strong enough in any man. Herbie, the cold professional, had gone rogue on them; and not surprising. Revenge and, maybe, bring out the woman – Electra. They all knew about Electra, in spite of Herbie. "Bit of comfort for his old age, what?"

"In lieu of pension," the Director snapped. "You on then, Tubby?"

Fincher nodded.

Once more the Director grabbed at the telephone, this time to speak to movements control: ordering something very fast from the RAF, to Berlin for Fincher. "I want a magic carpet," he said. Then, when it was arranged, he rattled off orders. Fincher was to assess and take action – the Director's responsibility. If things were very bad, and they managed to track

Herbie, Berlin Station could send the dogs in and pull him out. "But only if there's grave risk. Try and contain for as long as possible; and remember, it would be better if Herbie went the journey rather than being dried out in Moscow – the stupid clown. Kill him if you have to."

The Director was known for his calm under pressure. Now the voice and the ruthlessness of the orders shook Tubby Fincher. He reflected that the Director must be very, very fond of Big Herbie.

*   *   *

At that moment Herbie, now the American Herbert Kagen, bleeped the *Trepan* team from his room in the Metropol Hotel.

"Bloody hell," Tiptoes reacted as the map swivelled on the screen. "The bugger's installed himself in their one decent doss house."

"Nerve," Worboys said without betraying any feeling, controlling the quake in his bowels and knowing that it was for Herbie: fear for the lumbering giant.

In the background Charles was doing his nut about Max. He had gone on about Max ever since Worboys unzipped Herbie's message.

"For Christ's sake go out and find him yourself, Charles," Worboys turned in his chair, glaring at the lion-tamer. "Out," he shouted. "Out. You know which way they were heading when they left the Dahlmannstrasse. Follow your nose and get your little chum out." He added that he presumed Charles had enough instruments concealed about his person to open up a car.

Charles, taking Worboys at his word, turned and left without even thanking him.

Worboys said it would stop the rattle anyway. He had the volume on the receiver turned right up – a low hum in the background – and hardly took his eyes off the VUs in case a screech came over sooner than expected. Miriam leaned back, watching the screen, smoking another of Worboys' cigarettes.

"Done it now, young fella-me-lad," sneered Tiptoes. "Nobody to get coffee or grub."

"Just watch the bloody screen and keep reporting. I'm in the chair until they send someone else in."

"Soddin' SNAFU," Tiptoes snarled.

"Masterful," grinned Miriam Grubb.

Tony Worboys could not think of any retort. He stayed silent, pondering on the pressures that had sent Herbie over the Wall into the East. Poor bugger, he thought.

2

IN THE LOBBY of the Metropol they wanted to know if Herr Kagen required a car or taxi. They could arrange it in minutes. Herr Kagen said not today, thank you, in poor German, with an atrocious American accent. He would like a map, though. He thought a little stroll would do him good. Could they recommend a place to eat? The hotel restaurant was good; they thought he should come back to the hotel. Herr Kagen said he would think about it. He found it most interesting to be in East Berlin and, with that, left through the main doors, conscious of the hard black pistol, held with a makeshift harness – fashioned with a necktie – around his thigh. Not any good for the fast draw, he knew. But it was there if he wanted it, and had time to pull the tie end which would allow the weapon to fall down his trouser leg. Another trick they taught at the school, where a certain hypocrisy reigned, because they forbade the carrying of arms in the field – except under special authorisation.

It was starting to sink into dusk, but there were, oddly, more people about: the warm evening dragging couples from their workers' flats, or apartments, on to the streets. Whatever their politics Germans were all great evening strollers.

Herbie walked without purpose: a harmless tourist with an envied expensive camera on his shoulder. A big American. A big quiet American, he smiled. The aimless ramble had purpose. With nobody to watch out for him, Herbie did all the tricks of a singleton. He watched faces; the few cars; feet; shoes and headgear; looking for repeats. As if on a whim, he would suddenly cross the road – glancing carefully left and right – turn down streets, or double back. At one point he stood, close to a handy shop-front, where the glass acted as a mirror, as though examining his map, which he carried open, a passport to his tourism.

Yet, very gradually, going by a long and devious route, Herbie was getting nearer and nearer his goal. A clever street man would be able to follow the pattern. The dog-legs and angles he took brought Herbie in a series of ragged, zig-zagged circles, closing in each time on the apartment block he knew so well. The place where, on that November evening so long ago now, he had returned Ursula Zunder; to stand waving farewell and think about holding the magazines that had been so close to the secrets of her body.

There was a moment, when he began to close in on the area, that Herbie wished, with great fervour, that he had someone watching out for him. For no particular reason he recalled long talks with other field officers about whom they would choose to watch out for them. One American had been unyielding with his priorities. In a foreign country, alone and lost, he would prefer, first, the aid of Mossad, the Israeli service, because of their sense of survival; second, his own service which was, of course, the CIA. Herbie's Service – the British – ran third; while the man's fourth and fifth choices were, unequivocally, the KGB and the Cuban General Directorate of Intelligence.

In the same circumstances Herbie would have made similar choices, swapping the British Service and the CIA; but that was because of his personal familiarity with his own Service.

He was behind the block now. Circle once more. Check the lights in the windows. Make sure she's in, and pray there's nobody with her. In a sudden flurry of anxiety he wondered if the block still had the same house superintendent, who would certainly recognise him. Then he realised that was not possible. The fellow had been old and on the point of retire-ment; a new one would have replaced him long ago. Herbie would still have to try avoidance. The last thing he wanted was to be spotted, by anyone, going in or out.

There was a light in Ursula's apartment. The curtains were not drawn; the window open against the warm evening. Herbie went on walking, occasionally glancing up, hoping to spot movement. One or two people? He would have liked to know.

God in heaven, he wished he could have at least brought Schnabeln for cover. Again, impossible. If it was to be set up quickly Christoph would have his own work cut out that night: a feigned illness to get him away from the tourist bus, then a fast round-up of the rest of the Quartet, who would have to take to the streets in search of their personal Telegraph Boys. The messages, the timings, the meets which had to be prepared for tomorrow. Then, on top of that, the word passed for a woman who used to live in the Weibensee district, and was known as Luzia Gabell or Lotte Krug; depending on the light and year.

Schnabeln had said this would be relatively easy. There was an old buddy who worked in the Vopo Records Office. "Spin him the story. A flame from the past. He's a romantic. I make it sound good, and he'll go all starry eyed." Thus Christoph Schnabeln in the Dahlmannstrasse house, openly, for part of Herbie's brief had been to lay the ghost of Luzia Gabell. Max could pass all that to London. No problem.

He was approaching the doors to the apartment block now, again wishing he had a car handy, or someone placed at a good angle to signal safety. At least he was ninety-nine per cent sure there were no leeches on his tail.

The house superintendent was not in evidence. Low wattage bulbs burned in the bleak lobby – bare stone floor, walls of rough concrete on which some Party artist had tried to create a mural – great ugly figures, depicting the Workers' Struggle: agricultural on one wall, industrial on the other, with a battle raging on the third. A lot of people seemed to be lifting barges and toting bales. An equally large number appeared to be getting shot. The artist was good with blood. He was, Herbie thought wryly, probably an ancestor of Jack the Ripper. All the figures had square faces with big chins, and even the women sported shoulders like nightclub bouncers.

Slowly and heavily, Herbie began to mount the stone staircase. Ursula lived on the fourth floor. He knew the stairs almost by heart, and his memory had not played false. On the third floor he saw the door to the first flat. When he had been with Ursula, in this building, that particular apartment was owned by a couple of elderly people who seemed to have a vast army of sons and daughters. They would all come and visit every Sunday. One of the sons, Herbie knew, had been killed by the Grepos while trying to cross the Wall in '63. The couple had been prostrate with grief, and the SSD had men there, quizzing them for days after it happened.

At last the fourth floor. The crack in the wall, at the turning of the stairs, had not been plastered but had grown bigger with the years, like a jagged wound bursting from its stitches. Cement and plaster flaked away from either side in large lumps, making a map of tributaries and lakes from the broad river of the crack.

Along the passage. Still bare concrete, some areas scrubbed clean; dirty patches elsewhere. Ursula's was the third door on the right – a front-facing apartment.

The first door – Kurt and Karren Pilger. Good Party members. Dour and devoted. Communists from Hitler's day. The second door – they'd be dead and gone now, for they were an old couple, ailing, afraid of being separated and taken to different hospitals. The Händlers. Franz and Jessie Händler.

Just before he knocked at her door – their old, special knock: duh-duh-duh dump-dump – Herbie thought about Christoph Schnabeln, hoping that he had managed to get away: that he was making contact. Then he heard her feet; quick, still the agile, half-loping, run. Did he imagine the sound of hope in the noise of her feet coming towards the door? The lock and the bolts. Then –

The figure was still trim and neat. There were a few lines, small crows' feet around the eyes; and a greyness to the hair, but it was still Ursula. Really she did not look changed at all, the hair remaining copper in spite of the frost of grey; the eyes dark with flecks showing, even in the dim passage light; the nose, unchanged – Italian from her grandmother. The oval face seemed flat, the expression blank for the fraction of a second, then her hand flew to her mouth, and he saw the tears springing into her eyes, the mouth breaking open half in grief and half in joy, as the words came out in a long whispering wail of disbelief – "Herbie – Herbie. My God. Herbie, my darling Herbie," and she was in his arms, fragile but soft against him as though he had never been away.

Herbie held her, crushed her with his great bear arms. Through the blur of tears in his own eyes he saw, over her shoulder, that nothing had changed – the Dürer pen and ink drawing of the Avenging Angel hung near the door to the bedroom. The copy of the Meissen figurine stood on the shelf. And, behind it, the ruby glasses with facet-cut stems.

3

FROM THE SOUVENIR shop the coach party went as promised for a drink at the Budapest. They were then taken on a quick tour of the darkening streets – up the relatively new Lenin Allee, back through the Marx-Engels-Platz, then up the old Unter den Linden to view, from the coach, the Brandenburg Gate. It did not look much different when seen from the East than it did from the West.

After this pointless joyride the party moved on to the radio tower, where, in the bulbous, ugly functional restaurant, they were to have dinner. After dinner, Schnabeln told them, they would visit one of East Berlin's more famous night spots. He had forgotten which one was on tonight's itinerary, and had to refer to his colleague – Rudy Frettcher – who said that tonight, being Saturday, was a special occasion. They would be taken to the Metropol bar and restaurant where there was dancing and a floor show.

Christoph Schnabeln had missed that point. It consciously flicked through his mind that Herbie had better be out of sight when the tour arrived at the Metropol. The American lady from Des Moines had already asked him – quietly, thank God – if the big man who had been sitting next to her was all right. He assured her that everything was in order. She was not to worry if he did not show up again. "He wanted to spend the night with friends here. I've told him where to get permission."

At the radio tower restaurant Schnabeln made straight for the men's room, hefting his briefcase, never letting it out of sight for a moment. The room was empty, and he quickly doused his face with water, watching the elderly attendant

246

through the mirror as he combed his hair. The attendant was not interested in Schnabeln. In a few moments the male members of the coach party would be in, and the man's mind was on the possibility of tips in foreign currency. Tipping was not allowed; but nobody refused it.

With his head down, Schnabeln's hand closed around the bar of cheap soap in place on the wash-basin, sliding a thumbnail deep over one corner to break off a small piece, slipping it into his mouth, holding it there for a moment and then swallowing. The nausea came very quickly. The thought of swallowing soap had already brought on a queasiness. The act itself did the trick. Schnabeln retched, grabbed the briefcase, turned, and headed for one of the lavatories.

"Too much to drink, Comrade?" the old attendant shouted.

Schnabeln retched again. The soap genuinely made him feel ill. "No," he replied between the bouts of nausea. No, he had not taken anything to drink. A bug, perhaps. Or something he ate.

"Something you ate here?" the elderly attendant did not seem surprised. Then there were noises; people coming into the men's room.

Schnabeln swallowed, held on to the briefcase, and came out to see Rudy Frettcher acting as shepherd to the tourists. As he made for the wash-basins again, Frettcher spotted him, asking if he was okay. "You look terrible. Like the walking dead."

Schnabeln said he had not felt good all day. It was terrible now. He had been sick.

"Hoffer's outside," Frettcher motioned with his head. "Wants to see you. Seems anxious."

Schnabeln might have known that his boss would be on hand as soon as possible following the return from the West. He would be worried about the schedules. His threats before Schnabeln left were really caused by the man's own anxiety. Even the Germans in the East seemed to have caught the Russian disease of passing the buck, as the Americans called it. Hoffer's superiors would want to know if the regular tourist coach trips were to be reduced. If there were major changes which might affect the regular income they would scream at Hoffer. Hoffer would scream at Schnabeln.

He went unsteadily out into the main body of the restaurant.

"My God, you look terrible," Hoffer greeted him.

Schnabeln said he thought it was a bug. He had felt rotten all day, and had just been sick.

"What's the news?" Schnabeln's illness would not deter Hoffer from the main course of business.

Schnabeln asked if he could sit down for a minute, and his boss became solicitous. Eventually Schnabeln gave him the patter, just as Herbie had told him. The news was good. There was to be no reduction of coach trips for the time being – in spite of the high prices and the general recession. In fact the bookings appeared to be up for September, and the firm might even have to run two buses on some nights. However, they were not altogether happy about the evening trips. There had been some complaints. They would have to make certain that only the best places were used. He was sorry; that was mainly his fault. He would write a report tomorrow. Now, he felt too sick.

Hoffer scowled at the business about complaints, but showed obvious relief that the tours were not to be reduced. Christoph Schnabeln had better go home, back to the Metropol. "See the doctor. Maybe he'll give you something. You probably ate rich in the West. I would never trust the food over there."

Schnabeln thanked him, as Rudy Frettcher came out of the men's room. Waiters stood near, ready to conduct the party to their tables. Again, Frettcher asked how his comrade was feeling. Hoffer, with his most brusque pomposity, announced that Rudy would have to take over the tour on his own. Christoph was not well enough to see the evening through.

Schnabeln once more said thank you – starting towards the door, purposely only remembering that he held the passports in his briefcase when he was almost out of the restaurant. The nausea had begun to pass. With a weak, wry smile, he opened the case, handing over the passports to Frettcher. They included the American passport belonging to the large Elmer L. Krust, pushed down into the middle of the pile. As long as they had no trouble with a headcount – at the Eastern end of the checkpoint on the way back – the passport would be removed from the pile by someone at the control point at the Western end. Herbie had arranged all that.

"Some panic if I'd taken these," Schnabeln allowed the smile to fade, nodded his thanks again to Hoffer, apologised for the extra work he had loaded on to Rudy Frettcher, and left, weaving slightly.

Once outside Christoph Schnabeln shook off the sickness by walking fast: concentrating on the job in hand. The Wartburg was at the Metropol, and he would need that for making quick, personal contact with the other three members of the Quartet. Before that he could make the call to his Vopo friend, hoping the man was on duty, either that night or first thing in the morning. The tracing of Luzia Gabell would be impossible if the policeman – a sergeant – had the week-end off. Christoph could not push the old flame idea too hard.

Luck was a lady, and with him. At the Metropol he told the duty man on the desk that Hoffer had sent him back because of his upset stomach; but he was feeling much better now. He winked, as if to bring the man on the desk into a conspiracy. "I've had two days slogging away at those bastard tour operators in the West. I don't intend to work tonight, see?"

The desk clerk saw, and smiled as he watched Schnabeln make for the public telephone booth in the foyer. The Vopo sergeant was not at home. "Night duty shift for the next three weeks," his wife said, not sounding that unhappy about it. At the far end of the line Schnabeln thought he heard the sound of a man's cough. He grinned to himself, making farewells quickly, and dialled the Volkspolizei Headquarters, where his friend would be on duty.

Yes, anything for an old comrade, the Vopo sergeant said. There was not much doing tonight. Later it would probably get busy, but he would run through the files and call him back.

No, Christoph told him. He would be out. "I'll call you, later, from some bar. I'm really working, but I just got to thinking about her. If she's at a loose end . . . well . . . You know how it is . . .?"

The police sergeant knew how it was. Nobody better. He would be there until six. "If you find her and she's any good, I might look her up myself," the Vopo laughed. "Let me know."

Schnabeln went out to the Wartburg. There was no point in going to Walter Girren's place yet. He did not finish at the theatre until after ten o'clock. First he would see Anton Mohr, out in Köpenick; then a quick trip to Anna Blatte. If she did not leap on him he might have time to trace his own people – Hecuba and Priam. There was an emergency routine for urgent contact. But on a Saturday night, you could not be certain. It could be tomorrow before messages reached the men and women serviced by the Quartet, and Herbie had been adamant that his private meetings – using the only two safe houses available – should begin not later than eleven on the Sunday morning.

As he turned the car in the direction of the Köpenick district Schnabeln caught sight of his wrist-watch. Jesus. Every half-hour. He was supposed to bleep the West every half-hour. Setting the car on a straight stretch of road, Christoph Schnabeln brought his hands together on top of the wheel and operated the button, giving a thirty-second burst of his long bleeps.

*   *   *

"At last," Tiptoes Corn noted the bleep. Miriam Grubb logged the time. "Spendthrift," she said. "Moving, and very near the Metropol Hotel."

Worboys wondered, aloud, if Spendthrift and Herbie were together. Of Charles there was no sign. Still searching for Max, or prising open car doors. No more news from London, either. The Director had somebody coming over, and gave the impression that it would be from Berlin Station. They should be here by now. Worboys invoked every deity known to him, from the Trinity downwards. He could deal with the screech, but did not like the idea of being in sole charge of this lot.

Miriam Grubb saw his expression, and reached over, clasping Worboys' hand. It would work out, she said quietly. It would work out, and when it was over they would have Honeymoon Potatoes again – in better surroundings.

Tony Worboys gave her a weak grin, and felt the familiar stirrings of his body; reflecting that he lusted amazingly after Miriam Grubb. For a second or two his mind riffled through a few of the basic facts, in very clear vision, but without the sound.

Then the telephone rang, and the Director was on the line from London, his voice calm in Worboys' ear, while Miriam kept an eye on the VUs in case the screech came early.

*   *   *

In the building near Westminster Bridge, in London, the cipher machines had been speaking their own uneasy languages.

Tubby Fincher was on his way, by car, to Northolt where a Harrier jet stood by to ferry him into Berlin, cleared as military traffic and heading for Gatow.

As Fincher left the building the Director reflected that he looked less like a warrior of the secret world than any other man he knew – this rake-like figure, all skin and bone, carrying a light overnight bag. "Bloody white witch doctor, that's what he looks like." The Director watched Tubby climbing into the waiting car, then turned and walked back to the elevators, his stocky body moving as though he had to force his way through the atmosphere by sheer strength. It was a walk of purpose and determination. The Director knew exactly what he had to do now, and so took the elevator up to the very top of the building – to the C & C rooms, where he sought out the senior officer on duty: that same 'Jones the Spy' who had brought the Trapeze message from Stentor to his office only a couple of hours before. Two hours, which now seemed to have been a passage of days.

Together the Director and Jones the Spy sat down in one of the main cubicles containing a direct telex cipher machine. There they began to talk to the outside world – to Berlin Station in particular.

The problem was to contain most of the elements. The Director had no intention of revealing the *Trepan* operation to Berlin; or, for that matter, the fact that his senior expert in all things bright and beautiful within the DDR had gone over the Wall on a mission that was only partially sanctioned.

Yet two things had to be done. First, provide cover for Tubby Fincher's visit, without stirring anxiety and without having a street man constantly on his confidant's back. The Director also had to get a message into East Berlin. Not just a message – an order: instructions for the whole beehive to be evacuated.

Jones the Spy simply obeyed orders, working the machines. The Director himself did the encoding and unzipped the replies. The whole business took over an hour.

First, he talked in cipher – screeched from the telex – concerning Fincher's imminent arrival at Gatow. Head of Berlin Station knew Tubby Fincher personally and would recognise his work name.

Happily, Head of Station had not gone away for the week-end. It took the duty officer only fifteen minutes to get him into the cipher room, so that he was talking almost directly with London and his superior.

The first message was suitably ambiguous. A room was to be reserved – at the Kempinsky if possible – for Fincher (the cipher used the name 'Dombey') who was arriving at Gatow on a personal visit. Berlin Station would provide a private car, and then leave him alone. The matter was domestic, and Dombey was not infringing Head of Berlin Station's territorial rights.

Berlin came back with an understood and Wilco.

The second bit was more difficult. It was of the greatest urgency: to be acted on as priority. Head of Station was to open File Four: Source Six (a closed file, kept in the vaults near the shredder, and only to be opened on the Director's authority, against an emergency such as this). Head of Station was to check on the address, and immediate contact method, for Spendthrift in East Berlin. He was to examine nothing else, and reseal the file after completing the necessary logging procedure.

Head of Station was then to dispatch, with haste, one of his loners who had to make personal contact with Spendthrift. The Director went through the jargon which would convince Spendthrift he was not being sold a pup. Then the message, clear and simple. Decamp Quartet and all those they handled. Reason – Soviet intelligence was closing fast for the kill. Berlin's man was to offer any reasonable help in evacuating those to whom this referred. Berlin Station was to offer all reasonable help. No, repeat no, incidents: which meant no shooting.

Berlin came back with a Wilco and Wilrep-hour: which meant Head of Station would be back to London within the hour, with details of the man sent in, and when they could expect a report.

The Director nodded and left Jones the Spy at the machine, with threats of firing squads or transfer to the KGB if he deserted that post for a second. Jones the Spy was to call the Director as soon as any further word came from Berlin.

In his office the Director put through a direct, open-line call to the Mehring Platz penthouse, speaking a certain amount of double-Dutch with Worboys. During the course of this he learned that Herbie was installed in the Metropol Hotel, and that Spendthrift was nearby.

*　　*　　*

Worboys put down the telephone. He looked relieved, and both Tiptoes and Miriam glanced from their magic boxes, questioning with their eyes.

From what he could make out, Tony Worboys told them, all hell was breaking loose. Tubby Fincher, of all people, was on the way. Berlin Station was dealing with what the Director had called "the little problem concerning the surgeon and his colleagues". They just had to stay put, track the bleeps and rely on Tubby when he arrived.

He had just finished putting them in the picture when Charles returned, with a battered-looking Max who was making heavy weather of his minor injuries, and cursing Herbie Kruger with every jinx, enchantment, evil eye and cantrip he knew. Charles fussed around him playing nurse; and, between fetching hot water, a large brandy and bandages – which were totally unnecessary for the bump on the back of Max's head – he apologised for taking so long. "Had to stash the car away from Polly Polizei, Lieblings. Service motor with all the gadgets, and not known to Berlin Station. Max had a hidey-hole."

"You watched your own back, I hope," Worboys had found his measure again, and regarded the pair of lion-tamers with a stony eye.

"We're not bloody amateurs, dear," Charles spat. "Max is a very brave soldier. Walked under his own steam. Watched each other's backs. Clean as a virgin's –"

"The big hairy Kraut," Max blasted. "Blood-sucking son of an ape's whore. Slippery, uncouth reptile. Bloody Big Herbie sodding Kruger."

"Shut up, you," Worboys shouted, with such command that everyone looked at him, Charles' mouth falling open.

"Well," Max shrugged. "The madman hit me. In my own car. Threatened me with his gun as well."

Jesus, thought Worboys, how did Herbie pull that one? He had heard the Director give an express order concerning firearms. Charles and Max only.

"He should've shot your balls off," Worboys spat. "Now shut up and pull yourself together. Mr. Fincher's on the way.

"Old Scarecrow himself, eh?" Max, sotto voce.

Worboys gave him one more warning, telling him that he had got himself done by Herbie, and would have to answer for it. Max stayed silent after that, and Worboys quietly asked Miriam if she'd hold the look-out for a minute: he wanted air.

On the balcony Tony Worboys took in several deep breaths and looked out over the now-familiar view of Berlin. In particular, he gazed into the far distance, across the jagged, well-lit area of the Wall. Somewhere, among the far lights of the East, Big Herbie was on a personal quest. Young Tony Worboys thought he knew enough about Herbie to be certain that the man would never have taken such drastic and insubordinate action unless he thought it absolutely necessary.

Herbie's professionalism was sacred. He would not dash off in a fit of pique or spite just because the Director had forbidden it. He hoped, almost to the point of hysteria at this moment, that Herbie Kruger would one day be able to give a complete picture of his reasons. For a second Worboys almost saw him – in a kind of wish-fulfilment – lecturing at the school on the nature of taking independent action in the field.

Worboys had a lot of life to live: much to learn about stress, revenge and yearning. He was a long way off that time when a man – even a professional like Herbie Kruger – reaches the age of disillusionment and tries to take actions into his own hands, believing that right will not always prevail, and all stories do not have happy endings.

Before going back into the apartment Worboys gave a casual glance West. He could see the lighted broken tower of the Kaiser Wilhelmskirche, and the glare of neon and street lights from the Kurfurstendamm. The Ku-damm would be busy tonight. Saturday night.

*   *   *

The bars, hotels and clubs on the Ku-damm were indeed busy. One of these crowded, drinking places sported the English public house name of the Black Horse. Holding court at the bar of the Black Horse was one Curry Shepherd – a favoured regular customer.

Curry Shepherd had something of the ex-officer-gone-to-seed about him. Just occasionally, at the Black Horse, they would see him in a smart suit and shirt, wearing the tie of a famous British regiment. At this moment, however, Curry was in his usual old, almost threadbare tweed jacket and grey flannels. He wore an open-necked shirt, but the clothes somehow managed to give the impression that they had once been very good, but, like their owner, had seen better days and a lot of service.

Curry was a tallish man; sharp, penetrating good looks and what had once been blond hair, thinning now and in need of cutting. People said that it was the permanent tired look in his eyes that got the girls. There was a girl with him now: a dumpy little thing with a touch of the gypsy about her. She looked young enough to be his daughter, but hung on his every word, a hint of adoration in her eyes.

One large Shepherd hand was wrapped faithfully around the girl's shoulder, while the other clutched a glass of Schnapps – "to keep the cold out," he would say, even on the hottest day of the year. Curry was always good value, even though some of his little *bon mots* had long become repetitive.

At the moment he was telling the girl some story about his now-divorced wife and odd goings on with a local vicar back in England. The whole thing was ludicrous, highly embellished, but exceptionally amusing; as were all Curry's stories.

The regulars often marvelled at Curry Shepherd. Only a mad Englishman, they argued, could possibly hold down the job of foreign representative for a highly reputable firm of London publishers, yet manage to consume such quantities of alcohol. Also, only someone like Shepherd could dress so badly after once holding the rank of colonel in a famous British regiment. There were those who did not altogether believe that part of Curry's story; but there was no doubt about his present job, of which they had all seen evidence. The publishers produced a lot of books with a German flavour, but the job sometimes took him as far afield as Paris and Rome. Once a year he went to London.

Behind the bar the telephone burst into a harsh, commanding Teutonic clamour. Curry Shepherd made his usual joke about Alberich working on the Ring again, and the barman took the call, placing the flat of one hand over his right ear to blot out the noise.

The barman said *Ja* a couple of times, then picked up the instrument, placing it on the bar in front of the Englishman. "For you, Curry."

"Who the hell knows I'm here?" Curry looked genuinely surprised, even though every friend he possessed in Berlin was well aware that, when in town, Curry Shepherd could be relied upon to be at the bar of the Black Horse for a large portion of each evening.

"Hello," he bawled into the telephone. His voice bore the stamp of high-volume parade-ground training.

"Curry?" asked a quiet voice at the other end.

"We have mild or hot; Madras, Vindaloo or Biriani. Yes?" Which was his standard response.

"It's David," said the voice, and someone would have had to be looking very closely to spot the slight change in Curry Shepherd's eyes.

"David. Jolly d. What're you doing in the great divided city?"

"Passing through. Thought we might meet."

"Of course. Why not? I'm at the Black Horse on the Ku-damm. Come on over."

"Rather you came to me."

"Jolly d. Mind if I bring a bird?"

"Rather you didn't."

"Ah. She'll be a bit put out. Have to do a spot of the old glib-tongueing," he winked at the girl, moving his hand to tweak at her breast. She giggled and moved closer. "Where are you, David?"

"Hotel Les Nations. Near the Tiergarten."

"Know it like the back of my neck, old cocker. This is business, I presume, and can't wait? Rather had plans for tonight."

"I'm not here for long, and there's a book I really think you should see. I'm certain you'll want to follow it up: giving you first crack."

"Jolly d of you, cocker. When you want me, then?"

"Oh, I'll be here for the next couple of hours. Really, I'm doing you a favour, Curry."

"Okay, cocker. Business is business. See you soon." Curry Shepherd put down the telephone and grinned at the girl, speaking to her in English, because she was working on the language. "Sorry, angel eyes. Business calls. Literary agent in from London. Whistle stop and all that." Heaven knew if she really understood Curry's particular version of the English language, but she appeared to be getting the message. "Fella thinks he's found a German Tolstoy or something. Got to meet him, pronto." With that, he launched into negotiations for a date on Monday night, which, in the back of his head, he knew might be quite impossible for him to keep.

David was Head of Berlin Station, as far as Curry Shepherd was concerned. The Hotel Les Nations, near the Tiergarten, meant the safe house they kept in the Dahlmann-strasse; and meeting David there within the next two hours meant as quickly as Curry Shepherd's long legs could carry him.

Indeed Curry Shepherd worked for a London publisher: but only on a temporary basis. He was an old Berlin hand from way back, a street man with much experience under his belt, and the publishing cover gave him easy travel facilities. In effect, he led a pleasant life these days, as his particular talents were seldom on call. David's line, about "doing him a favour" indicated that this was something of high import.

He took his time, finishing the Schnapps and chatting with

the girl. Anything with a most urgent tag had to be treated like a bomb, or, as Curry would have put it, like porcupines screwing.

Once out on the Ku-damm he did not seem to hurry, though this was deceptive, as Curry's normal pace was a fairly fast, leg-stretching stride – the old tweed jacket open and billowing behind him like a gown.

He did not head straight up the Ku-damm, towards the Dahlmannstrase, but in the opposite direction. Blind 'em with science, he thought. Move around, check out the ground and watch for blowpipes in the bushes. He took a wide route, dog-legging the side streets until he was sure there were no look-outs or recce patrols about.

With this sort of care it took Curry Shepherd around forty-five minutes to reach the Dahlmannstrasse house. He was there for an hour, talking and listening – mainly listening – to the terse, specific orders given personally by Head of Berlin Station. Cover was well provided, and Curry took a straight route back to the two-room apartment he rented near the Zoo. He packed an overnight bag with the bare essentials; flicked through his passport, piled documents and contracts, bits of manuscript and notes, into a plastic zip-up folder, and was on his way.

Curry Shepherd, publisher's representative, was heading into East Berlin to do the rounds of the DDR publishing houses. Apparently there had been a mild panic earlier that evening when his secretary telephoned the Metropol to say he would be late arriving. They had no record of the booking. She had blasted them to blazes, claiming the room was reserved a month before. They ended up by apologising.

Before doing the rounds of the publishing houses on Monday he would drop off for a word with some fellow he had never seen. One Christoph Schnabeln. With luck he would get that done tonight.

4

It was as though Herbie had never been away from the little apartment: as though the separation had not existed.

Herbie was home, alive again: though discreet enough to excuse himself, within minutes of arrival, so that he could cache the pistol in the bathroom. At that moment with his guard down, the professional within him whispered he should trust nobody. Not yet: Ursula – like the others – would have to be put to the question: the Gorky phrase.

To begin with she cried a lot, and clung to him, pulling away to look at him, running her hands over his face, as if to reassure herself that it really was Herbie Kruger. Inevitably Herbie shed tears with her. The memories, the sense of time and place were so strong. The apartment felt the same as it had always done. It even smelled as it had at moments of brooding recall, far away in London. The aromas were of Ursula, and a hundred things identified with her: the soap she always used (and was obviously still able to obtain); the particular favourites of her kitchen, the spices and flavourings she hoarded; the mingled fresh scent of her laundry. Somewhere in the apartment there had always been a hint of nutmeg in the atmosphere. It was there still. This blend of odours was, to Herbie, as thrilling and sensually arousing as a million dreams, a thousand love poems.

Neither had her body changed. Herbie felt a twinge of guilt for allowing himself to deteriorate – even though he had kept to the bare minimum requirements of the Service. With Ursula even the texture of her skin was unaltered to his touch and sight: the firmness of her breasts unslackened by the passage of time. Later, her readiness for him – and his for her – dispersed the years like an incredible feat of magic.

She told him she always knew he would return; that she loved him, and had kept the faith, waited for him. Of course he already half knew it, if only because he had glimpsed the Telegraph Boys' reports, and taken special notice of the standard of raw information coming from the one called Electra.

When the shock of reunion was over they stood together in the cosy living room, the curtains now drawn as a precaution. Immediately on arrival, before Ursula had a chance to react, he told her to draw the curtains while he inspected all four rooms. Just to be certain – though he also used it to get rid of the weapon.

It was typical of Ursula to ask if he was hungry – if he wanted food – just as they plunged into a kiss of such heat and violence that the blood pumped, for the first time in years, into Herbie's loins. Food was the last thing either of them really needed.

Herbie gently held her shoulders, his massive hands curled around the thin material of her shirt, arms stretched to their full limit. "You haven't changed," grinning his mouthy, silly smile: shaking the great head. "Still you love me, eh?"

"Love? Could I love anybody but you, Herbie?" Her eyes lowered for a fraction. "My first love, and last. Is it so foolish to talk like a young girl? Like the young girls talk in cheap paper-books? Romances?"

"There's nothing foolish about love of any kind, Ursula: between two people, or countries, or for ideals. It is that we have to respect. Belief in love is happiness and grief. People kill for the love of ideals thought wrong or bad by others. Yet that is love. So, we love." A long pause. Then he said something about the time, the years apart having been hard to bear, and she looked up at him, biting a lip. Shy. Then, the little smile –

> "All right, shall I give you my heart?
> Will you always remember me?
> Take it, dear little boy, take it . . ."

pausing, a slight sob of pleasure in her voice as she completed the dialogue from *Wasted Effort* – their personal love-play game from *Des Knaben Wunderhorn* –

"... *take it, please!*"

Nobody, in the past few years, could have seen Herbie's smile break so radiantly over his face. Playfully, he pushed her away, walking slowly to the bedroom door –

"*Crazy little wench, I certainly don't want it.*" Hand to the doorknob, stumping inside as she came quickly behind him, her old loping walk, wrapping her arms around his waist, holding him and pressing her body against his back, as he pretended to pull away.

Then he turned, and they were fastened in a limpet kiss. Their fingers moved – an instrumental piece for four hands – over each other's bodies. Clothes fell away, the kiss broken, momentarily, only at instants when the removal of garments determined.

On this Saturday evening in East Berlin, Ursula Zunder and Eberhard Lukas Kruger once more became a single flesh: indivisible, conjoined in a fury and physical pleasure in the wide bed they had so often occupied – fifteen, twenty years before.

There was one point when Herbie seemed quite detached, for a second, and thought, for no reason, that the old movie makers had been right in using the sea, and breaking waves, as a pictorial analogy for passionate sex. The loving between Ursula and himself was like the sea – waves which crashed in splendour, followed by the slow, sifting runback of tide. The sea constant only in its changing moods, from storm to placidity.

Eventually a tranquil, satisfied peace settled upon them, and they lay naked side by side. As he rolled away Herbie glimpsed his watch and could not believe that almost two hours had passed.

They were silent, probably sharing similar thoughts: very close to one another in mind. Herbie was wrapped in so many memories of this room. The first time had been here; so much laughter was shared by them, under the white ceiling with its one hanging light bulb, and the same imitation vellum shade Herbie had brought there in the early sixties.

He recalled other things in their silence. As well as the happiness, comfort and laughter there had been anxiety – the day in 1961 when he knew, at last, that he had only one possible choice, the one he had tried to resist for months: that he would have to recruit Ursula as the sixth Telegraph Boy. He had tried, God knew, to be tender then, broaching the subject after they had made love, just like this.

He remembered that Sunday with an awful vividness – as one so often retains moments as if in sharp technicolor: even the timbre of voices staying quite clear, as though recorded on magnetic tape within the ear of memory.

He was supposed to be away for the entire week-end; on business – there was a week-end pattern by then, through force of circumstances – in the West; going through methods, technicalities, plans and the difficult problem of making a final decision regarding the last, sixth, Telegraph Boy.

The duty officer had wakened him in the middle of the night – early on the Sunday morning in reality. Sunday, 13 August 1961. My God, he had been staying at the Dahlmannstrasse house: the one they used for the meeting with Schnabeln.

"They've closed the border," the duty officer told him.

At first he did not really believe it. The hordes had been running from the East into the West for months. The DDR authorities had stepped up security. People were being questioned, even pulled off trains. There had been the usual talk, yet nobody really believed that Ulbricht and his government would take the step of stopping free access between East and West.

The rumours persisted, but still nobody in the West believed such action would come. For one thing, there was extreme political fuzziness over the issue, and a definite uncertainty about assistance, or even agreement from Moscow. In the French Sector the commandant and his deputy had both left for their summer holidays. The Head of Berlin Station had told Herbie on the Saturday afternoon that he would be taking his family to the Costa Brava in a few days' time – on 22 August.

Amidst the Moscow sabre-rattling, together with their uncertainty about backing East Germany, Ulbricht's establishment in East Berlin had for some months been putting on the pressure. Herbie had felt the thumbscrews himself several months before, while he was still using the cover of one who lived in the East and worked in the West – a Border Crosser; a *Grenzgänger*

Herbie's first intimation of trouble occurred one evening when returning from his 'job' in the West. He came up on to the platform of his usual S-Bahn station in the East to be confronted by a large, sinister hoarding – *DIESE GRENZGÄNGER SIND KRIEGSTREIBER*: These Border Crossers Are Warmongers. It was shortly afterwards that three Central Committee Communist Party members paid him a visit, issuing a stern warning that he must take work in the East or there would be serious trouble. One of them had been particularly vicious, calling Herbie and all like him *Schmarotzen* and *Speckjäger* – spongers and bacon chasers.

Herbie naturally took instructions from his masters in the West, but there was never any doubt. To keep the Schnitzer Group intact, and form the half-dozen Telegraph Boys, discretion had to be the better part of valour. From then onwards – until 13 August 1961 – he took a job in the East, which restricted operations for both the Schnitzer and Telegraph Boys. However, there was still easy access to West Berlin, so – much to Ursula's disgust – Herbie spent many whole week-ends in the West. For security, as well as his association with Ursula, Herbie varied the routine, sometimes going over for two consecutive week-ends, sometimes alternate week-ends. Occasionally there was a quick trip for one evening, when he would often take Ursula, and park her in a cinema until his business was completed. She remained compliant, asking no questions. Then came the early hours of Sunday 13 August. The sudden swoop upon the demarcation lines of the border, the troops and tanks, the barbed wire and the mesh (bought, ironically, from the British) – the harbingers of war: the blocks and bricks, steel traps and watch towers. All the paraphernalia of the Wall.

"They've closed the border," the duty officer had shaken him awake. "Looks very serious. Half the bloody senior people're away, and I'm having trouble raising London for instructions. But I've got your orders." They were letting people back into the East – mainly night revellers who found themselves stuck and parted from their families. Herbie was to return and for the time being use only the covert links and contacts. He had to work at establishing safer lines of communication. "They also said it's most urgent, now, for you to recruit your sixth man – if that means anything to you?" It meant more than Herbie could have told the duty officer, for he had fought all the way, trying to avoid the recruitment of Ursula Zunder, the woman upon whom he depended and lavished his emotions. But he dressed and tramped his way to the Brandenburg Gate, where things looked ugly, with barbed wire and machine guns set up, pointing into the West.

He remembered raising his hands, his identity papers in the left, and approaching a Vopo, who sent for an officer to interrogate him about what he had been up to in the West. "I usually go over on a Saturday night. It got out of hand." He shrugged his wide shoulders. "A woman. You know how it is."

The officer let him through with some lewd remark about having no more fun with the girls of the West, who all had the morals of whores anyway. Herbie went straight to Ursula – who had already heard the news, and had a radio on, listening to the bulletins. She asked if there was going to be war again. Herbie comforted her, telling her, no, there would not be war. She wanted to make a run for it into the West. "Herbie, let's get out now. While there's time." So often they had shared each other's feelings about the situation in the East and their hatred of the Communist régime: the Party itself. Herbie had gone as far as telling her he was a Party member in name only; to avoid trouble. Ursula seemed particularly frightened about the Soviet influence.

It was during the middle of that Sunday morning, in August 1961, that Herbie had brought her into this very room. They made love, quietly, gently, with great tenderness, as though to comfort one another. It went on until late afternoon, while out in the city individuals, whole families, were making last dangerous dashes to the West, leaving homes and belongings behind, risking death as they cut through wire or jumped from windows.

It was here, during the early evening, that Herbie laid the news on her: telling her the truth about himself, past and present, what he really did. She was not surprised; indeed, had suspected it, scented it for some time. Herbie recruited her that same night. Within a matter of weeks she was Electra.

Now she kissed his cheek, as though hauling him from his private thoughts. "It's unbelievable to have you back, Herbie. Tell me it's not a dream. You really are here, and you're staying tonight? Yes?"

He saw the wince of pain in her eyes as he broke it to her. There was work he must do. But he would be back. Herbie had always been soft about hurting her. When he finally left, in 1965: when there was no alternative but to take off – obey the orders, and leave her, working, in the East – he had adhered to the discipline of the Service. The cost, as he saw in Ursula's eyes, had been exorbitant. Even then he was too soft, though he knew it now. With the passage of time Herbie had become more prone to the ruthless ways of the secret world.

Again, in this room, he had told her – yet not told her – of his impending departure. Back among the familiar surroundings Herbie felt sickened by his own methods, hearing his voice all those years ago. "Listen to me carefully" – above her, looking down on the oval face, seeing the troubled, anxious look come into her eyes. "I may have to disappear for a time. Others will contact you. It will not be for long." He really had believed that: thought there would be a way back. Misinforming himself, when all reason told him that, if he wanted to live and carry on the work, he would have to be off within the next twenty-four hours. "Wait, Ursula, my darling." The nerve of him, asking her to wait. "I shall come back for you." It made the guilt send shivers down his spine to think of that moment. The last time he had been in this bed; in the spring of 1965. Fifteen years since he held her, and had her, like this.

Now the pain showed in her eyes like an image he had seen before: the fear that he was using her; leaving again. With a steady voice she asked if she would be an old woman when he came back next time. That made him smile, and he gave it to her in one rush of words. No. Last time they were already on his heels – the KGB, SSD, whoever. This time he had returned to do certain things. There would be trouble when they got back to the West; because what he was doing had not been authorised. This time it *would* be different. He had passports, and methods. Even a passport for her. He had it in his hotel: an American passport with all the correct stamps. A genius in cobbling documents had done the passports; the man had used Herbie's old photograph of her, adding fifteen years to the face, "Though you look older on the passport than in real life. That's not flattery. Just the truth."

Tomorrow, he told her, they would both go to the West. Tomorrow, when he had completed the jobs. Ursula wept again, and he held her close, trying to comfort her and, at the same time, be gentle in letting her know he had to get going now.

He dressed first, and watched as she put on her clothes – as she had always done in the distant past. She kept crying, repeating she always knew he would eventually return, as if to reassure herself.

"I am the White Knight, come especially for you, to carry you off on my charger," he said. Then, with a stab of conscience, but knowing that, professionally, the test had to be done, he said: "A man can teach another man to do good – believe me!"

She was doing up her stocking – she still wore suspenders, he was pleased to see: and the lacy underwear. Ursula was always careful about keeping it neat and clean. Herbie had smuggled a lot of that kind of thing into her before the crash of 1965, and she was still wearing it. He even recognised the bra and pants she wore now – the dark blue, one of his favourite sets, as though she had known he was coming. As they had made love, Ursula said she had experienced this strange feeling, all day, that he was close at hand – but she often had days like that.

Now Ursula gave a little tutting curse. Something was wrong with the suspender fastening. "Sorry," she looked at him, puzzled. "Sorry, what did you say?"

Herbie repeated the phrase.

She laughed. "I'm sure you're right, but what's that supposed to mean?"

Herbie said it was just a quotation from Gorky. Came into his mind.

"I suppose one man *can* teach another man to do good, when you come to think of it, darling, yes," as though humouring him.

Never mind, Herbie said – relieved beyond all measure, for she was talking again, questioning: he wouldn't let her down? He would come back? It would be tomorrow? What should she pack? What time would he come? It was all so sudden. Thank God he had chosen a week-end, and oh, she loved him so much, and had waited so long.

As he reluctantly prepared to leave ("There's so much we have to talk about. I want weeks with you. But that'll come. After tomorrow.") Herbie gave her the instructions. Her handler would be in touch – maybe very soon now. She would be called to a special meeting; in a safe place. She must show no surprise, but the meeting would be with him. There would be another man along, but Herbie would get rid of him. There were official questions which had to be put to her. He would ask the questions, and give her the time she should expect him at the apartment.

"We go from here," he held her close; telling her to put her prettiest and most expensive things in her case. "Only the best." She glanced at the Dürer drawing, and he shook his head. No. No personal household things. Just her prettiest clothes, and only those in case there was trouble at customs. She must look as though she had been spending the week-end in the East. Remember, she was an American.

"Just have your bag ready. I shall arrange transport. Probably a colleague, so that we can return to the hotel, then take a taxi to the checkpoint. I'll give you all the details at the meeting."

She was weeping when he left.

Once in the streets, Herbie had to make a great mental effort to wrap his professional cloak around him. He felt a little drunk, but knew all the risks were worth while. He would settle the double Telegraph Boy, and Luzia Gabell – both. He would resign once they were safely back in the West. Maybe they would take strict disciplinary action, but he doubted there would be any court proceedings. That would not be the Director's style, nor in the interests of the Service. They might just keep him at Warminster for a few years: that was possible.

Herbie pulled himself together: alert to the dangers, taking on the persona of the big American again, smiling to himself as he thought of his one small deceit with Ursula (he would tell her when they were out) – how he had excused himself, and gone to the bathroom to get rid of the gun; returning there, once dressed, to retrieve it; making up the tie harness again so that the weapon slapped against his thigh as he walked.

It was late, so Herbie took even greater care. His watch showed eleven forty-five. Schnabeln was meeting him in his room at midnight. Gathering his thoughts, Herbie wondered how successful Schnabeln had been in making the contacts. He hoped there had been some success in tracing the Gabell woman. If so, there might well be more work, and of an unpleasant nature, to be done before the night was out.

There was about a ten-minute walk still to go before reaching the hotel. Just in case the dogs were out Herbie bleeped the *Trepan* team. That'll confuse them, he thought.

*   *   *

"Herbie," Miriam Grubb called out as the dip-dah came up, the map swinging, trembling for a second on the screen. Spendthrift's signals had come up regularly, every half-hour since the late bleep, near the Metropol. They had all been carefully logged. Spendthrift had moved about a lot. "A busy little bee," Miriam said.

Now here was Herbie on the loose and in an unfamiliar part of town.

"Where?" muttered Worboys.

"Could be headin' back to the hostelry," Tiptoes proffered; and, at that moment, there was a ring at the main door.

Charles had a pistol in his hand, even though Worboys said it was probably Mr. Fincher at long last. Max was lying down: resting and licking his wounds – both the physical and the damaged pride.

The rake-like figure of Tubby Fincher stood in the doorway, then pushed past Charles.

"Where are they?"

They told him, and he went straight over to look at the log,

268

checking the positions and times of the bleeps, which had also been pencilled in on a smaller map of Berlin.

Tubby Fincher took it in quickly. Worboys was relieved to see that he had assumed command without even stating it, almost before he was in the room.

"Spendthrift's running to form," Tubby muttered, checking off names and places in his head. "If it's any consolation to you, friend Spendthrift is doing just what he oughta." He looked carefully at the last tracked position of Herbie's bleep, moving his twig finger in a series of small circles outwards. Straightening up, he nodded to himself, and said aloud that he thought he knew where brother Kruger had been. In his head he knew damn well where Herbie had been.

"Where?" Worboys asked without thinking.

Fincher gave a thin smile. "In the hope of not hurting anyone's sensibilities, it is my due consideration that Herr Kruger, our expert in East Berlin, has been getting himself well and truly laid. Now, can I have some coffee, please? My body's still in London. Ever travelled by Harrier, young Worboys? It's an experience I would not recommend."

Fincher, the keeper of so much secret knowledge, inwardly winced as the thought of Herbie Kruger slid painfully through his mind. The facts spoke for themselves: the driving urge to redeem his losses – the Schnitzer Group, the Telegraph Boys and the Quartet – had propelled Kruger into the East. But what of the other things? Fincher thought.

How, in God's name, would Herbie feel at this moment, out there chasing one victim, and clutching at his past? Tubby knew enough about Kruger and the woman they called Electra. What agonies would the huge, clumsy man be facing now?

A bleakness descended on Tubby Fincher, shrugged off only by his natural powers as a leader. Yet, from that moment until the end, his thoughts were never far from the crucifixion which had to be taking place in Herbie Kruger's head.

5

CHRISTOPH SCHNABELN HAD, as Miriam Grubb suggested, been a busy little bee. First, the drive out to Köpenick to contact Anton Mohr – Teacher – who, thankfully, was at home, reading by a dim light in one of the two shabby rooms he rented in the dank villa. One wall was completely covered with green mould, and there were patches of rising damp near the two windows, which looked out on to a strangely neat garden – gloomy in the street lighting now, but fresh to the nostrils, and obviously cared for. Schnabeln noticed this last fact as he walked up the flagged path to the front door. The garden was very much at odds with the crumbling relic of a house.

The furniture in Mohr's rooms was sparse, the floors uncarpeted, the picture adding up to one of general clutter, and extreme poverty – if not actual despair.

Mohr greeted Schnabeln with care, a shifty uncertainty in his eyes, head cocking constantly, as though listening for noises: though the only sound came from the old man coughing in the room directly above them. He was bedridden now, Mohr said; and the wife, who was the elder of the couple, appeared to be on her last legs. "So much for the medical care in the Workers' and Peasants' State."

Schnabeln commented on the garden. "The newly-weds," Mohr turned down the corners of his mouth. The newly-weds had the major part of this decaying building, but were good Party members. They spent most of their time smartening things up. The husband boasted that they were to get a grant to modernise their apartment. In the meantime the couple worked away at renovations during most evenings:

270

and in the garden at week-ends. Would Christoph care for a Schnapps?

"Let's take a stroll. It's a nice evening," raising his voice in case the newly-weds were hiding among the mould on the wall. "You must have a good bar somewhere around here."

Mohr agreed there was a bar, only ten minutes away. Ten minutes gave them enough time. Just to be on the safe side, Schnabeln thought, they should play it for real. He could brief Mohr as they walked to the bar and on the way back. Ten minutes at the place for a quick Schnapps. That would cut the time to half an hour. As they left the old villa, with its smell of damp, the cracks, mould and dirty façade, he bleeped the *Trepan* team.

Once clear Schnabeln began – "Your subject: the one you handle."

Mohr nodded, and Schnabeln told him what was required. Mohr said it would be difficult to make a crash meeting tonight. His man – Horus, Otto Luntmann – was on night duty. But he could bump him tomorrow morning, when he came off duty at six.

Schnabeln went over the exact details. It was up to Mohr to hand his subject over to Schnabeln. The time was fixed; and the place. Schnabeln had already decided it would be more prudent to use the safe house in the Weibensee district for the morning meetings. It was the worst of the two houses; but if they could get three meetings – at eleven, noon, and one o'clock – done there the other three could be fitted nicely into the Behrenstrasse house during the afternoon. With luck, and good, well-timed contacts, they could have all six done by five in the afternoon. Of course, the whole thing might be over much sooner, if one of the early meetings proved fruitful.

They arranged the pick-up for Horus so he could be first in at Weibensee: pick-up in time for the eleven o'clock date.

They drank their Schnapps, talking inconsequentialities, and Schnabeln reinforced the fine details during the return walk. His car was parked around the corner from Mohr's hovel, so they parted nearby – with a lot of loud laughter, and promises to meet the following week.

From the Kopenick district Schnabeln drove to the outskirts of Treptow Park, and Anna Blatte's apartment. She was preparing for an early bed; dressed in night clothes, and wrapped in a lurid robe. Anna was delighted to see him and could not wait to get him inside the apartment: her eyes glittering with anticipation. If Schnabeln knew anything about Anna she could not wait to get him into the bedroom either.

Christoph was fast, serious and commanding. "Work to be done." He used no names. "Get dressed. We're going for a short ride. Maybe you'll have to go on and do something else after that."

Herbie had been right about Anna. When the chips were down and things looked serious she could turn off the heat in her pants and get down to real work like a true professional. Anna Blatte nodded swiftly and disappeared into the bedroom; emerging within five minutes in street clothes. An admirable speed for any woman, let alone Anna, Schnabeln considered.

Herbie had given special instructions concerning Maurice's subject. Schnabeln smiled, as he always did, at the woman's crypto. It was probably one of Herbie Kruger's little jokes. Anna Blatte was no Maurice. This subject – Electra – was to be last on the list. As they drove around the perimeter of the park, Schnabeln gave the details. They arranged timings and the pick-up point. Blatte said there was no problem. A crash meeting with her target was simple and well-organised. She could do it from a public telephone booth in the morning: or tonight, in order to be certain.

For professional reasons they drove for almost twenty minutes after the matter had been settled, parking near Blatte's apartment, where, to her delight, they partook of a long fumble in the front of the car. For a few minutes professionalism disappeared, and she pleaded with Christoph to come up for what she called "a quickie". Much as he might have been tempted, there was a lot more work to be done.

His own people had to have the news laid on them. But first Schnabeln found a bar with a telephone to call his Vopo contact concerning Luzia Gabell.

"Old flame, indeed," the Vopo laughed.

Christoph asked what he meant, and the Vopo told him she was suspect as a common whore, still using the name Luzia

Gabell. "We do nothing about it, but she certainly has a lot of friends. Lives in a small apartment above an *Apotheke* near the Alexanderplatz. All nice prosperous-looking friends; but a lot of them, Christoph. Stay away, I should. We had four girls carved up in apartments just like that only last week." He added that it happened all the time. "At least two a week. Sometimes as many as six. Don't let them tell you there's no crime or violence in this city. It's always with us. Stay away."

Schnabeln said he certainly would. There was no address, but Herbie would have to make do with that information.

He then moved on to another bar. The two subjects he handled personally had to be set up, and he was wary about crash meetings with either of them. Particularly on a Saturday night. From the bar he dialled Hecuba's number, but there was no reply. That was worrying. She could easily have gone away for the entire week-end. He would try later.

The other call was further afield; right into the heart of the Soviets, for Priam worked and lived within the GSFG HQ at Zossen-Wunsdorf. Schnabeln had a drink in the bar and left, to find a less public booth which would be more secure.

A crash meeting call meant a security breach – whatever. That was particularly true of Priam. The Quartet knew the people they serviced, by sight and crypto, but not by name. Arrangements for a crash meeting with both Hecuba and Priam necessitated telephone calls. With Hecuba, Schnabeln would almost certainly get the woman herself on the line. There was a wrong number deal to fix times and fallbacks. The meeting place was permanently arranged for a crash. He presumed all the subjects had similar arrangements – crash meeting places that were never altered and only used in great emergency.

Arrangements for Priam were more involved. The civilian forces' maintenance staff out at the Soviet base in Zossen-Wunsdorf had their own quarters, but only one telephone, and this was used by the entire block. It was a direct line, so they had no added worries of going through a main Soviet military exchange. But, if Schnabeln wanted a crash meeting and telephoned, he was likely to get anyone on the line. He could not ask for Priam by name, as he did not know it. This was a handling flaw he had discussed in the past with Herbie. Promises had been made to look into it; in case of a rainy day. Now the rainy day was here.

There were two options when telephoning Priam. Happily, the man was blessed with a title – Foreman in Charge of Number Seven Section. He could ask for Priam by that title; or leave a prearranged message. There was always the possibility that someone without the patience or time to look for Priam would come on the line.

Schnabeln drove to a spot near the Lenin Allee, parking in a non-restricted zone, then walking for five minutes before selecting a small bar with a reasonably private telephone. From there he put in the call to Zossen-Wunsdorf, which was answered by a gruff, slightly petulant voice.

Schnabeln went through the routine. "I have to speak to the Foreman In Charge of Number Seven Section. Urgent." He used a clipped voice, underplaying a mild Soviet accent.

"Who wants him?"

Schnabeln said it was General Military Maintenance, Soviet Command, Berlin. That appeared to do the trick.

"He'll not be here on a Saturday night. Will anyone else do?"

Oh Christ. Should he leave a message? Nobody else would do, he told the gruff voice. Did anyone know where the Foreman could be found?

"I know he's in Berlin tonight. Saw him go," said the man at Zossen-Wunsdorf. He sounded distinctly unhappy.

"You know where he'll be found? I cannot stress the urgency sufficiently."

Reluctantly, the voice told him that Peter could usually be contacted at *Der Hengst*. Schnabeln asked, or rather commanded, to know what *Der Hengst* was. The fellow sounded shamefaced. *Der Hengst* – The Stallion – was a bar. He gave the address, just off the Lenin Allee – not ten minutes from where Schnabeln stood. Keeping in character, Schnabeln asked the man's name, thanking him for his help.

Schnabeln thought, 'Well, Priam's name is Peter something-or-other, and I'm not supposed to know that.' At least he would recognise Peter if he was at *Der Hengst*.

He returned to the car and drove near to the street off the

Lenin Allee, given as the address of the bar. He found the place quickly enough: a cellar bar, with a dim light over a small door at the bottom of steps, leading straight off the street: the basement of an old building, just on the fringes of all the modern, square, unlovely stuff which had transformed the Lenin Allee.

There was piano music coming from inside, vaguely American and jazzy from a long way back. The lighting made it almost impossible to see very far, until the eyes adjusted, and the place was filled with smoke and the low mutter of conversation. Nobody paid much attention to Schnabeln when he went up to the bar. It had an old-fashioned zinc top which did not go with the rest of the place. Like the music, *Der Hengst* seemed to have been decked out in a 1930s style: the kind of decadence frowned upon by the authorities. It struck Schnabeln as an odd place for the chubby and scruffy-looking man he knew as Priam.

The bartender was a young, good-looking boy, who contrived to touch Schnabeln's hand as he gave him change. A man already seated at the bar turned to look at Schnabeln, raising his eyebrows. Schnabeln ordered Schnapps, paid and retreated to a table near the door. He kept his back to the wall and, at least, could observe people entering or leaving. It would not take long for his sight to adjust. If Priam was there he would soon spot him.

After sipping the Schnapps for a couple of minutes, Christoph was suddenly shaken by his own naivety. As he began to see more clearly, he realised that there were no women in the place. He also took note of the kind of men gathered around the bar and at the tables. *The Stallion* was a homosexual haunt.

Almost as he realised it he spotted Priam, still looking scruffy and chubby, even though he wore a well-made suit. Priam leaned against the far end of the bar, talking to a tall man who kept reaching out to fondle Priam's shoulder.

Time was running out. He still had to contact Hecuba and make a meeting with Girren, when the latter left the theatre. Schnabeln threw back his Schnapps, got up and walked, as daintily as possible, towards his subject. All depended on Priam being quick enough to recognise his handler. If the man was drunk or if he did not pick up the signals God knew what might happen.

Schnabeln twisted his way down the room. The pianist, at the far end, was playing something he recognised as being by Noël Coward. A young boy reached out and grasped his arm, "Haven't seen you in here before. You want a drink?"

Schnabeln said he already had a friend, pushing forward, passing Priam, so that he could make his approach behind the man to whom his subject was talking, and, therefore, show his face.

"Hello, Peter," he said, trying to adopt a slight lisp. This camp business did not suit Schnabeln one bit.

Priam looked up; and, for a second, there was no recognition in his eyes. Schnabeln blurted out, "I haven't seen you since that terrible day I got the telegram."

The light dawned. "My God. Man, it's been a long time."

The fellow to whom he had been talking turned and looked aggressively at Schnabeln. If it was some rough trade he was after there'd be plenty in later, the man said.

"Do you mind?" Schnabeln all but minced. "He's an old friend, and I'd like a quick word with him."

Priam settled the matter with speed. "Is it about your Mama?" he asked.

Schnabeln said, yes; he needed to talk. Privately. It would not take long. "I'll return him to you in perfect condition," he glared at Priam's pick-up, who flounced off, saying he would believe that when he saw it.

In the street Priam asked what was wrong, and how Spendthrift had found him.

That did not matter. Schnabeln was precise, walking fast in the general direction of the car. It would not take a minute, he told Priam, but it was urgent: sizing up the man, making sure he was sober and able to take in orders, which he gave rapidly, stressing times and places; body talk; making him repeat everything.

It took about ten minutes. Schnabeln realised he should not have been so concerned. These people were all seasoned professionals – even the one among them who was doubling. They would obey instructions, though he had no doubt that, once the double was alerted, a lot of back-watching had to be done. He arranged Priam's pick-up for one-thirty. His would be the first afternoon meeting at the Behrenstrasse house: though, as far as Priam was concerned, the pick-up point would be the meeting place.

He walked back with the scruffy little man, who appeared to be thoroughly enjoying the whole business. They parted near *Der Hengst*, with Schnabeln's warning for him to be on time.

Walter Girren, like most theatre technicians, was a man of habit: not the best quality for one engaged in the secret war, but a necessary occupational hazard which, as it happened, suited the purpose of Herbie Kruger and his other masters.

Depending on what was playing, Girren left the Berliner Ensemble at roughly the same time each evening. Tonight Christoph Schnabeln was there about ten minutes ahead of him, sitting in his parked car, adjacent to the stage door: as though waiting to collect him by arrangement.

As the wraith-like Girren came out of the building so Schnabeln quickly opened the car door and hailed him. "Over here, Walter. I'm over here."

Never show surprise at crash meetings or contacts, they taught at the school. So far that night Schnabeln had experienced nothing but sound professionalism from all concerned. Walter Girren was no exception, raising an arm in greeting, and walking quickly to the Wartburg as though this was an old prearranged appointment. In fact the stage door keeper, who saw the incident – and had no cause to think about it until a long time after – muttered to himself, wondering where the thin, pale Girren was off to this week-end. Perhaps the country with friends?

Schnabeln pulled the car slowly from the kerb. Not mucn traffic, but they could drive quietly for fifteen minutes without danger. After that Schnabeln would have to use another telephone. Try for Hecuba again. The hotel was the last place from which he wanted to make that call: too many busy ears on the switchboards, and the public 'phones almost certainly had surveillance on a daily tape basis.

Girren was calm, lighting a cigarette as he asked if there was a flap.

As with the others, Christoph Schnabeln told him the

briefest, bare facts; though Girren needed more details than the rest. First, he had two subjects with whom crash contact had to be made; second, it would be Girren who would be watching Schnabeln's – and possibly Herbie Kruger's – back, through what looked like being a long, traumatic Sunday.

"Jesus," Girren breathed softly. "Saturday night. The best night, of course, for arranging crash meetings. I might have to cut a few corners." His subjects were Gemini, the little jokester who worked at the Soviet HQ at Karlshorst; and Nestor, the grey filing clerk at the National People's Army HQ. Real names – not known officially to Girren – Moritz Winter and Nikolas Monch.

"One's easy," Girren said, still speaking softly, as though he had a throat infection and was losing his voice. "I've got a brush drop with Nestor early tomorrow. I'll have to crash him and speak in plain language."

As the drop was early – "When he goes to collect his milk," Girren said – they mentally pencilled him in for number three on the morning schedule. Schnabeln did some calculations. At Weibensee he had Horus for eleven o'clock. Now, Girren would fix Nestor for one o'clock. He had Priam set for the three o'clock at the Behren Strasse house, and Electra for the four o'clock – final – meeting.

This meant that Gemini and Hecuba would have to be fitted for the noon date at Weibensee and the two o'clock at the Behrenstrasse. The pick-ups were to be scheduled on the half-hours – a crime in the school's book, for they hated meetings on the dot of hours, quarters or halves. By right you had to play the numbers and set meetings for odd times – twelve minutes past or twenty-two minutes before the hour.

Herbie had said forget the strict ground rules. Make it simple. There were six to be interviewed, backs to be watched, and no one subject had to bump into another. So they were doing it on the hour, driving the next candidate around until the coast was clear. The only real problem was getting Herbie down from Weibensee to the Behrenstrasse after the one o'clock meeting, and in time for that at two o'clock. Watching was going to be one hell of a problem. Schnabeln even considered using a sympathetic taxi driver who imagined he dealt with a smuggler.

Girren took the news that he would be looking after Schnabeln's moves without comment. That was easy. So was Nestor. Gemini was his headache. He looked slyly towards Schnabeln. "You fancy a trek around the bars on the Karl-Marx-Allee?"

Schnabeln did not have the time for games like that. "Have to do it myself, then." Girren sighed. He asked for a pick-up time for Gemini (Schnabeln told him eleven-thirty – for the noon meeting at Weibensee). Girren nodded. Leave it to him. He would wear out shoe leather finding Gemini. "I've picked up drops from him on Saturdays. Always on the piss. Probably ends the night with a whore. But I'll find him."

Schnabeln said that was good, but without much feeling. He then ran off a list of pick-up points, times and places of meetings. Girren repeated them back. He would be there, watching. There was an actor friend who would lend him a car. It was one of the first things he had organised for himself when the Quartet came into the field. An old and battered Merc. They had cobbled papers for him in London. He gave Schnabeln the licence number and colour – dirty, unwashed grey – then said he had better be dropped off in the Karl-Marx-Allee. There was a lot to do before his dawn patrol to bounce Nestor.

Both men were preoccupied as they parted, Schnabeln driving away and giving the *Trepan* team another quick bleep. He wondered what sort of panics were now raging there, and how London was reacting to Herbie's 'defection'. The tension was already stiffening the back of his neck: giving him a mild headache. It had sounded straightforward in the Dahlmannstrasse house. It appeared more complicated and dangerous now they were committed.

He stopped the car, to give Hecuba one last try, before going back to the hotel.

* * *

As Martha Adler had predicted to herself, the Russian, Major Kashov, had intended his presents to come off. Over dinner they had drunk a good deal – though Hecuba was careful to get rid of most of her drinks by pouring them under the table. The food had been good, and the major talkative: exceptionally so for the good KGB man he was. Now the time for payment had arrived, back at her little apartment, provided by the State for a good servant of the DDR's ruling establishment.

He was a lively man, very anxious to please, and a shade smooth in his approach, she thought. His kisses had not been unpleasant, and she was getting quite aroused by the time he had her skirt off. He smelled of expensive cologne, not the junk the Ivans usually wore to cover up sweat.

They had moved to the bedroom, and the last wisps of her underwear were just being gently removed when the telephone extension rang.

Kashov gave a small explosive oath in Russian, and told her not to answer. "It could be my mother," she lied. Her mother was old and ailing, she had told him the other day. Old she was, but still in high spirits, boasting that she had never had a day's illness in her life.

Kashov put his hand between her thighs, moving his fingers with the deft precision of an expert as she picked up the receiver. She never answered with a number. Just – "Hello. Yes?"

"Oh," said the voice at the other end. "It's possible I've dialled a wrong number. Quite possible."

Martha Adler was alert now, trying to anaesthetise her sexual senses against Kashov's hand so that she could concentrate on the caller, who had just given her the verbal signal for an imminent crash meeting with her handler. "What number did you want?" she asked; snappily, for Kashov's benefit.

"Hang on one moment, please. I have it written down here. There is not much light. I can't quite read it. Yes . . ." Then, very slowly, as they taught you in London, "92 13 30. Have I not got that number?"

"No, you haven't. Nothing like it."

"I'm so sorry."

She allowed her voice to lose its pique for a moment, "I understand. Good-night," turning to Kashov, "Wrong number. Always on a Saturday I get wrong numbers . . . Ooooh. *You've* got the right number, though." She curled her naked body towards him, and reached down.

The telephone number her handler had given was straight-forward. The 9 meant a crash meeting at the appointed place – which, for her, was at the junction of Invalidenstrasse and Brunnenstrasse, outside a cake shop which she often used. The 2 signified the following day – tomorrow, Sunday. The rest was simple: 13 30. Thirteen thirty. Half-past one in the afternoon.

Martha Adler slid her tongue between the major's parted lips and, with surprise, realised that he wore a dental plate.

*　　*　　*

All done. Everything organised. Christoph Schnabeln headed the Wartburg towards the Metropol and hoped to blazes that his boss, Hoffer, had not gone looking for him when the tour party arrived. He had time to spare before meeting with Herbie Kruger at midnight.

He parked the car and entered the hotel through a side entrance, surveying the foyer through one of the interior glass doors, making certain it was empty – but for the desk clerk – before he ventured in.

The desk clerk grinned, asking if he had enjoyed himself. My god, Schnabeln told him. You'd never believe. Legs all the way to her navel. Kiss like a vampire. Probably marked him for life. "Hope Uncle Hoffer hasn't been nosing around?" Casually.

The desk clerk shook his head. "Asked if you'd seen the doctor. I told him I didn't know, but you'd gone straight to bed. Asked not to be disturbed. He went with the tour. They've only just left. Herr Hoffer went with them to the checkpoint." He put an accent on the *Herr*: maliciously.

Schnabeln grinned and nodded. He thought he just might make it to his room.

"I'm off at midnight," the desk clerk called after him. "You give me her 'phone number?"

Schnabeln made a rude gesture, stepping into the elevator that would take him to the sixth floor and his room.

There was a guest – about to open his door – next to Schnabeln's room as he got out of the elevator. Friendly and polite, Schnabeln wished him the customary good night, and

281

unlocked his own door. The guest, who was a tall, somewhat rumpled-looking man, just stood and grinned, nodding his good-night, the key to his room still in his hand. As Schnabeln pushed at his door so the guest's strong arm closed around Schnabeln's wrist.

Before he knew what was happening Christoph Schnabeln was on his back, sprawled on the carpet in the middle of his room. The lights were on, the door closed and the tall guest leaning against it, still grinning.

"Pax and all that, cocker," the guest said in English. "Same flag. Spendthrift, isn't it? Sorry about the throw. Seemed the only way." He held out a hand. "Name of Curry Shepherd. Don't travel with a nom de plume or under false papers. Quick in and out job, that's me. Come to utter warnings and whisper in your ear. Give help if needed, cocker. Bring 'em back alive if possible."

Schnabeln shook his head. This he did not like. In English he asked, "Who played the Young Shepherd in *The Winter's Tale* at Stratford-on-Avon in the 1960 season?"

"Bloke called Ian Holm. Come on a lot since then."

"Who was the director?"

"Peter Wood."

Schnabeln nodded. Mr. Curry Shepherd was clean. "You have a message?"

"Everybody out."

"That it?"

"Just about. London says everyone's blown by some crypto called Trapeze. Moscow Centre. So, everyone out."

Schnabeln asked how quickly they had to go, and Curry Shepherd sat down, stretching his long legs in front of him. "London says it's probably too late now. Yesterday would have been a good idea."

Very coolly, Schnabeln told him that it would be tomorrow night at the earliest. "We have an operation running."

"Yes, cocker, I know. Other point actually. Take me to your leader, and that kind of thing. Good idea if I saw him."

"Who?"

"The Master. Big Herbie. The living legend. He's here, isn't he?"

Schnabeln said nothing.

"Well, isn't he?"

"Cat got my tongue," Schnabeln smiled.

"London's pretty upset with him. Really in everyone's interests if we can get him out – and the others."

Schnabeln said he did not think there was a chance in hell. As he said it, his hand moved to his watch, bleeping *Trepan*, wondering if they had already dismantled, and if it was a waste of time.

6

THE *Trepan* TEAM had not packed up and gone home. Worboys and Miriam had been taken off watch – sent to rest while Tubby Fincher and Tiptoes Corn kept an eye on the machines.

Max remained *hors de combat*, while Charles sat, curled like a cat, in the chair originally intended for Herbie. He looked about as lethal as a kitten, but for the pistol lying in his lap.

Before taking complete control, and organising a dual watch system, Tubby Fincher explained the situation, as authorised by the Director: therefore a truncated and incomplete version. The double, who was to have been gouged from the East under the original brief to the *Trepan* team, was probably a long-term prospect from Moscow Centre, known as Trapeze. "It makes a difference." Tubby laced his dry stick fingers together. "Herbie worked on the assumption that we were going after one of his people who had been spun in the wrong direction." Someone, he continued, trained, and a career officer in the Soviet Service, was a very different kettle of fish. The job these men and women were doing in East Berlin was important, but required only the minimum instruction. Their experience, though considerable in years, and – up until recently – their understanding of loyalty did not require full professional status. The double Herbie chased now was almost certainly a person of skill.

Berlin Station remained in the dark, just in case Herbie – who had taken the most rash and dangerous action, in a career full of danger – managed to pull it off. "I'm hoping, though," Fincher looked at the machines, and not the team, "that he will be persuaded to get out and come home before *Trepan* turns to catastrophe."

While they might have to call upon the full services of Berlin Station eventually, a small operation ("Limited to basics") was already under way. Head of Berlin Station had briefed one of their street men with good cover in the East. He was even now on his way with a message to Spendthrift.

Tubby had run a small subterfuge of his own. Berlin's man had been contacted – personally by Tubby Fincher – just before he left. "I got to him, and blocked any feedback to Head of Berlin Station," Fincher gave his thin, rather ruthless smile. "The messenger boy's taking a personal plea from the Director to Herbie. Come home now and all will be forgiven: there'll always be a lamp in the window for our wandering boy."

All they could do now was wait. Berlin knew Tubby was in town, on a domestic matter, but he had facilities to talk directly to London, through the Station's machines: if that proved unavoidable.

Worboys and Miriam Grubb, off watch, lay in each other's arms: the door safely locked against sudden intrusion. The loving had been subdued. Now Worboys smoked, while Miriam silently stared at the ceiling. Both had forebodings; gloomy and grey as winter. "You know him better than I," Miriam clasped Worboys' hand, asking the odds on Herbie's chances.

"He's got magic powers. That's on the record. Big Herbie's slipped his large self through tight nets before. But . . ."

"Are they all going to end up dead in East Berlin?" She did not look at Worboys, her voice quivering.

Worboys did not even reply. His thoughts were directed on Herbie who was at that moment walking into the foyer of the Metropol Hotel.

*   *   *

Herbie was smiling to himself, wondering how Spendthrift had fared. With luck everything would be arranged.

Unlike Christoph Schnabeln he had felt the tension before the operation started. Now that tension was turned into a driving force, almost a professional obsession. There was fear, naturally. Only fools felt no fear in the field. There were still grave question-marks drifting in his brain, like odd patterns made from cigarette smoke. They were with him always – Who? How? What means had Vascovsky used? Was Vascovsky's end game really an escape to the West? He hardly dared think of the consequences if this had not been the case – as Mistochenkov had sworn.

In spite of all these forces, now that Herbie had seen Ursula and was back on what he liked to think of as his old beat he was essentially at ease. Watchful, worried, frightened, but paradoxically at ease. Being in the field was really like swimming or riding a cycle. An old hand should be able to slip back into the second skin of that secret life as easily as a good swimmer could plunge into a pool.

Even with the ease there was no relaxation. When you were on your own, in the dark labyrinth, one thoughtless moment could spell disaster. The techniques of watching his own back were ingrained, and his actions were based on routines he had followed countless times before.

In truth, Herbie Kruger had never left the field: aware constantly that enemies, from other times in his long career, could pop up like trapdoor spiders to haunt, maim or kill, even in the most unlikely places. At least since being with Ursula, part of his body was at rest and his emotions salved.

Now a shadow fell over his mind. The reunion with Ursula, and its outcome – which he had never seriously doubted – was the relatively easy part. If Schnabeln had done his job there would be unpleasant work ahead, even within the next hour or so. The kind of work from which Herbie naturally shrank and detested. He had seen too much of it before.

A smiling desk clerk handed Herbie his key. He spoke immaculate English. No, there were no messages for Herr Kagen. Herr Kagen thanked him and said good night, in the assumed atrocious German.

Instinct told Herbie there was someone in his room. It had nothing to do with setting markers – matchsticks in the door, threads over the latch, tiny pieces of wax on the knob. In well-run hotels those old tricks were useless, because of the constant coming and going of hotel staff, chambermaids and the like. There was only experience – hunch, sixth sense, years of being alert and of living two lives in one body. Call it what you will, Herbie had it; the room was not empty. His heart lurched and there was a tremble in his thighs. Over the hill? he thought. The activity with Ursula? So near the truth, this would be a bad time to die. His stomach knotted, and with some alarm Herbie realised that his breathing had become shallow, his heart thudding.

He put the key into its lock, keeping his body against the wall, to the left of the door. It used to be an old trick: hide in the target's room, then shoot through the door at precisely the point where your target would be standing as he unlocked.

One hand on the key, the other grasping at the small length of necktie protruding from his waistband. One tug would release the automatic pistol from his thigh, dropping it down his trouser leg. Do it, Herbie. Come on, you know all the short cuts: all the sleights – the legerdemain of survival. He took a deep breath, turned the key and opened the door – pushing hard so that it swung in quickly, fully wide, combining the push with a swift kick.

Keep against the wall, out of any line of fire.

When he spoke it was with the American accent, German flavoured. "Come out quietly with your hands on your heads." He kept it soft. "The police are here. You have no chance of escape." Waiting for the eruption: the back-up man down the hall, or in the room opposite; or the sudden burst of fire. Maybe a grenade, or the silent death – the pellet with dissolving seals, like Georgi Markov. Even death in the field had changed since Herbie had been away.

The lights were on – or at least a standard lamp. Herbie had not seen it through any cracks, so presumed it had just been switched as he pushed the door open.

Then the voice, vaguely familiar, though he did not place it until he saw the face –

"Herbie, old cocker, it's okay. All chums together. Give you my word. Officer and gent, all that rot. Just come on in. Got your pal Spendthrift with me."

The last part of the speech was crossed with Schnabeln telling him there was no danger.

Herbie walked into the room, kicking the door closed behind him. Curry Shepherd was sprawled in one of the chairs. Christoph, looking green, stood by the other.

"Curry Shepherd. My God. It's been a long time."

"The old Big Herbie himself, in all that flesh. What's a large man like you doing in a place like this, cocker?"

Herbie's eyes flicked towards Schnabeln, then back to Curry Shepherd.

"What is it?" He was asking Schnabeln, his eyes still on Shepherd.

Christoph Schnabeln explained, using admirable brevity.

Herbie stood, legs apart, in the centre of the room where he had halted his entrance. Almost to himself he said, "Trapeze?" Then, addressing Shepherd, "They just gave you the crypto, Curry, Trapeze? No clues? Just Trapeze?"

"Sorry. Not very explicit, that part. Bit of added weight to convince you. Don't think they've any idea themselves: you know how it goes? Trapeze as in circus."

"Okay, Curry. So you have done your job. Always were a good postman. Now you should go, I think, before people get hurt."

"Dare say I should. But London really wants you back over that pile of East Deutsche masonry, PDQ Herbie."

"PDQ?" muttered Schnabeln.

"Pretty Damned Quick," Herbie snapped, fast, still not taking his eyes from Shepherd. "I put something to you, Curry – cocker," this last a credible imitation of Shepherd's irritating speech mannerism.

"Put away, old Kruger." Shepherd glazed his face with an affable smile.

"You argue that I have no right here. You bring orders. Get Herbie back, fast; abort the operation; close down the networks. You understand any of that?"

"Only the obvious."

"Right. You don't know what they're talking about when they say close the networks, get the people out. Okay, you give me an order from London. You pass a message to Spendthrift here. Now, I make you an offer, Curry. Either go or assist. There is no possible way anyone can get back to the West before tomorrow evening at the earliest." He hesitated, genuinely considering the full implications. "Oh, yes, probably some of Spendthrift's people can start moving first thing. Others may begin to get out by late morning. But nobody is going to move before tomorrow" – he glanced at his watch – "I mean today. Sunday." A grin at Schnabeln. "Bleep."

Their hands moved in unison. Back, high above the Mehring Platz, Tubby Fincher looked up from his chair.

"Both of them," Tiptoes whispered, as the bleeps showed up on the map, the audios crossing one another in the speakers.

"Snug in the Hotel Metropol." Fincher closed his eyes, asking if Schnabeln's bleep was out of phase. It was. Ten minutes out. Trying to tell us something? wondered Fincher, shifting his lean rump on the chair. His body was not made for long periods of repose. Had they got Shepherd's message? Were they trying to say, 'Here we are now; watch out, we're coming back'? A hundred times Tubby Fincher had gone over the thing in his head and come up with no stable answers. He also had doubts as to Herbie's knowledge of the truth; but at least – if Curry had reached them – Herbie would know what he was up against.

Back in the East, in his room, Herbie repeated, "Nobody is going to get back straight away. Not now."

"Told you: probably too late anyway."

Herbie, heavy on the sarcasm, said he had gathered as much. "But you see, Curry, I came over on my own initiative to clean up a mess. A mess I made years ago: my mess. Everybody out may be a good order, but it's one that cannot be obeyed. For one thing, I shall be seeing all the people concerned during the day. I shall be clearing up the mess. So either go now, or stay and assist."

Curry Shepherd gave what might have been taken, in other people, for a shrug. He was under orders. "Queen and country, all that sort of rot, cocker. Includes orders to give assistance and get you out, but fast."

If those were Shepherd's orders, Herbie said, they were instructions that would have to be bent to the facts. "Either help, as you are ordered, or go now. Get away and save your skin."

Herbie had known Curry Shepherd for a long time. They went back together into a past littered with betrayals and political polkas of great intricacy. During one of those times, like a thief in the night, Curry had occasionally come over the Wall – God knew how – to carry intelligence in or out. Curry had also been one of those who were involved with the sporadic handling of the Telegraph Boys during their period in the wilderness. For Curry, your skin came second to the job – particularly when the chips were down. Of this Herbie was fully aware. He did not even wait for a proper response; asking Shepherd about his cover, and getting the answer pat. He was free until Monday morning, when he really had to show the flag and trot around some publishers' offices. "Go through the motions."

"You don't want to waste all of this Sunday, Curry, do you? Not when Uncle Herbie's on the warpath."

Curry Shepherd grinned. "Try to make me leave, old cocker. But I have to put it all on the table, though I'm sure it's there in the old pate. The scarecrow – the Fincher – said I had to impress it on you." He repeated what Tubby had said, almost word for word. Adding that he did not follow it all himself. "You're not dealing with a simple double: someone given a bit of training and political propping by us, then let loose over here. It's not about a straight spinner any more, Herbie. Old Tub said you had to understand you were dealing with a died-in-the-wool, fully-trained Moscow Centre covert. Someone who's been at it from the beginning – whenever that was. Probably awarded the Order of the Red Banner with snowflakes, or whatever they get for the work. Old Tub said the bloke's a pro, and he'd suss you quick as John Peel's hounds on a cold and frosty morning."

Herbie gave a series of small nods. Tubby Fincher, Curry Shepherd, old Uncle Tom – whatever his name was in that odd English folk song – and all, were perfectly correct. If they were dealing with a Moscow-trained asset the odds were now heavily against them; if only because the asset would also have been wise to Vascovsky and Mistochenkov. It figured. The hush funeral for Jacob Vascovsky. The fact that someone like Kashov had flown in: Kashov, a low-profile operator, Herbie thought. The man even hung on to the rank of major when his true rating should really be something like full colonel, or higher. Kashov, whom Schnabeln had seen with Hecuba. Kashov, hit man organiser; chief weasel to the

Centre. Second from the top in Department V: the assassination bureau.

"Okay, Curry. You stay. Do as you're told, right?"

"Right."

Herbie moved for the first time, dropping into a chair, asking Schnabeln to go through the steps for him.

Like a bloody dancing instructor, Shepherd thought, but it only took a matter of three minutes or so before he realised how poorly he had been briefed. At the Dahlmannstrasse house Head of Station had, naturally, given him the bare essentials only. The old need-to-know principle working against itself, he thought. Listening to Spendthrift, whom Herbie referred to as Christoph, or even just Chris, was like hearing a new language for the first time.

He understood the basics because they were plain field techniques: mostly handling stuff, the gist of which a cretin could pick up in an hour or two – in a couple of lectures at the school. Less, in fact, because he had once heard Herbie's famous talk on agent handling, while he was at the school having an oil change. That was an eye-opener, and helped with the language now. He deduced two safe houses, and a series of meetings with six assets crammed into six hours. The handling of the assets was complicated, and not being played by the book. Someone was still setting up a couple of them.

Then they got into an area which froze even Curry Shepherd's blood, which he always reckoned had been treated with ethylene glycol at birth. The subject was one Luzia Gabell.

"Still using the same name, according to my source, which is sound." Schnabeln said there was no address, just that she seemed to be working as an amateur whore, in an apartment over an *Apotheke* near the Alexanderplatz.

Herbie went white. His body tensed to the point of shaking; his fists clenched. An apartment over an *Apotheke*, near the Alexanderplatz. If there was ever a clincher that was it. Vascovsky had used her – his mistress and adviser on the Schnitzer Group. When the Schnitzer Group had run for cover, or been killed off, nothing could be more appropriate than to set up his woman in a nice apartment, going begging. Where better than the Schnitzer Group's main safe house? It was the only apartment Herbie knew in that area located above a chemist's shop. Bitterly, he thought, the bastard probably had the place done up for her as well: so the smells could not percolate up from the dispensary.

As if by some Pavlovian trigger, Herbie Kruger let out a throaty cry of rage. "We go and talk with her . . ."

"Now?"

"Of course now, Christoph. This has to be done before anything."

"But . . ."

"I know. I know the Vopos question people more after midnight. I know they stop cars. But it has to be done."

"In the early hours, perhaps . . ."

"You got a set of picks?"

"Of course, but Herbie. If –"

"If we're stopped, too bad for those who stop us. Curry'll watch our backs. We go in. I know the damned place where she's living. That's what makes it worse. Main safe house of my old network – the one she fucked up."

Schnabeln saw there was no stopping him. Curry said that, at this time of night, he did quite a good lost drunk act for watching backs. That would not seem odd around the Alexanderplatz.

"What if she's got a man with her?" Schnabeln asked.

"Then he gets it first," Herbie still looked drained of colour – the white face of true rage and revenge. "I talk to her. Then . . ."

Schnabeln made a small choking noise. "You said," he began.

"I said you wouldn't have to do it. I do it. I recruited her. She blew a whole network – years of work – sky high. I talk, then I do her," his hand came up, palm flat, slashing violently over his own windpipe. The action was horribly realistic.

Jesus, thought Curry Shepherd, no wonder they want him back in London. He knew Herbie was not a natural killer – not equipped for those satanic arts. Yet any man, if driven by duplicity, can kill with no second thoughts.

Schnabeln took a step towards him. By the time he reached Herbie's side the big man had calmed. "It's what I came to do. First, the one who caused many brave people to go to their graves, and who played the double for a long, long time. Second, the one who's at it now. We go by car. Yes?"

Schnabeln said some of the way by car. They could do a roistering act for the last couple of blocks, and leave Curry watching them. A charade. Was Herbie sure of the place?

"I'm so sure it's almost killing me." The wrath was returning quickly. "It's Vascovsky's final pay-off, Chris. His little joke. Let's get on with it. There's some tough confessing to be done, and Fräulein Gabell to be sent to her damnation."

7

HERBIE DOWNED A swift, large vodka before they left the hotel. He also insisted on examining Schnabeln's wallet of lock picks. A change had come over him, almost terrible in its focused concentration. He issued one order after another: quick, clear and decisive. To Curry Shepherd Herbie suddenly seemed to have become a man with the scent of success – and possibly blood – in his nostrils.

Schnabeln explained separate and devious routes through the hotel to the car park. The trio moved off in different directions, sixty seconds between each departure, arriving in turn to where Schnabeln's Wartburg stood among a sad scatter of vehicles.

Herbie was the last to reach the car, having taken time to scout the park from at least three different angles. He needed action now: drive – determination – no hesitation. Having put his whole career on the block, Herbie did not intend to be let down now by any of the people upon whom he depended. After all, the reason he had come over the Wall himself lay at the heart of the premise that his own soul, the mainspring of revenge, could not be transplanted into another person: even a dedicated operator like Christoph Schnabeln.

Herbie had removed the Browning automatic from the tie harness. On emerging from the hotel to survey the car park the weapon was back in his waistband, butt down and muzzle pointing outwards.

Before reaching the car he made a brief detour to examine a small grey van parked nearby. Vans were, to Herbie, danger areas: the homes of those surveillance teams known, in the argo of his trade, as peepers.

The van was empty, and Herbie ninety per cent satisfied that there were no leeches on their backs.

Schnabeln drove with consummate care. Curry, murmuring something about always being the arse-end Charlie, slewed himself uncomfortably around in the back, so that he could watch the rear. Few cars moved in the streets, for it was now almost one-thirty. A policeman on foot patrol, near the hotel, hardly even looked at them.

Not one of the trio would deny the sense of vulnerability, for at this time of night East Berlin took on a look more menacing and grey than during the day: the sinister quality accentuated by the fuzzed angles of buildings, made eerie by the dim street lighting, which caused shadows to leap and blur in strange, unnatural shapes. The streets were more bare and deserted after midnight than in any other city Herbie had ever encountered.

"There is a door to the left of the *Apotheke*," Herbie told them. "It used to be open permanently, but there'll almost certainly be a lock on it now." He went on to express the hope that Schnabeln knew how to negotiate even difficult – probably Russian – locks at speed. "If you botch it I take over, right? I want in, and I want quiet. Stairs inside; then a landing. Door to the right. No shoulders or forcing. You pick that lock as well: fast. Only if there is a chain on the inside do we smash. Got it?"

Schnabeln said he had got it, though his voice indicated he did not like it one bit.

They parked in a deserted side street off the old Munzstrasse. Five minutes' easy walk to the place, Herbie said: but they did not plan an easy walk; not with a roistering routine. Roles were taken on from the moment they stepped out of the car – Schnabeln staggering a lot as he went around the vehicle, locking it and testing doors. Herbie and Curry Shepherd rolled around a little, giggling; making obvious attempts to subdue uncontrollable laughter. Curry and Schnabeln had been made to take quick swigs of vodka, just in case they ran into talk-out trouble. As it was, Schnabeln had already consumed his fair share of Schnapps during the evening; but he had the hard, clear head of a controlled drinker.

Eventually the trio linked arms and, keeping the noise down – making a great show of suppressing hilarity and mirth – they staggered and swayed their way up towards the Alexanderplatz: only a stone's throw from the Town Hall, meeting place of government.

Herbie had ensured the approach led them right up to the *Apotheke*, having gone through the routine with them before leaving the hotel. They were about three minutes from the place when he spoke quietly to Curry. "Almost there. If you totter across the road now, you'll see it. Plenty of doorways where you can watch; but get yourself right opposite. Come at the gallop if things get heavy."

Curry let out a swooping burst of laughter, unlinked his arm, slewed into the road and fell down. They called to him – with exaggerated softness – telling him to get up, which he did, in a series of strange movements: rolling on to his hands and knees then shuffling his legs forward, lifting his backside into the air, then finally making it to his feet, doing a two-step back towards them, spinning on his heels and, bent at the waist, projecting himself across the road with uncontrolled impetus.

Herbie swayed away from Schnabeln, almost falling into the gutter – in reality making certain of their position in relation to the shop. He spun around, then resumed his arm-linked progress with Schnabeln. The street was empty, he said. Only a few metres to go. Curry could be seen stumbling along on the far sidewalk, cannoning off walls, finally coming to rest in a shop doorway.

Ahead of them, in the Alexanderplatz itself, three sets of headlights swept the street, completing their circle and heading away. Herbie stumbled again. They were abreast of the *Apotheke*. He unlinked his arm, hit the wall with his shoulder, and sat down heavily close to the wall on the far side of the door, which was – as he had told them – to the left of the chemist's shop. Schnabeln went through the motions of helping Herbie to his feet and propping him against the wall – his back to the Alexanderplatz, facing Schnabeln, who now had his wallet of picks in his hand.

"Quick. Like lightning, Chris," breathed Herbie. The door, he noticed, even by the dull street lighting, had been cleaned up and painted since he was last there. A wave of nostalgia ran through him like a shiver at the onset of 'flu. So many hours of waiting, knowing one of the other members of the Schnitzer Group watched out for him – sometimes in the very doorway where Curry Shepherd now squatted. Stupidly he wanted, most strongly, to see how Vascovsky had redecorated the place. It had been a mess when they used it, in the late fifties and early sixties.

Schnabeln gave a short grunt. He had a pencil flash on the lock, working very quickly. The click as the lock gave was like a pistol shot, magnified in the empty night, vibrating down the street.

Herbie felt in his pocket, pulling out a pair of soft gloves, putting them on quickly as Schnabeln gingerly opened the door, using his shoulder to push it silently back. A light burned above the stairway. Herbie, conscious of an approaching car in the street, coming away from the Alexanderplatz, quickly followed Schnabeln inside and closed the door. The lock was the Russian equivalent of a Yale; easy enough to get out in a hurry.

There had been no carpet on the stairs in Herbie's day. Now a dark green covering filled the small hall, fitted right up to the landing. It was secured on each stair-tread by the outmoded method of polished brass rods; the short hand-rail and balusters had been painted white, and the walls – cracked and peeling, reeking from the dispensary in Herbie's day – were covered by a heavy, ornate paper, also in a green, matching the carpet.

Two prints hung, one above the other on the stair wall: Berlin in the late nineteenth century. One was of the Unter den Linden; the other, the Tiergarten in summer.

Herbie nodded Schnabeln up the stairs, both men moving on the balls of their feet, heels lifted, making sure the weight was equally balanced as they took each stair.

There was another print on the wall of the landing. Probably the same artist: certainly the same period – the Brandenburg Gate in winter, with the victory sculpture frosted white in the snow.

Schnabeln whispered that there was someone at home. Light showed under the door. That had also been changed. It had been a rough brown affair during the Schnitzer Group's tenure. This was a relatively new door, panelled and smooth, painted in the same dark green as before.

Schnabeln studied the lock, whispering that it was similar to the one on the street door. Then Herbie noticed something else. The door was not quite flush: on the latch, as though someone was expected. No sound from inside. Only the light, and the door not correctly closed.

Once more the intuition; only this time Herbie experienced genuine fright, feeling the short hairs on the back of his neck rise, like a dog's hair will rise at something fearful. Fearful was the word that came straight into Herbie's mind. The sixth sense seemed to be telling him that ghastly, horrible things had happened in this apartment, not long ago. He sniffed the air, catching the hint of something: fairly recent cigarette smoke hanging in the hall. Russian tobacco.

As they had watched Curry do his drunken pirouette across the road, Herbie – distracted for a moment – had thought a shadow moved, approximately from the street door area. Just a dark patch, caught in movement, from the corner of his eye. There one minute, gone the next.

Gently, Herbie pushed Schnabeln to one side, drew the Browning automatic, and placed his gloved hand on the door, just above the lock, using minimum pressure to swing the door inwards.

Vascovsky had done her proud. Very modern furniture. Swedish by the look of it – plain wood, glass, metal. One wall was taken up by an ornate mirror that was out of place among the modernity – the sleek table and matching chairs; the angled lights, high in the corners of the room; the slender standard lamp, and the big bed, covered with imitation skins. The window, which Herbie had used, many times, to watch for an expected visitor, was not visible, covered by wine velvet drapes matching the heavy, brocaded wallpaper, and thick pile carpet. The colour had been well chosen, it did not show the blood. There was a lot of blood.

Behind him Schnabeln retched. Herbie swallowed, because the blood smelled. The place reeked like an abattoir, the gore still warm. Some of it continued to run, like slime, from near the ceiling where it had jetted.

The horror, for Herbie, was the way in which she had died. It was as though his own violent pantomime of throat-cutting, performed in the hotel bedroom at the height of rage, had almost physically triggered someone into the action.

Luzia lay half on the bed, half off. Someone had taken a sharp knife to her throat, and with such force that the head was almost severed from her body, lolling back like a broken doll. There was no doubt that it was Luzia; a little older, but still the same perky features, even in the grotesque manner of her departing.

The face was ash grey, drained of blood, even to the lips; eyes wide and staring, but not with any horror – just looking out, sightless, in repose. The most repellent aspect was the mouth: lips drawn back, mouth open as if to scream, the gums and teeth displayed in what was almost a wolfish snarl. It seemed set for eternity.

Schnabeln retched again, and Herbie turned, pushing the pistol into his hand and telling him gruffly – covering his own feelings – to get out and watch the landing. The rage he had felt on hearing that Vascovsky had put Luzia Gabell into the old Schnitzer safe house now turned to something else – mainly memories of that unknowing time, when he still imagined, in his naivety, that Luzia was one of theirs – one of his – a faithful and loyal operator of the Schnitzer Group. Her betrayal had already been washed from his system. There was still anger; but it was the anger of having been thwarted.

Herbie needed to speak to Luzia, extract details from her – the minutiae of the picture: how she had been able to double on him for all that time. He had only wanted the briefest technical terms. After that he would have killed her. There was no doubt about that. It was one of the things for which he had risked coming over the Wall. Now both the act of revenge and the questioning were taken beyond his reach. It puzzled Herbie: all he could think about was Luzia Gabell alive, back in the old days. The guttersnipe face, the petite figure sashaying through the packed bodies at the Rialto. *The best little ass this side of dreamland.* Her old aunt who would not go west of the Brandenburg Gate. The rapes. *They're worse than the Nazis. Arschlöcher.* Luzia, on Herbie's bed, naked. Both of them young, virile and with a sense of purpose. Wasted by her; and now she in turn wasted.

He forced the litter of images from his mind, and began a fast, methodical search. On top of a small bedside table stood a framed photograph, instantly recognisable – the slim face, neat grey hair, combed back; the nose and mouth of a Frenchman, the eyes shining out in a look of adoration, lips slightly parted, as though he was about to tell her something. I love you? It was, naturally, her lover of all those years, Jacob Vascovsky.

He lifted the edge of the large ornate mirror to ensure it was not a two-way fitment, and went over any other likely hiding places for the mechanics of *son et lumière*.

Then Herbie went through the drawers, as quickly as he knew how. There was little, except in the small desk, where he unearthed a number of letters, written on blue, thin paper. They all began, *Lotte Darling*, and finished, *Your adoring Jacob*. He stuffed them into his pocket, and went on rummaging, finding two snapshots – one of Vascovsky, taken, he thought, in the early sixties. The other was of the pair of them, close together, sitting on a settee in some unknown room, her head on his shoulder, a look of happy contentment on both their faces.

On the back of Vascovsky's photograph were scrawled the words – *To Lotte, or whatever name she chooses, my love, ever J*. Herbie added the snapshots to the letters in his pocket. Another fast look around, trying to avoid even glancing at the body, before ripping the telephone cable from its box, low on the wall. He went to the door and put the catch down. Then, just before leaving, he did something which at the time seemed unaccountable. He bleeped the *Trepan* team in the Mehring Platz.

Only later did Herbie realise that the action was one of automatic subconscious technique. A psychiatrist could possibly even then prise from him the full logic of the way in which his mind led him. A long while later Herbie Kruger realised that it was in the old, transformed safe house – with Luzia Gabell's body on the bed – that he came to the inescapable conclusions about the whole business. Yet again, as any psychiatrist would have told him, Herbie could never have admitted the truth then; certainly not to himself.

In any case, Herbie was asking other questions. Why Luzia? Why at this moment, and in this manner? Schnabeln's Vopo friend had talked about a number of girls, working as semi-prostitutes, being murdered. A Jack the Ripper in East Berlin? The occupational hazard of these ladies? He doubted that. Luzia had friends in high places: being the late Colonel-General's girl she would rate as someone's prize. No, Luzia Gabell's end had come at this moment for one reason. The Telegraph Boys and the Quartet were blown. They must know that the news was out: maybe that Big Herbie was back in town – even that he had by now heard of Trapeze. Luzia had died because they did not want her pumped dry by any Western Service – particularly the British.

Closing the door, pulling it to make sure the lock clicked, Herbie gently took the gun from Schnabeln, who looked almost as ashen as the corpse. Then, with a nod of the head, he signalled his partner to follow him down the stairs. "Move, once we're outside." Go on ahead, Herbie told him. He would see to the street door and signal Curry to follow up. Straight back to the car. He would watch out for Schnabeln, and Curry would, presumably, keep an eye on him. Any sign of trouble at the car, disappear. "Lose yourself," Herbie hissed. "But be at the house in Weibensee in time for the first meeting. And work the dances" – by which he meant, get all their assets to the proper places at the arranged times.

In the fresh air the stench of Luzia's blood still stuck to his nostrils; and the pictures of her alive, happy and laughing would not go away.

8

THEY WERE ABOUT to change watch as Herbie's dip-dah bleep came through, and the map swivelled, the pin-point of light showing his location.

Miriam Grubb and Tony Worboys were just taking their places; Tiptoes Corn and Tubby Fincher had not yet left the room, so all eyes turned to the screen.

Fincher asked for a precise fix on the small map, though he knew already where Herbie's signal was placed.

Tubby's memory went back almost to pre-Kruger days. In his head, he held more confidential material than Herbie would ever see. He knew the files and places – not just in Europe, but world wide; and his secrets added up almost to the sum total of those held by both the Director and Ambrose Hill of Registry.

"I don't like you even leaving England," the Director said to him, before the dash to Berlin. "But you're the only one qualified." They both knew that Herbie, in reality, had little to give any confessors if he was nobbled; even though they refused him access to East Germany. There would be a few nuggets, of course, but nothing on the global scale that Fincher could provide. Herbie knew of Stentor's existence, of course, but with no details – not even the crypto.

Looking at the map, Fincher double-checked his memory, and came up with the right answer. That it puzzled him was an understatement. Herbie was bleeping from possibly the most insecure place in East Berlin – the old Schnitzer Group's prime safe house. A warning? Possibly. Aloud he said that at least they knew where one of them could be found. He tried not to look worried. He was tired and wanted to think. He and Tiptoes had tossed for sleeping quarters. Tubby had lost – condemned to a bedroll and blankets on the kitchen floor.

Lying there, trying to relax his muscles and at least get some rest, if not actual sleep, he worried at the complexities. From almost the outset Luzia Gabell had been Vascovsky's asset within the Schnitzer Group. No action taken, and Vascovsky seducing his own aide – Mistochenkov – into an ultimate defection. He recalled the Tapeworm confession reports. Vascovsky knew every move of the Schnitzer Group through Gabell. Then, in 1965 at the latest, Vascovsky knew at least the cryptonyms of the six Telegraph Boys. He also knew their purpose – so, presumably, the targets. There was a possibility, from Mistochenkov's own mouth and from the Psychological Stress Examination at Warminster, that Vascovsky knew about the Telegraph Boys even earlier than '65. Stentor's flash from Moscow indicated that every one of the Telegraph Boys was about to be blown; plus the Quartet.

Yet Gabell, Vascovsky's main asset, *couldn't* have known either cryptos or real identities. If Vascovsky had the ear of just one of the Telegraph Boys he could not automatically know the others – either their cryptos or identities. Why? Because only a handful of people knew: and the only person in East Berlin who had identities and cryptonyms in his head was Herbie Kruger – now over the Wall, chasing around places like the old Schnitzer safe house.

Tubby knew he had not revealed anything. Ambrose Hill was a guru who did not even speak to himself. The Director was above any suspicion. As much as he hated the idea, Tubby Fincher, putting Herbie's actions into perspective, could come to only one conclusion. The lovable, trusted Eberhard Lukas Kruger was the only person who had complete access. Ergo: the said Eberhard Lukas Kruger, Director of Special Projects, East Germany, was a Soviet asset. *Quod erat Demonstrandum.*

He could not believe it; but the logic was faultless.

* * *

The telephone bored into Martha Adler's sleep, like a pain drilling through her skull. Not again, she thought. Oh, please God, they're not checking again. It was going to be difficult enough getting rid of the lively little Kashov in time to make her crash meeting without any further complications.

Kashov had been ardent and most virile, to say the least. Martha had to admit she felt more sexually satisfied, when she finally drifted off to sleep, than she had done for years. At her age it meant a great deal. But by instinct she knew that neither the little Russian nor herself had been asleep for long. The telephone bell went on ringing. Whoever it was they were not going to give up.

Kashov made grumbling noises as Martha Adler stretched out and asked "Yes?" into the instrument. Her throat was dry, and the word came out as a croak.

The voice in her ear spoke German with a thick Russian accent. At first she could not understand him. Gradually it got through to her that the man wanted Major Kashov: urgently.

She had to pummel him awake, shouting that the call was for him. With great lack of grace, looking bleary-eyed and only partially awake, Kashov took the telephone, speaking in Russian. He listened for a few seconds, and Martha Adler saw him come more alive, his lips curling into a smile. He spoke a sentence, then listened again, putting his hand over the instrument and mouthing the word "*Kaffe*" at her.

She felt dreadful, switching on the lights, almost feeling her way to the kitchen blind, hearing the low mutter of conversation continuing in the bedroom; then the ping as Kashov replaced the telephone.

He stood naked in the kitchen doorway. "I'm sorry. There have been certain developments. I have to go and deal with things myself." He spoke in German, asking if he could possibly have some coffee before he left, to wake himself up. "They're sending a car for me." He repeated that he was sorry. He was also sorry, but he had left her telephone number at his office. "In case I was needed last night. I left this number, and the restaurant. I did not expect . . . You understand?"

Yes, Martha understood and told him so, wearily as she made the coffee.

*   *   *

304

Walter Girren was also making coffee in the small hours. Like Martha Adler it was not for himself. After covering a lot of ground Girren had finally run Gemini to earth – in a dangerously unauthorised drinking club at the far end of the Karl-Marx-Allee.

He had missed Moritz Winter twice. Once in a respectable bar, the second time in a place where they had told him Moritz had gone off with a girl called Mitzi. Mitzi he had thought was an obvious alias. When would these girls learn? Nobody knew where Mitzi lived, but she always worked this bar and would be back when she had taken care of his friend.

Mitzi – who turned out to be a tall busty woman of uncertain age, but definitely over forty – tried to persuade him to follow in Moritz' footsteps. He told her that was an odd way of putting it, and there was much merriment. "He was just like his friend, Moritz. Moritz was always full of jokes." He had talked about going on to this unauthorised bar which, according to Mitzi, was not good. The police often visited it, and none of the girls would go near.

Gemini had led Walter Girren a fair old dance, and when he finally caught up with him the prankster was too drunk to realise that Girren was his handler.

Schnabeln had given cause for Girren to assume – correctly – that the scheduled meetings were of vital importance, so he now broke every rule in the book: escorting the drunken Gemini into the street, holding on to him while he was very sick, getting him into a taxi – a very lucky chance at that time of night – and taking him back to his own apartment: a flagrant breach of field technique.

Black coffee – a great deal of black coffee – and a lot of walking the man around the small apartment, until at last a glimmer of hope. Moritz Winter took a long time to become sober enough to realise who Girren was: even longer to understand that there was work to be done.

Girren worked on him through the night, ending up with a sober, but very depressed and ill Gemini. He could sleep here, Girren told him. Here in his apartment. But he was not to answer telephones or the door. He was to remain silent as a tomb. Sleep if he could, but no going out, and no letting on that he was there.

Girren only left – to do his bump into Nestor, as this subject went for his Sunday morning milk – when he was quite satisfied that Gemini had grasped all the orders and the essential point of necessary complete security.

He did not even think – because there was no way of knowing the full extent of the situation – that there was any danger in leaving Gemini in his apartment, near a live telephone.

*   *   *

Big Herbie, with Schnabeln and Curry Shepherd, returned to the Metropol without incident, reversing the process of going back to their rooms by different and devious routes. Herbie wanted them all in his room exactly twenty-two minutes after Curry – the first one out – left the car.

They reported on the dot, and Herbie held a last briefing, leaving Schnabeln, who knew the exact footwork, to give Curry all the details and times. Once the arrangements were clear the party broke up – though Schnabeln still appeared tortured and shocked by what he had seen in Luzia Gabell's apartment. Herbie tried to reassure him as he left; but Herbie was himself in no truly tranquil state of mind.

Schnabeln had assured him that the driver of the taxi he had arranged was safe – "Because he is an innocent, and thinks he's dealing with a smuggling racket when he works for me. Besides, he gets well paid" – and would drop him on time at the appointed place in Weibensee.

Herbie was – as Service custom demanded – to be dropped short: five minutes' walk from the safe house. He constantly repeated to Schnabeln that it was essential he arrived by ten minutes to eleven, and that the first subject – Horus – did not see him.

Curry would watch Herbie to the house – and after. The itinerary was tight.

*   *   *

Nikolas Monch – Nestor – was prepared for a normal brush pass. He knew exactly where it would take place: about half way between his apartment block and the shop. He had over two dozen places for drops such as this, and had not used the present one for three months. It was the easiest, though he did not like passing intelligence so near to his home.

The wraith-like figure of his handler appeared on time, walking towards him. Monch only took a quick look, but he thought his handler appeared strained, ill almost. Certainly he looked very tired.

Monch transferred the small package of cigarettes in which his report was hidden into his right palm, so that he could pass his handler on the inside, thus shielding the passage of the cigarettes from prying eyes.

As he got to within a few paces of his handler Monch glanced back, making certain there was nobody close enough to observe the exchange. Then he pulled up short. His handler was slowing, looking at him, taking a cigarette from a packet of his own, and tapping his pockets.

As they drew abreast, Monch's handler actually approached him. "A light, comrade?" A hand on Monch's left bicep.

Monch, confused, looked around a little wildly. "Calm," muttered his handler. "This is very important. Listen to me; and for God's sake give me a light. There are orders. A special meeting with someone from the West. A crash meeting."

Monch's hand trembled as he lit the man's cigarette. He had always dreaded some moment like this. Through all the years he had carried on he knew the time would eventually come. Common sense told him that. Now it was here. The sudden order. The crash meeting. His first instinct made him wonder if anyone else was watching them.

*   *   *

Herbie Kruger dozed, woke, dozed again and then was fully awake, his mind turning constantly, following almost the same pattern as that of Tubby Fincher, over in the West, across the Wall.

Herbie did not doubt he would find the person who had blown the Telegraph Boys. The way he was going to make his pitch to each in turn would work. Maybe, if Curry Shepherd had not arrived with the warning that he was up against a trained Moscow asset, Herbie would have ruined the job. As it was, he was certain the whole thing had blown anyway. A straight play with the Gorky contact phrase was no good now. This had to be more devious.

If their target was from the Centre the warnings would already be out, the markers posted. Herbie, in those dismal small hours, faced the distinct possibility that this would be his last night of freedom; maybe his last night on earth.

He doubted that they would swoop on him before all six Telegraph Boys had been interviewed. That was common security. They would get him later – probably when he left the house on the Behrenstrasse, or when he got to Ursula. Maybe even just after that. He tried to work out ways around a final capture. Change the meeting with Ursula, for instance. No, he would just have to try a little nimble footwork. A mazurka.

If they got him – and they probably would – Herbie was determined they would have their money's worth. There could be no hanging about. Once the Soviet asset was fingered, Herbie would deal with him on the spot. Better leave him dead. They might know in the West, doing it that way.

When it came to the detection process Herbie was as logical as the next man. If you did it with the facts – as given by Pavel Mistochenkov, and through the files – there was only one conclusion any sane evaluator could make. The equation worked out to one answer alone – that he, Eberhard Lukas Kruger, was a double. That *he* was responsible for the treachery. Someone, he considered, shivering at the thought of Luzia's body with the head all but severed, had been very clever.

In a few hours he might have all the answers, and he did not want to leave any questions behind.

9

AT SIX O'CLOCK on that bright September morning, with the sky clear and the first slight hint of autumn in the air, Horus – Otto Luntmann – came off night duty at the Soviet Embassy. He felt happy. One or two tasty morsels had been retrieved from wastepaper baskets, where secretaries had dumped them instead of into the shredder. He had also managed to catch up on his reading of Gibbon's *Decline and Fall*.

In truth, Horus felt virtuous as he paced steadily up the Unter den Linden towards the Friedrichstrasse intersection. Even this early, some of the cafés were opening to catch passing trade: people on their way to or from work. Horus was tempted to stop and take a cup of coffee.

From a distance, on the other side of the road, his handler, Teacher – Anton Mohr – watched Horus leave, then started to walk quickly after him. Mohr overtook his subject before they reached the Friedrichstrasse. He crossed the road diagonally, putting himself slightly in front of his quarry, then slowed down to let Horus overtake him.

The virtuous feeling dwindled, like sand in an egg-timer, as Horus spotted his handler appear, as if by some trick, in front of him. He had learned much about the tricks of the trade, and knew this was no accident. His handler was slowing. Horus would have to overtake him, and, presumably, there would be some message passed or muttered. He would have to keep pace for just long enough to receive the message.

Anton Mohr heard his subject coming up on the inside. He prepared to quicken his step if necessary; but Horus slowed.

Looking straight ahead, Mohr spoke quietly. "Just say yes

if you understand. There is a most important crash meeting today. You will be at your appointed crash pick-up point at precisely ten-thirty. Be there. It is vital."

"Yes," breathed Otto Luntmann, lengthening his stride to draw ahead. To any casual watcher the two men had simply passed in the street, one overtaking the other.

Luntmann's guts turned. It was almost a quarter past six. His crash pick-up point was near his place of work. They always tried to plan it that way. At ten-thirty, in a little over four hours, he was required to be at the bus stop in the Franzosstrasse, not far from where he now walked. He did not know what was in store for him, but – after all this time – Horus had a fair idea. There was a lot to be done before ten-thirty: letters, telephone calls, possibly one other meeting. He increased his pace, trying not to run.

*   ·   *   *

Gemini, the trickster Moritz Winter, felt sick, lying on his handler's bed. He had expected something like this, but not quite yet. It was long overdue. He cursed himself for having gone out drinking; but at least he would not have to make the journey alone to his selected crash pick-up point.

His handler had given strict instructions. That was only to be expected. These people worked to schedules: old schedules, naturally, but schedules none the less. He must not open the door or use the telephone. Well, that was too bad, because he had to use the telephone. It was his only way.

He sat on the edge of the bed, shaking his head. After the telephone call he would take advantage of his handler's other offer – a bath and a shave.

Carefully Moritz Winter, face curving into the bright smile that broke the ice at parties, picked up Walter Girren's telephone and dialled the number at his place of work – the Soviet Military Headquarters at Karlshorst.

*   *   *

Peter Sensel had gone home with the man to whom he had been talking when his handler, Spendthrift, had pulled him out of *The Stallion*.

The man's name was Hans, or at least that is what he had told Sensel. Hans turned out to be no stallion. In all, the night proved very disappointing.

Priam, as Peter Sensel thought of himself, had a lot of time to kill before being picked up outside the State Library on the Unter den Linden: his crash meeting point. Hans was in the kitchen, making coffee. Maybe, Sensel considered, he should stay here, spin it out until the last moment. After all, the collection was not until half-past two.

He took a deep breath. This was it. The warning had come only a few weeks ago. He had been told everything, even to expect it at any moment. Perhaps the waiting was now over, and the crash meeting would take him on to bigger things. Yes, he would make the most of Hans; stay put; hole up until it was time. After all, the entire course of his life might well be altered after the meeting.

*   *   *

Ursula Zunder – Electra – had not slept since Herbie had left her the previous night. It was all too nervy, strained and desperate. She had known in her head and body that he would return. Of late that certainty was strengthened by a kind of inner knowledge.

At a little after eight, on Sunday morning, she received the call from her handler – just as Herbie predicted. The woman's voice on the telephone did the wrong number routine. She wanted 91 15 30.

So, Ursula thought, that's it. Fifteen-thirty. Half-past three, at her crash meeting-place: a bench on the West side of Treptow Park. She gave the right answers, put the telephone back on its rests, lit a cigarette, picked up the 'phone again and dialled a number, just as they had taught her.

*   *   *

Martha Adler did manage to sleep once Kashov left. It was easy. She groped her way back to the bed, which still smelled of his cologne; checked the alarm; switched off the light and closed her eyes.

The alarm went off just before ten-thirty. She did not feel in the least rested. Her body was tired, her eyes hurt, and her head had the entire tribe of Nibelungen hammering away inside. The only good thing was the trace of physical satisfaction remaining from Kashov's ministrations.

Too bad she would not see Major Kashov again. At one-thirty she had to be at her appointed place outside the cake shop. However she felt in the morning, Martha clearly remembered the order. Particularly this order.

Martha Adler had been hoping for weeks for the call to such an interview. Now she could only feel elation, mixed with a slight sense of fear, at its imminence.

She dragged herself to the kitchen and put on the coffee, much as she had done in the small hours for Kashov; then went back to retrieve the lacy wisps of underwear from the floor, where they had been thrown during last night's sexual cavort.

Sensible clothes today, Martha, she told herself. Sensible from the skin out. And the large handbag, to carry the most unauthorised of her possessions: the small pistol, just in case anything went wrong.

10

It WAS FOR technical reasons that the Quartet's safe house, in the western area of the Weibensee district, was deemed the worst of the two available.

Schnabeln had acquired the place at a time when an extra house was badly needed. In his cover job with the East German Tourist Office he was able to make many contacts with the criminal classes in the classless Workers' and Peasants' State. Among certain people Schnabeln allowed it to be rumoured that he had a handly little smuggling operation going for him. Indeed, he was able to produce small fruits of these ventures. It was a cover within his cover, providing people like the tame taxi driver and the girl to whom he leased the Weibensee safe house – on the under-standing that she would lose herself for certain periods of time. To be on the safe side Schnabeln insisted that she make herself scarce for the whole Sunday.

The reasons which contributed to the safe house being unpopular were numerous. It was a basement flat with three rooms, accessible only from the small set of stone steps that led directly down from the pavement. The windows at the front looked out upon the stone wall and on the steps themselves, giving no chance to watch the street. There were no windows in the rear; and, possibly worst of all, no rear exit. There was also no telephone. It was not essential, but was certainly an inconvenience.

The place was in a good neighbourhood: which was about all it had to commend itself. Apart from this, the Weibensee house was a model of what a safe house in the field should not be. A great shame, because the park-like terrain, with its greenery running down to the lakeside, made Weibensee particularly attractive.

Herbie knew about the drawbacks of the house, and did not like the idea of being cooped up, a sitting duck for three hours, while he talked to three of the Telegraph Boys. Any one of them could be a Moscow heavy, trained to pitch by a service that had gone from strength to strength in the years since it bungled, and was blooded, in the most active days of the Cold War.

The taxi dropped Herbie at the exact point Schnabeln had indicated. Herbie paid the man, adding a generous tip, even though he knew Schnabeln was seeing the driver right. If anything did go wrong at least the fellow would probably keep quiet for a few hours.

By ten forty-five the nip had gone from the air. The sun shone on the lime trees, like the ones planted in the Unter den Linden in an attempt to return it to some of its past glory. The air was mild.

People were already out and about, some of them even giving Herbie odd glances – recognising his clothing, the camera and briefcase as the natural accoutrements of an American. This area was not deep into the Weibensee district, but it was impossible for Herbie to cast thoughts of Luzia Gabell from his mind. She had lived not far from here, in a section that had suffered much during the war. It was uncanny to see how little of this particular part had changed since the nineteen-thirties. That was Berlin, though – vast tracts laid waste, with islands of the old buildings left intact. It was exactly the same in the West.

The key was where he expected it; Herbie let himself into the basement flat with caution. If there was trouble he would rely on his hands and body skills, for the pistol was again secured by the harness, the end of his old necktie peeping out from the waistband of his trousers.

As a precaution he travelled light. Since the dispersal orders arrived with Curry Shepherd, Herbie had decided the Metropol could do without his custom. After the final meeting – with Ursula – Schnabeln would drive them back to her apartment and collect her case. They would go straight on to the checkpoint from there – and pray. The few things Herbie had brought with him were still at the hotel. In the briefcase he had only the bare essentials – the documents and a spare passport for Ursula, who was to become Mrs. Herbert Kagen at the checkpoint.

The basement flat smelled musty: damp mixed with some oddly unpleasant frying smells from the tiny kitchen. Herbie opened the windows then went out to place a small pebble, he had carried in his pocket, on the bottom step outside the door – the signal that it was safe to enter. He had seen no sign of Curry Shepherd, but he would be around: the knowledge made Herbie feel a good deal safer.

He went back inside, closed the windows of the small front room and arranged the furniture – the table centre, a chair at each end. There was to be no informality. These interviews would be professional and without feeling. Every Telegraph Boy had to sense Kruger's anxiety – for one of them it should be the signal, the gradual talk-in before Herbie played the Vascovsky code phrase.

He opened the briefcase. Most obvious among its contents was the book containing the special fast-sender that Schnabeln would operate – from the prescribed place – the moment it was all done: just before the final flight back, should they get that far.

At dawn Herbie Kruger had encoded the message, and made the recording. All that was left to be done was the addition of the name – Gemini? Horus? Electra? Priam? Nestor? Or Hecuba?

Deliberately he looked at his watch. Two minutes to the first meeting. Two minutes to eleven, on a bright Sunday morning in East Berlin. He pressed the watch button and bleeped the *Trepan* team.

*   *   *

Half an hour earlier Horus – Otto Luntmann – waited ready at the bus stop on the Franzosstrasse. He was there slightly early, his copy of Gibbon's *Decline and Fall* under his left arm. Any book would do; that was the language to tell them he was prepared, and that it was safe.

At a minute to the half-hour he saw his handler approach

from the direction of the Friedrichstrasse. He carried a newspaper. Otto Luntmann adjusted his glasses, watched and waited. He was not sure of the exact moves. They had always been vague about crash meetings, saying only that the handler would be there. The pick-up could well be done by someone else. The sign would come from the handler.

Indeed, someone else was walking towards his handler now.

Schnabeln approached Anton Mohr with a wave and cheery smile. They shook hands, engaging in friendly, chance conversation. The dialogue was, in fact, terse.

"Lead me to him," Schnabeln smiled, as though he was really saying good morning. "Tell him to follow us, and get into the car with me."

"Okay. That all?" Anton Mohr sounded quite cheerful, the smile dying on his lips as Schnabeln continued.

"Unhappily no. Walk. Walk past him and tell him." They began to stroll in Luntmann's direction. "Once I've taken him, you get out."

"What?"

"Out. Use your dismantle documents – your escape route. The Quartet's finished. Take care. See you in London – if we get back. Just, good luck, my friend. For your own sake, move when we get into the car."

"My things . . .?"

"Forget it. We're blown."

They were abreast of Luntmann now, and Mohr had to pull himself together in order to mutter the orders.

Schnabeln knew that before the day was finally out he would have to go through this routine several times. Next to Herbie he would be the last man out. Schnabeln did not even think about the possible consequences: it was difficult enough to keep last night's horror out of his head.

As Schnabeln's Wartburg pulled away from the kerb – where it had been parked, in a side street near the bus stop – so Walter Girren put the old borrowed Mercedes into gear, steering into the traffic, keeping well back.

He had collected the car from his actor friend only an hour before, and knew the route. Christoph had talked it with him already – doing the footwork by mouth. Girren, driving as a tail, was as good a man as any, knowing the rules and technique down to the fine print. *Like they used to tell the fighter pilots,* his instructor had said, when they played these same games in London traffic, *watch out for the one in the sun.* By which he meant, keep looking in the mirror.

With this minimal traffic it was almost a joyride. When Schnabeln finally pulled over, a few minutes' walk from the Weibensee house, Girren accelerated past, heading for his next destination – home to get Gemini for the noon assignment. Schnabeln would be around Weibensee for a while, seeing this client safely in.

*   *   *

"Hallo Otto, glad you could make it." Herbie did not rise from the table, nor did he sound at all pleased that Otto Luntmann could make it.

The thin, scholarly figure peered, narrowing his eyes behind the thick glasses. "My God. Herbie? After all this . . ."

Herbie said, yes, he knew it had been a long time, but they had work to do. Would Otto – only he called him Horus – sit down? Schnabeln took up station at the door, and Herbie started an exceptionally quick-fire question-and-answer routine. Luntmann's recent work? How had he kept going through all the years, before the new handler had taken over? What was the real strength on the latest reports? How was his personal life? Had he noticed any distinct changes in the way the DDR was being run? Had he any indication that he was being watched? Suspected? Herbie hardly smiled through this whole business, which went on for some ten minutes.

At length Herbie turned to Schnabeln. "I think you can disappear now. I'll take care of things."

Schnabeln gave an unsmiling nod, followed by a look of deep suspicion at Horus. Before leaving he placed the pebble – the 'enter' sign – on the table by Herbie's elbow. Herbie hardly seemed to notice. Deep inside, he thought the timing was right. Schnabeln had to get back to the Lenin Allee for the Gemini pick-up.

For ten minutes more he continued the questions, gradually easing into a slightly more mellow approach – asking mainly

317

about Luntmann's welfare. Then he got up, went to the door and looked out. This time, when he turned, the familiar broad stupid smile creased his face. "Otto, my dear old friend. Sorry about all that, but I have to be careful with him. How are you really? It's so good to see you."

Luntmann, who was just regaining his poise, smiled back, shoulders slightly hunched – the ancient schoolmaster manner, worn like a favourite coat.

Herbie came over and embraced the scholarly man with great affection. The tension visibly ebbed from Otto Luntmann. Never, in his long relationship, during recruitment and training, years ago, had he known Herbie Kruger to be as brusque as this. The experience had made him fear the worst.

Herbie repeated it was good to see his old friend, who now asked what the meeting was really about.

"You don't know, Otto?" The stupid, idiot smile as Herbie turned towards the window, looking out on to the grey stone wall. He noticed the pits and cracks in the wall, heard the clip of feet passing on the pavement above, and glimpsed ankles, trouser bottoms, shoes and women's stockings as he glanced upwards. He allowed a carefully-timed sigh to escape his lips. Casually, he said they were safe enough now. Alone. Then he spoke the Gorky phrase, low but clear, moving his head slightly so that Luntmann would catch the whole sentence – "A man can teach another man to do good – believe me." As he said it Herbie turned quickly. Luntmann was sitting at the table again, looking at him through the thick lenses of his spectacles.

Watch the hands, Herbie thought. Hands, fingers, feet, that is where you should look. It was a common misconception that guilt or fear shows first in the eyes. *Look 'em straight in the eyes: innocent, even bewildered* was one of the first things any service taught about being interrogated. Particularly with a trained operator, or a cool professional, you watched the eyes last of all.

There was no agitation, no odd movements of Luntmann's hands or feet. Now Herbie could look at the face.

"What do you mean?" Luntmann asked.

Herbie repeated the quotation.

"I'm sorry," Luntmann looked genuinely puzzled now. "I'm sorry, I don't understand, Herbie."

"Isn't that what they told you? Perhaps you didn't expect it to be me, Otto. A surprise, yes?"

"Herbie . . ." he began, his hands making a small pleading gesture: a few inches of movement. "Herbie, I'm sorry. Perhaps there's been some mistake. What was it?"

For the third time Herbie repeated the Gorky phrase. Luntmann continued to look puzzled.

"I'm obviously in great error, Herbie . . ."

By this time Kruger was as sure as he would ever be. Otto Luntmann was not his man.

"It's okay, Otto. Just a reaction test" – one big hand flapping the air – "I'm afraid I have bad news. The worst."

It was as Otto Luntmann feared when he had the news of the crash meeting that morning. "Blown?" He could hardly get the word out.

Herbie nodded. Sky high, he told him before issuing the final instructions, making certain Horus still had his get-out papers – issued to all the Telegraph Boys after recruitment – and knew the escape route.

Luntmann said he suspected as much. He had removed his papers to a dead-drop. In a waterproof wallet, this morning, taped under a bench for old people: a good kilometre from where he lived.

Herbie thanked God for that. He did not want Otto going back to his lodgings. "You leave now. Straight away. I have money for you, to help. Swiss francs and West deutschmarks." He turned the briefcase away, so that Luntmann could not see inside, taking the first wad of notes, made up and secreted under the lining. In the original scenario Schnabeln was to have brought the money in.

As they finally embraced, Herbie cautioned Horus to go very fast, and with care. He wished him luck.

"I think you will need luck also, Herbie. Coming over to do this is a brave act." Luntmann did not smile.

Foolish and stupid, Herbie thought. Not brave, though. To be brave was something quite different.

One cleared. Five to go.

*　　　*　　　*

The whole of the *Trepan* team were in what they now called the Operations Room ("Bit grand, isn't it?" Worboys commented) when Herbie's bleep came from the Weibensee basement. Schnabeln's bleeps were arriving every half-hour, and seemed to have no pattern. "Buzzing around like a fly in a colander," Tiptoes muttered.

But Tubby Fincher was following the pattern. He could read it as easily as the morning paper. In spite of Big Herbie's blatant folly and criminal disregard of orders, Tubby Fincher had a sneaking admiration for the man – whatever side he was really playing. So strong had Fincher's final deductions become that, at dawn, he had gone over to Berlin Station, taking Charles to mind him. There he was given access to the machines, and talked to London for over half an hour, laying out the only possible and logical answer to the problem. However difficult the Director might find the solution, Tubby was in no doubt that his chief would have already come to the same conclusion – even if only in his subconscious.

The bleep, he knew, came from one of the two Quartet safe houses. Schnabeln's movements were those of a man doing the crash pick-ups. If Herbie was with the opposition the charade was very professional – seeing each of the Telegraph Boys in rotation, warning the double, letting the others go away satisfied but, almost certainly, with markers on them.

On the other hand, if Herbie was still their man, the actions were coolly brave – a filtering job: seeking out the culprit, then . . .? Then what? If – if – if Herbie were loyal, would he take the law to its final course in the field? Would he kill?

That was academic, Tubby thought. All he could do was sit back and watch developing events.

*　　　*　　　*

Schnabeln sat in the Wartburg, waiting at the appointed place for the Gemini meeting. The switch here was to be smooth and simple. Walter Girren, doubling as handler and watcher, would pick Gemini off the street – Schnabeln presumed, not knowing about the moves Walter had made to keep Gemini in tow. Gemini would be driven past the parked Wartburg, Girren marking his subject's card, dropping him –

perhaps around the corner – so that he would merely walk back and climb into the Wartburg. Schnabeln figured that Walter Girren was experienced enough to drop his subject at a point and distance that would just allow enough time for him to place the borrowed, battered Mercedes in position to tail the Wartburg out to Weibensee again.

It went off as smoothly as that. Quick, and very professional; even though Gemini looked as though he had fallen into a vat of alcohol.

On returning to his apartment Girren found his subject in better humour, though it had taken most of his precious store of coffee to do it. Gemini had shaved, bathed and was reasonably presentable. On the way over to the switch point Water Girren told his subject exactly what was going to happen. Presentable Gemini may be; hung-up he certainly was.

Schnabeln was away with Gemini sitting beside him before the subject even had time to close the passenger door properly. Gemini tried some bright conversation, but Schnabeln was in no mood for that: telling him to keep his mouth shut and eyes skinned. He'd have plenty of time for talking later.

Within the hour Schnabeln knew he would be seeing Girren again – for the Nestor pick-up. That one would be more difficult. The signal for need-to-talk had always been scratching his right ear with the left hand. He would have to be out of the car, praying that Girren spotted the sign in time to park nearby. At the Nestor pick-up it was essential that Schnabeln should break the news to Girren: order him out with his dismantle documents: tell him to run for cover. Though not until he had watched Schnabeln all down the line to the last drop.

That would leave only Anna Blatte to be warned – late in the day – at the three-thirty pick-up for Electra. After Nestor the next two were Schnabeln's own subjects: the leggy ash-blonde, Hecuba; and Queen Priam. He smiled at his own weak joke.

Schnabeln drove with great care towards a slightly different drop near the Weibensee house, twice catching a glimpse of Girren tailing him in the Merc. Then his mind drifted for a few seconds, thinking of how near he had come to not starting the day on schedule because of running slap into Hoffer in the main foyer.

Hoffer looked queasy after his night with the tourists, but had the grace to be concerned about Schnabeln's health – "Did you see the doctor as I suggested?" No, Schnabeln had just gone to bed and slept. He felt fine now, and would deal with tonight's tour. He might even go across with the driver and bring them in from the West. (On alternate nights, by arrangement with the tour company, the driver came from the East and was passed through the Friedrichstrasse checkpoint with no problems.) Hoffer was glad to hear Christoph would work tonight, "It would have been inconvenient for me . . . tonight would not have been easy . . ." He actually blushed. Everyone in the hotel knew Hoffer was two-timing his wife with a dumpy fat brunette waitress. Frau Hoffer imagined her husband worked with the tours on at least three nights each week.

Spread across the road in front of them, hanging between the trees, a large poster proclaimed *LONG LIVE THE WORKING CLASS*. Schnabeln thought he would drink to that. In the West nearly all the people he knew were working class, only some of them worked harder than others – hours the Trade Unions would never allow.

He pulled himself up sharply, bringing his mind back to the business in hand, feeling his guts sink. Already, this early in the day, Schnabeln was anxious. It would get worse, he knew; but his old friend Walter Girren, riding shotgun on his back, was a comfort. He pondered on what might happen if anything went wrong at one of the safe houses: how would Curry Shepherd react? Come to think of it, Curry was very good. Schnabeln had not spotted him all day.

*   *   *

Curry was good. Over the years, as an old Berlin hand, he had collected cobbled documents as a schoolboy hoards stamps. Among those he had brought with him – mainly in the linings of his jacket – was a complete set of identity papers which, as long as the light was right, would pass him off as a plainclothes member of the Volkspolizei.

322

At nine-thirty that morning Curry Shepherd had taken what he would call a 'look-see' at the basement – so-called – safe house, and picked out his best vantage point. Almost directly across the road was an old, opulent building, standing a short way back from the sidewalk.

After a couple of circuits Curry decided the place had been turned into apartments – about four, he thought, deducing from two of the occupants who were departing as he passed that they were student flats. It was all rather Richmond Park; though, when he heaved at the bell pull and the door was opened by a bent elderly man claiming to be the house superintendent, Richmond Park seemed as far away as the moon.

Curry only used his fluent German, with its perfect Berlin accent, when necessary. The Service knew; but few of his friends heard him speak German with anything but an atrocious English drawl.

He also managed to assume that threatening, dour attitude recognisable in most parts of the Soviet Bloc. Flashing the documents he spun a story about keeping an eye on a building across the street – not the one Herbie was using. He needed complete quiet, and one of the windows to carry out his observations. He would be there for at least three hours, and he might need to use the telephone in order to call a patrol. The house superintendent was to allow him these rights and make sure no word got out.

The couple he had seen leaving were happily off for a day – "She has a sick mother in the Charité Hospital" – and the old man was only too willing to open up their apartment: three rooms and a nauseating smell of cabbage.

So Curry was not seen. He had yet to conquer the Behrenstrasse job; but knew that would be easier, because there were cafés in the Behrenstrasse. Cafés always helped with surveillance. In his safe hide, Curry watched Schnabeln's arrival with Gemini, and nodded to himself at the timing. "On the button, cocker," he muttered.

The pebble was in place again on the steps, and Schnabeln took Gemini straight in, bleeping *Trepan* as he closed the door. Smack on time the noon meeting was under way.

Big Herbie went through his routine with Moritz Winter;

using exactly the same technique as with Otto Luntmann. First, the hard, cold, brusque manner: the questions, flung like a machine gun switched to automatic, and with no sign of sympathy for the subject. By the time Schnabeln was dismissed the usually joky Moritz Winter was sweating and looking very frightened.

The fear was quickly replaced by an almost dog-like devotion once Herbie did his quick personality change act.

"Christ, you had me worried, Herbie," Winter mopped his brow. The sweat gave off a high odour of last night's booze.

"I have to be careful: but you know that, Moritz." Herbie had begun to pick out faces among the cracks in the wall outside the window. He stood looking out in silence for a moment as he traced the outlines of ex-President Nixon's face in the stone. A good place for Nixon, he thought, this safe house in Berlin.

Just before he gave Moritz Winter the Gorky signal, a young girl passed along the pavement above him, swaying near the edge, her dress billowing, giving Herbie a quick but vivid view straight up her skirt. When he turned to face Moritz – after saying the magic words – Herbie was smiling with genuine pleasure.

Moritz Winter's hands lifted fractionally from the table, but his feet remained still, anchored and unmoving on the floor. "Sorry, Herbie?" he frowned.

"A man can teach another man to do good – believe me," Kruger repeated.

"Yes. Yes, I suppose so." Moritz grinned. "A woman would do it better. Is it a joke?"

Herbie said he thought Moritz would know. For good measure he added that Moritz would probably be surprised that it was him, Herbie, delivering the message.

"What message?" Winter looked at him, blankly, then started to sweat again. Finally he became angry.

Within five minutes it was plain to Herbie that Moritz Winter was clean. He sat down quietly, facing his old recruit across the table, and told him he was blown. That Gemini had to get out fast.

The details took less than seven minutes. The farewells, thirty seconds. "See you in London," Herbie said, the darkness inking over his mind with the knowledge that his own chances of getting back were far from high. Who in God's name was Trapeze? Curry's information had been basic. Was Trapeze and the Soviet asset, among the Telegraph Boys, one and the same person? Herbie longed for peace, quiet and some of Ambrose Hill's files. He needed a good think with, probably, the Mahler Seventh running in the background.

As he left the basement, Moritz Winter thanked God he had used his handler's telephone that morning. His escape documents were stashed at the house of a friend, who held on to a locked steel box for him, and he could be trusted not to tamper. Those he could get easily. The telephone call, from Girren's rooms, had been to his co-worker – another civilian storeman at Karlshorst. They had planned to meet that afternoon, as they did on many Sundays. Moritz told him a tale about being shacked up with this tart from Eberswalde: calling off the meeting. His co-worker was a good Party member, uncertain about Winter. The word that Winter was missing would have been out before evening if he had not telephoned.

*　　*　　*

Girren spotted Schnabeln's need-to-speak message and pulled the Merc over, parking only four cars away from the Wartburg. He told Nestor – Nikolas Monch – to stay where he was. If he called or waved Nestor was to come fast to the Wartburg, which he had pointed out as they drove past – just before he saw Schnabeln leaning against the bonnet, scratching his ear.

"Blown?" Girren scowled, a sullen kind of fury.

"Stay with it until you've seen me leave with Electra and the Big Man. Wait until then. I shall have to make one trip out before then – during the last meeting. But wait until I take them both away." Schnabeln said it might not be so bad. They may not have to wait that long, but everyone had to be told. "Watch out for yourself, Walter."

Girren was not a fool. Something was really up, and he had known it since the crash meetings were ordered: yet somehow he had not thought it to be as serious as this.

They made things look as natural as possible, with Schnabeln walking calmly over to Girren's car, chatting for a moment through the window to the grey, taciturn filing clerk who worked at the Nationale Volksarmee Headquarters: Nestor.

Finally Schnabeln opened the door and Nikolas Monch climbed out. There were handshakes, with both Girren and Schnabeln telling Nestor to behave naturally. "Smile a lot and walk slowly."

Girren, feeling a new hollow nausea deep in his stomach, kept his normal distance as they drove for the final trip out to the Weibensee house. Now that he knew, Girren tried to induce calm into his nervous system. His watch was sharper, his head more clear.

Once he saw Schnabeln and the subject make the drop, he accelerated away. He had half an hour. Schnabeln was managing incredibly, making the various pick-ups in less than fifteen minutes from the Weibensee house. Thank God the rest were nearer home, in the Behrenstrasse.

Girren had to be ready to follow Schnabeln from the pick-up point outside a cake shop at the junction of Invaliden-Brunnenstrasse. A blonde, Schnabeln said. Well, it would be a change of scenery. Now he had best make plans for himself. If he hurried, Girren reckoned he would just make his apartment, get his escape documents, and reach the cake shop in time for the collection.

His actor friend was unlikely to see his car again for a while. Girren's escape route was out through East Germany, crossing into the West from a point high up near the Baltic. His emergency documents would not tally with those he had cobbled for use with the car; but at least the old Mercedes would get him some of the way.

He parked about three minutes' walk from his apartment block, almost running to make up the time. The set of papers lay where he always kept them, under a loose floorboard – for Girren lived in one of the old, undamaged houses.

He made it back to the car in less than three minutes, leaped in, and was about to start the engine when the door was suddenly yanked open.

There were four of them, two in civilian clothes, and two

Vopos, each with a machine pistol – one at the front, and one at the rear of the car. The smallish man, who had pulled the door open, spoke with a distinct Russian accent. "Major Kashov. KGB," he said. "We would like to see your documents, please. A routine matter."

*   *   *

Possibly, if they had been better equipped and able to keep strict surveillance, one on another, Herbie might have quickened the pace with Nestor. But, with Nikolas Monch, you did not work fast at the best of times. One of the factors in his original recruitment had been his taciturn nature.

Even now, on seeing Herbie for the first time in years, Nestor showed little surprise. The hint of a smile, a friendly nod, that was all.

Herbie remained impassive, as before; motioning Nestor to sit down and starting the question-and-answer routine almost before the man had his backside on the chair.

As always Nestor took his time answering questions. This worried Herbie. The man had been like that from the beginning: now the habit could be construed as cover – always giving himself time to think, avoid traps, swerve from the truth.

Yet he *did* answer each query: clearly and, in some cases, with a lot of detail. Eventually Schnabeln left, and Herbie went through his little act – getting up, relaxing, saying it was good to see Nestor after so long.

Over to the window, chatting almost casually. Then –

"A man can teach another man to do good – believe me." Turning as he said it: watching the hands, fingers and feet. Then the face.

Nikolas Monch's brow creased. "I should know that from somewhere," he said slowly. Herbie's stomach turned over.

"It's from a play. I'm sure. Russian. Chekhov?"

"No," Herbie snapped, moving close. "Come on, Nikolas. Where did you hear it? Who told you? How recently?"

Nestor shrugged. He did not know. From childhood, maybe. Certainly not recently. No, he could not even place it. Anyway, what was it all about?

For about five minutes Herbie pressed, hinted, probed, until it became obvious that Nikolas Monch did not have the connection. He was clean.

Returning to the table, Herbie sat down, leaning on his elbows, and calmly began to go through Nestor's escape procedure.

11

CURRY SHEPHERD SAW the grey, silent man who was Herbie's one o'clock appointment scurry up the steps and set off down the street as though all hell was after him.

A few moments later Herbie came out, carefully locking the door behind him. He did not hurry, but walked quietly in the opposite direction from the last subject. From where he sat Curry thought Herbie looked concerned, his shoulders stooping slightly as he strode slowly out of sight.

Get your skates on, Curry, old cocker, he thought. Big Herbie's got transport laid on. You've got to hoof it, or find a jolly bus.

Assuming his Berlin accent, Shepherd told the house superintendent that his period of surveillance was now complete. This operation must not be discussed, except with other officers who might call at the house in a day or so.

The superintendent did a Uriah Heep act in the hallway, and Curry finally made his exit with a dismissive nod. He was wary and concerned. During his period of watching there had been hints – only unconfirmed clues – that a surveillance team, using four cars and two men, were on the prowl.

Curry Shepherd had been right about Herbie, who now sat in the back of the taxi. The driver, more than delighted with the tip – and the money he knew had yet to come from Schnabeln – was already waiting. Herbie, however, was becoming increasingly anxious. Nikolas Monch had been absolutely one hundred per cent clean. He would swear his life to that. Ursula had been proven clear the previous evening. This left only two real possibles, neither of whom

Herbie had thought capable of deception – though Peter Sensel's homosexual tendencies had worried others, particularly Tubby Fincher, who regarded him as a grave risk.

If Herbie had been a betting man he would have put his money on either Luntmann or Moritz Winter. The thought that it was now certainly either the sexy Martha Adler or Peter Sensel depressed him.

The crowds were out in force now, the pavements and cafés filling up. That Sunday turned out to be one of the warmest for weeks, and the citizens of East Berlin were heading to their favourite pleasure haunts, or strolling amiably along the broad thoroughfares of the city.

The safe house on the Behrenstrasse was a different matter compared with the hole in which Herbie had been incarcerated during the morning. The Behrenstrasse house was small but modern, in reality a worker's apartment, suitable for a family of three. Once again Schnabeln had procured it through his semi-criminal contacts. It was lived-in: Herbie cursed as he tripped over a child's tricycle in the small hallway. Like the Weibensee girl, the family would not return until everything was over.

A ground floor apartment: there were good forward-facing views from the main room, off which a narrow corridor led to a pair of bedrooms, bathroom and kitchen. The kitchen had a rear-facing window, looking out on to a small yard – the drop to the yard being only a matter of a few feet. A low wall at the end of the yard was easily surmountable, and the place had a feeling of space about it. At the Weibensee basement Herbie had been overpowered by an almost claustrophobic depression. Here, in the centre of the city, he was more at home.

He secured the door to the passage, and began to move the furniture around so that once more he had a table in the centre of the room, with a chair at either side. The free-entry signal was the front window – slightly opened. Closed signified keep out.

Herbie opened the window to the prescribed amount, then sat back and waited, realising with a sense of some horror that he had moved the furniture and locked the exit to the other rooms because he wanted the subjects enclosed. Resting his hand on the pistol, still hanging at his thigh, Herbie shivered.

It was quite likely he would kill either Martha Adler or Peter Sensel in this place.

*   *   *

Curry Shepherd sighed with relief. He had ambled along the Behrenstrasse until he spotted the apartment block and the window. It was open, which meant the two o'clock appointment had not yet arrived. His watch showed a couple of minutes to go.

There were three cafés to choose from. Curry took a spare chair at the middle, most crowded place, giving him a good view of the premises. As he ordered coffee he spotted Schnabeln, arm in arm with a tall, attractive ash blonde woman whom he wouldn't mind, thank you very much, at two in the afternoon. If they really did manage to dismantle this lot he would almost certainly be required to appear before a board in London. Maybe he would meet the blonde there. Curry Shepherd grinned to himself, thinking, 'Curry, you sly old dog.'

Inside the apartment Herbie gave the *Trepan* team a treat. A good thirty-second burst with the homer.

Schnabeln, opening the main door for Hecuba, did the same thing. He was a very worried man, and wanted to tell Herbie. Girren had not been at his back: not at the cake shop, or anywhere along the route. He could not believe Walter would cut and run at this point – though it was not impossible. More likely the Trapeze act had begun. Curry Shepherd was on station, though, sitting at the café over the road. It was the first time he had spotted Curry all day.

Herbie did not even get up from the table. His eyes stayed dull, almost accusing, as Martha Adler was ushered in.

Her mouth dropped open. "Herbie? Herbie, darling. What a surprise; God, you're the last person –"

"Sit down, would you," said Herbie sharply, hardly looking at her.

Schnabeln crossed the room, whispering his fears concerning Girren into Herbie's ear. The big man remained impassive.

*   *   *

Back in West Berlin Max had joined the others in the Operations Room. He seemed much recovered, and Tubby Fincher twice had to tell him and Charles to stop chattering. Worboys was at his machines, while both Tiptoes and Miriam manned theirs. Fincher had pulled the chair, originally prepared for Herbie, to a point directly behind the technicians.

Nobody showed any surprise when Herbie's long bleep showed up in the Behrenstrasse. "Make sense?" Miriam asked, turning slightly towards Fincher.

He said it made a lot of sense: remaining silent about his real thoughts. Herbie had moved to the second safe house. It would only be a matter of hours now, if that. Then they would know. A voice seemed to whisper in his head, asking, "Then you'll know what? Where Herbie stands? Who's the dodgy Telegraph Boy? If they're all done for?"

"And Spendthrift," Tiptoes said quietly, as the long bleeps came up from almost the same point where Herbie's signal had appeared a minute or two before.

"Still make sense?" Miriam smiled. For a disquieting moment Tubby Fincher seemed to recognise the smile: it had an enigmatic quality. Mona Lisa? Fincher knew Miriam Grubb's father; he was also quite conversant with the story of the girl's personal tragedy – in fact, even more than Miriam herself, because he knew the full details: the facts they did not dare tell her about her husband's death. Her smile, now, was oddly unnerving.

"Mr. Fincher, how long's this going to go on for?" Tiptoes asked. He sounded tired, fed up with the whole business.

As long as it takes, Tubby told him; and as long as he, Tubby Fincher, decreed.

Tiptoes snorted. Bloody Kruger and Spendthrift were darting all over the place. "It's like a soddin' flea circus. What's it in aid of now? Big Herbie gone over, has he?"

Fincher said that time would tell.

"Important?" as though Tiptoes Corn had detected a note of stress in Fincher's voice.

Silence. The whole team had shifted to look at him. "Probably more important than any of you will ever realise." Tubby's voice *did* show stress. He could hear it himself.

"For all your black boxes, your sound and sight stealing, the satellites and mechanical garners of intelligence, it boils down to human beings in the end." He spoke distinctly, slowly, knowing it sounded like a lecture.

"No matter how advanced the technology, it is human beings who have to make final assessments; human beings who can give us access to the minds and forward planning of the opposition." He said that might sound old-fashioned to some of them, but it was true. Black box intelligence still needed what Herbie Kruger always called 'bodies on the ground' – street men, field men, handlers, runners, watchers. Those they were tracking now dealt with covert assets, living cheek by jowl with discovery and death every day of their lives. The operation was vital, and they should know it.

"It's also altered drastically since Herbie Kruger briefed you." He paused, wondering if he should really give it to them, warts and all. "What you're watching is two-fold: and it's a tragedy – for those concerned and for our Service. You're watching the disclosure of a traitor – for want of a better word. You're also witnesses to a retreat: a small catastrophe, the ripples of which will cause not just inconvenience but genuine danger to ourselves and our allies. You're watching a secret dam being breached; people being drowned. In the end, someone else will have to go in there to repair the damage and bury the dead." This was not just a chauvinist matter – not a question of Service pride – but the almost certain removal of a very important section of the West's defensive strategy. "It's like having one of your eyes plucked out." He ended. "Put that into personal terms, and you'll come somewhere near to the true ramifications."

*   *   *

"Herbie, darling, what's the matter with you? Where's the smiling boy we all used to know and love?"

"Gone on vacation. Just sit down, Martha." He used her real name. Puzzled, Martha Adler started towards the chair opposite Herbie. He suddenly seemed to change his mind, holding up a hand, palm towards her, like a traffic policeman. On second thoughts would she mind a search? He was sorry there was not a woman to do it. She had a choice – himself, or the agent who had brought her in – Spendthrift, her handler.

She smiled, nervously, and made some joke about having always fancied Spendthrift. "Search away," she said, putting her handbag near the chair, turning towards Schnabeln and raising her hands.

Herbie nodded and, without embarrassment, Christoph Schnabeln began a complete body search.

Soundless, almost cat-like, Herbie reached under the table, drawing the handbag towards him, unclipping it, slowly pulling out the contents. It contained only the normal paraphernalia of a woman's bag, except for the small, Austrian .25 OWA automatic pistol.

Martha giggled as Schnabeln patted the inside of her thighs. "I'd have worn silk if I'd known."

"And where would you get silk from, Martha, these days? Your Russian friends?" Herbie asked.

She still had her back to him. Of course, she said. All part of the service. The Russians she pumped ("and I used that word in all its possible meanings") seemed to be able to bring anything in from the West. "Silk's no problem, Herbie. Never was, or have you forgotten your youth and dreams?"

"She's clean," Schnabeln pronounced, stepping back.

Not quite, Herbie growled, with a menace that frightened even himself, holding the pistol as Hecuba turned to face him. "What you want to carry this toy for, Martha?"

Her mouth formed an *Oh*, eyes flicking between the handbag and Herbie.

"It's against everything you've ever been taught by us. For your own protection we do not allow you to carry arms."

"And for my protection I carry that; under certain circumstances."

Herbie gestured her into the chair, unloading the little pistol as she sat down.

"Look, Herbie." No fear emanated from her, but you would not smell fear from a woman like Hecuba. Her voice remained calm, even persuasive. "Something's up. Crash meetings. Now you; back here after deserting us for so long . . ."

"You didn't know I was here. When you set out for the meeting you didn't know."

"I knew something was very wrong. Christ, I'm not an idiot. I've carried on, even when your people seemed to forget our existence. Then, suddenly, I find myself being wooed by the KGB."

"Wooed?"

"Literally. Not in your sense – the trade sense. Presents; little favours; being screwed." She lifted her eyebrows. "When you trained me, Herbie, you said a crash meeting usually meant the worst. I was a star pupil. I can even remember how you put it. *The crash meeting should be looked upon as a warning of thunder: a prelude to lightning. If a crash meeting is ordered, treat it like a time bomb. Take more care than ever before.*" She laughed, throwing her head back. "You were a randy devil in those days, Herbie. You even said to me, 'If there's a crash meeting wear two pairs of drawers,' remember?"

Unsmiling, Herbie nodded. "So this," gesturing at the pistol, "was your spare pair of drawers?"

She said, yes, if he wanted to think of it like that.

Where did she get the pistol? How long had she had it? Martha told him: a gift from a Russian officer, a couple of years ago. "There'd been a number of attacks on women in the Pankow district. He was doing me a favour. Promised me a certificate, but it didn't arrive."

The authorities always had an excuse to pull her then; hold her for questioning. Unauthorised possession. His harshness did not diminish. Herbie leaned over the table and began to give Martha Adler the full treatment – harder than any of the others. He wanted to know everything: the names of all her contacts in the last years; particularly the Russians. How much of the information she passed came directly from them, instead of her personal observation? Her target was the Soviet Attaché to the DDR's Political Headquarters, so how much of her reports was culled from hearsay? How much from reality – her own experience?

Schnabeln, by the door, stayed longer than usual. Priam, the next appointment, was his own man, and could be picked up within ten minutes. It crossed his mind that Herbie might even forget his presence in the room, so concentrated was his attention on the woman Hecuba.

How did she feel, all those years ago, when she realised

Herbie's appointed handlers had deserted her? She knew why it stopped. There was talk. Herbie should not forget that she worked in the political HQ; that she had access to most of the gossip. "I knew, Herbie. I knew some had got away and that some were caught, some shot down. I didn't know about you – though I discovered later, from a chance word."

"What kind of chance word?"

"At a party, in the political compound. There were some SSD and KGB people there. It's surprising how indiscreet those boys can be. They actually used your name – Schnitzer *and* Kruger. You put their noses right out of joint."

So what had all this got to do with the way she felt?

She understood. She did not feel deserted. "You always said that, if anything happened, I was to carry on. Someone else would take over. They did – badly and unreliably, yes: but I got stuff through; remained loyal. It's been worth it." She leaned forward over the table, looking at him. Just as she must look at men when trying to lure them to her bed, Herbie thought. "I hate them more than ever, Herbie. I've kept faith; done my job."

Herbie grunted – "In spite of temptations?" he said.

She answered, yes. The one word, clipped and angry.

Schnabeln thought, God, he's getting her. A ratter with a big rodent caught in the barn: worrying her until she gives in. Dies.

Indeed, it was really only at that moment Herbie put the pressure into top gear: sweating her in every way he knew. Details? Details? More details – as though he knew her file by heart: memorised every piece of raw material she had sent over.

Almost as an aside Herbie glanced towards Schnabeln, telling him he could get out. Even that was said sharply; and as Schnabeln left he wondered what he would find on his return.

The questions went on. Hard, heavy, probing, until he sensed she was getting angry, losing her balance. Only then did Herbie ease up, entering the mellow phase which, in turn, would lead to the moment of truth.

All memories of past dealings with her had flown. In the core of his intellect Herbie Kruger was certain he had their double. Martha Adler. Under the table, he gave the *Trepan* team another bleep. Then he rose, looking at her, without sympathy, asking the questions concerning her own welfare and condition. She had a wildness about her now: the poise gone, even the beautifully-groomed ash blonde hair tousled by the constant running of her hand – a gesture of distress. When the questions went deep, Herbie noticed, she plunged the splayed fingers of her right hand into the heavy hair.

He did not want to turn his back on her; but it was time to put the question. He went and stood by her, placing a hand on her shoulder, then sliding it along the back of her neck, starting the personality change; beginning by laughing, low and pleasant.

She appeared to be even more puzzled, so Herbie went to the door and peeped out; then to the window. He spotted Curry Shepherd, sitting at a sidewalk table, sipping coffee and reading an English newspaper. It flicked through his mind that it must be an old edition.

"Martha, my darling girl. It's good to see you."

"Herbie? What the hell. That was my line. What . . .?

But he took her in his arms, embracing her, kissing her cheeks, then pulling away. She looked wary: confused. He had to be careful, he told her, just as he had warned the others. "They watch me also, you know. By rights, I should not be here. It was the only way."

She asked what he meant, and Herbie gave her his big smile – the one you reserved for the publicity stills. Then he put her to the question – "A man can teach another man to do good – believe me."

She did not seem to even notice what he had said. Why had he been so rough on her? She of all people? Hadn't she been his most trusted person? Hadn't he picked her – out of all those who must have been around at the time – to do this one very special job? Now he treated her like some faithless whore: or like a priest trying to test someone's faith. "Well, my faith's kept up to scratch, Herbie. Right up to scratch. Yes, I've stolen for my faith in the West; lived under this accursed régime; stolen, lied and whored for freedom. God, if you only knew the times I've wanted to run for it: make up for the years I've missed. Now you, of all people, come back and treat me like a whore."

"A man can teach another man to do good – believe me."

Her brow wrinkled. "Yes, I know what you mean. You taught me to do good for the cause of what I like to think of as freedom: democracy. I believe you, Herbie. But do I deserve all this?"

Herbie did not go for it. Something about her could not convince him. Yet the reactions appeared genuine. If she was the Moscow-trained double then she was very, very good, and now he had lost her. There was one more card he might play; though it would have to be left to others.

He slumped into the chair, glancing at his watch, realising time was running out. Slowly, the weariness pervading his voice, Herbie told her that she was blown, then ran the dance steps for her escape. He spun it out, going through her route – making her repeat it to him – asking where she had cached her dismantle identity papers; if she could get to them quickly?

During all this, he went over to the window and opened it, giving the sign that Schnabeln could come in with Priam. He then locked the door of the main room, in which they sat: taking these precautions without explanation, trying not to draw attention to them.

"The man I sent away will be back," he explained. "I want him to help you get out."

She said he need not put anyone else at risk.

"He won't be at risk. I just want to make sure nobody's on your back when you hit the street. He'll pull off as soon as he's certain. Okay?"

She agreed, and Herbie went through the money routine. He had only just closed the briefcase when he heard Schnabeln returning with Priam; Schnabeln trying the handle of the door; then knocking.

Herbie shouted for him to wait, telling Schnabeln to send his subject back to the car. It was insecure as hell, but the uncertainty about Hecuba meant taking fast, possibly unwise decisions. When he called out to Schnabeln Herbie even tried to disguise his voice – for Priam's benefit. There was always Priam; he could not altogether rule out that possibility.

The front door closed. Herbie motioned Martha Adler to wait, while he let himself out into the small hallway.

Schnabeln's face was creased with anxiety, relaxing a shade as Herbie told him what to do. It should only take a few minutes. Christoph Schnabeln nodded and left, murmuring he hoped Priam had not been scared off. Herbie shrugged. "Get it done fast. Wait until she's out; then bring Priam in."

*   *   *

Curry Shepherd looked at his watch. He was distinctly uneasy. Schnabeln had taken the woman into the house. In due course he had left; the normal run of events. Then the come-in sign had gone up, even though the woman had not gone from the house. Perhaps she had left by the back. That was the only reasonable explanation, because he saw Schnabeln arrive with a roly-poly, scruffy man who looked almost down at heel, in spite of what seemed, even at this distance, quite good clothes for East Berlin.

Curry was on his third coffee. Really time for him to change venue. Then he saw the scruff come out and run a loitering act, tying his shoelace. Schnabeln followed a few seconds later and the pair walked back the way they had come.

In fact, Schnabeln was taking no chances with Priam. He returned him to the car, telling his subject to stay put: that he was being watched. This was a serious business, and Schnabeln's friends would collar Priam very fast if he took so much as a step out of the car.

Peter Sensel, well-rested, having spent most of the day in bed, was not going anywhere. He made that quite plain to his handler.

Curry signalled to the waiter, paid his bill, and was just about to leave – he would walk a bit, with the house in view, then go to one of the other cafés – when he saw Schnabeln coming up the pavement towards him, giving a friendly smile.

Shepherd left the café, sauntering towards Schnabeln, shaking hands, making it look very good: laughing occasionally, nodding away while Schnabeln talked.

The girl was still in the house, Schnabeln told him. But the big fellow was not happy. In a minute she would leave. Curry was to put his hooks on her, but be careful. Quickly Schnabeln recited the number of the safe house telephone, making Curry say it back. If the girl made contact with anyone suspicious he was to telephone and do a bit of double-talk.

In his drawling English-German Curry said it was so nice to have seen him again, but he really should get going. As they shook hands Schnabeln recited what the woman's movements should be. If she was clean she would go back to her apartment in Pankow, stay for about five minutes, then leave for the Ostbahnhof.

Curry waved cheerfully and set off along the sidewalk, eventually crossing the street, bringing himself on to a reverse track down the far pavement; lingering as he waited for the woman to leave.

His timing was slightly out, forcing him to start the tail from the front; for he had passed the house by the time the woman emerged. She walked fast, though, and Curry had no difficulty in letting her overtake. Within minutes he was in no doubt she was heading for the nearest S-Bahn station that would take her to the Pankow district. He tried to look happy, though Curry was now even more sure than before that the opposition had their surveillance people crawling all over the place.

*   *   *

Big Herbie's rage stemmed basically from suspecting Martha Adler yet not pinning her down. The schedule was so tight that it was impossible to leave Priam alone for long. He also had to set the record straight with Ursula, and that should be done here. Just a few questions, in case anything went wrong.

Schnabeln gave him the nod as he ushered Priam into the room. Curry was leeching Hecuba. Then the whole business started again with Priam. By now Herbie was really into his role. Priam looked more disturbed and shocked than any of the others when Herbie gave him the brusque treatment.

By God, Herbie thought, I'm going to sweat blood from this one. If the Adler woman was clean – despite his reservations, that was how Herbie had to think – Priam was now on the rack. Here was his man.

He started by the roughest treatment yet – making Schnabeln go over Priam, doing a heavy body search.

"But Herbie," Sensel almost whined. "It's been so long. For God's sake, haven't you got even the hand of friendship for an old comrade?"

Schnabeln said Priam was clean.

"Then sit down there and answer my questions. I know the truth, so I want the truth back from you. This is not a picnic with one of your boyfriends." Herbie started with that: the sexual aspect. How many affairs had Priam experienced with Russians?

From there he moved on to the question of loyalty during the time when handling was bad. How had Priam managed? Then down to specifics: the detailed raw information: Herbie harsh, uncompromising, almost brutal in the way he pounded questions at Sensel.

By the time Schnabeln was ordered out, Herbie had the subject almost in tears, claiming he had done everything possible. "You cannot fault me on any of the material, Herbie. Nor on the way I got it over. Even during the bad times. Are you accusing me of something? Tell me if you are, so that I can prove . . ."

"Prove what? That you are one of our biggest risks in the East? A man constantly in sexual contact with Russian males. Ripe for blackmail."

Peter Sensel shook his head wildly. Nothing like that. No. Nothing like that had ever happened. He was careful. His work for the British had been immaculate.

Schnabeln had gone by this time, but Herbie still kept up the pressure: refusing to lapse into the mellow attitude. As it happened, Peter Sensel's work had not always been immaculate, as he claimed. On three occasions Priam had put in reports concerning his target's movements (the target being the Commander-in-Chief, General Soviet Forces in Germany) which had turned out not only to be inaccurate but highly misleading.

Herbie knew this could happen – particularly with surveillance from within a military base where rumour was rife and dummies often thrown: especially when it came to the movements of important personnel. It did not stop him hammering at these three reports until he had taken Priam to the outer limit. Time for the change of course.

The stern visage turned into the more friendly, smiling Herbie, whom Peter Sensel recognised of old.

At the window – having made his peace with Sensel – Herbie Kruger tensed. It was the moment. If he was wrong, it meant the Adler woman had duped him, or . . .? But he could not even think of that possibility.

"A man can teach another man to do good – believe me," he said slowly, gritting his teeth.

"Jesus," breathed Peter Sensel from behind him.

For a second, Herbie hardly realised what had happened. He had been through it, acted the part to no effect, too many times already. He turned, smiling, saying the now-familiar words, "You are surprised it's me, Peter?"

"Just say it again," Sensel now relaxed completely; smirking as if he recognised what had been going on.

"A man can teach another man to do good – believe me."

"Jail doesn't teach anyone to do good, nor Siberia, but a man – yes!" Sensel said. Mistochenkov had mentioned nothing about an answer; but this was typical Russian method – the contact giving the second section of the whole quotation.

"My God," Sensel smiled, rising: walking towards Herbie. "My God, I'm so glad it's you. I've waited."

"Since when?" Herbie wanted it over quickly. Never in his life had he really desired to kill, but as he looked at the over-ripe, mincing Sensel the whole ghastly betrayal exploded in his head.

"Since Trapeze sent me the message from Vascovsky – sorry, I should have said Auguste. Sloppy."

"Good for Trapeze," Herbie forced a smile. Sensel came even closer. "You know who Trapeze is?"

"Vascovsky's girl – sorry, Auguste's girl – wasn't she? Until Auguste . . . My God, Herbie, you're a clever old bugger." He actually reached forward to embrace Herbie. It was at that moment Kruger hit him for the first time, a great roar rising from his soul – "You're blown, you little bastard."

Herbie's fist took Sensel in the stomach, knocking the wind out of him, and, by the force, probably doing internal damage. Sensel jack-knifed, and Herbie brought a fist up under his chin.

Sensel had breath enough left to scream Herbie's name, then the next punch took most of his teeth away; and another broke his nose. The man whom the Service had trusted as Priam landed, sprawled in one corner of the room. Herbie leaped on him like a huge bear, lifting him bodily, slamming another punch into the face. Knee to the groin. Punch to the face – to the stomach – to the ribs – the ribs again; and again – he felt the bone crack under his fist. Then the face – again; the face – now a pulp of blood – yet again.

Sensel was probably dead long before that last blow; and Herbie would certainly have gone on beating away at him had it not been for the ringing of the telephone.

Through the wild mist of rage and hatred, red, clouding his head, choking the emotions, Herbie became conscious of the bell. Slowly he released the thing he had been punching and striking, in that terrible moment of uncontrolled anger. Why? Why go berserk and blood mad? His mind threw back the questions, and the answers – sounding hollow now. Because this man had betrayed; because he had removed the truth that was the heart of Herbie Kruger's whole life. From what appeared to be a long way back in his life, Herbie seemed to hear somebody quoting a poem to him: *We are the hollow men; we are the stuffed men.*

Panting, amazed at the awful loss of restraint which had driven him to the madness, Herbie stumbled over to the telephone. There was blood on his knuckles, he noticed. They hurt: stinging and throbbing.

"Ja?" he asked, looking with a lack of comprehension at the obscene, red-splashed doll crumpled in the corner.

"We need a surgeon," the voice said.

"Who is that?"

"A friend has had an accident. I'm speaking from near the church of the Good Shepherd in Pankow."

Curry Shepherd, doing his best to double-talk his way out of something terrible, Herbie realised. Sanity slowly returned. "Curry?" Herbie asked, because the double-talk seemed pointless now.

"Okay. They snatched her. Two uniforms and two plain-

343

clothes. Took her off in a car. One of them was from the Centre. Name of Kashov."

Herbie told him to get out now; speed. Use his normal papers. Go. It was over. "I got him, Curry. Got the bastard. If I don't make it back, tell them: Priam."

"Priam," Curry repeated from the telephone booth in Pankow. "Well done, old cocker. Good luck."

Herbie stood for a moment, looking at his blood-stained hands. Yes, he was probably well over the hill, but what do you do in the field? All his life, in the dark secret places of Europe, probing other people's secrets, Herbie Kruger had been taught you should use your common sense and initiative. He had done just that by coming over the Wall.

Wearily he walked over to the huddle that had been Peter Sensel. Then he unlocked the door to the passage leading to the rest of the apartment. Like a huge child towing a toy, Herbie dragged Sensel's body through to one of the other rooms, then set about cleaning – both himself and the room.

Whatever they might say about his insubordination Herbie Kruger had dealt with the cancer. Information came from human beings; human beings had to be in the field. Days, weeks of playing Sherlock Holmes with the files and reports would not have put right the errors of his past. Luzia Gabell and Peter Sensel had either posed or sold themselves. Between them, the pair rendered all Big Herbie Kruger's past efforts – his credo, his loyalty – to nothing but a blotch on the Service's history.

So now, in an almost sacramental action, he bathed his hands in the bathroom, washing away the blood, looking at the broken and hanging skin. Herbie Kruger had righted his own wrongs. The record was straight – or as straight as it could ever be. He recalled a fragment of childhood, when he had scalded his fingers accidentally plunging them into hot water. They said you could not recall pain, but that hurt was just like this – the throbbing and sting.

As he started to tidy the main room of the apartment, Herbie thought, with rising anger, that it was now all blown away. Finished. Gabell had been Trapeze. Trapeze must have talked – to somebody in the secret hierarchy – before her death: hence the message from Curry Shepherd.

Walter Girren probably gone. He wondered about the others. Martha Adler gone. With the place now tidy, the window open to signal Schnabeln in with Ursula, he sat down, wondering how long they had to go. And what a fool he was to have put Martha Adler at such risk; to have been obsessive with uncertainty about her.

He was as guilty as the rest of them; and, if they had picked up the Adler woman so quickly, the opposition must be well and truly around them. They were all boxed in. Surrounded.

Probably they would get him. Herbie had to be a realist about that prospect; but he still had a few tricks. There were ways out, over the Wall, that did not entail using the checkpoints. He looked at his watch, and used the button, giving the *Trepan* team a long burst, letting it continue for a couple of minutes as he worked.

It was almost four o'clock and the tape had to be completed. He reached for the briefcase and took out the hollow book, removed the machine, set it, added the one word – *Priam* – to the tape, before rewinding and switching to *send*. Schnabeln could get out and screech the message to the *Trepan* team. That would take only a short while. The correct place for sending was near the Brandenburg Gate. Ten minutes, fifteen at the most. It was a waste of time now for them to go back and get Ursula's luggage, but they should do it, if only to keep her calm. Maybe – much later that night – they would go over by the normal route, through Charlie; though Herbie thought it unlikely. His face and build would be in every Vopo's head, every KGB man's mind. Every member of the SSD would have it burned into their brains.

12

ANNA BLATTE HAD been feeding the birds at the western corner of Treptow Park when Schnabeln arrived, a minute early. Electra had not shown yet, she told him. Electra was prompt. She would be there dead on three-thirty.

It gave Schnabeln time to break the news. Anna Blatte took it well. Then she laughed. She would have to hole up somewhere overnight. She laughed again. "I thought I had been so clever with my dismantle documents. They're cached in the Town Hall – the Alexanderplatz. I can't get in until tomorrow." On Sunday the Town Hall was closed. "Never on Sundays," she laughed again. Wasn't that the name of a film? Schnabeln said it was, looked up and saw Electra, sitting on the bench as though she had materialised there by some act of magic.

He told Anna Blatte, good luck, instructing her in what she should say to Electra. Just whisper for her to follow him. The car was five minutes away.

Schnabeln surprised himself at his own calm. The last visit to the house on the Behrenstrasse had been unnerving. Again, he dreaded to think what might be waiting for him when he got there.

She followed like a docile child, observing all the procedures: dallying at one point, stopping at an intersection, as though making up her mind which way to go. A woman with time on her hands, on a sunny Sunday afternoon, taking a stroll.

She wore a light raincoat, open, with a blue skirt and blouse underneath, her head covered by a matching scarf.

Her shoes, he noticed, were sensible – lace-ups: comfortable probably.

In the car she quietly placed her handbag on her lap, and said good day to him; asking no questions.

* * *

He heard the outer door: Ursula – his woman. Herbie rose from the table as Schnabeln ushered her in. There was none of the brusque treatment for Electra. He smiled, at ease, even looking happy, taking her in his arms and kissing her. She clung to him as if he was a log of wood in a river and she could not swim.

For Schnabeln the embrace seemed to be endless. Then Herbie, still holding Electra, pulled back. "Got him," he grinned.

"Priam?" Scowling, realising the insecurity of his remark, Schnabeln cursed.

Herbie said it was okay. Christoph Schnabeln asked, almost in a whisper, where the man was. Herbie tilted his head towards the passage. Schnabeln mouthed a final question, and Herbie shook his head – like a doctor in some TV melodrama signifying they had lost the patient.

There was no hint of alarm in Herbie Kruger's voice when he said they were possibly all under surveillance. Schnabeln would now go and do the final act of the *Trepan* operation. Herbie handed him the book.

They spoke for a few moments, Schnabeln insisting that he come back – that they all go in the Wartburg. Herbie said at least he would be sure, then, that the screech had been transmitted. He supposed they had better go to Ursula's place: pick up her case.

"Please, darling. I need it, don't I?"

Herbie was not certain. They might go out another way. He would have to run it ad lib. See what the opposition were up to. Yes, they would go and get her case.

After Schnabeln had left the house Herbie kissed her again, and she asked if they were really going – like a child, excited, not quite able to believe, he thought.

"We'll get out. Don't worry. I haven't waited – and

347

allowed you to wait – all these years for nothing. There'll be comfort of a kind, peace of a kind, in the West. For a few years more, anyway."

Again they embraced, Ursula kissing him with that same abandon as the night before. He wanted to have her, make love to her, there – now, here in this place where he had beaten out the germ with his fists. To love her here would be a cleansing action.

But there was no time, for Schnabeln would not take long, and there were still a few questions. He asked her gently; things about the way she had made contact with the new handler; who had handled her material during the period of what he called the long silence? Had she ever suspected that she was being watched? Had anyone made another approach: even obliquely? The standard questions, in case he made it and she did not – though he asked them automatically, without thought for the reason, carefully stowing away her answers against the day of his return. Lord, they would sweat him at Warminster. The full declaration.

"All done." Schnabeln smiled on his return, handing the book back to Herbie who took out the tape, crushed it, destroying the thing, by fire, in a metal waste basket. They would take the machine with them.

It was just after four-thirty when they left the Behrenstrasse safe house, walking the seven minutes to Schnabeln's parked Wartburg. Herbie's mind was clear, and he stayed silent, going through every possibility: knowing that he would wait until the last minute to make up his mind about the route out.

*   *   *

"Spendthrift's in Treptow Park," Miriam announced as the long bleeps came up.

Tubby Fincher glanced at his watch. Exactly three-thirty. Wait, he thought. It cannot be long now.

Miriam reached over to adjust the homing monitor.

"What are you playing at?" Tiptoes had become more edgy, hunched forward, occasionally drumming the fingers of his right hand.

"That last picture was fuzzy before the lens settled."

"Warm day, isn't it? Considering all the static, you expect some blurring. Settled down, though."

Miriam gave a tutting reply. "Temper, temper."

"Oh, shut up and concentrate."

Worboys leaned over to squeeze Miriam's hand. "Soon be over."

She smiled, blinking slowly, and helped herself to another of his cigarettes. Worboys raised his eyes to the ceiling. "As soon as we get out, I'm going to march you into the duty free at Tegel and make you buy them all back for me."

They laughed.

At three forty-two exactly Herbie's long signal came bleeping loudly out of the speakers.

"Still in the Behrenstrasse," Miriam said quietly, expecting the regular ten to fifteen seconds. When the bleeping went on – a minute, two minutes – Worboys asked if Tubby thought Herbie was trying to tell them something.

Fincher said it was possible. "I'd stand by, son, if I were you. Maybe we're going to get the screech."

Worboys put on the earphones, adjusting the receiver and tape controls. He did not look at Miriam or Tiptoes, concentrating on the hiss in his ears and any fluctuation on the lighted VUs in front of him.

At twelve minutes past four he heard it, the fractional zip, in his head. Less than a second. "Screech," he shouted, pulling off the 'phones.

"You're sure?" Fincher asked. Very quietly. Controlled.

Worboys already had the tape running back. "Absolutely certain."

Schnabeln's bleep came up at the expected sending point, just east of the Brandenburg Gate. "That's it," Fincher sighed.

Miriam leaned forward to make a fine adjustment to the map picture on the screen, her right hand steadying the consol.

Worboys, earphones draped around his neck, concentrated on transferring the screech to the cassette machine, and going through the slowing process.

The bang came from within the scanner: a series of pops, followed by a small flash and a lot of smoke.

"Shit," said Miriam.

Tiptoes shouted, demented. "You stupid cow. She did that on purpose. Silly bitch altered the voltage selector switch." Tiptoes had already reached down to throw the wall switches and pull out the plugs. Worboys' machines worked from another set of power points.

"You did that on purpose. She's blown the valves, fuses, transistors, the lot. Buggered, Mr. Fincher. We'll get no more homer signals. We've lost them."

"Sorry," Miriam shook her head. "I'm sorry, Tiptoes, it was an accident."

"You don't make accidents like that. Can't be done. You soddin' did it on purpose."

"Don't be stupid, Tiptoes. Christ, I'm sorry – but why would I want to screw up the tracking?"

"Indeed why, Miss Grubb?" Tubby Fincher's voice was so startlingly cutting that they all turned from the machines. He held a small automatic pistol pointing directly at Miriam Grubb, and had already gestured for Max and Charles, who were closing in on the girl.

"Hang about –" Worboys began.

"Get on with sorting out that screech," snapped Fincher. "She did it on purpose. I watched the whole thing. Blatant. Nicely timed, Miss Grubb, but deliberate."

Fincher told Max and Charles to pull her away from the machines. "Gently," he said. "Go over her. Mouth, ears, the lot. Take away the armament."

Worboys had found the screech and set the open-reel tape deck in motion, transferring the noise to the cassette in the unraveller. He was appalled at what was happening. "What in the name of –"

"Get on with your work and leave this to the experts," Tubby cut him off with a warning glance.

Miriam Grubb, eased from her chair by Max and Charles, had been taken to the far end of the room, while Tubby Fincher went through her handbag.

Miriam still protested. "Why would I want to do it on purpose?" A harsh note added to her voice.

"You tell me?" Tubby Fincher was perfectly at ease: speaking softly. "Because we are not to know, at this point, what happens to Spendthrift or Herbie Kruger? Is that why? Or don't they tell you the details?"

"Oh, come on."

"What was the enticement, Miriam? Your husband? They tell you we sent him to a certain death? Revenge? Hatred of the Service?"

"What?"

"The Director argued for you. For this operation. I tried to keep you out, Miriam. Even warned Herbie. Just straws in the wind, my dear, but *that* was a deliberate act of sabotage. They dangled the truth about your husband in front of you, did they? Said *we* did it?"

"This is nonsense."

"No, Miriam, it's a fair cop. A professional piece of work — from you, and from the opposition. Felt it in these old bones; I'd put down my pension they've spun you, girl."

"I'm not hearing you straight, Tubby." She had gone a grey-white: trembling slightly, anger pinching the corners of her eyes.

"They'll get it all at Warminster, love. A lot of pressure, I should think; and excellent moves when they suborned you, as I'm dead certain they did. Gave you proof, I should think? Proof that we set your husband up." His manner altered, hardness in the tone. "Nearly disallowed the wedding, Miriam. That's why they put a block on you knowing you'd married into the Service. The danglers were right: we *did* set him up."

"Yes," she gave a lopsided smile. "If you know it all, there's nothing more to be said."

"Unless you want to come clean on why you blew the tracker. Was I right? We're not supposed to follow what happens next, over there?" His head nodded in the general direction of East Berlin. "Big Herbie enticed, was he? They going to chop him, Miriam? Or don't they tell all the subtleties to temporaries, out for revenge? Big Herbie in it, is he? Spun? Are we not to follow him because he's being briefed for the return journey?"

She stood, glowering at Fincher; mouth tightly closed. Then — "Don't be bloody stupid, Mr. Fincher."

As Charles and Max took her away, into the other room, a

351

dazed Worboys was reaching the final stages of unzipping the screech, tapping out the groups, so that they came up *en clair* on the print-out. He stopped for a moment, eyes oddly damp; an unusual storm he did not recognise brewing in his emotions. "Tell me, will you, Tubby?"

"Later, lad, when we know it all. She claw your heart a bit, did she?"

Silently, Worboys nodded.

"Known for it. In the Service." Fincher did not seem surprised. "Hard life, young Worboys, especially with politics the way they are these days. Old loyalties dying. Every man for himself. She took her husband's death very hard, and he wasn't worth it. Headstrong; rose-tinted glasses – Miriam, I mean. Behaved oddly after it happened. Went on that way. She was excellent material for a temporary spin by the opposition. Technician, of course, so no real secrets hidden up her knickers. Kind of inmate one spins on a temporary basis, and they've made good use of her: poor bitch."

He gave a short sniff. It was not really Service style, what they had done to Miriam's husband, Fincher drawled. "No option, though. We had to take him out. She saw nothing wrong with him, but he drank a lot. Bit of a blowpipe," by which Worboys understood that Miriam's husband had become gabby. "Got himself caught between the juggernauts. Came a purler. Could've put him into solitude for the rest of his natural, but there would have been questions. So we chopped him. Only way. KGB spin squad probably had some solid evidence. Easy as pulling a tooth, spinning Miss Grubb."

After a short silence, Fincher said, "Think of Herbie." The words sounded like a death knell.

Tiptoes coughed, his eyes not leaving the now useless machines.

Worboys, troubled and confused, completed the decipher, tearing off the print-out, passing it silently to the senior man.

It read:

TRAPEZE POSSIBLY LUZIA GABELL NOW DEAD SOURCE UNKNOWN. AM TRYING TO GET EVERYONE OUT EXCEPT JUDAS. NAME WILL

BE ADDED CLEAR TO THIS MESSAGE. IF SO
JUDAS WILL BE DEAD. HOPE TO COME HOME
THEN. SURGEON.

Then the one word, unciphered – PRIAM.

"Got him then," Worboys smiled: weakly, still shaken by
events he did not fully understand.

"I wonder . . ." Tubby Fincher looked like a corpse – not
just the body of skin and bones. His face appeared to have
altered, becoming drawn, haggard, a terrible parchment, as
though the blood had been pumped from him. He was
thinking. Miriam blowing the tracking system. Herbie
making contact with the man sent in by Berlin Station, and
knowing about Trapeze. Spendthrift's final message coming
from the right place. Priam exposed and dead. His previous
logic had to be wrong. Herbie was still alive, well and on their
team. But Priam discovered and Miriam under orders –
presumably – to put the tracker out of action *after* the final
message was delivered. Tubby Fincher's logic read that as
meaning Priam's death did not end it all. There had to be
someone else – another Trapeze? Or the real Trapeze? Who
in Hell?

"I wonder," he said again, almost whispering. "Herbie's
been lured, that's for sure. Miss Grubb's job was to see we
couldn't follow the dance to the end." He gave a humourless
chuckle. "Dance macabre."

"Is there . . .?" Worboys did not complete the question. He
already knew the answer, and it was stupid anyway.

Fincher put it into words – "Anything we can do? No,
Tony. Not a bloody thing."

*   *   *

Herbie Kruger watched the rear all the way to Ursula
Zunder's apartment block. Nothing. He also took the precaution of releasing the gun tie, retrieving the weapon from
the floor of the car and sticking it into his waistband, butt
downwards, hard.

Schnabeln was told to stop well short of the actual apartment entrance.

"Your case heavy?" Herbie asked Ursula, eyes never still. It was quiet; hardly anyone about.

Ursula told him, no. She had done exactly what he had ordered. "An overnight bag. Just my best things, and very few of those. Come up with me, Herbie?" She was, rightly, nervous: hand shaking as she smoothed her hair.

Of course he was coming up. She would not be out of his sight from now on. Herbie, still alert, gave quick orders to Schnabeln. "Watch. Everywhere. Get out fast if there's any sign of trouble. Vopos, anything. We'll make our own way. Just go, yes?"

Schnabeln did not seem happy at the prospect. "Hurry then," he said.

Herbie nodded and spoke to Ursula. When he said go, they would leave the car – fast. "Not running, you understand. Not attracting attention. But we don't loiter. You keep your eyes on the door, don't look around you. I shall do that for both of us." He told her that, as soon as they were inside the building, they would go up the stairs as quickly as possible. "It is then we run. Right?"

She nodded.

"I go first up the stairs. You stay behind me and have the key ready."

She nodded again. Herbie put one paw on the door handle and the other inside his jacket on the butt of the Browning.

As they crossed the open space leading to the apartment block doors a dog barked, and Herbie was conscious of the sound of traffic coming from somewhere behind the building. He stayed to the left and slightly behind Ursula, in the classic bodyguard position, his eyes restless, watching windows and the sight-lines on either side – picking vantage spots for hidden eyes. At the door he turned to look back. Down the road he saw the car with Schnabeln. A man and a woman walking, deep in conversation, arms linked, on the far side of the street. For a second he recalled how many times he had walked the same way with Ursula.

"Okay. Me first," he spoke quietly to Ursula as they reached the stairs, his right hand withdrawing the Browning, flicking the safety and keeping the weapon just within his jacket – hidden.

354

He took the stairs in big, long bounds, two at a time, landing on the toes as feet hit each tread. For a man as large as Kruger he made little noise. Ursula's shoes clicked on the uncarpeted cement as she ran up after him.

At each floor, he paused, listening for a second, glancing down the passages leading off the landings.

At Ursula's door Herbie motioned her to use the key, then stand back. She nodded, unlocked the door and pushed it open. He could see through the crack as it swung back. Nobody behind the door, but he would not expect that. The movies usually have it all wrong, they say at the school: hiding behind doors is not a safe ploy.

The gun in his hand now Herbie almost jumped into the room, one hand holding Ursula back, ears straining. Long instinct told him the place was empty. Quietly, he asked where she had put her suitcase. She nodded towards the bedroom door.

"Okay. You get it quickly."

She was away, crossing the room with her loping stride, while Herbie stood just inside the door, his free hand on the edge of the wood, eyes taking in what he knew would be a final look. The Dürer: the avenging angel – he had carried that vengeance to its final limit. The ruby glasses with their facet-cut stems. Ursula disappeared inside the bedroom.

He heard her moving, but suddenly sensed something was wrong in the other silence. Sensed it only a second before it happened.

The sense was so strong that he was starting to turn when the cold, unmistakable touch of a pistol barrel pressed hard into his neck, and a voice whispered quietly in his ear. "This is very real now, Mr. Kruger. I shall stand back and kill you if you make one move. Place the gun quietly on the floor, then straighten up. Hands on your head." Somewhere from the distant past Herbie recognised the voice, the inflection in its German speech. As he obeyed the order, knowing there was nothing to be done immediately, the voice spoke to someone else – "See to the woman."

A figure brushed past him, heading quickly for the bedroom. He thought Ursula cried out as the door closed; just as he was certain the flitting figure was Kashov.

By this time Herbie had his gun on the floor and was standing erect, hands on his head. "It's nice to meet you at last, Herbie Kruger," the voice said. "You may turn around now."

As Herbie turned the man spoke very slowly, a whole mass of mockery in his tone, "A man can teach another man to do good – believe me. Eh?"

He had hardly changed – though, in the past, Herbie had only viewed him from a distance. Slim, the iron grey hair and deceptively kind blue eyes. Maybe there were a few more creases around the eyes, but the same delicate features had stood up well to the passage of time. He looked very French – elegant in civilian clothes. Most un-Russian. They always said, Vascovsky had French blood in him. It showed close up. Vascovsky? A spectre? No, this was flesh, blood, bone, sinew, intelligence.

There were other men outside the door. With a flick of his hand Vascovsky unleashed a pair of them towards the bedroom.

"Don't . . ." Herbie started to speak; but, softly, and with a certain amount of charm, Vascovsky told him to move. "Downstairs, quietly, and as quickly as we can, I think. We have your man – the one you left in the car. We want no fuss, Big Herbie – they still call you Big Herbie, I understand. No fuss, though. My people have to work through the Germans, but you know all about that from your side of the fence – neutral Berlin." He gave a small laugh, derisive but not unpleasant. "We are here only to help. I think we move now."

Herbie felt hands on his arms. He did not resist, or shout back. When they have you it is better to remain silent.

13

A FLY, SETTLED on the grille surrounding the one naked light
bulb in the stone ceiling of the cell, would probably have
sensed the awful, bitter, malign atmosphere – had it the brain
and intelligence.

The cell was bleak enough. Cold, so far below the ground;
old, also, with stone flags and damp grey walls. A simple
pallet in one corner, a bucket in the other, the usual heavy
metal door, the graffiti of past inmates scratched into the
walls. In the centre, a small metal table and chair, securely
bolted to the floor. There was no window, and, even in the
cold, a sour smell filled the small dungeon.

The big man, dressed in sagging denim prison drab, sat
upright, at the table. He did not shift or move. Even a fly of
great intellect could not have known that the large man was
trying to compose his mind by listening, in his brain, to
Mahler's Fifth Symphony.

For once, though, the ploy of musical memory did not
work. Herbie Kruger remained confused and bewildered – in
mental chaos for many reasons: not least of all the sudden
appearance of Vascovsky's ghost. Though this was no ghost.
Jacob Vascovsky had not died, either by sudden heart attack
or bullet fired into a water-filled mouth.

That was chaos enough for Herbie. He was trapped, and
knew what would follow. Russia, probably. Almost certainly.
The successes of the past had been revealed as failures. Now
the present successes had led to the disaster of entrapment.

His mind had been so shocked by Vascovsky's appearance
in Ursula's apartment – reeling under the effort to focus on
the facts; wild with concern for Ursula herself – that he had

hardly been able to follow the route once they had bundled him into the car and driven fast.

He was almost certain they had taken him to the grim old SSD's Magdalenenstrasse jail, though he thought the place had been out of use for some time. It would make sense, though – even if he was its only inmate.

Vascovsky disappeared soon after the arrival, when Herbie was made to suffer every possible indignity, from a crude medical examination to the dressing in rough denim and, finally, the cell.

He reckoned two to three hours had passed, and the only consideration had been a mug of tepid, foul coffee, some black bread and cold sausage. Apart from that Herbie Kruger had been left alone.

The main concern, which endlessly repeated itself – try as he would to blot it out with memories of the Mahler – was Ursula. Was she here? What was happening to her?

He heard the footsteps long before they stopped outside the cell door. Then the rusty clunk of the key, before the heavy metal swung back and Vascovsky entered, sniffing the air; wrinkling his face in disgust. Herbie just looked at him without a word.

"I'm sorry about this," Vascovsky began. "We'll have you away from here into more suitable surroundings, as soon as possible. In the meantime it's safe: for us and for you."

Holding his real concern in check, Herbie asked where he was. Vascovsky lit a cigarette. Then, as an afterthought, handed one to Herbie. They were British: John Player King Size. Vascovsky gave an amused shrug.

Herbie asked, flatly, where he was; coughing on the cigarette.

"Alive," Vascovsky smiled. "Alive, Herbie – I shall call you Herbie for I have known you as Big Herbie for many years. Alive, and in my safe keeping. You are confused, yes?"

Not particularly, Herbie told him.

"My entrance was not a shock to you? After what you believed?"

Of course it was; Herbie had to admit that.

"Pride is not encouraged in our profession; but you know that better than any of us. However, I cannot deny feeling a

358

small pride in this operation. It took a long time." He inhaled deeply on his cigarette and looked hard at Kruger. "We will have to talk a great deal, my friend. You understand this? I shall have to ask many questions – but in more conducive surroundings than these, I think, also that some gaps – which may puzzle you – will have to be filled in. But we do that later. I bring you a letter." He felt inside his jacket and produced a thin blue envelope, which he held lightly between finger and thumb. "A letter from Ursula Zunder."

Herbie could hold back no longer. He started to speak, but found his voice abnormally weak. He coughed and spoke again, from the beginning. "What have you done with her? Where is she?"

Vascovsky looked blank, emitting a sound half way between surprise and irritation. At this Herbie was suddenly very alert; his head clear; the first signs of disbelief beginning to appear over the horizon of his mind, like the early warning of thunderclouds.

"I am sorry," Vascovsky looked serious.

"You haven't? . . . You . . .?"

"I foolishly imagined you had cleared your mind. Worked it all out. That's why I left you alone in here – to give you a chance to adjust." He paused again, placing the cheap blue envelope on the metal table. It was addressed to Herbie, the writing unmistakable: clear and bold without flourish. Ursula's handwriting had always struck Herbie as being the least feminine thing about her.

"I should leave you alone a little longer." Vascovsky began to edge towards the door. "If you don't understand all of it, no matter. But you have to know, now, Herbie. You went for my necromancy all the way. Ursula Zunder was mine from the very start. She is Trapeze, Herbie."

The door closed behind the Russian. For a second or so Herbie Kruger's mind went blank. A trick, he thought. It has to be some kind of horrible, sadistic trick. Then, looking at the envelope, and seeing Vascovsky's face – hearing his voice – in the mind, he knew this was no illusion.

The demons broke from inside Herbie's head, a snarl from his lips, followed by a long howling scream, as he scrabbled to open the letter. Far away, he seemed to be looking at himself, and clearly thinking this was the kind of echoing noise Shakespeare intended King Lear to make on finding Cordelia dead – *Howl. Howl. Howl. Howl! O – you are men of stones.*

Slowly now, with his hands shaking, Herbie unfolded the thin paper, covered in Ursula's writing. There was a bitter stab as he read the first line –

My Darling Herbie – it began –

I have no right to call you that, it is true, yet you will forever remain so. You will not feel anything but hatred for me. That is punishment enough, for the rest of my life. You will feel and know that I have betrayed you, and your personal standards of loyalty will revolt against that. I understand. I wish to try and make you understand also. For me, and for my people, there is one thing more sacred than the love of two human beings. That, as you well know, is the love and loyalty one must bear for country and ideal. In this case, you should know by now that I am Russian-born. I am also a true believer in the right of my political creed, which you will call Communism. There is no changing that. It is like the true Roman Catholic refusing to marry a Protestant unless he changes his faith. I have no illusions that you will ever alter your way of thinking, even though my whole heart and mind cries out, calls to you, pleads with you to do so.

Remember that, in spite of my deceptions, I loved, and still love you as a man. You are the only man with whom I have ever found the qualities I could respect; the only man with whom I have truly felt the rewards of physical, emotional and mental love – except in the most vital sense for me: the political creed. Please try to forgive me. Remember me.

Once, on a happy evening, in what I still like to think of as our apartment in Berlin, you asked me how people clung on to the faith of Communism, when they saw the injustices, and had seen suffering during bad political leadership. Your question, then, was rhetorical. I would have been foolish – in my situation – even to have attempted an answer. Now I feel free to do so. I do it by illustration, and know you will understand. Have you ever heard of Daniel Averbuch? He was a leading member of the Communist Party in Palestine – in the nineteen-thirties. In fact he was sent by Moscow to promote Communism in the Mid-East. He fell foul of Moscow and, in the end, was not even allowed to leave Russia after his return: accused by

360

Stalin of working against the Party. Many, many years after this a friend of mine met Daniel Averbuch's widow – poverty-stricken, old and infirm. She told him – "My husband, my sons, my brother, my husband's brother – they were all arrested and assassinated. I'm the only one still alive. But, you know, in spite of what happened, I have not stopped believing in Communism." This may help you to understand, my dearest Herbie. I can never stop believing in Communism – though it has assassinated your love for me; and rent us apart. I love you for ever. Forgive me –

Ursula

Herbie Kruger smoothed out the paper, gently folding it with his huge hands. At that moment he felt nothing – a numbness, perhaps; maybe disbelief. It was not that he wanted to bury his head in the sand of time. Time was what he needed. There were too many questions to be answered if Ursula's letter was, in truth, real.

He was still sorting it out in his mind when they came for him. This time he was taken to a more comfortable room. There was coffee and plenty of cigarettes. There was also Vascovsky, and Herbie reasoned that this might be the start of what he knew must be a long interrogation.

He remained dumb, accepting coffee and a cigarette, waiting for Vascovsky to begin, which he did: coming to the point quite quickly.

"It is best that I fill in some of the gaps, those you cannot work out for yourself."

Herbie tried to assume indifference. Since the arrest and reading Ursula's letter, he had set his mind upon two of the puzzles. If it was all true, Ursula Zunder had to be a professional, even when he – Herbie – had recruited her. But as there was a hermetic situation, no interrelationship, between any of the Telegraph Boys, how had she lifted the information from the maze? There was no real way. So had Peter Sensel been the real villain? The one who helped lead her to the others: watching, following, keeping their eyes on the handler's backs?

Also, why the elaborate charade? The faked death for Vascovsky? Mistochenkov's defection? Why did they need him, Herbie Kruger, to be lured into the East again?

Reluctantly, he concluded this was an entrapment of monumental complexity.

"You know my situation," Herbie said quietly. "I am in your hands. What is done is done. Am I to be charged? A show trial?"

Vascovsky told him it depended very much on what happened during the next few weeks. "What you tell us. Even how much you know."

Herbie did not smile. With no feeling he answered, "I am not at liberty to tell you anything, Colonel-General."

"Please, you must call me Jacob. After all, we have known one another for a long time."

"There is very little I can offer you, Jacob."

They would see how things went, Vascovsky smiled. Herbie found the constant smile irritating; half way between the sardonic and a smirk.

"As I have said, it is only fair that you should know certain things." How much of the picture had Herbie managed to paint? the Russian asked.

"You tell it." Better admit to nothing than give away any strengths without really being aware.

"You must have some questions?" Vascovsky had a habit of touching the bridge of his nose with a forefinger. Later Herbie would realise that the Colonel-General wore spectacles — but only when absolutely necessary: a question of vanity. The frames tended to slip on to the bridge of his nose, and the habit was acquired by pushing them back.

Herbie allowed a small concession. "How much did Pavel Mistochenkov really know? He fooled me. I admit it."

"Poor Pavel," Vascovsky leaned closer. "Pavel was always a dupe. You really imagine that Pavel Mistochenkov could have kept much from you? Misdirected you, Herbie? No. There were certain things, easy things, things that I thought *you* would *wish* to swallow. In fact Pavel Mistochenkov is the start of the whole story."

The way Vascovsky told it he had recognised the faults in Pavel's character from the first day the man was assigned to him. "I almost asked for him to be transferred immediately." He had thought better of that, though; seeing in Pavel Mistochenkov two traits which might just be put to some use.

First, he had a leaning towards reliance. "There always had to be someone, or something, upon which he could rely. A prop. Without his prop little Pavel was lost: not a good feature in a man of our profession, Herbie. Pavel – when he came to me – was not self-reliant. He was therefore most pliable."

Jacob Vascovsky decided to keep the man. Maybe, in time, he would find a use for him. Meanwhile, he would shrewdly mould the weak Pavel into his personal zombie. "It's a wonder he was ever allowed in our service at all. But there you are."

There was no particular plan in Vascovsky's mind; nothing for which he could groom his aide. "So I began to play games with him. Test his strength. To see how his political convictions would hold up."

Caustically, Herbie said that Mistochenkov had no true political convictions. Vascovsky agreed. "That was my strength. I could direct him: feed him half-truths. He soon became very reliant upon me."

Yes, Herbie realised that; just as he now understood how Vascovsky had played on Mistochenkov's fears by implanting dissatisfaction. That had been a dangerous game, Vascovsky admitted. Originally he had a vague plan to cast Mistochenkov in the role of a defector; send him over, and see if Herbie's Service played him back. "I could have run a nice double that way. But Pavel would not have stood up to it."

In any case Vascovsky's signals to Pavel Mistochenkov were working well. "I let him know I was seriously thinking about going over: sang all the old capitalist tunes. It took time, but he swallowed it. The hook, the line and the rod." All this happened, however, at the moment when the Schnitzer Group were becoming a nuisance. He congratulated Herbie on the way that Group was run. "We knew – of course we knew – there was a definite organisation, a network, in operation. Before your Schnitzer Group it had all been Lone Ranger stuff. But here was a real organisation. Admirable."

Herbie thanked him for the praise, adding it was not all that admirable. Vascovsky had got under their guard: penetrated the Group, "That was the clever part, Jacob. I just didn't spot Luzia Gabell as your lady friend, Lotte Krug."

A smile flickered on Vascovsky's face. He shook his head, with the hint of a frown. No, Herbie would not have spotted Luzia Gabell. "She wasn't Lotte, my friend. She was yours. Nothing to do with us. I'm sorry; that is why Kashov's people had to silence her before you got near. Did you like the photographs we planted in her flat, by the way?" He did not wait for an answer. "No, our man within the Schnitzer Group was Emil Habicht. We got to him quite early on. Mistochenkov did not know, of course. He knew Habicht was having a fling with one of our secretaries out at Karlshorst, but nothing more."

Herbie asked why? his mind screening a film he had not witnessed: the death of Emil Habicht in the Alexanderplatz, shot from a car.

"His heart went out of it. I think he wanted to warn you – and confess. The Last Rites. You know."

It made sense, and Herbie could hardly conceal the shock. He felt the familiar churning of his stomach, and the hint of facing that reality he had not fully faced on reading Ursula's letter. "But Luzia?" He knew he was showing confusion, thinking of Pavel Mistochenkov fingering Luzia Gabell's photograph in the Charlton house.

The Colonel-General seemed not to have heard. "You must not be too hard on yourself for not spotting Habicht." He leaned forward, resting a hand on Herbie's shoulder for a moment. "He tried to remain very loyal. It took us a long, long time to marry you up with Schnitzer. You were simply Big Herbie. A courier – almost small fry – for many years."

"But he gave you the lot in the end?"

Vascovsky lit another cigarette, the smile returning, then going quickly. "In the end we all give the lot, Herbie. You know that."

The first true hints forming the answer to the puzzle began to take shape in Herbie's mind. He had tried not to dwell on the matter of Ursula – waiting, to see, in hope, that it was only a ploy. Now he was near to the truth, which began to form with horrific clarity. It was physically as though a huge crystal bowl had been shattered – the fragments, sharp, left to cut and fester within his emotions. He shook his head, repeating the original question. "Luzia?" he asked. "Mistochenkov gave me Luzia Gabell on a plate. Lotte Krug, he said. Lotte Krug, your mistress. If it was Habicht, and not the Gabell woman, was there a Lotte Krug?"

Oh yes, Vascovsky looked away. Yes, there was a Lotte Krug. That was one of the vital pieces of deception implanted within Pavel Mistochenkov. "I drilled him like a sergeant. Whatever happened. If we both went over, or only one of us – there was never any question of both, you understand – this one act of misdirection *had* to be performed. He obviously did well. I'm proud of him. Little Pavel *had* to identify Luzia Gabell as my lady friend. It was the one positive thing Pavel knew was not true. I ran film for him; showed him photographs. Pavel was a good name for him – Pavlovian. He learned his lesson like one of Pavlov's dogs."

"Lotte Krug, then?" As he asked Herbie dreaded the answer. He supposed that even then he already knew the truth; but when Vascovsky spoke, the splinters of crystal cut deeper than he expected.

"Lotte Krug was your Ursula, Herbie. But if it gives you any comfort I knew that she loved you far more than she could ever care for me. My association with her was professional only. Her feelings for you actually put her under grave suspicion for a while. But Lotte Krug was Ursula Zunder."

*   *   *

Much later Herbie had time to reflect on Jacob Vascovsky's actions at that moment. If the roles had been reversed, he concluded, he would have gone for the kill then – carried on, pressing home the psychological advantage. Instead, Vascovsky rose and said that was enough for one night. They would talk again in the morning. By the following evening he hoped to have Herbie out of these surroundings and in more comfortable quarters.

They took him back to the cell, where Herbie lay on the pallet with a single blanket for warmth, the light burning throughout the night.

At one point he took out Ursula's letter and carefully read it over again. Twice.

After the second reading the big man crumpled the thin

paper between his huge fists and wept as he had never done, even as a child: for he wept with the whole range of his senses, each sob and tear being a kind of prayer for mankind, and the barriers men put up against truth, love and peace. In a way, Herbie's tears were a Mass for traitors: wherever and whoever they may be.

14

DURING THAT MISERABLE Sunday night Miriam Grubb was taken from the building in the Mehring Platz and flown back to England. Worboys imagined they would get her to Warminster quite quickly.

"What'll happen to her?" he asked Tubby Fincher as they waited for the news that did not come from the other side of the Wall.

Probably nothing, Fincher told him. "Might send her to them; or keep her – rehabilitation. Who knows?"

"Will she admit . . .?"

Fincher put his hand to his thin lips. She did not need to admit anything. Miriam Grubb probably knew little enough anyway. By now Fincher was certain Herbie had been deviously enticed into the East, and Miriam instructed to pull the plugs at the right moment. She had probably also supplied a lot of background material concerning the electronic hardware to whoever was controlling the operation across the Berlin Wall.

What remained of the *Trepan* team stayed on for another couple of days. By the time they decamped Fincher knew Herbie was in Russian hands and that, in due course, the Minister would make representations through the proper channels.

Curry Shepherd and Anton Mohr were the only two who escaped the net, and came home – to Warminster and massive debriefing. Worboys eventually went back to his office and waited. In the Annexe he missed the bulk and presence of Big Herbie Kruger. It was some time before Worboys learned of the horror of that particular Sunday night for

Herbie; or of the worse hell that was to come on the Monday morning, at his next session with Vascovsky.

*   *   *

They took Herbie from the cell early in the morning. He was allowed a comfortable bath and his own clothes were returned. Then, in the room where Vascovsky had broken the news that Ursula Zunder and Lotte Krug were the same person, Herbie ate a hearty breakfast – or at least picked at it, for he was still in no mood for anything hearty. Vascovsky came in eventually, and the two sullen Vopo guards who had stayed with Herbie since taking him from the cell were dismissed.

"This afternoon we really start," announced Vascovsky, almost jovially.

Herbie did not even have to ask what they were to start. He had other questions which, at that moment, appeared more pressing to him. The wounds inside were still suppurating, and he wondered if they would ever heal. He asked, quietly, if he might continue where the Colonel-General had left off on the previous night.

Vascovsky sat down, helping himself to coffee, nodding an affirmative.

"If Pavel Mistochenkov was briefed by you to play this one piece of misdirection to me, he really must have believed you were dead," Herbie stated.

Of course. Vascovsky looked at him with surprise. That was a set-up. "Did he tell you straight away, or invent some story? Kashov told him that nobody was to know. It was a heart attack, not suicide. It was to be the official line. How did he hold up?"

Herbie asked if it was necessary for Pavel to hold up. "We all read the official reports."

The smile again. "Come on, Herbie. We planted the suicide story directly through your man, Girren. You knew before Pavel came over that I had committed suicide. You would not let that go for long."

They had used the body of a man roughly the same build as Vascovsky. "He died of natural causes, of course."

"Of course," said Herbie, not knowing what to believe any more. He sat back on his bed, crossing his arms.

Poor little Pavel, he swallowed that. They told him the story must not get out; that suicide was never to be mentioned on any account. "How did he hold up?"

"Not for long." Herbie was not going to give satisfaction. "So your Lotte Krug was my Ursula?" His voice surprisingly steady.

Before the incident with the magazines Ursula had been putting out signals for weeks. "She is Russian by birth. German educated. Trained by Centre. Yet she could not get you. She tried three times before the magazine business did the job."

Herbie was silent, and Vascovsky said he understood how this must feel.

"You have no idea at all," Herbie snapped. "You cannot have any idea how it feels."

Vascovsky apologised. It was their good fortune that Herbie had recruited her as one of his Telegraph Boys. They would have had no suspicions, but for Ursula – Electra.

"And I suppose she organised the back-watching, so that you could track the lot?"

For the second time Vascovsky showed surprise. "You still don't understand?"

What was there to understand? "You knew the Telegraph Boys long before I left in a hurry. In '65."

"We knew their cryptonyms," Vascovsky appeared almost shocked. "Why did you think we enticed you back? Used Pavel? We needed to finger each of the Telegraph Boys. The order came from Centre. We were to detect, identify and expose all Western surveillance teams. Particularly your Telegraph Boys in East Berlin."

"You . . .?"

"Why else would we want you? You can give us little things, possibly. One or two things. You must know that I shall be your confessor – is that what you still say? You may prove useful; but the real objects of our affections were your Telegraph Boys. There are some other surveillance teams within our territories. We have a few leads. But we needed you, Herbie, to take us into the heart of your people. We were

369

aware that six at least did the job here. Naturally we had some anxiety – a lot of water under the bridge, Herbie: you could have had eight or ten little Peeping Toms at work."

Herbie smiled, as though he still held a dark secret.

"So we used innocent Pavel. Set him as the catalyst, and, of course, dangled the emotional bait – Pavel was most carefully prepared. Really he did not know what kind of pressures he would be putting on you, personally."

"The Telegraph Boys?" Herbie spoke almost to himself, musing, brow lined like a patch of ploughed earth. "You knew the cryptonyms, though, Jacob," turning to face the Russian. "You knew them years ago. And Sensel? What about Peter Sensel?"

Blood on his hands. The gore-streaked rag doll beaten to death. Herbie looked at his knuckles. Christ, he had beaten an innocent man: beaten him to death, broken his face, probably ruptured the spleen, crushed his ribs, smashed the windpipe.

"Only the cryptos, Herbie. For a long time we only had the cryptos. You should be proud of your people; they were very, very good. Too good for us – even though we had one of them. We tried everything – watching the drops and letterboxes used by Ursula. Leeching on to the handlers. Every time, they lost our men: even when we worked full street teams: cars, walkers, quick-change actors. Every time, they slipped away. They led charmed lives. Lost them every time," he repeated, "just like we lost you, Herbie, when your Schnitzer Group broke and ran. How did you do that, by the way?"

Herbie opened his mouth, closing it rapidly. Years back, in his head, he saw a particular stretch of the ground between the barricades and the Wall – a section which had been the façade of a street, shored up with extra timber and stone. An opening of bricks, loose and removed at a precise moment; bribed Vopos and Grepos. He must beware. In his head Herbie carried the names of seven Grepos still available for sweetening. He smiled at Vascovsky, moving his head in a negative gesture. "Can I ask how you got those six cryptos – five, I suppose, because you already had Electra?"

The smile vanished; replaced by a mask, as he heard Vascovsky say lightly: "But you, Herbie. You gave us the cryptonyms of your Telegraph Boys."

Had all reality gone? He was adrift, the sea stormy and not even a straw to which he could cling. Herbie had to put the brakes on to his whirling mind, for Vascovsky was asking something else – did Herbie ever remember being ill? Was he ever taken ill at Ursula's apartment?

He struggled to collate the memories. Time was a tunnel, dark, lit by small, well-remembered lights, and huge moments of either happiness or fear, etched there for ever. Ursula Zunder's apartment? There had been a bout of 'flu. In the winter of '63, he thought. Nothing else. Oh, except for a couple of very bad hangovers: they had put it down to some cheap brand of vodka Ursula had picked up. Those hangovers? Yes, he had been terribly ill: never experienced anything like it. "There must have been anti-freeze in that stuff," he said to Ursula.

Then the pinpoint of truth grew into a floodlight, filling his brain. "Hangovers?" It was half a question, whispered.

"You have it now? You've got it?" Vascovsky looked pleased with himself, one hand held out elegantly; smoke running upwards from his cigarette, clouding at the top of the rising stream. You might expect a Genie to appear from the smoke; or perhaps one had already leaped through the star-trap of the past.

"What did you use on me?" Herbie sounded cowed, the awful truth gradually filling him with the greatest horror of all.

"Sodium thiopental," Vascovsky shrugged. "It was the best we had in those days; and you are not a good subject."

"But I'd have known – felt the bruising: the injection."

"That's why we had to do it twice. You nearly died. If it's any comfort your Ursula pleaded with me not to try again. No injections, Herbie. We gave it to you orally. Ursula put it in your last drink."

"But that's . . ."

"Not easy: no. Risky also. The dosage is tricky at the best of times. It's pure murder trying to hit on the correct amount when you have to swallow it – particularly as you had been drinking. But then that was necessary to cover the taste. We've come a long way since those days, eh, Herbie?"

At first he did not reply. The tangled skein of deception

changed to a vast hall of mirrors, an endless series of Chinese boxes. Ursula? Ursula, who had written the letter saying she still loved him, pouring grief into his body; showing it was burned into her own emotions for all time. Ursula had given him sodium thio – pentathol – in the cheap vodka.

Soap – as the Service called it – would sometimes produce spectacular results: the so-called first truth drug. *In pentathol veritas*. It also occasionally did nothing but put the subject to sleep; or, more than often, produced a particular stubbornness – especially if the subject was trained. Many doctors claimed a trained man would refuse to reveal that which he knew should not be spoken aloud. But many doctors have been proved wrong.

"What happened?" Herbie asked, trying to strengthen his trembling voice.

On the first occasion he had passed out cold. They could not get to him at all: not even as he was coming out of it. "That was risky anyway, because we needed you to remain innocent." There had been an experienced doctor there all night. "As I told you, Ursula did not want to do it again."

"But she did," Herbie shouted, raising himself from the pillows, fury raping his mind. "The bitch did it again."

Vascovsky spread his hands, as though trying to make him see it was an inevitable course of action. "There was no other way. In any case, you are a difficult subject. We could only get the cryptonyms, and, of course, there was no way of knowing if we had them all. Priam; Hecuba; Nestor; Horus; Gemini, and Electra."

Herbie venomously said it was very tough they could only get the cryptonyms. He was so sorry about that. But what of Priam? Peter Sensel? The man he had killed with his bare hands?

Vascovský had to admit luck. "You knew he was *schwül*?" He used the slang German for gay. "He chose a boyfriend who put in a report. The boyfriend found some evidence – one-time emergency stuff." Vascovsky laughed. "The lover thought he was having another man – you know how jealous they can get? That's why he searched the room. We watched Sensel pass information." Another chuckle. "As usual the handler got away. But we had Sensel; and he did not know. So we used Electra. Mind you, we spent much time trying to plot Sensel's contacts. How do you train those people to be so good, Herbie?" Once more the laugh. "We had your Sensel, and we did not even know his cryptonym. Ursula played him right off the cuff. Bumped him and passed a message for a meet. A special message directly from you. His regular handler was not to be told. She even used the name 'Schnitzer'."

They had filtered delicate words, sensitive instructions, to poor Peter Sensel. He was chosen for a special job. A new job. A prime piece of work. Silence was absolutely golden: more than ever before. Schnitzer had a new asset in East Berlin. Right in the heart. His crypto was Auguste. ("You know what an 'Auguste' is, Herbie? A red-nosed clown who wears baggy, ragged clothes.")

After Vascovsky's faked suicide Electra had let Sensel know that Auguste had been Vascovsky. Because of what had happened there were even more important things to be done. She told him that she was Herbie's agent, Trapeze: even showing herself. Sensel fell for the whole yarn. He was to wait. Say nothing to his regular handler. Someone new would be coming in. She gave him the sentence from Gorky.

"Mistochenkov already had that password. I gave it to him without pushing the matter: just told him that our man within the Telegraph Boys was expecting the Gorky sentence. I did not labour the point, and he obviously gave it to you along with everything else. It's a good rule, Herbie – implant and then let the seed grow: that's the secret of making it look natural."

That was exactly what Colonel-General Vascovsky was doing now, to Big Herbie Kruger. Vascovsky, in giving details of his operation to lure Herbie, had planted seeds: performed the first part of what, he knew, would be a long haul of delving – panning for the small facts that Herbie might give him. The implanted seed was the fact that Herbie Kruger was his own traitor: the betrayer of his own trust.

"I killed him. In rage I killed him," Herbie said quietly.

There was no feeling. Just a numb agony. Like no pain or sensation Herbie had ever experienced. The worst thing, he supposed later, was the fall of pride. They had hooked and

dangled him as neatly as clever anglers – caught him between
the twin poles of duty and love. Then they brought him down
with a bludgeon, filling him with the sense that he was the
cancer: the one who had betrayed.

His own people had forbidden him to go into the garden of
weapons, to play with the deadly flowers. But Herbie had
already, unknowingly, touched their poisonous pollen, filling
him with the need to avenge his own reputation: see his duty
through to the end.

He looked, blank-eyed at Jacob Vascovsky, hearing close
within his head the last words of the *Song of the Night Sentry*:
wishing that he had listened to them properly; wishing he had
understood them –

> *Anyone who believes it is far away.*
> *He is a king!*
> *He is an Emperor!*
> *He is making the war!*
> *Halt! Who goes there? Speak up!*
> *Clear off.*

15

HERBIE HAD BEEN right in his assumption that he was in the old Magdalenenstrasse jail. He was housed in a refurbished wing, and it was there that Vascovsky carried out his initial interrogation.

Being a senior executive of the British Service, Herbie was a rare prize. Any man like Herbie Kruger, who had dwelt in the world of secrets since the age of fourteen, had to have grains of information within his mind which might eventually be turned into vast pastures of usable intelligence.

But the labourers who toil in the secret places of the world learn quickly how to tie their knowledge in screened parcels, which they drop deep within their memories: allowing these facts to lie dormant until *they* wish to retrieve them.

Vascovsky's job was to search for the parcels in Herbie Kruger's memory. The Colonel-General was aware – as indeed Herbie was aware – that, no matter what techniques were known and used, the professional is always at greater risk, if only because he already knows the techniques. Police officers subjected to interrogation are apt to give away more, because they are watching for the pitfalls inherent in the techniques. So it is with those trained in the arcane life.

The preliminary part of Herbie Kruger's interrogation was, from Vascovsky's viewpoint, the most important. From the moment he placed Kruger in the loser's corner, by giving him the facts, he knew the big man would be most likely to provide him with small clues very quickly: possibly without even knowing it.

On one point he was quite open with Herbie. "We shall

stay here in Berlin for a week or two only," he told him. "After that we go to Russia: to a pleasant *dacha* we keep near the Black Sea. There we have everything – doctors, the proper conditions . . ."

There was no need for him to continue. Herbie knew the course his questioning would take. First a long series of face-to-face sessions – the establishing of the relationship, and the early signs. 'Panning for gold', they called it at Warminster. Sometimes this process was enough. Herbie had imagined it had been enough for him when interrogating Pavel Mistochenkov. Now he was determined to let Vascovsky think it was enough for him also. The hatred which welled from Herbie, with the truth in the open, seemed to give him strength. This he would need, because the next phase, at the *dacha* near the Black Sea, would slowly strip him bare. The technology of interrogation had advanced a long way, and – though the road may twist and turn; lead off at tangents; double back on itself – the end would be a total drying out. The injections, the black boxes, the freak sessions. All would be used against such a man as Big Herbie.

So, for almost four weeks, he played the game with Vascovsky – attempting to reverse the roles, even ingratiating himself with the Colonel-General; for it was important that the relationship should appear friendly.

Within himself, quite coldly, Herbie Kruger knew they must not get him as far as Russia, and the specialists. Either he had to make one last throw at an escape (and he saw no way from this secure place), or he must, in some manner, do away with himself.

He worked hard to make Vascovsky believe he would be pliant; that he was not a grudge-bearer. "In England criminals have a phrase," he smiled his daft smile at Vascovsky. "Some, when arrested, say, 'It's a fair cop,' meaning the police have won, and they accept their situation. To you I say, 'It's a fair cop.'"

Vascovsky nodded, smiling. Inside himself, for a second Herbie felt the smouldering ruins of his life flare into flame again.

So the first sessions of questioning continued each day, with Herbie storing every question and answer into his memory

Eventually he would need to be able to repeat these sessions verbatim. If he lived that long.

He tried to see the traps as they were set, long before Jacob Vascovsky attempted to spring them, and was aware that, on two occasions, he nearly fell headlong into his confessor's hidden snares. Some of the Colonel-General's questions led back to sources of years ago – other lives, other times.

"Man is never the same man two years running," Herbie said often. "Jacob, are you the same man now that you were three, four, five years ago?"

It was a counter ploy to Vascovsky. An attempt by Herbie to get the man looking back into his own past, so that he, for a second or two, became the victim of interrogation. A couple of times it almost worked.

Herbie knew a few days before the departure for Russia was imminent. They did not tell him anything, but provided him with a new suit. The food got slightly better. There was an air about Vascovsky that said they would soon be leaving – indefinable, yet almost tangible. In the end the Colonel-General told him on the night before departure.

They usually had an early evening session, starting around six o'clock, going on sometimes until after dinner. On this night Jacob Vascovsky told him they would not be eating together. "I have to go to my office at Karlshorst. Clear up a few papers. Then, check out some things in my apartment." He ran a hand lightly over the iron hair. "Tomorrow, my dear Herbie, we take a plane to Moscow. Very quietly, just the two of us, and a reception committee at the other end."

Herbie allowed himself to react with some pleasure. "It will be good. I have been looking forward to seeing Russia." He spread his hands wide, the huge palms upwards. "There are things I can speak of more freely there. Things I don't wish to talk of while I am here – so near to the West."

Jacob Vascovsky raised his eyebrows. "So?"

Herbie steeled himself. "You read Ursula's letter?"

Vascovsky nodded.

"You know how much she means to me – meant to me? There is, perhaps, some kind of deal we can do. In my heart of hearts I am aware that, in the end, the final struggle will come. Maybe I just want to be on the winning side; maybe my contact against your system has made me respect it.''

"You're making me an offer?" Vascovsky leaned forward. "A genuine offer?"

"Maybe. Can we talk about it in Russia?"

Vascovsky laughed. "Oh, we can talk. I've no doubt what your kind of deal would be, Herbie. Go back and work for us in the West, yes?"

Herbie shook his head. "I very much doubt that. Personally I think I could be of more use to you in Moscow. In the West, Herbie Kruger is a discredited man – you've seen to that."

Vascovsky nodded slowly. "But, if we did some kind of a deal, as you call it, we might want you to go back. Stranger things have been arranged."

"In Moscow," Herbie made motions with his ham hands, indicating that he really did not want to talk here.

That night he wondered for a long time if Vascovsky would seriously rise to the bait. If so he might lower his guard a little before they got to the airport. Already Herbie had decided not even to try and take his own life until every avenue had been explored. He would only do it if they were on the brink of really deep interrogation with drugs.

The next morning they told him he would be leaving during the early afternoon. He was always aware of the guards, though did not see them often. He ate lunch alone. Vascovsky came down at two o'clock.

"Well, my friend. We have plenty of time, but I have to drop off at my apartment to pick up a case. A nice quiet drive to the airport, eh?"

"A scheduled flight?" Herbie looked at him, face bland.

Vascovsky's mouth flickered in a smile. "Scheduled for us. A small military transport. I can trust you to behave, I think," he opened his civilian jacket to show the holstered little Makarov automatic under his left shoulder.

Herbie laughed aloud. "You are joking, Jacob. Remember what I said – it's a fair cop? I go even further once we get to Russia. I'm not an idiot.''

"No." Vascovsky's hand hovered over the large German's shoulder. "No. We go then? Right?"

378

Herbie nodded, and they left his room for the last time.

It seemed too good to be true, thought Herbie. Far too good. First, they were using an elderly black, unmarked Mercedes; second, apart from the driver, only Vascovsky and Kruger were travelling in the vehicle; third, the driver was a uniformed man, almost as large as Herbie himself. He carried a pistol on his belt.

Three of them. There had to be a trail car, either in front or behind. Yet nothing showed. He was careful not to call attention by looking around often; but the odd glance was enough. There was no trail car. Vascovsky's vanity had taken over, thought Herbie. The Russian did not want to call attention to this part of the operation. After all, he was bringing in Eberhard Lukas Kruger, an executive of the British Security Services. He had panned a little gold from the man, and there was no question, in his mind, that his prisoner was undergoing that strange phenomenon, known well to analysts as 'transference'. So Vascovsky reasoned. He would arrive in Moscow with a pliable captive – a potential recruit. His superiors there must see this to be the case.

Herbie's mind was also racing. They were heading towards the Soviet Embassy – Pavel Mistochenkov had spoken of the apartment Vascovsky kept near there. No chance of a run for it, he argued. Near the Brandenburg Gate; but that was a hot area. It crossed Herbie's mind that all the Wall areas were hot now. Even the couple he knew about could be unsafe. He was out of touch, and would have no time to make new contacts. Going over the Wall was not possible.

His mind flicked back to the old days – the experienced men and women who used to go over; who had their own places. Then the desperate ones – the people who just took chances. Vividly he recalled the reports and photographs. Christmas 1963. A white Christmas, and there were special Christmas passes: permits allowing West Berliners to visit relatives in the East, valid for twenty-four hours. People had been stunned, a month before, by the events in Dallas – Kennedy's assassination.

Yet that Christmas there seemed to be a spirit of compromise abroad. On Boxing Day there was still a sense of Christmas in the cold air. People were still making their visits, taking presents to the East. The bells of St. Thomas' church, right on the Wall, pealed a message of good will, even at nightfall when the two figures climbed the wall of the church, heading West.

Both got to the top of the wall and were just climbing the barbed-wire barrier, silhouetted against the sky, when the bells were drowned by the crackle of machine-gun fire. One of the boys – for they were only boys – jumped to safety, the other threw up his hands and fell, with bullets ripping his chest and back. A glove hung from the wire, and the boy's blood dripped scarlet into the snow under the arc lights. He was only eighteen years old – Peter Schultz from Neu Brandenburg. Herbie remembered that the deputy mayor of West Berlin claimed the death had undone a lot of the good will forged by the Christmas permits. Willy Brandt declared, "The bullets which hit Peter Schultz have hit us all."

Why could Herbie remember all this so vividly, when he had been much occupied at the time? Certain pictures, words and phrases stick more constantly in the memory, he thought. But it did not alter the fact that going over the Wall was not possible. If he were to make an escape, Herbie would have to go through, not over. Hang around until evening, then mug some poor devil for his documents, perhaps? No, that would not work. Within minutes of making a successful run, the border checks would be doubled. Unless . . .? The idea scared him, but the risk might just be acceptable. He noticed a street clock: nearly three in the afternoon.

"What time do we leave?" Casually as he could muster.

"Four-thirty; five. The aircraft will be ready at four-thirty." Vascovsky was looking out of the window; but the driver, Herbie noticed, appeared to be very alert: eyes everywhere.

They turned off near the Embassy, into a side street, pulling up in front of the entrance to a modern apartment block. The place, Herbie thought, where Pavel Mistochenkov had been supposed to find the Colonel-General's body; the place where Vascovsky entertained his mistress, Lotte Krug – Ursula. He had ceased to be clear about Ursula, uncertain of the real truth. Had Vascovsky lied to him? Was she really mistress to the two men at the same time? Or, as Vascovsky claimed, only lover to Herbie? There were even moments – which the large man dismissed, usually quite quickly, as sentimental delusion on his part – when he wondered about the reality of Ursula's last letter. Was that true? Or had she been forced to write it under Vascovsky's duress?

The Colonel-General was speaking to him now. "I think it best if we stay together." He flashed his smile. "Not that I don't trust you, Herbie. I just want to have my eye on you all the time. I'm sure you understand."

Herbie merely laughed. The driver, silent, his hand never far from the holster on his belt, moved from behind the wheel to open the door. Vascovsky alighted first, waiting on the pavement so that, as Herbie emerged, he was between his captors. They went into the building in file – Vascovsky, Herbie, then the driver.

Into the lift. "I shall miss this little place. So convenient," Vascovsky said, adding that he would be returning when they had sorted out matters in Russia. "Who knows, you may even be with me, Herbie?"

Then the apartment. It was pleasant enough, if a shade gaudy for Herbie's taste. He did not care for the décor at all – chintzy; like a pouf, he thought in English slang. A fairy castle. Maybe it was for the benefit of the ladies?

The place was of standard design – one main room and three doors off. Bathroom, kitchen and bedroom, Herbie decided. A small, ornate desk stood below the window. It had been cleared of papers, but a telephone remained. Vascovsky said he would not be a moment, walking quickly to the bedroom.

Herbie turned to face the driver, whose hand still hovered over his holster. Silent and very fast, Herbie's brain told him: very fast indeed.

There is an empty-hand, silent-kill technique which is a more severe variant of the neck-chop to the carotid artery – a movement which if firmly applied will render a person unconscious for a short period. The silent-kill technique is one in which you catch the victim with a faster, more accurate blow. The recipient feels nothing. His carotid artery is ruptured and the neck broken, all with one correctly-placed blow, using the right amount of force.

Herbie had been first taught methods of silent killing years ago. Even now he did the annual refresher course. Technically he knew how to perform this particular action, but had never used it.

Herbie grinned at the driver, and the driver grinned back. He did not even see Herbie's arm move. Herbie rationalised that the driver was dead before his brain even gave out danger signals. For the smallest fraction of a second Herbie registered surprise that it really worked, the way they always said it did. The driver was dead on his feet from the one terrible blow – standing there, head lolling and eyes glazed.

There seemed to be all the time in the world for Herbie to step quietly behind him, to catch the weight under the body's arms, lower him gently and remove the pistol from the holster. He even had time to check that the large Stechkin APS was cocked. He made no noise in sliding the safety from *on* to *off*.

When Vascovsky came back, carrying a small suitcase in one hand, a smart briefcase in the other – less than thirty seconds after he had gone into the bedroom – he found himself facing the ugly eye of the automatic, gripped, almost to the point of invisibility, in Herbie Kruger's paw.

The Russian stopped, eyes shifting. "Herbie . . .?" he began.

"Very gently, Jacob. The case on the floor, please. Then the pistol out. Finger and thumb on the butt. You know the drill, and don't forget: it doesn't worry me to kill you."

Vascovsky did not hesitate.

"Now kick it over here." Herbie caught the weapon between his feet. He did not make the mistake of picking it up.

"You can't get away. There's no way out for you, Herbie. Don't be foolish."

"You want to die?" Herbie heard the seriousness in his own voice, knowing that he would prefer to take the man with him, or kill him first.

"You would not get further than the elevator. Certainly never out of Berlin. Never to the West."

Herbie said he thought it could be managed – with Vascovsky's help.

"If I help you I'm probably dead myself anyway. You might as well shoot me and get it over with."

Herbie laughed. The Colonel-General was flattering him. "You can talk your way out of anything, Jacob – even a prisoner getting the drop on you. Certainly I'll kill you now if that's what you want. But I leave you here, trussed like a chicken, after you have helped. You'll talk your way out of that. A small demotion, maybe . . ."

Vascovsky thought about it for a minute, then asked Herbie what he wanted.

Herbie told him – a written, official order, under the name of the now dead driver ("In a minute, I want you to remove his papers for me to look at"), giving instructions to cross into the West, to collect one of Vascovsky's officers, ostensibly visiting Spandau. "Come on, Jacob. We all know your people go in and out on that excuse all the time."

"It wouldn't work. A Control Point has to be informed personally."

Herbie smiled. "Yes, I know. You will do that also. You will cover me by telephoning the adjutant at Karlshorst as well, just in case there's a smart duty officer at the checkpoint. I'll use Charlie, like your people normally do. Maybe your driver's photograph won't quite match my ugly face, but it may just work. I shall tell you what to say. Don't forget, I speak Russian as well as German. This is something you just remembered driving out to the airport – what you say on the 'phone."

Herbie kicked Vascovsky's gun away again and told him to approach the body of the driver, unbutton his pockets, and take out his identification. The Colonel-General looked resigned, but one could never be sure. He was very slow and careful in his movements, keeping his hands well away from his body. Herbie stood back. If he could perform a silent kill that quickly, heaven knew what Vascovsky would manage in a corner as tight as this.

With a sudden horror Herbie realised that he was overwhelmed with the desire to kill the man. He remembered the old saying, *Er hatte Blut geleckt* – he who tastes blood gets to like it.

He made Vascovsky move over to the desk and place the

driver's ID flat in front of him – pleased to notice that, as long as there was no really close scrutiny, he might just get away with it. Or was he fooling himself?

Next he ordered the Russian to open the desk drawers one at a time – starting at the bottom. He knew what he was looking for; and there it was, in the second drawer up on the right: printed and headed official stationery, complete with Vascovsky's rank and non-existent cover unit number at Karlshorst.

The driver's name was Oleg Tavorin. He was a sergeant. Herbie made Vascovsky write the order twice – once in Russian, then in German.

"But they'll . . ." Vascovsky began. He was going to say they would query it at the Western post, then realised Herbie would clear himself if he ever reached the West alive.

"Just do it, Jacob."

Vascovsky signed the document, and Herbie laid it to one side. He still stayed out of the Russian's reach. "Now the telephone book."

Jacob Vascovsky smiled, asking what telephone book? Crisply, Herbie suggested his private book. "The one *I* would carry in *my* briefcase."

"I carry numbers in my head."

Herbie told him to open the briefcase anyhow.

"Why not trust me for a change, Herbie? It can't work. They'll spot you whatever I say."

"Open the briefcase, Jacob."

Herbie moved back a step further. Better be safe, they always taught this one – tell a man to open something, and always presume he has a weapon concealed. As Vascovsky clicked the locks Herbie found himself automatically taking up the first pressure on the trigger.

But there was no weapon in the case. Merely papers, and, on top, two small black notebooks.

"Riffle those books through for me, Jacob." The voice commanding; all the cheerful, stupid co-operation gone. Herbie was his working self again.

Vascovsky glanced up, his face showing hatred, the eyes shifting, signalling that the brain was desperately trying to formulate some plan.

The second of the books was crammed with telephone numbers – mainly Berlin, confidential. Herbie told him to turn the page to the Karlshorst numbers and extensions. "Hold it up so I can see," he snapped.

The Karlshorst list covered two entire pages. "Roskov?" Herbie read. "He seems to be your adjutant. Extension 497. You will get through to him and say exactly what I tell you. Any changes and I kill you now. This minute. Understand?"

Vascovsky did not reply, so Herbie went on, slowly going through the form he wished Vascovsky to use.

He watched carefully as the Colonel-General dialled, then asked for the extension. Some underling obviously came on the line. "Major Roskov," Vascovsky said. Then, in answer to a question, "Colonel Vascovsky."

There was a click, then a voice, quite audible. Herbie had instructed Vascovsky to keep the earpiece slightly away from his head.

"Sasha," Vascovsky spoke flatly into the telephone. "I am running late, heading for the airport now. I forgot to tell you. This morning I issued an authorisation for Tavorin to take the car into the West. It's cleared on the other side. Tavorin is picking up one of my people at Spandau."

The voice at the other end asked a question. "Not on the telephone, Sasha. He'll report to you personally after Tavorin gets him back. I thought you should know in case the Control Point get on the line. Just clear it, will you? I must go, otherwise we'll not get back to Moscow tonight." The man at the other end tried to say something else, but Vascovsky put down the handset. "Are you satisfied now?" he said, looking up with loathing.

Herbie hoped he was satisfied. It seemed to have gone as he wished, but one could never tell. The voice at the other end of the line appeared to have stayed unruffled. The only extra word had been the man's christian name – Sasha. For all Herbie knew that could have been a warning.

He stepped behind Jacob Vascovsky, who had begun to say he supposed Herbie now wanted a call to the duty officer at Checkpoint Charlie. Herbie hit him once – the hard heel of his hand right on the back of the Russian's neck, high up. Just enough force to put him out for the best part of an hour or so, and cause possible concussion once he regained consciousness.

Using a belt and service tie, Herbie trussed Vascovsky, emptying his pockets as he went, throwing the contents on to the desk — ID, official passes, everything.

In the bedroom he found more ties, with which he made a long rope. Vascovsky's feet were secure, and the hands tied high up behind his back. He passed the knotted ties around the man's wrists, turning the body over so that the Russian lay face down. The ties were now looped around the captive's neck, and passed back to the wrists, tightly; then, down to the feet which Herbie bent upwards, finally securing them with the tie. If Vascovsky struggled a lot he might even choke himself.

The number for Checkpoint Charlie (duty officer) was easy enough to find in the black book. Herbie dialled and a voice answered, naturally enough, in German.

Herbie could do a fair Russian-accented version of his own natural language. He used it now to ask for the duty officer, introducing himself as Colonel-General Vascovsky, Special Section, 4th Motorised Infantry, Karlshorst. "You have heard from my office?" he asked. The duty officer had heard nothing. "As I thought. Inefficient. I am leaving Berlin shortly. It is good that I checked. Has one of my people been through yet? Driving a Mercedes? Licence number 234 7658? The driver is in uniform. A sergeant. Name of Tavorin, and travelling on a special order issued by myself."

The duty officer said he would check. He was away for almost two minutes. No. No driver of that name had been through on the Colonel-General's orders. Herbie cursed in Russian. "He is running very late. It is most important he is passed through with speed. He should be with you any minute. He will be in the West for about one hour, returning with a passenger. Speed is essential. I have to go now, but if you have any query, just call my adjutant — Major Roskov at extension 497, Karlshorst. Good?"

The Colonel-General was assured they would delay his driver for as short a time as possible.

Vascovsky was still out cold when Herbie left the apartment, even though it had taken him almost twenty minutes to prepare himself. Most of that time was spent in getting the uniform jacket with the high neck off Tavorin's corpse. The jacket fitted: just. It would be impossible to get the trousers off – in any case, they were probably soiled. Tavorin's gun was back in the holster. His ID and the newly-written Vascovsky pass were in the top right-hand pocket so that Herbie could use his left to get them out – leaving the right hand clear and near the holster.

All Vascovsky's documents were tucked into other pockets. The briefcase – which contained a number of highly-interesting files – was locked with the other automatic inside.

Taking the car keys in his right hand, with the briefcase, Herbie hefted the suitcase into his left hand, and walked from the apartment, most conscious that the uniform cap was at least one size too small for his massive head. He had stretched it as far as possible – even the sweatband had split and torn under his ministrations.

The suitcase he stowed in the rear of the car. The briefcase was at his feet. He would pass, as long as they did not order him out of the car.

The Mercedes reached the main street by the time Herbie thought of Vascovsky's telephone. He had made mistakes with telephones before. Now he realised that it would have been wiser to tear the wires from the junction box. He shrugged, crouching over the wheel. It would probably be safe enough; after all, Vascovsky would take a long time to recover consciousness, and even longer to get himself near the telephone – even trying to roll towards the desk would cause extreme discomfort and the symptoms of strangulation from the loop of ties around his neck.

Herbie concentrated on the late afternoon traffic, driving carefully towards the control point which had, during the height of the old Cold War, been almost a symbol – Checkpoint Charlie.

There were two cars ahead of him, both civilian; pulled up at the long buildings where you could sometimes queue for hours. The place was swarming with Grepos – the East German border police. Two Grepos were going through the first car – looking under it with the wheeled mirror, examining everything inside.

Herbie's stomach churned. Was there already an alert out? Or – as it was a quiet afternoon – were the Grepos merely passing time? Ahead of the control point was the first striped barrier, with its metal skirt to stop low sports cars from racing beneath it. Past this, the slalom of low walls, through which cars, lorries and buses had to negotiate with zig-zagging care; slowing down the passage towards the final barrier, and the stretch of road which was the no-man's land leading towards the first barrier on the Western side.

Herbie crouched again and looked upwards. As ever the two miradors – the searchlight and machine-gun towers – were well-manned: the nozzles of the machine-guns turned to face both East and West. They could pick off anyone in the no-man's land; or at the Control Point itself.

The Grepos continued to take their time, moving listlessly. They were in no hurry.

Herbie took a deep breath. He had given so much. If he managed to cross now at least he would be able to take back something – the papers in Vascovsky's briefcase, the little he had learned during interrogation, the facts about the whole operation. At least he could do that. If he got part way and died . . . Well, that would be an end to it all.

Slowly, and with a great firmness, he put his huge hand on the car horn and pressed.

The Grepos looked up, one of them motioning with his machine-pistol for Herbie to keep quiet. He took his hand off the horn and began to give strong, loud toots to attract attention. A Grepo sergeant, on the small covered walkway which ran the length of the control building, looked hard and walked slowly towards the Mercedes.

Herbie lowered the window, keeping one hand over the holstered automatic, the other unbuttoning his jacket pocket for Vascovsky's pass and Tavorin's ID.

"You shut up and wait your turn; otherwise we take longer," the Grepo sergeant said sharply. He had a heavy Berlin accent. Herbie replied in halting German, Russian-accented. "I have papers. My Colonel's orders – Colonel-General Vascovsky. I should have been in the West over an hour ago. It is most urgent official business. See . . ." He waved Vascovsky's handwritten order under the sergeant's nose.

The man took the paper and read it quickly. "Your identity papers," he snapped. Then, as Herbie handed over Tavorin's ID, "Pull the car forward, sergeant. In front of the one they are searching."

"I stay in the car." Herbie phrased it flatly, not as a question.

The Grepo sergeant said, "Yes," as he moved off; and Herbie put the Mercedes into gear and pulled out from behind the waiting cars. He was conscious of the sergeant shouting something at the Grepos who were searching the first car, then pointing back towards him. One of the Grepos nodded and waved Herbie on into a place in front of the car he was examining.

Herbie left the engine running, but another Grepo appeared and told him to turn the engine off. The Grepo stood in front of the Mercedes, his machine-pistol slung almost casually over his shoulder, but with the muzzle pointing forwards and down, roughly in Herbie's direction.

In the silence, once the engine was stopped, Herbie could hear his heart thumping and the blood pounding in his ears. He kept one hand near the ignition keys, the other resting on the butt of the gun in its open holster.

Lines from the *Serenade of the Sentry* again crossed his mind; then recrossed, as though his whole life, with its errors and mistakes, its triumphs that had been poisoned, his successes which might still be saved, was distilled down to this one point in time: sitting, waiting for escape or death, at a control point on the Berlin Wall —

Halt! Who goes there? Speak up!

Clear off!

Time appeared to stand still. Like a trick in the mind: a clock ticking on and on. He realised it was a childhood memory — a clock in his grandfather's house; you could hear the tick-tock through the night, and, as a small boy, he had the impression that time was not passing at all. Herbie looked at the Grepo near the car. He was young — very young, eighteen, nineteen, perhaps, with grey eyes caught in the light. Then Herbie looked ahead again and tried to remember the names of those who had been caught at a checkpoint: gunned down, or hauled from cars. There was one who had tried to get out under a lorry and failed, but he could not remember the name.

Odd, he had remembered Peter Schultz with great clarity. He could also recite other names, still kept alive in memory with little markers of wood and barbed wire, flowers, and boards on which their names were carved – Ida Siekmann, Rolf Urban, Olga Segler, Bernd Lünser. But they had all died crossing the Wall, not at a control point. Herbie's memory could not dredge up a single name, out of the many, caught or killed at places like Checkpoint Charlie. Eberhard Lukas Kruger? he wondered. Would he be remembered as one who died at this place, in the no-man's land ahead?

A door opened to his left, and the Grepo sergeant came out carrying the papers. An officer stood framed in the door, shouting something to Herbie. He had to lean over and wind down the other window to hear.

"We had orders about you," the officer was shouting. "Your Colonel wants you over as quickly as possible. You are due back in an hour."

Herbie waved a kind of salute and shouted back. "Less than an hour."

The Grepo sergeant was at the window, thrusting the papers at him. "You had better move," he muttered. "My officer says your Colonel is furious you are so late."

"Traffic," Herbie shrugged, and looked towards the officer again. He was a young man, blond, not wearing a cap. He had that sharp efficient manner – like the SS in the old days, Herbie thought, turning the key in the ignition. Already they had raised the first barrier for him. As he turned the key he heard a telephone ringing from behind the officer, who hesitated for a second, then wheeled around and went back into his office.

Herbie drove slowly towards the slalom. Don't rush it, he thought; but, by the time he reached the low walls, he was gaining speed. He took the car through the obstacles, gaining a little speed with each turn. Then through, and on to the other side. They were raising the barrier.

He glanced into the mirror, and saw the officer running out on to the walkway, shouting, pointing towards the Mercedes. The barrier was fully up, and it flashed through Herbie's mind that there may well be a metal safety barrier in the road, before the centre of the no-man's strip – a big flange that could be raised in his path. He put his foot on the accelerator and took off towards the barrier. As it got closer he saw it waver and begin to descend.

He changed into third and tried to put his foot through the floor, felt the car leap forward, and heard the metal scrape as the barrier apron hit the roof. Then the shots came.

At first a couple of bursts of fire. He felt the bullets jar into the rear of the car, and the back come round as the tyres went.

He was flat over the wheel now, his foot still down on the accelerator, and the Mercedes slewing and grinding. Another burst of fire – probably from above, from the miradors. The rear of the car seemed to buck, and he felt the roof behind him being torn away. Ahead, the paving was moving: a metal barrier, set flush with the road, now slowly rising on a series of hydraulic jacks.

Herbie pulled at the wheel as though he was in an aircraft, trying to lift the machine over the slowly rising metal, the bullets chewing the rear of the car to pieces.

The front wheels hit the rising barrier at an angle – it could not have been up more than six inches at that point – and the whole car juddered, then leaped forward.

Herbie felt the rear dragging; it was as though he was moving solely on the engine, front wheels and the driver's seat. But he *was* moving, and fast. Far from straight; bucking, grinding, straining.

Ahead, the Western barrier had been raised, and he saw the West German troops taking cover, their weapons pointing towards the Eastern Control Point. Dimly, Herbie realised that the shooting had stopped, and he was moving more slowly – the Mercedes limping under the Western barrier.

He was home.

They took him out of the car at gunpoint, and would not let him carry either of the cases. He did not bother to look back at the damage, just allowed himself to be hustled into the Control building, through a passage and into an office. A major was standing in front of his desk, face like thunder. Then the thunder went and his jaw dropped open.

"Take that hat off," the major ordered.

Herbie felt an odd chill. On the wall, behind the major, were a number of photographs. One was of himself.

The major was talking to him. "You are Eberhard Lukas Kruger?"

Herbie nodded, motioning towards a chair, asking if he could sit down.

"We do not like such incidents," the major said, then quickly shouted for coffee to be brought. "I have special orders about you."

They would have special orders, Herbie thought. Very special orders. Next time he looked up the major was speaking into the telephone.

"I shall need to take the cases," Herbie said when the major had replaced the telephone.

"Naturally. Some of your people will be here soon."

They brought the cases, and the coffee, which Herbie drank slowly. He had barely finished by the time two men arrived. He recognised neither of them, but they spoke gently. One of them even said it was all well done. They agreed he should be custodian of the cases.

Herbie did not even try to follow the route. The destination was a safe flat he did not recognise – very new, bright, and in a tall, modern building.

The two men were English, but did not speak much. They fed him and made him comfortable, but did not let him out of their sight for a moment.

*   *   *

That night young Worboys arrived with a couple of lion-tamers he did not know. So they had sent young Worboys, Herbie thought. Not a senior officer, not even Tubby Fincher. Tony Worboys and a pair of nameless heavies.

"You made it, Herbie. Thank God. You made it. Well done." Worboys was like a puppy, delighted to see the big man, pumping his hand and grinning.

Herbie merely nodded, looking over Worboys' shoulder at the two bodyguards.

"Herbie, they had you, and you got away. Did they get anything from you? Information? . . ." He seemed to be about to ask if there had been torture. Worboys still had a spark of the romantic in him; he needed a lot of training yet.

Herbie gave his daft smile. "Nothing," shaking his head. "Nothing from me, I think. I got things from them."

They took him downstairs; to the car that would carry them to the airport, and the plane that would take them to England. Big Herbie Kruger looked at Tony Worboys.

"They fed me a cargo of old rabbits," he said, the bitterness on his tongue. "A cargo of old rabbits." His eyes were stinging.

Young Worboys looked up at his old boss, smiling, "And I bet you fed them a bigger cargo in return," he laughed, loudly. "At least you've come back a sort of hero."

A sort of hero? Herbie grasped hold of the straw. "There are documents. Papers. I got some of Vascovsky's papers . . ." he began. Then the old depression sluiced over him. They had taken him from the very start. Even Ursula had taken him . . . And now the confessors would be waiting. The questions would follow; the court of enquiry. The long days' journeys into the past. And the even longer nights.